ADVANCE PRAISE FOR *CAROUSEL TIDES*

"Sharon Lee is one of my all-time f~ ~~~~~~~~ gifted storyteller whose work neve~ ~~~~~ ~ousel *Tides* she gives her fans an~ ~~~~~ ~ime with fascinating characters, br~ ~~~~~ ~~ that becomes so real you can sme~ ~~~~~ ~und you. Her fine hand with detail never lets ~~spense falter, as mystery, folklore, and magic are artfully interwoven into a thoroughly engaging tale. *Carousel Tides* will leave you eagerly awaiting the next novel by this master."

—**Jan Burke**, author of *The Messenger, Bones,* and *Bloodlines*

"*Carousel Tides* is a gripping, enthralling read that I didn't want to put down for any reason. From its beautifully detailed small-town Maine setting to a cosmology that manages to be unique and familiar at the same time, this book demonstrates the best of what urban fantasy can be. It's rare that I find a book I can recommend without any reservations; *Carousel Tides* is one of those books."

—**Seanan McGuire**, author of *Rosemary and Rue, A Local Habitation* and *An Artificial Night*

"Proof that contemporary fantasy is alive and well and living beyond the big city limits—*Carousel Tides* is a worthy inheritor to Charles DeLint's Newford series, and magical in its own right. Delightful."

—**Laura Anne Gilman**, author of *Blood from Stone*

BAEN BOOKS by
SHARON LEE and STEVE MILLER

THE LIADEN UNIVERSE®
Fledgling
Saltation
Mouse and Dragon
The Dragon Variation (omnibus)
The Agent Gambit (forthcoming omnibus)
Ghost Ship (forthcoming)

Duainfey
Longeye

Carousel Tides

Sharon Lee

CAROUSEL TIDES

A Baen Books Original

Baen Publishing Enterprises
P.O. Box 1403
Riverdale, NY 10471
www.baen.com

ISBN: 978-1-4391-3395-8

Cover art by Dominic Harman

First printing, November 2010

Distributed by Simon & Schuster
1230 Avenue of the Americas
New York, NY 10020

Library of Congress Cataloging-in-Publication Data

Lee, Sharon, 1952–
  Carousel tides / Sharon Lee.
     p. cm.
  ISBN 978-1-4391-3395-8 (trade pbk.)
  1. Maine—Fiction. I. Title.
  PS3562.E3629C37 2010
  813'.54—dc22

                                2010029988

10 9 8 7 6 5 4 3 2 1

Pages by Joy Freeman (www.pagesbyjoy.com)
Printed in the United States of America

Thanks are due to...

J. Ahronheim, University of Michigan, for providing a list of books of Abenaki legend

Lou McIntosh, for shiplore, stories, and just the right mix of patience and impatience over the years

Woodchucks' Revenge, for *Voices in the Hills*

Mike Barker, Jennifer Dunne, Elektra Hammond, James A. Hetley, Merle Hetley, Jennifer Jackson, Irene Radford for eagle eyes, comments and encouragement

Joseph Fessenden of the Maine Department of Marine Resources

Steve Miller for lending me his snallygaster, his love, and his support for 30 years now, and counting

Jennifer Jackson, for not freaking

"The Blimp," WBLM FM, 102.9, out of Portland, Maine, for providing inspirational music

The f'list on LiveJournal; you guys know *every*thing!

Archers Beach, Maine, is a fictional town, though it owes portions of its history, coastline, and geography to the communities of Old Orchard Beach, Ocean Park, Kinney Shores, Camp Ellis, and to the Rachel Carson National Wildlife Refuge.

The Chance Menagerie Carousel at Palace Playland in Old Orchard Beach occupies roughly the spot where one would find the Fantasy Menagerie Merry-go-Round in Fun Country at Archers Beach, if either existed.

ONE

Tuesday, April 18
High Tide 2:29 A.M.
Sunrise 5:54 A.M. EDT

I almost missed the left onto Route 5, which would've been embarrassing as hell. Luckily, I recognized the intersection before I was through it, snapping dry-mouthed out of a quarter-doze. Luckily, the Subaru answered quick to the wheel.

Luckily, there wasn't anybody else fool enough to be driving this particular stretch of Maine highway at this particular ungodly hour of the morning-or-night. If there had, I'd've been toast.

Route 5 twisted, snakelike, between parallel rows of dark storefronts and shuttered motels. I pushed myself up straighter in the seat, biting my lip when the pain knifed through my chest, and tried to stay focused on the matter at hand. Not long now. Not long.

Going home, after all this time.

No matter how many words they use to say it, people only ever leave home for two reasons. Money, that's one. Love—that's the other.

The reasons people come home again . . . it could be there are more than two. Me, I was worried about my grandmother. Worried enough to risk a homecoming. Trust me—that's some kind of worried.

Mind you, the crisis or calumny that Bonny Pepperidge—that

1

would be Gran—couldn't settle with her off hand while cooking breakfast wasn't something that was likely to roll over and play dead for the likes of me. Still, there was the bothersome fact that the phone had rung empty the last six times I'd called—and it was *just* like Gran not to bother with an answering machine or to pick herself up a cell—and the downright terrifying reality of the foreclosure notice from Fun Country management.

Perfectly reasonable for Fun Country to contact me; my name's right there on the lease as co-owner. But I'm only an Archer—a half-Pepperidge, and not the best half, either. It's the Pepperidges who've owned and operated the merry-go-round at Archers Beach since right around the dawn of civilization, Maine time; and Gran who's had the care and keeping of the thing since well before I'd been born. The size and shape of the disaster she'd allow to threaten the carousel was—almost unimaginable.

Unfortunately, I've got a vivid imagination; and Gran's my last family, so far as I know. Given the combination of circumstances, I could no more have stayed away than flown to the moon.

Not to say that Gran didn't have a lot of friends in town—as old or older than she was, some of whom didn't look kindly on me. And of course, there was the family lawyer. But Henry'd been out of town when I called, according to the message on *his* answering machine, due back some days after Fun Country wanted their money.

Which is why I was here, driving uncertainly down Maine Route 5 at oh-my-God-o'clock in the morning, toward the home I'd forsaken, and trying not to think of what was likely to be waiting for me there.

The headlights picked out a deserted parking lot on the right. I pulled in next to the boarded up ice cream stand, "For Sale" sign hanging at a crazy angle from the storm shutters, slid the car into park, and fingered my cell phone free of its pocket on the outside of my backpack.

I hit speed dial and held the unit to my ear, listening to my grandmother's phone ringing, ringing, ringing on the other end.

Sighing, I thumbed "end" and sat holding the phone in my hand, staring out into the dark. No doubt about it, I was going to have to go in—back to Archers Beach, which I hadn't left on the best of terms. That would teach me to burn my bridges.

Or not.

I slid the phone back into its pocket, ratcheted the stick down to drive and pulled back onto 5. Soonest begun, soonest done, as the saying goes. And the devil take the hindermost.

Mist began to creep across the road as I went on. I kept my foot on the gas, and I won't say I wasn't holding my breath when the Subaru crossed the town line, which was a waste of perfectly good anxiety—nothing out of the ordinary happened, unless you count an increase of mist.

Breathing carefully, I turned off Route 5 and headed down into town.

The street lamps were out on Archer Avenue, and the Subaru's headlights illuminated swirls of sea mist pirouetting before boarded-up storefronts. At the bottom of the long hill was the Atlantic Ocean, hidden by a full-fledged fog.

I rolled the window down, shivering in the sudden cold breeze, and took a deep breath of salt air. My eyes watered—which was the salt, or maybe the breeze—and slammed on the brakes as a dark form loped across the street directly in front—but no. It was only the mist, playing games.

I took my foot off the brake and let the car drift.

At the bottom of the hill, where Archer Avenue crosses Grand, I tapped the brakes again. It was five-ten by the clock on the Subaru's dash; twenty minutes shy of Gran's usual rising time, though I told myself I no longer expected to find her at home. That last phone call, made just outside the town line, had been pretty definitive. Even Gran isn't stubborn enough to ignore her phone ringing at four-thirty in the morning.

I should, I thought, go straight on to the house, but habit decided me otherwise. Habit and the fact that I could hear Gran's voice just as plain as if she sat in the passenger's seat beside me—"Did you pay your respects to the sea?"

The fog played its game of hide and seek as I felt my way 'round Fountain Circle and pulled the Subaru head first into the center of the five municipal parking spots that face the ocean across a wide stretch of fine, pale sand. In Season there would be signs posted, warning drivers of a ten minute limit on parking, and a strictly enforced tow away policy.

In April, the signs were still in the Public Works garage, and you could park facing the ocean for weeks, and nobody'd notice. Or care, if they did.

I put the Subaru into park, turned off the engine, and sat, taking stock.

My head throbbed and my chest ached—nothing unusual, these days. Not to mention that I was standing on the chancy edge of being 'way too tired, which driving three days non-stop'll do for you, even if you're in the pink of health.

Damp breeze danced in the window, chilling my ungloved hands. Faintly, very faintly, I could hear the sound of the surf, slapping and sizzling against the sand.

"Walk light on the land," I whispered to myself, which was something I hadn't done since I was a kid, new-come to the Beach and afraid of it all. "Walk light on the land and everything'll be fine."

Or not. And it wasn't like I had a choice, anyway. Peril Number One, and counting.

I rolled up the window, popped the door, grabbed my cell, on the vanishingly small chance that I'd get a call; and went down to the water.

The tide was going out. I slogged through shifty dry sand to the firm wet stuff, the fog running cold fingers across my face; a blind thing trying to puzzle out my features. Turning up my collar, I pushed my hands deeper into my pockets, wishing I'd remembered how cold an early morning in April could be, here on the Maine seacoast.

Shivering and out of breath, I stopped at the water's edge, the toes of my sneakers on the tide line. I shook my hair back out of my eyes, squared my shoulders, and waited for what the sea might bring me.

Wavelets struck the shore and fizzed. The breeze swung 'round, freshened, trying to push the fog back out to sea.

A wave smacked against the sand, sudden as a shotgun blast, and water splashed over my sneakers.

Swearing, I jumped back, and looked down.

Wet sand was all I saw; that, and a little rag of foam.

I bit my lip. What had I expected? It was my good fortune that I'd gotten nothing worse than wet shoes.

I pulled the cell phone out of my pocket and took a look at its face: five-thirty-five. The sea had taken its own sweet time getting back to me. Turning my back on the water, I squinted uphill, barely making out a blue smear that was the Subaru, waiting patiently where I'd put her. To my right, the Archers Beach Municipal Pier hove out of the fog like a ship out of stormy seas; to my left Fun Country sat like a broken dream, sea mist toying with the shrouded rides. The carousel was invisible, gray steel storm gates absorbed by the gray fog.

I lifted my soggy right foot and shook it; did the same for my left—and stood for a moment, weighing the cramped agony in my chest against the long slog back up to the parking lot. Up above the fog, a gull screamed an insult, and somehow that decided it. I turned right and started walking, keeping to the damp sand, but well out of the splash zone. Under the Pier I went, making for the townie side of town, and one particular old house facing the water across the dunes.

"'Mornin'." The voice was deep, soft as the fog itself.

Gasping, I spun, wet sneakers skidding on wet sand. The owner of the voice stepped out of the fog and raised his hands—one empty, one holding a Styrofoam coffee cup—and stopped where he was, letting me get a good look at him.

Tall—'way taller than I am—broad and powerful-looking. His face was high-cheeked and brown; his black hair cropped, except for a thin braid that snaked across his shoulder, falling almost to his waist. His jeans were as soft as salt and weather could make them, and he wore a brown leather jacket open over a green work sweater. He looked to be maybe thirty, thirty-five. I didn't recognize him—but, then, there wasn't any reason why I should.

"'Morning," I answered, on the general principle that it's prudent to be polite to guys who're bigger than I am. "Pleasant day for a walk."

He laughed, deep in his chest, and lowered his hands. "Well, it's not. But I was up anyway, hoping it would clear in time to go out." He had a sip from his cup, and jerked his head at the fog-shrouded ocean. "No going out in this, and by the time she burns off, the tide'll have turned." He gave me nod. "I fish Mary Vois' boat for her, since the sea took Hum, couple years back." A pause for another sip from his cup. "Don't believe I've seen you around before. Visiting?"

It was on the tip of my tongue to tell him that my business was none of his—and then I thought better of it, recalling small town manners that were rusty with disuse. He'd given me info, and now he was asking for info in return. Fair enough.

"Visiting," I agreed, trying to reckon how much I needed to put on the table to balance my social debt. I was 'way too tired for that kind of subtle calculation, though, and in a couple seconds I gave it up and just told him what passed for the truth. "I grew up in town, and my grandmother's still here."

"Don't say." He sounded genuinely interested, which of course he would be. Parsing lineage is an ancient Maine pastime. "Who's your gran, then?"

Should've seen that coming. I sighed lightly, but forked over. It wasn't like it was a state secret, and if I spent more than two hours in town, he'd hear it from somebody else anyway. "Bonny Pepperidge. She runs the carousel."

"Sure she does!" He grinned. "You must be Kate."

"Yep, I'm Kate. And you are?"

"Borgan." He gave the name readily enough, and between it and the information that he fished Mary Vois' boat, I had enough to pin him down for any townie I met. Just in case I should need to, which I really hoped I wouldn't.

"I could use a cup of coffee," I said, which was nothing less than the truth. The fog had chilled me straight through while we'd played Twenty Questions, and I was shivering inside my denim jacket. "Anything open this early?"

Borgan held out the Styrofoam cup. "Bob's."

There wasn't any reason why I should've been startled, but I was. Exhaustion, maybe. "Bob's is still there?"

"Was ten minutes ago."

"Well, I'm going in the right direction, then." I cleared my throat and gave him a civil nod. "Morning."

"See you around," he answered easily, and raised his cup to his lips.

Social obligation discharged, I put my face into the wind and began to walk. Happily, Gran's house on Dube Street was only three blocks up from the Pier, and Bob's Diner was conveniently located at the bottom of the street. I'd check the house first, I thought, and glanced over my shoulder.

All I saw behind me was the shadow of the Pier, black inside the fog.

TWO

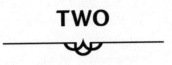

Tuesday, April 18
Low Tide 8:51 A.M.
Sunrise 5:54 A.M. EDT

I'd expected the house to be locked and empty, and it didn't disappoint me. For form's sake, I tried the doors, and every window I could reach, checked the empty mailbox and took note of the fact that the porch was free of yellowing newspapers. By the time I'd done all that, I was shaking with cold and damp, and really wanted that cup of coffee.

It was good, I thought, as I walked down quiet, fog-filled street, that Bob's was still there. Bob was one of those old friends of Gran's who didn't think so much of me. And if anybody knew where she'd gotten to, it would be Bob.

The bell on the knob jangled as I pushed the door open, and again, when I shoved it shut behind me. Heat blasted down from the overhead blower and hit me in the face. My eyes started to water, which was likely just the eyeballs thawing out.

The place hadn't changed any, from what I could see through the tears. There was Bob himself at the back counter, white-haired and pixie-faced, pouring coffee for one of the regulars. I didn't offhand recognize the wire-thin woman in the salt-stained work sweater and patched jeans, but it went without saying that she was either a regular or a townie—and probably both.

For a minute—no longer—I stood on the threshold, taking it all in. The radio was tuned to WBLM in Portland, just like it'd always been, bellowing classic rock music into the din of conversation and clattering silverware. The booths on the right, away from the windows, were crowded; the tables along the windows, not. The dividers were still up, sequestering the so-called "summer dining room." On the walls between the windows were the photographs famous people had signed to Bob over the years. It seemed there were a few more since the last time I'd been in, which surprised me. I didn't think famous people came to Archers Beach anymore.

That's what I noticed, inside that first minute, then Bob straightened up from pouring, looked down the room and saw me.

The woman he'd just served saw him stiffen, and she turned on her stool to sight along his line. A couple fellas in the booths noticed her interest and turned to look, too.

I nodded, casual and friendly as I could manage, heart hammering and short of breath as I was.

"Bob," I said, by way of greeting.

I saw some of the starch go out of his shoulders and he gave me back my nod.

"Kate," he answered, civil, if not exactly welcoming. He hefted the pot. "Coffee?"

"Coffee'd be good," I said, though it wouldn't be, unless a miracle had occurred since the last time I'd had Bob's brew. It would, however, be hot. I moved forward, walking careful on wobbly legs.

The guys in the booth went back to their talk, and the woman at the counter turned away, showing me a narrow back. I slid into the empty stool next to the wall, and watched while Bob hooked a thick brown mug from the peg, filled it and set it down on the counter in front of me. He turned to put the pot away; I reached for the cream and doctored my cup. The coffee was strong; rich dark odors rising in the steam. I finished with the cream and wrapped my hands around the mug, wise enough not to try to drink just yet, grateful for the uncomplicated warmth.

Bob's face, when he turned back to me, that wasn't exactly uncomplicated.

"You come for the keys, I guess," he said. "Bonny said you'd be by."

I sighed, quietly, one guess to the good. Go, me.

"I'd like the keys, sure," I said to Bob's waiting eyes. "Also some idea of how long she's been gone, and where she went. I tried to call..." The kitchen bell rang, sharp, signaling a meal up, and Bob turned to deal with it. Me, I cuddled my coffee mug, and concentrated on the music, laboriously piecing "Born to Run" out of the surrounding din.

"You're Bonny Pepperidge's girl." The voice was low and raspy. I glanced to the right. The thin woman in the sweater was watching me. Her eyes were pale gold, like old ale; her face was brown, spare and pointed. There were creases at her eyes, and lines around her mouth. The hair wisping in mist curls from under her gimme hat was a sort of rusty brown. She might've been thirty, or sixty, or anywhere in between.

"I'm Kate Archer," I admitted, nodding at her, and gave the obligatory lineage. "Bonny Pepperidge's granddaughter."

She chewed on that a bit, then washed it down with a gulp of coffee.

"Nancy Vois," she said, with a nod of her own. "I helped out with the merry-go-round couple Seasons back."

Not much of a conversational gambit, even if I was good at small talk, which I never had been. I made what I hoped was a noncommittal noise, raised my mug in both hands, and sipped carefully. Hot, bitter, and just slightly oily. Wake-up coffee, yessir! Just what a girl who was half-frozen, half-frantic, and half-dead needed on an empty stomach at the end of a long, long drive.

I had another sip.

Next to me, Nancy Vois drank down what she had left and thumped the mug to the counter. She flipped over the check, sighed, and slid from her stool.

"Stayin' for the Season?" she asked me, pulling a couple crumpled bills out of her jeans pocket.

"That depends."

Fortunately, she didn't ask what it depended on, since I didn't know myself.

"Need any help on the ride, I'm an able mechanic," she said, just letting me know, and smoothed the singles between thin, knobby fingers before putting them carefully across the check.

"Thanks," I said; "I'll remember that."

She nodded again and took herself off; I sipped some more,

feeling the coffee wash away a layer of stomach lining, and squinted at the menu hanging over the kitchen window.

"Here." A manila envelope briefly obscured the menu, and settled on the counter in front of me. A ring of keys jingled and landed on top. "Bonny left this for you, 'round the middle of October. She said I was to tell you it's up to you."

I frowned. "*What's* up to me?"

Bob, predictably, shrugged. He might be one of Gran's oldest friends, but it doesn't naturally follow that he knows her mind, nor thinks he should. Her business was her business and she was fully capable of taking care of her business—be it the carousel, or the town council, or the sullen, sickly girl-child who had landed on her doorstep bearing news of her daughter's death.

I sighed, and held the mug out, two-handed. "More coffee, please?" I said, nice as I could, and waited while he reached 'round for the pot and poured.

"Bob," I said, serious and steady. "Where's Gran?"

He shrugged again. "It's in the packet, I'm guessing," he said. "You want anything else?"

I looked at the envelope, my name written on the front in old-fashioned cursive. Sighed again and met Bob's eyes.

"I'd like a cheddar cheese omelet," I said. "With home fries and wheat toast. Please."

"Sure," he said, and turned away to write up the ticket.

I'd taken my time—not to say dawdled—over breakfast. By the time I was done, I'd stopped shaking, and the ever-present pain had settled down to what I'd come to consider normal levels. I paid my tab, put the keys in my pocket, tucked the unbreached manila envelope under one arm, and strolled back to the Subaru through nothing worse than a light mist, silvered by the sun.

It would've made sense, I guess, to open the envelope right there in the car, and get down to cases. I thought about it, then put the envelope on the passenger's seat, started the Subaru and drove over to Ahz's Market. Displacement activity.

'Round about eight-thirty, having displaced as well as I was able, I was back at the house, sliding one of the four keys on Gran's ring into the lock of the second-floor apartment.

Grocery bag in the crook of my arm, pack slung over the opposite shoulder, I pushed the door with an elbow. It didn't budge, of course. Tupelo House had been built right around the turn of the century and it has its crotchets.

Sighing, I juggled the bag, settled myself firmly on my left foot, raised the right and brought the flat of my still-damp sneaker smart against the center of the door.

My technique was still good; the door popped wide. Inside, it was dim, and I hesitated.

"Oh, right," I said out loud, sarcasm mode *on*. "So now you're afraid of the dark?"

Overhead, a gull laughed, caught an air current and whisked away, still laughing, its shadow flickering over the dunes.

"It wasn't that funny," I muttered, and got my feet moving— right, left, right; that's all it took to get inside. I dropped my pack to the dark linoleum floor, yanked the key out of the lock, and used my hip to shut the door.

Tupelo House is three storeys tall, what they used to call an "oceanside cottage," built with extra income in mind. Half of the ground floor is a rental; a comfy studio apartment with a patio nestled against the dunes. Upstairs, the main floor of the owner's quarters consists of a great room, the French doors presently hidden behind winter-weight curtains opening onto a porch—the so-called "summer parlor." To the rear, overlooking the alley/parking lot, is the kitchen; bathroom/laundry combo down a short hallway, and the stairs to the third floor, where two long bedrooms run the width of the house, each with a window overlooking the sea.

I carried the groceries into the kitchen, put the bag on the counter and sighed. The refrigerator's doors were open, the inside a gleaming wasteland. And dammit, I thought crankily, slamming the freezer shut and reaching into the main compartment to turn the temperature dial and give the light bulb a half-twist to bring it on—dammit, if she'd had time to clean out the fridge, she'd had time to call me. What on earth ailed the woman?

That the answer to that was probably in the manila envelope I'd shoved, still unopened, into my pack, I ignored for the moment. It felt better—safer—to be annoyed at Gran. That was familiar territory.

The fridge hummed, and I slammed the door before moving across the room. The window over the sink was dark; Venetian blinds rolled down and folded tight. I yanked on the cord, and the blinds rattled up, letting the weak April sunlight into the room. Then, I went down the hall to the bitter end and fiddled with the thermostat, nodding in satisfaction when the furnace gave a low, irritable rumble.

On my way back to the kitchen, I detoured into the great room, and pulled the heavy curtains back. Outside, Saco Bay sparkled and flashed in the sunlight, the early morning fog gone like it had never been. I paused with my hand gripping the edge of the curtain, staring at the scene I had once professed to loathe.

Straight out, waves broke against Blunt Island and Strafford, perfectly visible now. Down beach—south—there was the Pier, the sand stretching wide and straight beyond it. If I squinted, I could just make out the black blotch of Googin Rock, and the notch at Kinney Harbor. Out again, further south and to the east, I could see Wood Island Light.

To the north, the beach begins a long eastward arc; the communities up that way are Surfside, Grand Beach, Pine Point. At the far end of the arc is Cape Elizabeth Light, and beyond that is the open sea.

It's a mesmerizing view, and maybe I stood there a little longer than I had intended, asleep with my eyes open, more or less. No surprise after all that driving, even with a quart of Bob's coffee in me, and, anyway, I tended to phase in and out nowadays. Part of the process, that's all.

The shadow of a gull flickered over the glittering waves; I blinked, shook my head, and turned away from the window. My pack squatted by the door like a reproachful hound. I walked past, giving it plenty of room in case it decided to jump up and get mud on my jeans.

In the kitchen, the fridge was already cooling. I made quick work of stowing my loot—skim milk, coffee, a vacuum-sealed pack of Swiss cheese, and a loaf of off-the-shelf whole wheat; a bottle of cheap chardonnay, half-dozen eggs, a pound of margarine— folded the bag, and put it between the fridge and the wall. There were maybe a half-dozen other bags already in residence, which homey touch delivered a sharp and completely unexpected little twist of anguish.

Closing my eyes, I swallowed hard. I hate to cry; always have. I don't think that's something Gran taught me.

I spun. Stretching high on my toes, I opened cupboards at random, discovering canned goods, paper towels, dishes—none of which made me feel any better. I forced myself to turn away, and leaned on the back of one of the kitchen chairs, gripping it so hard my fingers hurt, and concentrated on breathing slow and easy until the tightness in my chest eased off to bearable.

"I'm too old for this," I told the kitchen at large, my voice rasping in my own ears as I half-laughed. Ayuh. And Gran could give me a couple centuries, local. Both of us were 'way too old for games.

Some more deep breathing and I managed to get myself steady—or at least steady enough. I didn't like the way this was shaping up. The state of the apartment not only spoke of a woman who had time enough to tidy up before she'd taken herself off, it also showed a state of readiness that indicated she'd expected to return.

Except she hadn't returned. And she hadn't felt it necessary to share her plans with one of her oldest and closest cronies.

Which did make one wonder what the *hell* was going on.

I sighed, and pushed away from the chair, heading for the hallway and my pack.

There was only one way to find out.

I ran my finger under the flap to break the seal, and gingerly slid the contents of the manila envelope onto the kitchen table.

A green bank book in a cloudy plastic sleeve slipped free first, followed by an old button folder, well-smudged and tattered, the word "Legal" written diagonally across its face in rusty black ink. Last to emerge, almost as if it were as reluctant to be read as I was to read it—a single sheet of Gran's stationery, folded in half.

I put the envelope aside, and reached—not for the letter, but for something a little easier to deal with.

The flaking gold stamp on the front of the bank book read "Archers Beach Community Federal Credit Union." It was the account we'd set up years ago; the first page listed joint owners Ebony Pepperidge and Katharine Fae Archer; the last page revealed a balance that was enough to pay the Season lease on the carousel's space in Fun Country, and a tidy sum left over.

I closed the bank book and sat holding it in my hand, wondering if this whole business was nothing but an elaborate charade to drag me back to Archers Beach, where I'd sworn I'd never set foot again. All it had taken to break that oath had been a half-dozen unanswered phone calls and a letter from the bean counters.

"And you call yourself a Child of the Ozali," I muttered, slipping the bank book back into its sleeve and reaching for the Legal folder.

The string that wrapped 'round the button and kept the flap in place was thin and grimy. I unwound it with care and pulled out four documents, each stapled in a crisp, new cover.

I had, as they say, a Very Bad Feeling about this.

Carefully, as if it were a live thing that might at any moment take it to mind to bite me, I fingered the top document off of the pile, and considered the folio notes. *Pepperidge: Transfer of Real Property/Tupelo House,* that was the title. The date was October of the year previous, and the lawyer—no surprises there—was Henry Emerson.

"This plan was not brought together in an instant, Malvolio," I muttered.

Malvolio, typically, didn't answer. Where's your straight man when you really need him?

For form's sake, I opened the document and scanned the first page. "...transfer of real property located at 100 Dube Street, Archers Beach, Maine, known as Tupelo House, from Ebony Pepperidge to..."

Sighing, I put the document aside and pulled the others to me. After the first, I knew what I was dealing with, and quickly shuffled through the documents transferring the carousel and the business wholly to me.

The fourth document, though—that *was* a surprise.

Gran had deeded the land on Heath Hill, that had been Pepperidge land since this little bit of Maine coast had been settled—to me. Wholly to me. And that was—just wrong.

I closed my eyes, but all I saw was spangles of colored lights, swirling. Soon, I was going to have to voluntarily get horizontal and grab some sleep, or sleep was going to ambush me and put me flat on my face in some uncomfortable and embarrassing locale.

First things first, though.

I opened my eyes, took a deep breath, and finally picked up the letter.

A leaf fell out when I unfolded the sheet. I gave it a look—enough to establish that I didn't offhand recognize what sort of tree had put it forth—and began to read.

Dear Kate,

If you're reading this, things have not gone as I had hoped and expected they would. I'm afraid I've left you a pretty mess, my dear, and it's yours to decide whether or not to clean up after me.

The obligations of kinship...of love...are not always easy to bear. But, there, I haven't told you anything you didn't learn as a babe.

If you're reading this...I'm glad you came home, Katie.

All my love,
Gran

THREE

Wednesday, April 19
High Tide 3:17 A.M.
Sunrise 5:53 A.M. EDT

It was dark when I woke, feeling considerably more rested than usual, and rolled over, squinting at the alarm clock's palely illuminated face. Twelve-fifteen. Perfect. If I didn't dawdle, I could catch Nerazi at the usual place, assuming it was still the usual place, and that Nerazi bothered to come to the mainland anymore.

I pushed the blankets back and went determinedly down the stairs, surefooted in the dark. Snapping on the bathroom light, I slipped past the washer–dryer unit hulking in the corner, pausing long enough to skin out of sweat pants and T-shirt before hitting the shower.

Twenty minutes later, hair blast-dried and sticking on end, in clean jeans and a Google sweatshirt, I let myself out into the night.

On the porch, I paused, looking over the ocean as I shrugged into my jacket and buttoned it. The waning moon was high; the stars bright and brash. The waves showed lace at the leading edges, and a light mist was rising, softening the blare of starlight. The tide had turned and the wind was off the ocean, heavy with the scents of salt and sand and fish.

Out and east, a sword of brilliance leapt from Wood Island Light, slicing through the mist.

I took a deep breath—and another—before going down the steps and across the dunes, keeping scrupulously to the marked path until I reached the beach. There, I paused again, hands in pockets and face against the wind, tasting, tasting... salt. And sand. And nothing else.

"Good," I whispered, and turned up the collar of my jacket. Putting my back to the town, I headed up coast, toward Surfside, angling across dry sand to wet, and more certain footing. Out beyond the lacy break of waves, I could see patches of subtle blue and green riding just below the surface of the water. From ahead, the no-nonsense sweep of Cape Elizabeth Light illuminated waves and rock.

At the little notch in the beach that marks the beginning of Surfside, there's a rock. Not much of a rock, by the rugged standards of the Maine coast, and not nearly as impressive as Googin Rock, 'way down to the south of town. Still, it's big enough to serve as a landmark, as well as a boundary stone. From the sand to its flat pinnacle, it stands twice as high as I do, and measures considerably wider, side to side. At low tide, it wears a skirt of shiny sea grass; and its pockets are numerous, some secret, some not. Below the sand, its roots are deep and wide. So wide, I've heard it said, that the hidden portion of the rock is as much on Surfside's portion of beach as on ours.

That might be true. The one I heard that from liked to spin a tale or three, and I can't think how she might have gained the knowledge. Still, it's true that no violence comes near this rock, unlike its brother to the south, and a sliver worn 'round the neck, or carried in a pocket, is rumored to be a powerful ward.

I paused a few steps out, listening to the waves and to the wind singing in the wires; watching the mist rise up to cocoon the stars. In an hour, the sea would be lapping at the base of the rock; in two hours, it would be mostly submerged. I flexed my fingers inside the pockets of my jacket and wished I'd remembered to bring gloves. The wind gusted off the waves, yanking my hair with something more than playfulness.

And a hat, I thought.

"Good morning, Princess." The voice was low, and slightly sibilant; possibly, she meant to surprise me. If so, she was disappointed.

"Morning already?" I asked, not arguing with *princess*. Might as well argue with the tide as with Nerazi.

"Courtesy," she told the singing wind as I mooched toward the rock. "Gentle courtesy is as rare a commodity upon the mainland as ever it was, I apprehend."

I felt my lips twitch and straightened them with an effort.

"Good morning, fair Nerazi," I said, moving closer across the sand.

"Nay, nay, keep your sweet words close, my lady, and be niggardly in their spending! For when those are gone, there will be no more, I warrant."

"You're probably right," I said, coming around to the lee side of the rock. Cross-legged and quite naked, Nerazi sat with her back against the rock's rustling grass skirt, her rump cozy and warm on a sealskin blanket, braiding her silver hair.

I braced my own rump against a thin, low ledge, which put the rock between me and the wind, and sighed.

"You should wear gloves, my lady; the wind has teeth."

"Every time I wear gloves, I ruin them," I told her, truthfully.

"And thus your wisdom teaches you that it is better to ruin your hands." She turned her head and looked up at me from wide eyes that reflected the moonlight greenly, her hands moving along her hair. "I shall provide you with gauntlets suitable to your station."

"I don't think—"

"Now, *that* has ever been the case," she said with asperity, and I laughed. The rock thrummed with the rhythm of the waves.

Nerazi gave me a small, secret smile from behind her hair before her gaze moved, looking across the line and up coast.

"Quiet, is it not?" she said softly. "Protected and peaceful. Men sleep soundly in their beds, unworried by the wind or the rattle of water across beach stones. And if a selkie were to come out of the sea and walk their streets for an hour, observing what she might of mortal ways, none would see her—nor, seeing, believe."

"Normal folks see what they want to see," I agreed. "And we're lucky that they do."

"Perhaps. Perhaps. Though surely some see what they would rather not, else your father's mother would not have pledged herself to an Ozali and followed him to the Land of the Flowers."

"Special case," I said, keeping my voice matter-of-fact with an effort. "Guardians get to see—and do—all kinds of things they'd rather not." And die of them, more often than not, as Lydia Archer had.

"Privilege has its price, surely." Nerazi's hands paused among the long strands of her hair, and I felt the whole of her regard suddenly upon me.

"Are you quite well, Princess?"

I took a breath, gauging the ache in my chest. "Not dead yet," I answered, shifting against the rock. "Nerazi, where's my grandmother?"

"I do not know."

That was a little more straightforward than I'd been hoping for—okay, it was a *lot* more straightforward than I'd been hoping for. Nerazi could parse a twisty sentence with the best of 'em; most *trenvay*—that would be *earth spirit,* to you—could, and did. Relating facts in ways that made nothing seem less likely was kind of a hobby of the breed. I'd've been relieved if Nerazi had spun me an improbable yarn; it would have meant that Gran was—safe. That unadorned denial, though...

I shivered, and adjusted my lean against the rock, fists shoved deep into my pockets.

"She must have told you *some*thing," I said, and was horrified to hear the naked pleading in my voice. At least it was Nerazi, who was, or had been...kindly disposed toward me. In general.

"In truth, Princess," she said, more gently than she was wont, "I am as uninformed as you appear to be. She told me that she would be absent for a time, and to look for her at the turning of the year." There was a pause, filled by the sound of the waves against the shore. "More than that she would not say."

When Gran doesn't want to say, there's no power here or there that can force her. I know. Nerazi's formidable, but Gran's *stubborn*. And yet—

"The year turned," I pointed out, mild as I was able. "And she didn't come back."

"One year turned," Nerazi agreed. "There are others."

Right. I sighed. "I'm thinking it was the calendar year she had in mind," I said, still sticking with mild. "She left me a letter, which is considerably less informative than it could be, and a handful of legal papers, putting the house, the carousel, and her land all in my name."

"In your name alone?" That came out right sharp; I'd surprised her.

"That's right."

"Well," said Nerazi, and after a bit she said it again: "Well."

Back in the days before I'd repudiated the land and left Archers Beach forever, I'd seen Nerazi flummoxed exactly once. Seeing it again wasn't nearly as much fun as I might've imagined it would be. So, I waited while she finished up her braid, put a knot in the end, flipped it over one smooth, plump shoulder—and waited some more while she just sat there on her sealskin, staring off into the night...

"You will wish to inspect your landhold," she said finally, and with that she rose, bringing the sealskin with her, and turned away.

"Nerazi—" I said, coming away from the rock so fast my foot skidded in the sand. "Hey!"

"Keep you well, Princess," she said, not even bothering to look at me over her shoulder, which is a hell of a way to treat royalty. "I will send the gift I promised."

She passed beyond the rock. I got my feet coordinated and went after her, but she was already at the surf line, the sealskin wrapped around her shoulders and snapping in the wind.

I watched her walk into the lacy waves. When she reached the shelf, she simply dove in, the skin still caught about her shoulders.

The waves came in and the waves went out. Beyond them, a seal rolled in dark water—and vanished.

FOUR

Wednesday, April 19
Low Tide 9:42 A.M. EDT

Despite my early social call, I was at the door of Fun Country's on-site office at eight o'clock sharp, only to find that "off season" hours were from ten to three. Typical, really. If there's anything that Fun Country or its agent-in-place, Marilyn Michaud, can do to discommode a tenant, by golly, that's exactly what they'll do.

Discommoded, not to say aggravated, I glared at the door. A piece of canary yellow paper was tacked below the card elucidating those very convenient hours of operation, printed with faded red ink.

Attention All Tenants! Fun Country will begin operating on a weekend-only schedule May 14. All Name Rides are expected to open at noon on that date. Park closes at 10 P.M.

Great, I thought, and sighed. The Early Season was a blessing and a curse. On the one hand, it let you work out any kinks that might've developed in the ride over the winter. On the other hand, there was precious little money to be made during Early Season.

Not that there was all that much to be made during the Season, anymore.

Well. Nothing to be done here until Marilyn unlocked the door—on the stroke of ten and not one second before, if I knew my woman. Might as well move on to the next agenda item. Gran's letter hadn't exactly left me with the impression that I'd find her safe and cozy at Heath Hill. Trouble was, I didn't have the idea that Nerazi thought Gran was under tree, either. And yet—

Look to your landhold. Not the kind of advice I could afford to ignore, coming as it did from the oldest and most potent *trenvay* in Archers Beach.

Walking down Grand Avenue, I distracted myself by noticing changes in the neighborhood. Several of the motels had re-invented themselves as condominiums, and a number of surprisingly upscalish business enterprises had moved in, apparently to service those with deep pockets and plenty of leisure. In one short block, I passed a deli specializing in high-end cold cuts and artisan breads; a day spa offering sea salt body scrubs; and a boutique wine store. Made the east side of Grand, with its seedy diners, T-shirt stores, ice cream shops, and pizza stands, look downright tawdry.

Which, come to think of it, was one thing that hadn't changed. The townies were still scraping by, borrowing against that day when their ship stood in or their pony came through, while the people from Away never seemed to want for anything.

At Harmon Street, I took a shortcut across a vacant lot between Gentleman Johnnie's Mini-golf and Seaside Rentals, and leaned against the fence for a couple minutes to catch my breath. There were a couple guys working the grounds at the Gentleman's, unwinding the blue tarps that had protected the course from winter, and piling them in the back of a lawn tractor. They were stripped down to T-shirts, their discarded flannel draped over a handy salt cedar. I wasn't ready to lose my jacket, personally, though I might unbutton it if the temp climbed another five degrees.

I went up the Hill from the east, off of Heath Street, which is the gentle slope. The side facing the ocean is sand-covered stone, and the side toward Kinney Harbor is rock stitched with sea rose. There's a trail that comes in from the top, through the abutting land, which has been in the Rogers family a good couple hundred years. Once, there'd been a small house and garden plot there, but it'd been let to go wild.

I'd gone to school with Randy Rogers. The land passed to him before we graduated, after his father went over the side as a result of putting his lobster boat too hard by Googin Rock. Back then, Randy's plans had included joining up and getting the hell outta Archers Beach, which his dad had opposed. Last I saw him, Randy was getting on the Navy bus with the rest of the new recruits. He hadn't come back, as far as I knew. I wondered if he'd survived the war.

The wind picked up as I came up out of the protected zone, and by the time I hit the top of the hill, I was blowing like a grampus, bright flecks swarming at the edge of my vision, my chest edgy and raw.

I paused in the shadow of the sentinel trees, breathing shallowly, until the flecks went back to wherever they called home, then stood some more, looking out over the ocean. The sun struck sparks from the busy water, and I narrowed my eyes against the brightness, regretting the sunglasses I'd left sitting in the Subaru's change tray. Squinting, I could see the islands silhouetted against the turquoise sky. Closer in was Googin Rock, as weird and as black as a moonscape in the retreating tide.

I closed my eyes again, and took an experimental breath, deliberately drawing the salt air down deep into my lungs. Different—so different from the stuff I'd been breathing. Air was supposed to invigorate you, to give you a reason to rise and do battle with the challenges of the day, setting your blood to bubbling and your brain to jigging. Anything's possible, with ocean air in your lungs. City air's all weighted down with car exhaust, diesel fumes, and feelings of hopelessness. All that stuff gets into your system and it makes you tired, too, the heavy metals alchemize in your blood, turning your gifts into burdens and your joys into sorrows. Breathe enough of it and it'll kill you, sure.

Which was, after all, what I had wanted.

One more deep breath, my chest hardly hurting at all, before I turned and approached the trees. The air changed again as the breeze filtered through leaf; I breathed in the scents of bark and mold, and felt the gathering regard of the forest.

The shadows melted before me, and a path opened for my feet—that was the good news. But the wood was still, no bird song or insect sound, nor stirring of rabbit or squirrel in the fallen leaves, only a whisper of breeze in the branches. Around me, the trees were poised, on the edge of what action, I hadn't a clue.

Thinking it might be me that was making them tense, despite the fact that they'd let me in, I stopped, took my hands out of my pockets and opened my fingers wide.

"It's Kate," I said, and waited.

Leaves rustled; stilled. I took a breath, tasting the spice of green growing things—then the breeze was back, tickling inside my ear. *Welcome, Kate...*

All righty, then. Whatever the problem was, it wasn't me, for a novel change.

The wood on Heath Hill is a mixed stand—hardwood and soft—and I moved on, sneakers soft on fallen needles, then crunching loudly on dead leaves or downed sticks. Somewhere, not close at hand, I heard a scream of maniac laughter—a pileated woodpecker; not exactly what you'd call bird song. Still, it made me feel better to know I wasn't the only living thing in that place. Excepting the trees, of course.

In due time I came to the Center. Here, the trees thin a bit, ceding pride of place to the soaring black gum which is the heart and soul of the wood.

Nine feet around, is that tree, and somewhere over a hundred feet tall, with great, twisty, wide-reaching branches already showing oval leaves so brilliant they seemed blown from green glass.

I walked up to the giant and put my palms against the rough silvery bark.

"Anybody home?" I whispered.

Silence, the wood beneath my hand rough and cool—only wood, that was all.

"Damn." I leaned in, setting my forehead against the trunk, and closed my eyes. All around, the trees were still, tense leaves smothering the breeze.

"Damn," I said again, some while later; I'd phased out again. I pushed away from my grandmother's tree with a sigh, brushing my hands together to clear off the bits of bark.

Clearly, Gran wasn't at home. Well, she'd said as much in her letter, hadn't she? The comfort was that she couldn't have gone far. That, and the fact that her tree was hale and healthy, green leaves sparkling in the filtered sunlight. The only thing I needed to do was figure out where the devil the woman was holed up, and fetch her back.

Piece of cake.

I came out of the woods on the side abutting the Rogers' land. Overhead, seagulls shouted insults at each other, or maybe at me, and the breeze whipped right sprightly, unimpeded by leaf and trunk. Stepping from the shadow of the trees, I looked to the hilltop—and caught my jaw just before it hit the ground.

Above me, at the top of Heath Hill, on what had been the Rogers' landhold, stood a . . . a—well, I suppose the folk who'd built it thought it was a Maine summer cottage in the grand Bar Harbor style. What I saw . . . was a monstrosity; a house that overfilled its land and its location, its windows afire in the sunlight, a sneer at the sea and the sky it overlooked, a slap at the groundlings who groveled in the town.

"Randy sold the land?" I asked, and a moment later the breeze brought me the confirmation of the trees.

. . . sold the land . . .

The new owner had cleared his parcel, brought in dirt and made it all nice and level. 'Way up by the house, a man sat on the flagstone patio, sipping from a mug, a newspaper held between him and the sea. Walkways stretched out from the patio, lined with tame flowers, well-pruned cedars, and marsh pine. The grass was a uniform, unlikely emerald green, and—over the line by a good six foot.

"Now, *dammit*," I snapped, and my temper flickered. Not good. I look a breath and sighted upland.

Bearding strange men on their patios at half-past breakfast isn't on my top ten list of fun things to do. Nevertheless, the thing had to be dealt with, one way or another, and I was the captain of this particular ship until such time as Gran got her ass back from wherever it was she'd gone to.

Firmly, I walked toward that towering monstrosity of a house. At my rear, I could hear the trees murmuring among themselves, expressing a lively interest in what I might be going to do.

I'd've liked to have known that, myself, but I figured something would come to me. It usually did. Unfortunately.

Up on the patio, the man turned the page of his paper without ever once looking up.

I stopped walking precisely at the edge of my—of Gran's—landhold, feet cushioned by emerald grass. Six feet over, right enough. I caught my breath, and considered the matter, feeling the spring of the grass beneath my sneakers, and sighted along the deeded markers, taking my time.

Certain of my markers, I stepped over to the tree line, finding a stout stick suitable to my purpose obligingly close to hand, and went back to the boundary.

This time, I paced the line, double—and then triple—checking, while the new neighbor kept on with his paper, oblivious.

I finished my third check and paused, heart hammering and breath coming a little short, which was the exercise, and the excitement. *Easy, Kate,* I told myself. *You don't want to be losing your temper.*

Right. Losing my temper would be a very foolish, not to say life-threatening, thing to do. I concentrated on taking deep, even breaths until I was feeling steadier. Then, I hefted the stick, drove the sharp end into the emerald grass and began to cut.

"Hey!"

I looked up. The man from the patio was rushing down toward me across his pretty, soulless lawn, newspaper—*The Wall Street Journal,* I could tell by the type—still clutched in one hand, an expression of disbelief on his soft, well-kept face.

"Hey!" he said again, stopping just t'other side of the cut-line. "That's my lawn you're defacing!"

"That could be the case," I allowed, looking him in the eye and giving him a nod. "But it's on *my* land."

He stared at me. His eyes were pale blue; his hair was blond, lightly silvered, and cut within an inch of its life. He'd dressed himself straight out of L.L. Bean: chino shirt, casual khakis, and moose hide moccasins all looking brand new out of the box.

"*Your* land?" he repeated, obviously having a hard time believing such a thing.

"That's right," I told him. I turned and used the stick to point at the stand of old wood, out to the seaward edge of the hill, over toward Kinney Harbor, and back to where we stood, making sure to plant the point of the stick right where I'd been cutting. "I'm Kate Archer, and I own this piece of land. You're six foot over my line. You might not have known that, so I'm marking it out for you."

The pale blue eyes glinted. "Prove it's your land," he said, and there was a note of pure meanness in his voice that I didn't like at all.

"You'd've seen it on the survey and read it in your deed. The deed would've said something about being bounded on the seaward side by property owned by Ebony Pepperidge. I'm Mrs. Pepperidge's granddaughter, and the deed's in my name now. You might not have known that either, but you sure did know that this strip here wasn't any of yours."

"That deed is ancient!" my man told me, which in fact, it is. "We surveyed as well as we could, but when the markers are old rocks and trees that rotted fifty years ago—"

"Not rotted," I interrupted, which wasn't polite, but in spite of my best intentions, I was beginning to get irritable. I raised my stick and leveled it at the solid reality of the five foot granite boulder that was the northern boundary listed in the deed.

"Old rock," I said, and had the fleeting pleasure of seeing him flush. I shifted the stick again, sighting along it to the second boundary, 'way down on the Kinney Harbor side of the equation.

"Tree, not by any means rotten. Black gum live a long, long time; that's why the original survey picked it as a marker." I considered him. "What's your name, if it isn't a state secret?"

"Joe Nemeier," he snapped. "I don't care who you are or say you are. You're vandalizing my lawn and if you don't cease, and repair the damage immediately, I'll call the police and see you hauled away in handcuffs."

That wasn't very likely, for a grass vandal, but there was that certain something about Joe Nemeier that put my back right up. The little flicker of irritation was in danger of becoming a full flame-out of temper, which, I reminded myself, I could neither support nor afford.

With that thought in mind, I took a deliberate, ocean-rich breath, to steady myself, and looked straight into Joe Nemeier's pale blue eyes.

"Here's a counteroffer," I said, as calm as I could. "You get your lawn service out here to take up the grass from this line down. Do that, and I'll call us square."

He laughed, which I might've known he would. Turning away, he snapped over his shoulder, "I'm calling the cops. If you're smart, you'll leave before they get here."

And of course that was all she wrote. Orange flame coursed up my backbone, and likely smoke came out of my ears. That quick, the Word had formed, and there wasn't anything to do but let it loose.

"Hear me, Man," I heard myself say, hard and chancy as the surface of Googin Rock. "The boundary will be honored." And then the Word spoke itself, soft and gentle, like dew.

Joe Nemeier had spun to stare at me, as well he might. Me, I held his eyes with mine for two long heartbeats, feeling the Word settle. When I was sure it'd taken, I looked down, and Joe Nemeier followed my glance.

"What the *hell*!" he shouted, staring at the blight creeping across the brilliant green. "You poisoned my grass! I'll have your ass for this, whoever you are!"

"My lawyer's Henry Emerson, down in town," I said, barely able to see him through the spangles filling my vision. *Stupid!* I told myself. But, there, I've always had a lousy temper, and if I'd been able to control it, I wouldn't be in my current state of disrepair declining toward obsolescence.

Careful of wobbly knees and legs gone to rubber, I turned away, pitching my stick back into the wood, and headed for the downward slope into town.

"Come back here!" Joe Nemeier yelled. I heard his feet moving over dry grass and whispered a request to the trees. Shadows loomed, sudden, menacing, and cold, and I heard the sound of footsteps again, retreating. When I looked back, there was no sign of Joe Nemeier out of doors, and the line between our properties was marked with a wide ribbon of dead grass.

FIVE

Wednesday, April 19

Sometime between leaving the scene of the crime and reaching Heath Street, I phased out.

When I came back to myself, I was standing in front of Fun Country's door, and it was ten minutes to nine by the midway clock.

"Kate," I whispered; "you're a damn' fool."

Which was a proposition that had been proved more often than not during the largely misspent course of my life.

I tried the knob, but the door was still locked. Naturally. Marilyn was a woman of her word. When she said ten o'clock, by God, she *meant* ten o'clock.

Still feeling a little gone in the legs, I wobbled over to the gate. The chain was off, so I tripped the latch and slipped through. A moment later, I was heading across the lot, taking it slow by necessity.

It was quiet in the park, the neighborhood of the carousel being no exception. The Oriental Funhouse was still boarded up, the giant samurai straddling the doorway mummified in blue tarp, but somebody had been at Summer's Wheel: four gondolas, still in their winter wrappings, were sitting haphazard on the platform, and the plastic had been peeled back from the control panel. Across the square, Tony Lee's concession was locked up, storm hatches down and secured. I caught a whiff of old grease, and a wistful memory of fried rice before the breeze whisked the odors down the plaza toward Dodge City.

Across from Tony Lee's, next to Summer's Wheel, in the corner nearest the sea, there sits the Fantasy Menagerie Merry-go-Round. I leaned against the storm gates to catch my breath, and to let the shakes settle down. It wouldn't do to let the animals see me weak. No, no, not at all.

As I leaned there, panting and shivering, I felt a...twitch...at the edge of my consciousness, like a child tugging at an adult's sleeve.

The breath caught in my throat.

Visiting the Wood, frying a man's grass for him—not exactly walking lightly on the land.

And the land had taken note of me.

Back when I'd first come to Archers Beach, fresh from my grandfather's castle and the horrors therein, Gran had explained to me how it was that an Archer had always been Guardian of the Land—like Lydia, my father's mother. And that, as the last Archer around, it was my duty to take up the charge.

I was new in this place, having lost my family, my home, and my integrity before what passed for my thirteenth birthday. It was work and worth I wanted—I'd been born royal, after all, and rigorously trained in my obligations. I took up the charge, and offered myself to the land.

My offering was enthusiastically accepted; the land and I forged a bond—and it happened that Gran was right. The connection and the duty healed my wounds and settled me into my new life.

I was a kid. I didn't know then that there are some things we can't be healed of. Because they're inborn, part of the warp and woof of our being, running black in the blood, tainting every action and turning every good intention.

It hadn't been long until my nature caught up with me, and even my bond with the land wasn't strong enough to withstand it. Horrified and soul-sick, determined not to infect or destroy anything else that I loved—I broke my oath, and cut myself free of the bond.

Crippled, I left Archers Beach and embraced exile in the desert lands, where the granddaughter of a sea king could scarcely hope to thrive—and where the poison that blackened my heart could do no further harm.

Cutting the bond should have been enough to kill me—at least, those few of Gran's stories which dealt with the topic strongly suggested as much. Unfortunately, the sea king's line was a hardy one. The amputation hadn't killed me outright.

But it was killing me in stages.

And now here I was, where I'd sworn never to come again, and ironically, with an imperative to stay alive for just a bit longer.

The land had recognized me. I could infect it, if I renewed the bond.

Assuming the land would have me.

And assuming I was idiot enough to try.

The twitch at my metaphysical sleeve came again, somewhat stronger.

Biting my lip, I concentrated, visualizing a high stone tower and myself in the topmost room. A third twitch came, tentative now. Grimly, I kept to my tower, tasting salt from my abused lip, until I was at last rewarded with the feeling that I was alone.

I sighed out the breath I'd been holding, leaned my head against the storm gate and closed my eyes. Overhead, a gull screeched an oath, and I heard a motorcycle winding out, away down on Grand Avenue.

It was silent inside the storm gates, as if the space occupied some reality where gulls, motorcycles, and even the ocean didn't exist. Shadows were deep along the walls, hanging in hungry shrouds from the beams, roiling inkily 'gainst the ceiling: A winter's worth of frigid shadow, which would be what you'd expect. Beneath it, glowing with a silver-pink light like fog coming off the waves at dawn was—the carousel.

It's an old machine, as machine age gets counted—a menagerie, like the name says; three across, twenty-three animals and a chariot. The decking's hardwood, dark with age; the rounding boards and the swan chariot carved and gilded tupelo. Inside, boxing the center, and behind the orchestrion, are four oil paintings, depicting a tree in Spring, Summer, Fall, and Winter. Each overhead beam supports its own army of incandescent bulbs. The poles and the hardware are every damn' one of them brass; the orchestrion has brass grace notes and plays music off a perforated spool of Violano paper.

The animals are tupelo wood, like the boards and the chariot, the figures fanciful: dolphin, seal, seahorse, dragon, unicorn, goat, giraffe, ostrich, and leaping deer; a bobcat with tufted ears, a brute of a brown bear—there're those. Horses, too, if you didn't mind that some are a little odder than others. One's an Indian pony, with a blanket saddle and no reins; another's tall, broad and bejeweled, a lance set through the rings in its armor; still another's a dandy little gray with fangs, and batwings half-furled against its sides. I remembered them all—some more fondly than others.

Gingerly, I took a single step forward.

Force flowed and flowered, prickly against my skin; the wards resisted me, then yielded. I tasted mint and honey—a tattered remnant of Gran's signature—and then I was inside.

I took another step, which wasn't as easy as you might suppose— and one more, going by touch and memory, senses dazzled by the interplay of force...My fingers touched a clammy metal door; I yanked it open and hit the switch.

Electric light filled the space, melting the worst of the shadows. I sighed and sagged, shivering, against the post, considering the reality of the situation.

The animals looked dull in the ordinary light, their jewels clearly faux, the unicorn's horn listing a touch to the right. The bobcat was slightly misshapen, the bear a bit mangy, the brass bits on the orchestrion cloudy and showing a greenish sheen. Nothing that couldn't be put right with spit, polish, and paint, though it would be a job for one person working alone—but that wasn't the worst of the work to be done.

And how it was going to get done before the start of the Early Season on May 14, God alone knew. Just my luck the carousel was one of Fun Country's treasured Name Rides.

I sighed. Forcefully. Dammit, I was *so* going to give Gran an earful when I caught up with her.

A little voice muttered a worried *if* from the back of my head, but there wasn't any use borrowing trouble. Her tree was healthy, and she had to be somewhere in Archers Beach. Unfortunately, *until* I got hold of Gran, the carousel—and its occupants—were mine to deal with.

And may God have mercy on my soul. So to speak.

SIX

Wednesday, April 19

Bob's was empty when I arrived; "Hair of the Dog" coming down the airwaves from WBLM, perfectly audible over the moderate and genteel clatter from the kitchen.

"Coffee's on the plate!" Bob yelled from the back.

"Thanks!" I yelled back. "Is it too late for a grilled muffin?"

"Never too late for a grilled muffin," he answered, sticking his head through the hatch, and giving me a nod, downright affable. "'Morning, Kate. Blueberry?"

"Please."

"Get yourself settled, and I'll bring it out when it's ready."

"Thanks," I said again, and moved over to the hotplate.

The coffee didn't look any worse than usual. On the other hand, it didn't look any better. I carried my mug over to the center booth, right next to the radiator, slid into the corner, and administered a liberal dose of cream. The radiator was pumping out the heat; and I propped myself up in the corner of the booth, letting my eyelids droop. On WBLM, Nazareth finished up and the DJ came on with the weather. According to him, we were looking for afternoon highs around fifty-five, lows on the overnight in the upper twenties. He promised U2, The Cars, and

Tom Petty on the other side of the commercial break. I wrapped my hands around the coffee mug.

We were halfway through the second ad for MickeyD's when Bob appeared with my muffin. He thumped the plate down in front of me, with a knife, fork, and spoon all wrapped up in a white paper napkin. I sat up and put my mug aside.

"You let me know how that stacks up to them muffins Away, now," he directed.

Away is the pocket where your typical Mainer keeps anyplace that happens not to be Maine. Simplifies geography something wonderful.

"I will," I promised, and looked up to catch his eyes. "Bob?"

He frowned, shoulders stiffening. "Kate..." he said warningly, which, unfortunately, wasn't entirely unjustified. I raised my hands, showing him empty palms.

"I just have a question, okay?" I sounded snappish in my own ears, but Bob wouldn't find anything odd in that.

His shoulders stayed stiff, but at least he gave me a nod. "So, ask."

"How do I get a message to Nancy Vois?"

The shoulders eased a fraction. "She's usually in for coffee early. You can catch her then, or I can pass a word."

"I'd appreciate it if you'd pass on that I've got work for her, starting tomorrow at eight, if she's willing."

Bob damn' near smiled.

"I'll do that. You're staying the Season, then?"

"Probably not. But the ride needs to be ready to go, anyway."

I broke the paper tape and freed my utensils. The muffin smelled *wonder*ful, and I was suddenly and entirely ravenous.

"Right you are," Bob said softly. He stood by while I took my first taste of muffin.

I sighed, blissful. "*Nobody* Away understands grilled blueberry muffins," I told him honestly, and smite me if he didn't blush. I had some more muffin, trying to act like a lady and not bolt my food. I set the fork down, which took a major act of will, and reached for my mug.

"Another question," I said, looking back to Bob. "If you're willing."

He watched me while I sipped coffee, then shrugged. "I'm willing enough."

"I appreciate that," I said, meaning it. "Seen Mr. Ignatious?"

Bob snorted. "Him? He comes and goes—just like always, no rhyme or reason to it. Haven't seen him recent, if that's what you're after. Likely he'll turn up in time to get the Knot running for the Season. But whether he'll make Early Season—" Another shrug. "What d'you want him for?"

I had another forkful of muffin, taking my time about chewing. "I thought he might know where Gran's gone to," I said mildly.

There was a small pause.

"Even if he knew, will he know now?" Bob said, surprisingly tactful. "That's the question, Kate."

And honestly, it *was* the question. Mr. Ignat' isn't just a little foolish, though he'd been Gran's beau since I'd known her. I once asked her what she saw in him. "He makes me laugh," she'd said, after taking some time to consider it. "And he keeps me honest."

Which, all things considered, were reasons enough. Myself, I valued him for his warmth, and the uncounted simple kindnesses he'd bestowed on a surly, frightened halfling.

I chased the last bit of muffin around the plate, and didn't sigh.

Bob cleared his throat. "None of my business, but didn't that packet—"

The door to the street came open with a bang, bell clattering. I jumped, losing that last piece of muffin off my fork. Bob turned his head.

"Sorry, sorry!" The gray-haired man in the navy blue overcoat grabbed the handle and pushed the door closed. "She slipped away from me, is all. Didn't mean to disturb any illicit conversations— Oh, there you are, Kate!" He came over to the booth, hands at his rumpled hair, smoothing it down into perfection. "You might've phoned, you know, instead of letting me find out you're back home through a third party. 'Morning, Bob."

"You don't mean to say that Joe Nemeier actually *called* you?" I asked in disbelief. *Honestly*—flatlanders.

"'Morning, Henry," Bob said, heading back to the kitchen. "Coffee's on the plate. You want anything else, give a yell."

Henry nodded. "Not only did he call me with the news that you've poisoned his grass, but he was so obliging as to leave me the name and phone number of his lawyer in Boston," he said, smiling. There's nothing Henry Emerson likes better than to be calling attorneys in Boston and straightening out their view of the law.

"I'm glad to see you called Mr. Nemeier's lawyer right away," I said, mouth full of muffin.

"As it happens, I attempted to contact the gentleman as soon as I hung up with Mr. Nemeier, but—he was in a meeting. Left a message to call me on an urgent matter regarding his client. Then I called Tupelo House, but no one answered. You *will* get an answering machine, won't you, Kate?"

I swallowed. "I'll think about it."

"As you like, my dear, but tell me—what did you do to Mr. Nemeier's lawn?"

"He's over our line," I said. "I tried to explain the situation and he told me he was above property lines drawn on trees and rocks. Words were exchanged and—I lost my temper. The upshot being that nothing Mr. Nemeier plants on our land will grow."

Henry stroked his baby smooth chin with a long, well-manicured hand. It wasn't that he disbelieved me, I knew. The Emersons might not be as old as the Pepperidges, or as tied in with the land as the Archers, but they've been in town a good long while, and they've seen and heard tell of odder things than the simple hexing of a swath of grass.

"Kate," Henry said now, "where exactly was the boundary boulder?"

"Six feet into Mr. Nemeier's lawn," I told him, feeling my temper sparking again. I reached for my mug and drank more than I wanted of tepid, oily coffee.

His eyes gleamed. "Oh," he purred, "was it?" He smiled. "I think Mr. Nemeier's lawyer and I will be able to work out an accommodation," he said. "Do you want damages?"

"No, I don't want damages. I want him to honor the line."

"Consider it done, my dear. Call the office a little later today, all right?"

"Sure," I said, and put my mug down, eying him. "What're you doing here, by the way? The message on the machine says you're out until next week."

Henry's blue eyes widened. "Did it say that? Silly me. Of course, I meant I would be back in the office today."

"Really?" I asked, not buying it for a second.

"Really," Henry said emphatically. "Do me a favor, Kate, and try not to get angry again today. For my sake?"

"No promises," I told him. "I've got to see Marilyn about the lease."

Henry sighed, reached into an inside pocket and put a business card on the table next to my mug. "Keep my number handy," he said, and headed for the coffeepot.

"What the hell do you mean, I can't pay the Season up front?" I glared at Marilyn, who wasn't impressed. Historically, Marilyn was unimpressed. She'd been the resident agent for Fun Country since before I'd graduated high school, and I've never been able to figure out if she's unflappable, or just stupid. Purely academic, you understand; the end result was just as annoying.

"New policy," she said, turning her back on me to haul open the listing file cabinet and finger through the paper-choked drawer.

"What new policy?" I asked, sarcasm mode full *on*. "Fun Country's going to stop skinning its tenants?"

"The new policy is that Fun Country is now accepting park space lease payments in three equal installments throughout the Season," Marilyn said, in her Number Three Neutral Voice, not even bothering to turn around. "Corporate hopes that this move will ease the financial burden on our tenants."

Yeah, sure. Like Fun Country Corporate cared about its tenants except as cash cows. Something was going on that would shortly be found to not benefit the tenants one whit, but I was too tired to try and scope it out right now. All I wanted to do right now was pay the damn' rent and go home.

"Look, Marilyn, I got a certified letter from the boss down in Jersey, giving me a deadline of tomorrow to pay up the whole Season's rent. I've got the money right here—in cash. So just write out the receipt and I'll stop taking up your air."

Marilyn slammed the file cabinet and came back to her desk, settling in to the chair before finally looking at me.

"Katharine," she said, patiently, like I was maybe four and on the verge of a tantrum, which, come to think of it, was pretty much the way I felt. "I'll be happy to accept your first payment. Since you're paying before Corporate's deadline, according to regulations now in force, you won't need to take any further action at this time."

I sighed, loud.

"I want to pay the whole Season and get it over with," I said, keeping it reasonable and calm.

"I'm sorry, but that's not possible," Marilyn answered, folding her hands together on the desk top and looking like she could wait all day for me to Get It. Which personal experience has shown that she can and will do.

"All right," I said, giving her the round. Bob's muffin had been amazingly restorative, but I wasn't about to risk phasing out in front of Marilyn.

I pulled the bank envelope out of my pocket, counted a third of the bills onto her desk, then reached into my jeans pocket and dropped three dimes and four pennies on top.

"You can keep the extra two-thirds of a cent for your trouble, deah," I told her.

Marilyn didn't even look at me. She swept the change into her palm, picked the bills up off the desk, counted them twice, then leaned over to unlock the cash drawer. She put the bills away nice and neat, like paired with like and all facing the same direction, and dropped the dimes and the pennies in their assigned pockets.

That done, she relocked the drawer, pulled the receipt book to her, and flipped it open, carefully slid the overworked strip of carbon paper between the next two clean sheets. Picking up a generic blue ballpoint, she clicked it and wrote the ticket out in her round, neutral handwriting, bearing down extra hard, wringing the last bit of ink out of the carbon. That done, she turned the book around and filled out the stub, too. Then she clicked the pen closed, and used both hands to tear the receipt out of the book.

She handed it to me without looking up.

"Thank you, Katharine. Your next payment is due on June first. Have a nice day."

I took the receipt and left, pausing outside the door for a deep breath of ocean air.

Well, I thought, as I folded the receipt and slipped it carefully into the pocket of my jeans, I hadn't set Marilyn's hair on fire. Wouldn't Henry be proud?

I walked slowly across to the square and sat down on the edge of the fountain, still in its winter wrappings. The sun was warm and welcome, and I closed my eyes, half-drowsing, until the wail of a siren 'way up on 5 startled me awake.

Right. I pushed myself to my feet and took a deep breath.

Next stop, Gregor's Electronics.

SEVEN

The sun was bright and busy about melting away the last of the morning mist when I strolled across Fountain Circle at a few minutes shy of a quarter 'til eight. I'd slept twelve hours straight through, which was somewhere between an oddity and a miracle, and was decidedly the better for it.

Someone had gotten it together to run the American, Maine, and Canadian flags up the triple flagpoles at the center of the circle, and they were snapping smartly in a brisk off-shore breeze. Seagulls swung in a complicated do-si-do overhead, their shadows flashing across the cobblestones.

Inside Fun Country, the storm gate was open at Tony Lee's Kitchen, and the breeze brought me the scent of fresh-frying egg rolls. My stomach grumbled like I hadn't fed it perfectly good scrambled eggs and toast not twenty minutes before. I bribed it with a sip of coffee from the commuter mug I carried—good coffee, the last of my morning pot, not any of Bob's paint remover—and bore left.

A shadow clung to the carousel's storm gates, thin and tremulous. It moved before I could get worried, resolving into Nancy Vois.

"You're early," I said, as she came forward to meet me, hands tucked into the pockets of her jeans.

She smiled slightly, the lines around her pale gold eyes deepening.

"Want to make a good impression," she said in her raspy voice, "my first day on the job."

"I'm impressed," I assured her, and she nodded like she'd expected it to be so.

I opened the hatch and shouldered it wide, releasing a gust of ice-cold air. Nancy slipped by me and used the toe of her work boot to shove the door-stop brick into position.

The shadows retreated a mite from the rectangle of sunlight, and I gave Nancy an approving nod before going across to the fuse box and hitting the switch.

Electric light flared, and the shadows retreated further.

Or so I told myself.

I had a sip of coffee and set the cup down next to the post. When I turned around, Nancy was standing quietly just outside the tattered wards, hands in pockets, gimme hat shoved back off her forehead, considering the animals with that kind of bland indifference that makes you think somebody's seen something they'd rather not have, and are trying very hard to pretend they weren't ever going to see anything like it again.

"When I worked for your gran," she said, not looking at me, oh, no, not at all. "Couple Seasons back. She had me to bring the mechanicals up to spec, polish the brass, and see to the organ. Herself, she did what was needful for the critters." She slide a pale gold glance in my direction. "I'm agreeable to a similar arrangement. But you ought to know right off, I'm no hand with them animals."

As if anybody but a powerful *trenvay*, or a mage of note—or, in Gran's case, an extremely powerful *trenvay* who also had some small skill in magery—could handle the animals. I nodded to show I understood her position.

"I'll need you to do exactly what you did for Gran," I said. "I'll take care of the menagerie."

She was quiet a a beat too long, her eyes still on the animals. "That's all right then," she said finally, and shifted her shoulders.

"Saw the one with the batwings take a nip out of a fella come down to talk with your gran," she said abruptly. "Plain fact. Your gran, she didn't much care for him, that's how I read it." A sigh, another shift of thin shoulders under the shapeless sweater. "Bill collector, he looked like to me." She shook herself and turned to face me. "I'll need to get into the tool locker."

"That'll be the next stop for both of us," I agreed, leading the way around to the metal shed against the permanent wall that stood between the carousel and Summer's Wheel.

The door shrieked when I opened it, and of course I jumped a foot, gasping like a fish out of water, and damn' near knocked Nancy over.

"Sorry," I muttered, and skinned inside, barking my shins on something, and reached up to turn the light bulb in its socket. Tools and brushes were illuminated, hung on pegboard along two sides of the interior; solvents, lubricants, and paint cans sorted by color sat on the shelves beneath. All nice and orderly, just like Gran always kept things. In the center, right at shin-barking height, stood two wooden sawhorses, a paint-spattered tarp folded neatly across the pair of them. Nancy helped me shift them out onto the concrete, then went back inside for a can of WD-40, which she used liberally on the metal door hinges.

"That'll keep 'er quiet," she said with satisfaction, moving the door back and forth to show off the silence. I gave her a smile.

"'Preciate it," I said, and carried the tarp out to the utility pole, where I rescued my mug and drank what was left of the tepid coffee, considering the task at hand.

Of the twenty-three creatures on the carousel, seventeen are ordinary tupelo wood carvings, much in need of repainting. Not an easy job, but doable, stipulating I started doing pretty quick.

The remaining six—those being the seahorse, unicorn, goat, wolf, the armored charger, and the dainty batwinged gray—were something else entirely. Specifically, they're criminals in their homelands, exiled by order of the Wise, who seemed to think rustication would do them good.

There are, as you might imagine, a couple of problems about that.

The first is that the climate hereabouts is terribly hard on the bindings that tie the wrongdoers to the carousel creatures. Which means that, at the end of every Season the bindings are renewed, and the extra protection of industrial-grade wards and warn-aways are put in place.

At the beginning of the Season, the bindings are strengthened, though obviously you don't want to ward a public amusement. Most people aren't sensitive enough to notice the bindings, or that some of animals are a little . . . strange. Still, it's a risky enterprise, with the potential for being Extremely Unhealthy for the average man on the midway. Not that the Wise care. Given to odd notions, the Wise, and with lots of firepower to back them up.

It was just such an odd notion that fixed on the carousel as the perfect instrument of incarceration. According to Gran, they figured the local climate would eventually work beneficial changes on their criminals.

The operative word being "eventually."

Second problem is that the nature of the criminals and their jail more or less requires constant oversight by a skilled magic-worker. If that sort of supervision isn't on tap, the whole operation goes from risky to stupendously dangerous.

I sighed. As far as I could see—which, let's be honest, was somewhere just shy of the end of my nose—the bindings on the creatures were still strong. The wards fraying was—troubling, but not critical. Hell, it was even theoretically possible that I could use some the remaining energy in the wards to craft new bindings.

Unfortunately, all I had was theory, though I supposed I'd have to put it to the test if a better answer didn't present itself. The optimum solution being that Gran showed up within the next fifteen minutes and took a hand.

Failing that, I could at least start with the repainting.

One thing at a time.

We'd left the hatch propped open, letting in the noise of the day to disturb the deep silence inside the storm gates. Nancy was down deep in the workings, making a good bit of noise herself.

But up on the carousel, inside the wards, it was as quiet and breathless as the ocean air just before a nor'easter.

I cleaned and repainted the broad work on the chariot first, leaving it to dry before I went back with a fine brush for the scrolls, then cleaned the Indian pony and spread the tarp around the base, paints open and brushes to hand. The work demanded concentration; more than it should have, really. I started at the ears and moved down, trying to work fast, but careful. Trying to take simple pleasure in the simple work.

My hand shook at first, but eventually I settled into the rhythm, and by the time I'd gotten 'round to brightening the feathers braided into the wild mane, I was actually beginning to enjoy myself.

Which is when something nipped me, sharp and secret, and I jumped, smudging yellow into black.

What have we here? A wounded soldier at the front? The voice was oily and insincere and the instant I heard it, I wanted it out of my head.

It laughed, not nicely, and I recognized it now—the batwing horse.

Halt, lame, blind, and failing. But not deaf yet, eh? Where is the old one? Rotted at last and leaving only you between Is and Ending?

I took a breath, used the rag on the smudge, and touched up the feather edge, pleased to see my hand so steady.

"You'll get your chance," I said, and my voice was steady, too.

Indeed. I am quite looking forward to it. Don't tarry too long at your mundane tasks, halfling. It wouldn't do for you to die before the challenge. There was a blast of wind, bitter and edgy, rocking my brain in its holdings—and I was alone again inside my head.

I put the brush in the turpentine jar, and sat back on my heels, shaking all over. Which was bad, very bad. If they thought I was too weak to stand against an attack...

I took a breath, tasting turpentine, and wobbled to my feet.

It was definitely time for a break.

I stepped off the deck, and crossed the floor on rubbery legs, the wards so much white noise against my senses. When I broke through, it was like coming into clear air after a long dive, lungs burning, eyes tearing, muscles shivering with effort.

My ears cleared first, filling up with metallic clanks, the distant scream of a seagull, men's voices, the spit of hot oil...

I gulped a mouthful of air, blinked my eyes clear—and blinked again.

He had one shoulder against the pole supporting the fuse box, sipping coffee from a Styrofoam cup emblazoned with the proud scarlet legend, "Bob's Diner, East Grand Avenue, Archers Beach, Maine. Where the Stars Come to Dine."

"Afternoon," he said comfortably. "We met yesterday morning, over at the Pier—you might remember it."

I took a breath and gave him a nod. "Borgan."

He smiled and raised the cup in salute. "Always nice when a pretty lady remembers my name," he said and had a sip from his cup. "Hope it's all right that I'm here."

It was slightly worrisome that he was here, frankly, though I'd told him right out straight who I was. I didn't need a stalker—especially one twice as big as I was, in all directions. On the other hand, I also didn't need an enemy.

So I shrugged. "It's a public amusement," I said, and pointedly didn't ask him why he had come.

It wasn't much of a conversation starter, but he didn't seem to be the sort who was bothered by silence. He stayed in his comfortable lean, cup in his left hand, right tucked into the pocket of his jacket, and considered me out of deep-set black eyes in a way that reminded me uncomfortably of the batwing horse.

I sighed, shoved the sleeves of my sweatshirt down, and tucked my hands into my back pockets, meeting those deep ironic eyes square, determined to wait him out.

Borgan's mouth twitched, but the nod he gave me was as bland as a Mainer could want it. "You're looking well," he said, in that polite tone people use when they trot out a pleasantry that wasn't exactly true.

"You don't look bad, yourself," I replied in the same tone, which was downright niggardly. I don't usually cotton to big men, but Borgan had an air of placid competence about him that was damned attractive. Not that I was about to tell him that. I pressed my lips together and waited.

More silence, during which the racket Nancy had been orchestrating came to an abrupt, unharmonious end, followed by muttering, and approaching footsteps. I turned my head, breaking Borgan's gaze, as my help came 'round the carousel, cap set at an irritable angle.

She checked when she saw him, just a tiny hesitation between one step and the next, then picked up her stride again, giving him an off-handed nod. "Cap'n Borgan."

"Nancy," he answered easily. "How are ya today?"

"Doin' well, sir. Thank you for askin'." She moved her attention to me. "Need some solvent and a quarter-inch socket wrench," she said. "I'll go on up to the hardware and put 'em 'gainst the tab."

I nodded. "Anything else?"

"Nothin' apparent," she said. "You want anything while I'm goin'?"

"I'm good," I told her, which was nowhere near the truth, and, give her credit, Nancy didn't fall for it.

"You're looking a bit peckish, if you don't mind my saying. It's coming on to noon. Why don't I fetch you along a sandwich?"

Noon? My stomach bunched up again. I'd been inside the wards for *four hours?* That wasn't—

Nancy was waiting. So, unfortunately, was Borgan. I gave her a half-smile and a head shake. "I'll step over to Tony's in a few and get myself an egg roll," I said. "You take some time for lunch while you're out."

She hesitated, then nodded. "Right, then. Back in a shake." She moved off, giving Borgan a glance and a nod. "Cap'n."

"Nancy," he said again, and the two of us reposed in silence until her shadow was gone from the hatch.

"Nancy's sound," Borgan commented. He gave me a grin. "Despite she doesn't like me."

This was disturbing news. "Why not?"

He lifted a shoulder. "I'm fishing her mother's boat, like I said. Somebody's got to do it since Hum went and got himself killed. Only thing he had to leave Mary and the girl was the boat."

"But Mary gets her piece, right?" I asked. He nodded.

"So what's Nancy's beef?"

"Mary's piece is sixty-five percent, and I'll tell you it took some clever tacking to settle it there with her believing the whole thing to be her idea. Nancy was a mite less distracted, though, and she's not one to take charity."

"Oh." I sighed. Charity was what you did for others, not, no never, what you took. And sixty-five percent of the haul, owner or not—

"Maybe Nancy wonders how you can live on thirty-five percent of the take."

"I don't have many expenses," he said. "Own my own place, and all."

There wasn't much to say to that, and I didn't. Borgan was starting to wear out his welcome, and it was on the tip of my tongue to ask him why the hell he was—

"Before I forget," he said, straightening out of his lean with easy, boneless grace. He reached into his jacket, came two steps forward and held out a broad hand. "Nerazi sends these to you."

I started, barely sparing a glance at what he held, looking hard at his face, at the leather jacket, at the thin, beaded braid snaking over his shoulder...

"You're *trenvay*," I managed, after a moment, and my voice sounded accusatory in my own ears.

Borgan raised a lazy eyebrow. "You say that like it's a bad thing."

I glared at him. "Why didn't you tell me?"

"Didn't come up," he said, reasonably enough. "You want these or should I take 'em back to Nerazi with a no-thank-'ee?"

"These" being a pair of old work gauntlets, stained, scored and battered; the wide cuffs were blue, badly faded, the palms and fingers a mottled pinkish-red. I blinked, then threw back my head and laughed. Gloves according to my station, indeed.

Borgan waited, patiently, gloves extended, until I'd gotten it out of my system.

Slightly out of breath, I did some fast calculations.

Taking a gift from a *trenvay* is always a risky proposition. There's no such thing as a free lunch in their worldview, where everything given requires a thing given in return, sooner or later, and usually at the worst possible time. It was just better all around not to go there, and while you were at it, to never invite one into your house or guarded space.

All that being so, it wasn't in me to refuse a gift from Nerazi—for one thing, it would offend her, and I couldn't afford that. And for another, Nerazi was Gran's oldest friend.

I stepped forward and took the gloves out of Borgan's hand.

They were warm from their nestle inside his jacket. I took a steadying breath and retreated the two steps I'd advanced, hands dropping to my side, gloves fisted in the right.

"So," I said nastily. "You're Nerazi's errand boy?"

He shrugged, taking no visible offense; coffee cup held negligently in his left hand. "Nerazi knew I'd be looking for you, and asked me to bear them along."

My chest tightened. "Why would you be looking for me?" I snapped.

"Why not?" he returned, and lifted his empty hand, fingers spread wide. "Look, Kate. Why don't you let me buy you a cup of coffee?"

I gasped, startled into a laugh.

"No, thanks," I said, shortly. "I've got work to do."

His mouth tightened; then he gave me a brief nod. "Right. Dinner then. I'll pick you up at eight." With that, he was gone, moving quick and quiet, across the room and out the hatch, leaving me blinking stupidly at the place he'd been standing, the battered work gloves clenched warm and forgotten in my hand.

EIGHT

Thursday, April 20
Low Tide 10:52 P.M.
Sunset 7:31 P.M. EDT

I held the bottle with both hands, so as not to spill wine on the counter; my hands were shaking that bad. Also, somebody had a jackhammer going inside my right temple, and my peripheral vision was filled with a haze of spangled pastels.

Other than that, though, I was cool.

A brief tussle got the cork back where it belonged and the bottle into the door of the fridge. I got a two-handed grip on the glass and had a healthy slug, wishing I'd thought to buy something with a higher alcohol content.

Second shift inside the wards had been—nightmarish, even for somebody with a high threshold for horror. The batwing didn't speak again, but as the afternoon wore on, the others wakened and begin to test their limits. Metaphorically speaking, I'd been pushed, pinched, slapped, cut, and burned all afternoon, to the increasingly cruel and raucous laughter of those who had no reason to love me or mine, and every reason to oppose us, heart and will.

Well.

I gulped some more wine, got my eyes open and my feet under me and went over to check the answering machine I'd gotten at

Gregor's yesterday. Henry still hadn't returned my call. It was too late to catch him in the office, but I dialed the number anyway, and had another swallow of wine while his machine picked up and ran through its recorded message.

At the tone, I cleared my throat. "Henry, it's Kate," I said, my voice a creaky whisper. "I'm wondering how it went with Nemeier's lawyer. I'll be at the carousel tomorrow, or you can call and leave a message on my machine. Bye."

That minor chore taken care of, I went to the fridge, topped off my glass, and wandered out into the great room. My laptop was sitting on the coffee table where I'd left it last night, lid up and ready-light glowing, cell phone charging beside it. My books—what few I still owned—were in the case, hobnobbing like old buds with Gran's collection. My clothes were taking up about half the available space in the closet upstairs; my jacket and keys hung ready on the hook by the door, next to Gran's old brown sweater.

It was . . . a relief . . . to see how little impact I had on my surroundings. Pretty soon, the process would be complete and I wouldn't take up any room at all. Before that, though, I had to get Gran back on the case, and clean out such stuff as I did have, so as not to leave a mess.

I had another sip of wine and thought about going to bed, but I knew I wouldn't be able to sleep with the echo of the batwing's voice still caught inside my head.

Instead, I moved over to the fireplace. Wood was laid in, newspaper and matches to hand, the grate swept clean. The winter I came to live with Gran, the fireplace had been my best friend. I spent hours kneeling on the brick hearth, watching stories unfold in the flames, telling them out loud, not once looking over at Gran, or at Mr. Ignatious, who'd been there more often than not, where they sat quiet over book or handwork, and never let on that they were paying any mind.

The stories I told the flames were hardly happy. I told how my grandfather had contested with Ramendysis of the Storm and fallen, his power and his property forfeit. I told how Ramendysis drank my father's power, and that of all our House, until they were but dust blowing upon the scented breeze. All gone, except my mother and myself. I whispered to the flames the story of my shame, and how my mother had bargained for my freedom with her soul.

It must've been beyond creepy, the hoarse little-girl voice reciting the atrocities of another time and place. I remember thinking at the time—believing—that the fire took the stories as I said them, and unmade them, so the histories I recited had never... really... happened.

It's a wonderful thing to be a child, and to believe in fairy tales.

I moved my gaze from the cold firestones—up to the crowded mantelpiece.

On the far left, wedged between a clam shell full of sand dollars and a smooth gray beach stone, framed in shiny red plastic, was a group shot—the end-of-Season blow-out at Bob's, when all the townies get together and drink to the absence of tourists. Front and center was Gran, tidy and cool in canvas slacks and a flowered shirt, hair wrapped 'round her head in that complicated knot she favors, a beer in one square, capable hand and the other on the shoulder of a gremlin, dark hair hanging in witches' locks, eyes as giving as peridot in a surly pointed face, oversized Black Sabbath T-shirt emphasizing her thinness. Nerazi stood on the other side of the gremlin, elegant in a yellow sun dress.

Behind Gran was Mr. Ignatious, smiling his sweet, absent smile; then Brand Carver, who owned Summer's Wheel, Jelly Lee of the Oriental Funhouse, Millie Bouchard of Dodge City, and Skip Davies, who ran the games of skill and chance spotted around Fun Country. Back behind was Bob, his arm around a washed-out looking woman—Lillian, that would have been, right before she died—and various of the street artists, bit players, roadies, and hangers-on who appeared at need every May and faded away again in September, like the shoemaker's elves, only with a longer term contract.

I sipped some more wine, moving on to the next picture—slim and lithe, light brown curls tossed by the breeze, a smile on her face to melt stone—Gran's daughter, Nessa. My mother.

Next came another picture of the same girl, dressed in drifty white lace, one hand up, pinning the wide-brimmed hat to her head, the other held in a death-grip by a black-haired gremlin of a fellow, wild hair tamed by a liberal application of pomade, dark eyes feral in a pale, pointed face—my father, Nathan Archer.

Not for the first time I wondered how Gran could tolerate that picture, considering everything that happened, later. Gran, though—Gran never spoke a word of anger or criticism of my father, not in my hearing, not ever. And if she held it against me that I'd survived while her Nessa had not, she'd kept that to herself, too.

Turning away from the mantle, I wandered across the room to the French doors, and stood watching the smooth, glassy roll of the waves.

"I am," I confided to the room at large, "*so* cooked."

If I took a lesson from today's adventures it was that I was long past the point of being able to bind the prisoners.

Trenvay who are separated from their land waste and die. That's what happened to Lillian, dead of the toxins that had leached into her pond.

I wasn't *trenvay*, but I'd given myself and all that I was to the land. Cutting that bond had wounded me. It had taken some while, given who and what I was, but I was dying of it. I no longer had access to the land's—oh, hell, call it magic. Everybody else does. And while I could still draw on my inborn power—witness the death of Joe Nemeier's pretty grass—the cost was . . . steep.

Problem being that there's magic—and magic. The trees up on Heath Hill, aware, awake, and interested—that's magic, all right. Mouse magic. Homey magic.

The carousel, the geas set upon the prisoners, and that which I had been born into—*that* was magic of a very different order.

The High Magic, if you like it that way—that's predicated on *jikinap*, which is—roughly—personal power. The more *jikinap* a particular mage possesses, the greater her ability to manipulate High Magic. Every magical encounter has the potential of leaving the winning magic-worker higher on the food chain. Given that High Magic is intoxicating *and* addictive, this leads to a certain competitiveness, not to say the wholesale destruction of entire Houses. The more power a mage acquires, the more dangerous it—and they—are. It's unfortunately not uncommon to learn that a particularly ambitious mage's power has eaten him.

Ozali. That's what you call a master mage. Aeronymous, my grandfather, had been Ozali, much good it'd done him.

There are a few who've managed to stay sensible and not accumulate so much *jikinap* that it turns on them. Those beings are called the Wise, and in council they stand as the ultimate magical authority across the Six Worlds.

Those who don't care for the acquiring of *jikinap,* or who, for one reason or another, choose not to exercise their power—they're nobody.

Like me.

I leaned my forehead against the window, the glass cold against my skin. Outside, the sea rolled, pastel pink beneath the setting sun, keeping its counsel close.

I towel-dried my hair, pulled on my oldest pair of jeans and a denim shirt, and mooched sock-footed down the hall, headed for a grilled cheese sandwich, and yet another glass of wine, on the admittedly shaky theory that if I drank enough, I'd be able to sleep.

Not bothering with the light, I put my hand on the fridge—and jumped a foot straight up when the doorbell gave tongue.

Brrrrrrrrrrrrrrrrrriiiiinnnnnnnnnnng!

I hate that damn' doorbell. Always have. The first time I heard it, I thought it sounded like a hunting Hound, and the years haven't altered my opinion any, or the ice-creep down my spine.

Grounded again, I turned—and the bell gave tongue a second time. I leapt into the hall and yanked the door open before the third offense, ready to gut whoever'd—

"Good evening, Kate," Borgan said. "We made a date for dinner."

He'd dressed for it, too—black jeans, open-collar white shirt under the leather jacket, and a nacre stud in his right ear. He looked clean, calm, competent, and—beautiful.

Of course, he was also *trenvay* and could make himself seem any damn' way he cared to.

I took a hard breath. "*You* made a date for dinner," I snapped. "I didn't agree to go anywhere with you. And I *hate* that doorbell!"

He tipped his head, and settled into a half-sit against the railing, hands in his pockets.

"Didn't know that," he said. "Now that I do, I won't use it again."

Like he was going to be stopping by as a regular thing. The cool assumption left me momentarily speechless.

"You like Italian?" Borgan asked. "There's a new place up on Two that might—"

"I'm not going to dinner with you," I said, as clearly and calmly as I could manage. "I am not going to let you give me a cup of coffee—or anything else. I am not inviting you into this house, or into any other place that's mine. I might look like a blind, blithering idiot, but that doesn't mean I'm going to make it easy for you."

His mouth twitched; not quite a smile. "Believe me, I never once thought you were gonna make it easy for me," he said, a shade too seriously. He pulled his hands out of his pockets and turned them up, showing me broad palms calloused with work and weather, and empty of any overt threat.

"Kate. I want to talk, that's all." He turned his head to look out over the sand and the sea, then back to me. "Take a walk with me."

"Am I not getting through to you, here? I *said*—"

"Just down the beach a way," he interrupted, and shook his head, rueful, as I read it. "I'm not such a fool as to mischief Bonny Pepperidge's granddaughter, y'know. For one thing, Nerazi'd gut me, and for another your Gran'd break a board over my head."

I stared at him. He waited.

I broke first.

"What do you want to talk about?" I asked, with scant grace.

"Things in town you might not know about, being gone so long."

Well, that certainly sounded innocent enough; light years better than being alone with my thoughts. And the beach was neutral territory.

More or less.

"All right," I said, stepping back inside. "I'll be out in a minute." I closed the door.

Two minutes later, shod, jacket on, pockets a-bulge with the old work gloves, I stepped out onto the landing, pulling the door closed behind me.

Borgan was still in his lean against the railing, face turned to the sea, the breeze toying with his braid like a lover.

He looked 'round and came to his feet, hands out in plain sight, and the ghost of a smile on his lips.

My chest constricted; not the long-familiar pain, but something...else. I took a deep breath. I knew *trenvay* glamor when I felt it. So much for Borgan's assurances of good behavior.

I looked up at him, and jerked my chin toward the stairway.

"After you," I said, shortly.

NINE

Thursday, April 20

The wind was blowing up from the south, directly into our faces as we headed toward Kinney Harbor. I shivered and buttoned my jacket, more conscious than I liked of Borgan turning his head to look down at me, a puzzled set to his shoulders.

"Cold?" he asked, voice shaded with disbelief. I sighed.

"My blood got thin, Away. All right? Just pretend I'm a tourist."

"Don't believe I can do that," he answered, and there was silence between us for a while as we walked along the edge of the quiet sea. The tide was going out, and Borgan walked on my right, courteously ceding me the firmer sand nearest the water.

"What did you do," he asked suddenly, "all that time Away?"

Not the direction I had expected the conversation to take, but maybe Borgan needed a round of small talk to warm him up to the advertised topic. Whatever. I shrugged. "Went to university, got a degree in computer science. Wound up working for a start-up with its tail on fire."

"You did okay, then?" he persisted. "Out there in the dry lands?"

"I did all right," I allowed. "'Til it all went to hell." I looked out across the dusky water, shivered again, and tucked my hands into my pockets, knuckles nestled against the rough fabric of the work gloves.

"The dot com bust," Borgan said wisely. "I read about that. Lose your shirt?"

"Nah, I was just out of work, with a whole bunch of useless stock certificates to show for my time." I sighed. "After, I got some gigs here and there—contract work. Enough to keep heart and mind together." *While the dying took its course,* I finished silently.

I slid a glance in his direction, but he was looking over my head—at the sky, maybe, or the early stars.

"You're not interested in what I did Away."

He looked down at me, black eyes glinting. "Actually, I am," he said, and he sounded serious. Worse, he *looked* serious.

Trenvay, I reminded myself, and sighed.

"I thought you wanted to bring me up to speed on all the changes since I've been gone," I said.

"I did want to do that," he acknowledged, and then didn't say anything more. Ahead of us, the Pier was a stern shadow against the dusk, the beach beneath it as black as one of those painted tunnels you see in Road Runner cartoons.

"Your gran might've told you about the city trade coming up the coast?"

I shrugged, hands deep in my pockets. "I didn't exactly keep in close contact." In fact, all the contact-keeping had been on Gran's side. When she stopped calling, I'd just thought she'd finally realized that I wasn't worth her trouble. Until the overdue notice from Fun Country arrived in the mail.

"Well," Borgan said.

We went under the Pier, and walked silent through the shadow. A gull shouted overhead as we came out on the far side, turned on a wing-tip and sped away over Fun Country, on a heading for Heath Hill.

"So," I prodded my companion. "Drugs are coming up-coast from Boston, are they?"

"Boston—and other places, too," Borgan agreed. "That fella bought the Rogers' land's got a piece of it. You'll want to sail wide of him."

It was just like me, I thought resignedly, to first off run into the biggest trouble in town—and piss him off, too.

"Day late and a dollar short," I told Borgan, and he flicked me a glance.

"What happened?"

I sighed. "He didn't like my suggestion that he honor our property lines. I lost my temper and a couple feet of grass in the disputed territory fried and died. Henry had a call in to Mr. Nemeier's Boston lawyer yesterday. I haven't heard back, but he didn't seem to think there was going to be a problem."

"Might not be, so long as it's kept between lawyers," Borgan allowed. "Still, he's not a man to cross. Don't provoke him."

I shrugged. "He doesn't provoke me, I don't provoke him. Win–win."

Borgan stopped walking, so I did, too, wondering if we'd reached the end of what he'd wanted to tell me, and if I could go home now. I was aching all over, and cold, not to mention light-headed and drifty. The wine must've been more potent than I'd thought.

"Kate." Borgan raised a hand like he was going to touch my shoulder, then thought better of it. "Joe Nemeier and his crew're running loads of never-you-mind up through the town, and the so-called abandoned places."

It wouldn't be the first time; Archers Beach has a long association with smuggling. Seven miles of sand beach, a long shelf, and a fair number of little inlets giving on to unpeopled land make it attractive to those who aren't particularly interested in calling attention to themselves or their work.

Problem being that *trenvay* live in and care for most of those so-called abandoned places. And *trenvay*, like most Mainers, don't much care for having strangers on their land.

"You'll want to be *careful*, if you've got any understanding of the word, and not only of the man himself," Borgan said. "His crew's no better than it should be, and the town's on edge. You need to be watchful and on guard, like you never had to be careful on the Beach, years back."

A speech, forsooth—all said out as solemn and firm as could be. Which wasn't much like *trenvay*. I looked up into his face and saw no shred of mischief; only an earnestness that matched his tone.

"All right," I said, keeping my own voice serious. "But if Mr. Nemeier and his crew are running illegal substances up into Archers Beach, then that's a job for the police, or the Coast Guard."

"Yeah, well." He sighed. "Comes about the Coasties can't even *see* 'em. The *trenvay* who belongs to the rocks at the Notch got tired of all those strange feet traipsing through his living room, and tried to put a stop to it himself."

Not unreasonable, I thought. A *trenvay* in his own territory was formidable. Not quite invincible, but more than a match for a mere man, no matter how—

"Damn' near got himself unmade," Borgan interrupted my comfy train of thought. "Told Nerazi the only thing saved him was that he *was* standing on his own stones. Never did lay a hand on 'em, though the same couldn't be said for them."

I frowned. "That's—funny."

"If you got a certain sense of humor," he agreed. "Anyways, it turns out we can see 'em fine, but not one of us can touch 'em—and I'm counting me and Nerazi among those who've tried."

Oh, really? I thought, but Borgan was going on.

"We're thinking maybe they've got some downcoast help. Nerazi sent a couple of hers to ask around. In the meantime, we're watching, and keeping as secret as we can."

"You can't touch *them*," I said slowly, as the idea took shape. "But what about the goods?"

"Now, then..." Borgan shifted his gaze. Silence stretched while he considered the sea over my left shoulder. At least, I thought he was looking at the sea, though it could've been the sky again, or the ragged blotches of Blunt and Stafford islands—or a fleet of Viking ships. It was impossible to tell which—or any—from his expression, though I told myself I'd hear an invading fleet of Vikings.

The wind gusted, spraying sand against the side of my face, and I shivered again in the sudden burst of chill. Borgan blinked, and sent a sharp look down into my face.

"Here I invite a girl to walk out with me, then keep her standing 'round to freeze," he said wryly. He turned and continued down the beach, keeping his stride short, so I didn't have any trouble pacing him. He didn't say anything else, which didn't bother me as much as it maybe should have. I kept on walking at his side, still feeling a trifle drifty, though warmer, with the walking; comfortable in and comforted by the ordinary sounds of the shore.

Fun Country was well behind us now. Ahead, a shimmer of rippling reds and oranges pulsed against the deepening sky, like the Northern Lights, but much, much too close to the earth.

Googin Rock.

You have to be sensitive to...magic...to feel the pale, hot colors coming off the Rock like they do, and hear the way the sea sizzles and boils around it. You don't have to be anything but human, though, to see the pockets and the edges along that jagged surface phosphorescing in the dark, and know deep in your gut that it's no good place to be.

I caught glimpses and glimmers out the sides of my eyes, enough to notice that the fell-fire over the Rock brightened as we approached, and to see how the outgoing waves struck the surface hard, unlike any other place on the beach. Beside me, Borgan shook himself, and looked over to it.

"Irritable this evening," he commented, and I nodded agreement. The water spat as we passed by.

Beyond the Rock, the beach curved hard 'round the foot of Heath Hill. The persistent breeze brought me the creak of lines and the splash of water against hull; the sounds of Kinney Harbor, where the working boats of Archers Beach put in to sleep.

Sand gave way to rock underfoot—a portion of the old jetty. To the right was the harbor with its drowsing boats, and a two-master tied up at the dock, lantern glowing over the wheelhouse and her sails rolled tight. I stopped at the foot of the pier, the better to take her in.

"Come aboard and let me give you a cup of coffee, Kate; warm you right up."

"Aboard?" I blinked, and turned to look up at my companion. "Yours?" I asked. "She's a beauty."

"Got 'er from family up to Halifax," he said, easing onto the dock. "Been up on blocks since Uncle Veleg died, and needed a touch of work. Happened I had a couple minutes on my hands..." He let the rest drift off.

I couldn't say how much work it had taken to refurb the boat, though I imagined, from the over-dry tone, that it had been considerable. Let it stand that she *was* a beauty; a classic Tancook Schooner, deck gleaming and paint sharp. Gray she was on the dark water; a fine, fresh-looking lady, with just the right amount of sass and salt to her.

I sighed, letting my eyes rest on the smooth lines of her, drifty and unfocused, feeling myself slip sideways, the boat softening in my sight—until I didn't see anything at all.

TEN

Thursday, April 20

When I came to myself, I was lying on my back on a hard surface. My muscles felt like water, and it seemed . . . tremendously difficult . . . to form thoughts. I took an experimental breath, and thought about opening my eyes. It seemed like an awful lot of trouble, but after due consideration I supposed I really ought to know where I was.

To prepare for this arduous undertaking, I took a deliberately deep breath—and another, tasting salt and sand. Thus fortified, I opened my eyes.

The night sky spread above me, stars so close I could reach up and grab them, if only I wasn't so . . . very . . . tired.

"What," a careful voice said from somewhere behind my head, "was that, exactly?"

Regarding the stars, I sighed.

"Phase . . ." I whispered, then cleared my throat and managed a stronger second attempt. "Phased out."

"Ayuh. And phased out is what?"

"Part of the process," I told the stars. "All according to plan."

Silence. Then a sense of movement, a scrape of heel on sandy stone, and Borgan was kneeling beside me, his face obscuring the sky, the end of his braid tickling my cheek. It would, I thought, be very satisfying to kiss him—and then I remembered that I only thought so because he was *trenvay*.

"Kate," he said, very seriously. "How sick are you?"

"Not sick," I told him, and laboriously raised a hand to catch his braid. It was unexpectedly heavy, the beads smooth and cool against my fingers.

"What then?" he asked, his voice drawing my eyes up to meet his.

"Dying."

His eyes widened slightly. "I . . . see." he said. "And that's according to plan, is it?"

"Right." Reluctantly, I released the braid, closed my eyes and took stock. Oddly, I felt warm. Strength was returning to my watery muscles and my brain had gotten into gear sufficiently to be horrified that I had phased out in the presence of another—and not just any other, but a *trenvay* who put himself on a level with Nerazi in terms of power and effectiveness.

Trenvay will twist a lot of truth for the befuddlement of mere humans, but they keep a meticulous hierarchy among themselves. Boasting more power than you could deliver was a good way to get a hiding.

And the last I'd known, Nerazi was the most powerful *trenvay* in Archers Beach—and maybe on all of the Maine coast.

"Kate?"

"Sorry," I mumbled, opening my eyes again. I got my elbows braced on the rock and pushed myself upright, feeling about as coordinated as a sack of potatoes. Borgan sat back on his heels to give me room, but didn't offer assistance.

"Sorry for what?" he asked, when I was sitting up, legs laboriously crossed, and spine more or less straight. The breeze had died, and I sighed, content to be warm.

"For phasing in front of you," I said. "I—it hasn't happened before in . . . company, and I don't imagine it was pleasant to see."

"It wasn't unpleasant," he said carefully. "Startling, but kinda pretty. I hadn't expected you to go all to green-and-blue sparkles, and I had a bad couple minutes when I thought the breeze would shred you. Then you came solid again and folded up on the rock." He tipped his head. "This happen often?"

"More often, lately. Like I said, it's part of the process." And the process must be moving into the next stage, I thought, tiredly.

"Usually, I sort of—drift out and snap back. At least, that's how it feels to me. The fainting thing's ... new."

"So you're getting on with it, then," Borgan said, and sighed lightly. "I don't suppose you want to tell me what's worth dying for?"

I shrugged, and raised my hands to rub my face. Sand scratched my cheeks, smarting. I dropped my hands and met Borgan's eyes.

"I killed somebody," I said steadily. "Worse, I killed a friend."

Silence for the beat of three. "And that's worth this death?" he asked, sounding sincerely puzzled.

I gasped, swallowed sand, coughed.

"What do you think's a fitting punishment for murder?" I asked when I could, my voice harsh, and louder than I'd intended.

Borgan lifted a shoulder. "Depends," he said gravely. "Killing a friend—that's complex. Circumstances—nuances—mean a lot, in a case like that. Wants some serious weighing and measuring before settling a fitting punishment, if there's any needed at all." He looked down at the sand, then back to me.

"Who set that punishment on you? Your gran?"

I looked aside, letting my eyes rest on the Tancook Schooner there at dock, a dark silhouette against the spangled sky.

"I did," I whispered. "I set the punishment. There was no one else ... competent to judge."

"And why's that?"

I sighed, and shook my head. "Because I was born in the Land of the Flowers, and I used High Magic to kill him. Gran—Gran's a pretty good mage, but she's rooted here in the Changing Land. It was mine to judge." I swallowed. "Mine to pay."

Borgan laughed. Mouth open, I turned to stare at him, which got me a headshake along with the laugh.

"Funny, is it?" I snapped.

"No, no, now, Kate—" He raised his hands in mock defense, the laughter distilled into a grin that I didn't like any better. "Don't skin me. When'd you do this murder, if you don't mind saying? Last week?"

"Ten years ago," I said, still snapping. "You probably didn't know Tarva—"

"I knew him," Borgan interrupted, completely serious now. "Always up for a game, and no thought at all for the hurt he might do."

I blinked. Tarva had been high-spirited and tricksy to a fault, but— "He *was* a selkie," I pointed out, startled into mildness.

"Oh, aye. And the salt in Nerazi's sea, as well. I'm not saying the pup couldn't charm the fins off a flounder, only that he was heedless and disrespectful, and caused care to honest folk who'd never done him a stroke of harm."

I looked out over the sea, the reflection of stars rippling on the busy surface, and chewed on that for a bit before looking back to where Borgan sat on his heels, to all appearances content to wait until May Day, if it took me that long to come up with something to say. I sighed and said the only thing I could think of—an unvarnished fact.

"You weren't on Archers Beach back then."

"Now, that's true. I wasn't. I was up to Halifax, like I told you. But the sea knows what the sea knows. And the sea knew Tarva right well."

I shook my head. "It wouldn't have mattered if he was an ax murderer," I said tiredly. "I overrode his will and compelled him to act like I wanted him to—and he died because of it." And even if he hadn't, I added silently, I would have still deserved to die. Subverting someone else's will is very, very, very wrong. Trust me on this.

"Hmm." Borgan said. "And that's why you determined you were fit only to die, eh?" He paused, then shrugged slightly. "Up where I'm from the Old Ones would've prolly given you an atonement and a life-guide. A death hardly ever balances a wrong."

"In the Land of the Flowers," I said, "it does."

"In case your compass is off, this ain't the Land of the Flowers," Borgan said tartly. "Kate—" He paused, then started again, milder this time. "Kate, you were Guardian. You share a soul with this land. Have you taken a good look 'round Archers Beach? You're not the only one dying. The *trenvay* can each keep their little territories safe, but with the Guardian holding herself aloof..." He shook his head, his voice low and intense. "For the love of the sea, Kate, touch the land!" He held out his hand.

I looked down. His palm was brown and broad and calloused, the fingers curled a little in invitation.

Touch the land, was it? I'd repudiated the land, broken my oath, cast away my duty. There was nothing for me here except despite and vengeance. I looked back to Borgan's face.

"Well," he said, and cleared his throat. The steady brown hand fell out of my range of vision. "You'll be wanting to think it over, naturally."

Right. The breeze chose that moment to come up again with a vengeance, and I shivered, the warmth I had felt on coming out of my faint dissipating in an instant.

Borgan jerked his head toward the dock. "Looks like you might still be needing that coffee. Come on aboard."

"*No*," I snarled, my temper flaring dangerously. "I am not coming into your space, or letting you give me anything. That hasn't changed."

His face tightened. "*My* space, is it?" he snapped back. "Let me tell you something, Kate Archer—I knew the instant you crossed into town yesterday morning. Woken right up out of sound sleep with the land singing like to deafen me. While that boat's tied up at dock, it's more your place than it is mine—but have it your way." He took a hard breath, and came to his feet in one fluid move.

"Bide a tick," he said, sounding as tired as I felt. "I'll bring the coffee out."

I watched him cross the dock. He stepped onto the deck of his boat and disappeared below.

Me, I took two deep, careful breaths and got to my feet with considerably less grace. I paused a moment to look up again at the jewel-filled sky before I turned my face north and walked away.

I was halfway between Googin Rock and Fun Country when I noticed the plovers running along the water line. Getting on to nest-building season, now that I thought about it. Ice Age or no.

At least my hands were warm, if my nose and ears weren't. The battered work gloves were astonishingly cozy, and fit like they'd been made for me. I smiled slightly, and rubbed the canvas palms together as I walked. *Thank you, Nerazi.*

"'Evenin', Missus," a high voice declaimed from somewhere in the vicinity of my left elbow.

I turned my head carefully, and gave a nod to the sand-colored birdling pacing me.

"Heeterskyte, good evening to you," I said politely. Heeterskyte have delicate sensibilities; they also tend to pick up interesting bits of this and that, which they're more inclined to share with those who treat them like they ought.

A satisfied blink of a beady black eye. "That's well-spoke," it allowed. "Always did speak well to us smallkin, no matter what the other ones said."

A compliment, by God.

"Thank you," I said sincerely, and then, as it continued to walk along with me—"Is there some little thing I might do for you, Heeterskyte?"

"No, no. Just noticed you'd lost yer escort, is all. Not safe, these times, bein' out on the beach after dark. Not even fer such as yerself."

I considered this in light of Borgan's news of the drug trade. Pirates weren't likely to interest the smallkin much, unless they were threatening the nests. Still, it never hurt to be sure. "Is there a danger of which I ought to be aware, good Heeterskyte?"

It clacked its beak. "Only willie wisps, Black Dogs, and snally-gasters, deah."

What? I blinked. "In Archers Beach? That's not possible."

"No? Here's a question fer ya, then, Missus: Who's been gone Away a good long while, and who's been here the whole time, marking how the possibles do change?"

There was that.

"I take your point," I said moderately; "and I thank you for your escort. But tell me—do these dangers manifest nightly?"

"Near enough," it answered, and added, grudgingly, "Haven't seen a one since you been back."

"Maybe they're gone, then," I suggested. "And won't come back."

The heeterskyte hesitated, and I could almost taste its doubt, but all it said was, "Could be yer right, Missus. It's early days, and it ain't like they don't take a night off now and then."

"Of course not," I murmured, and we walked on several paces in silence, the wind at our backs. Ahead, Fun Country showed dark spires and fantastic structures against the starry sky, like the silhouette of the alien city everybody but the heroes of the sci-fi film know better than to go inside.

"Tell me," I said then, because, damn it, the heeterskyte *did* hear all kinds of things. "Do you have any idea where I might find my grandmother?"

My escort was silent. Silent, we passed beneath the Pier. On the other side, it clacked its beak, and spoke apologetically. "There's a bushel o'rumors about the old lady. Always is. This time, they're spoutin' all manner of nonsense. Some'll have it that she's just taking a rest. Others say she's keepin' low, to lull them night-hunters into what you might call a false sense of security."

Another beak-clack. "Trouble bein', Missus, that not one of them that's sayin' has anythin' approaching a hard fact to bless themselves with. All we really know is—she was here, and then she wasn't." Two clacks as we came up to the dune-bridge that led to home. "If Seal Woman don't know where she is, nobody does."

Which was, unfortunately, about what I'd thought. I angled left, toward the dunes—and checked as I realized I was alone. I turned and squinted; barely picking the heeterskyte out of the dark sand.

"Thank you," I called to it, and raised my hand. "I'm grateful for the escort."

"Take care now, Missus," it replied and suddenly darted away, legs moving in a blur.

I grinned and turned to trudge across the dry sand to the plank walk between the sea roses. The planks followed the contour of the dune, and I paused at the top to survey the street beyond. Full of shadows, and empty of everything else. In other words, Archers Beach in pre-Season. Just like it'd been for 'way too long.

With the exception of your odd willie wisp, Black Dog, or snallygaster, of course.

None of which ought to be anywhere near these environs, damn it. I frowned at the empty street. Granting that the heeterskyte wasn't likely to mistake a snallygaster, how the devil had it crossed? I mean, sure, any middling good mage can sing herself from one of the Six Worlds to another. But snallygasters, Black Dogs and willie wisps are—critters. Vermin. The only way they'd be able to move into the Changing Land from the Land of the Flowers was—if a mage deliberately sent them through. And if *that* were so...

Someone needed to send up a shout to the Wise.

"Great," I muttered, and rubbed my gloved hands together, moving down the plank walk toward the street.

High Magic exists in all the Six Worlds, though it's by no means evenly distributed. The Real World, like we like to say it, has the least. That's because there's so much *change* here—or so my tutor had it, back when I lived in my grandfather's house. According to him, the change creates an energy state that polarizes *jikinap*, and makes it hard to do mage-work.

Critters from another of the Six Worlds, though, with just their instincts and their appetites to guide them... They could operate here, right enough, and do damage, too. Especially if whoever was letting them through also brought them back home from time to time, so they could renew their essences.

Definitely something to shunt up to a Higher Authority—though not without proof. The Wise aren't summoned lightly, and certainly not before every single duck is bathed, combed, brushed and standing at full attention.

I angled toward Tupelo House, still chewing on the information. I wondered, specifically, if Nerazi had any news of snallygasters. She hadn't mentioned them—but, then, I hadn't asked her. First thing, then, was to talk to her.

Something moved under the stairs, a darker blot against the darkness. I froze, straining my eyes—but my dark-sight didn't bring me anything more than the impression of tightly coiled bulk. I felt a tingle of force, and moved forward, a Word I doubted I had the strength to speak forming on the back of my tongue. Beneath the stairs, the shadow drew in on itself—and exploded out into the street.

I shouted, Wordless—and then shouted again, with laughter this time, as the black cat shot across the street in front of me and dove for the sea roses and the dune.

"Sorry!" I called after it. "Thought you were somebody else!"

The cat didn't answer, which was fair enough. I went up the stairs to the front door, unlocked it and let myself in.

ELEVEN

Friday, April 21
High Tide 5:14 A.M.
Sunrise 5:49 A.M. EDT

It was light when I woke. I lay in bed, staring up at the feature-less white ceiling; unwilling to let the dream go.

It's rare that I dream—and rarer still that the dream isn't a nightmare. This one had been . . . peaceful; a memory, really, from about six months after I came to live with my grandmother.

When I was well enough to walk, Gran had packed some sand-wiches into a basket with a thermos of cold tea, bundled me up, and the two of us strolled over to Heath Hill. There, she introduced me to the wood, insisting on full court manners. The trees had been dressed in yellow, orange, green, and brown, the colors soft as velvet.

After I had made my bow and the trees had discussed me among themselves, Gran took my hand, and we entered the wood, branches lifting out of our way to clear the path before us. Straight to the Center of the wood we went, and picnicked at the foot of the great black gum tree, the sun streaming in golden ribbons through the leaves.

The line of sunlight creeping across the ceiling was distracting. There was something about the morning light that—

Right. I sighed sharply and turned my head. Six o'clock, according to the clock on the bedside table—which meant I'd missed my chance to chat with Nerazi about the reported incursions of natives from the Land of the Flowers.

"Damn." I threw the blankets back and slid to my feet. "Set an alarm tonight, Kate."

It seemed the sleep had done me good, though; I was feeling clear-headed and supple as I pulled on my clothes, which was all to the good. I was going to need every advantage for today's work.

I went downstairs, got the coffeepot primed, and had my hand on the fridge when there was a sound at the door.

Not much of a sound, really—a rustle, like a shrew moving through dry leaves. Except there weren't any leaves on the porch, and nothing for a shrew to want.

The sound came again, slightly louder, accompanied by a soft thump.

"Oh, for . . ." I crossed the hall and yanked the door open.

"Eek!" shrieked the small person crouching on the porch, crushing a paper sack to their meager chest. "What did you have to go and do that for?"

"You're the one rustling around at my door," I pointed out, a little breathless, myself. I squinted, trying to get a good look under the brim of the grimy gimme hat.

"Just come to give due, that's all!" my visitor exclaimed, and put the bag down on the porch between us, unrolling the top with trembling hands. "Fiddleheads. Picked 'em myself this morning. Best to eat 'em now, while they're fresh."

Fresh fiddleheads. I blinked, catching the edge of the face, the hint of shape inside the layers of mismatched clothing.

"Gaby?" I asked.

"Who else would be bringing you fiddleheads?" she demanded. "*I* remember how much you like 'em, if you don't! Best when they're fresh!" She toed the bag nearer to me, hands tucked behind her back, then darted down to the first step.

Well, they are. Best when they're fresh, that is. The breeze brought me a mouth-watering scent of moist, spicy greenness. I looked down. The bag was full of tight gray-green coils enclosing an intricate lace work of new leaves. New growth of the Ostrich Fern, fiddleheads are an acquired taste—and I'd acquired it bad, during my mostly misspent childhood. Some folks said they tasted like asparagus, but they're better than that.

Fiddleheads. It'd been *years.* . . .

I took a breath, tucked my hands into the pockets of my jeans, and considered Gaby, a rag-tag creature in earth-colored motley, cap jammed down over straw-like hair, dark eyes looking at me furtively from beneath the brim. The thing to remember when dealing with *trenvay* is that there's *always* a price—and it's best to get it stated out plain as soon as possible. Always remembering that the *trenvay* national sport is obfuscation.

"What do you want," I asked bluntly, "in payment?"

She ducked her head. "Only the returnables..." Her nose twitched, and she licked her lips. "And a cup of sweet coffee."

Maine buys back things like soda cans and beer bottles for a nickel apiece via the process locally known as "redemption." Most people save their returnables in a sack and take them down to the redemption center once a month or so. The throwaways on the side of the road, or in the trashcans, or on the beach, though—those are the legitimate prey of scavengers like Gaby.

"You won't get much from me," I said, "but you can have what there is."

Gaby fairly quivered. "Thank'ee, thank'ee. That's generous. And... and the coffee?"

I bent and picked up the bag of fiddleheads, stomach growling. Best when they're fresh, but not when they're raw.

"I'll get the water started and bring you a mug of coffee," I said, and Gaby settled herself on the top stair.

"Thank'ee," she whispered.

"Just a minute." I went inside, leaving the door ajar, knowing there was no danger of Gaby following me into the house.

In the kitchen, I filled a pot with water and set it on the burner, fetched a yellow mug painted with delphiniums down from the cabinet, poured coffee, added sugar until my teeth hurt just looking at it, and carried it outside.

Gaby was right on the step where I'd left her, sitting as still and as quiet as a garden gnome. I put the mug next to her— you don't hand things directly to Gaby—and she snatched it up, gulping half the contents at once, not seeming to mind the heat.

"You make sure and clean 'em good," she said, and had another gulp, finishing the coffee. She sighed hugely, and set the mug gently on the porch.

"Thank'ee kindly. You get to them fiddleheads, now. Best when they're fresh!"

And with that she was gone, scampering down the stairs like a squirrel. I looked over the rail, but she was already halfway down the street, all but invisible in her motley. Shaking my head, I picked up the empty mug and went back inside.

The fiddleheads, I scaled carefully before boiling, and served them to myself on toast, dressed with margarine.

It just doesn't get any better than that.

What with the fiddlehead negotiations, I was a few minutes late to the carousel. Nancy was over at Tony Lee's; Anna, Tony's wife, was leaning on the counter, and both were bent over a single sheet of sun-yellow paper. The air was redolent of hot oil and strong coffee.

I strolled over, mellow with fiddleheads and toast. Anna looked up and gave me a smile, shaking glossy black bangs out of tip-tilted blue eyes. She didn't look a day older than the last time I'd seen her, ten years gone.

"Kate, it's good to have you back."

"Thanks," I said, and smiled. Anna's one of the few genuinely nice people I've ever met, and it's easy to smile at her. I used my chin to point at the paper on the counter. "What's up?"

"Chamber's asking us all to open early," Nancy said.

I blinked. "We're already going to be opening for May 14."

"Wants earlier'n that." She scooted the paper in my direction. I caught it and frowned down at the gray letters. Somebody at the Chamber of Commerce office ought to see about changing the cartridge in their inkjet.

"They applied for a hospitality grant—oh, almost a year ago," Anna said in her soft voice. "And now they find that they're one of three finalists..."

"And they want everybody to be open and ready to receive customers on the twenty-sixth—that's Wednesday!" My stomach hit my heels and stayed there, ice cold. I shot a glance at Nancy. "We can't have the carousel ready by Wednesday."

"Sure we can," she said soothingly. "'Nother couple hours'll put the mechanicals to rights, then I'll get right onto the organ and the brass." She hesitated, before suggesting, delicately. "Maybe there's somebody in town can give you a hand with the critters?"

Stipulating that Gran was in town, which she had to be, dammit-alltohell. I gave Nancy a shrug, trying for noncommittal. "Maybe there is," I allowed, and turned to Anna. "Seen Mr. Ignatious lately?"

She frowned slightly, trying to remember, then looked over her shoulder and yelled into the kitchen. "Tony! Has the old gentleman been around yet this year?"

A shout answered her, words unintelligible over the spit of grease. Anna shook her head. "Haven't seen him."

My disappointment must've shown on my face, because Anna put out a hand and touched me lightly on the arm. "That doesn't mean he isn't here, Kate. Lots of times, he'll just come in from the beach side and go right to the Knot."

"Knot doesn't always open for Early Season," Nancy commented, canceling any comfort I might've taken from Anna—then added hastily, "Though like she says, he might be down there right now, for all we know about it. No need for him to pass this way."

"Though it's early in the day for him," Anna said musingly. "He likes to work late, when he works."

True enough, on both counts. I sighed, and tried to buy off the dread in my stomach with an easy fantasy—*I'll go down to the Knot in an hour or two and Mr. Ignatious'll know exactly where Gran is*—but my gut wasn't having any.

"Well." For lack of anything else to do, I looked down at the paper in my hand again. "Five hundred visitors," I read. "Where in God's name are we going to put them?"

"The Chamber's trying to talk the motel owners into opening early, too," Anna said. "In case that doesn't work—" She gave me a look so earnest in its blandness that I felt myself grin. "If that doesn't work, they cut a backup deal with the big new Holiday Inn in Portland. They'll sleep in the city and bus in during the days."

"Not the way to win a hospitality competition," Nancy muttered, and I had to agree with her.

I rattled the paper before putting it back on Anna's counter. "Says here, if the Chamber wins, they'll split the prize money with all participants," I said. "If that comes to pass, I'll split the carousel's piece with you fifty–fifty."

"Sixty–forty," Nancy corrected, using one finger to nudge her cap back off her forehead. "Management's got expenses."

"You drive a hard bargain, but—have it your way," I told her, and moved off toward the carousel. "Looks like I'd better get cracking."

"Me, too," Nancy said, coming along.

"We'll send lunch over," Anna called. "And coffee!"

❋　　　❋　　　❋

The shadows had melted a bit more on the overnight; only a few black rags were clinging to the high rafters. Unfortunately, the degradation of the wards had also accelerated, leaving them looking like old lace. Or maybe Swiss cheese. A clammy breeze wafted through the holes and into the larger space, bearing giggles and dire mutterings.

Pretending not to hear, I got my paints, rags, and brushes together, while Nancy commenced in torturing the machinery.

I hefted the work hamper and the tarp, and walked forward, keeping my shoulders square and my face smooth. The wards clung to me like spiderwebs when I passed through them, which was not what you like in wards.

I carried my hamper to the dolphin, set it down and spread the tarp.

Looks tired, doesn't she? Poor lame creature, the batwing cooed, making me want to gag.

Lazy slut! That was the goat. *She needs a fire lit under her, that's all!*

Naturally it wasn't a real fire, and the goat hadn't been able to work up all that much juice, even with the wards fraying. Oh, it stung, right enough, but I've taken worse, and smiled.

I finished settling the tarp, brought the hamper closer, chose my brush and my color, and got to work.

Fifteen jostles and nips later, I put the brush into the turpentine jar, sealed the paint, and walked—slowly and deliberately—off the deck and through the wards.

My hands were shaking—with temper, mostly, though one of them had come up with enough juice to smack me a good one in my left ear, and I'd jumped, and smeared a long line of hibiscus red down the dolphin's smooth blue side. Adrenaline was roiling in my stomach, making me regret my good breakfast.

I took a deep breath—and another one, concentrating on the everyday, outside-of-my-head sounds: the clanks and clatters Nancy was producing; the rise and fall of Anna's voice, and the sudden sparkle of her laughter; a car horn; the ringing clang of a delivery truck's door being rolled up. One more breath and I opened my eyes, fishing my cell phone out of the pocket of my jeans. A few minutes shy of eleven o'clock. It could be that

Mr. Ignatious was down at the Knot by now. And if he wasn't, the walk over and back would give me some time to settle and fortify myself for the next session inside the wards. I bit my lip.

Gran, I didn't say aloud, *what were you thinking?*

I took a breath, the snickering from the peanut gallery bouncing around inside my skull.

Graaaannnn! wailed the goat, to considerable merriment. *Save me, Gran!*

My temper flared—and I spun on my heel, snatched up my jacket and strode out of that place, shrieks, howls, and hoots following me until I hit the plaza.

The sudden absence of racket brought tears to my eyes. I stood there, blinking, while I got my jacket on, and watched as Brand Carver ran Summer's Wheel 'round, positioning it with the deceptive ease of long practice to receive the next gondola.

The Wheel settled to his satisfaction, Brand locked it, turned away from the control box, and paused, hand shooting into the air.

"Hey, Kate! Long time, no see!"

I raised my hand and went forward to the end of the ramp. "Hi, Brand. How's it going?"

"Staggering, but still upright," he said, the breeze ruffling his red hair. He was wearing a bright blue windbreaker half-zipped over a T-shirt, the sleeves pushed up his forearms, elastic stretched to the breaking point. "Here for the Season?"

"The Season, the Early Season, and the Really Early Season," I admitted, and he laughed.

"The Chamber—what a buncha screw-ups. Still, I ain't in a position to let a few extra bucks pass me by. You?"

I made owl eyes at him. "What is this 'extra' of which you speak?"

He laughed, and waved a hand, encompassing the Wheel and the line of plastic-shrouded gondolas awaiting his attention. "Back to work. Good to see you!"

"You, too," I said, but he was already moving across the platform, utility knife in hand.

I moved off to the right, deeper into Fun Country.

Baxter Avenue—that's the thoroughfare that runs from the park's outer boundary down to Dodge City—Baxter Avenue was deserted. The duck-pick and lobster toss were still wrapped in plastic, the tarot reader's cubby and the T-shirt shop adjacent still wore their winter shutters. Oriental Funhouse was dark, no sign that Jelly Lee or any of his helpers had been around. Might be he hadn't gotten the Chamber's letter yet, though it wasn't like Anna not to give him a call and a head's up.

The wind gusted over my shoulder, picked up a cupful of grit and swirled it. I reached into my pockets and pulled out the old work gloves, hauling them on as I followed the dust devil down to the end of the avenue toward a growing rumble. At Dodge City, I paused with my hand on the rail, watching the bumper cars dance under their dark canopy, sparks spitting from the interface of ceiling and contact wire.

"Well, if it ain't Kate Archer!" a high voice screamed above the noise. I turned my head and raised a hand.

"Millie!" I shouted, and she nodded, grinning.

"Good to see you! Come talk to me when it's quieter!"

I nodded and moved off, between long rows of corrugated metal. Later—or sooner, if the Chamber had its way—the storm gates would be drawn up to reveal a wonderland of games: squirt gun races, ring tosses, balloon darts, and the like—everyone a winner!

I went across the service alley and between the boarded-up ticket booths, following the scratched Plexiglas splash-guard along the bottom of the dry log flume. At the corner, I turned left, threaded my way between the shrouded kiddie yachts and dancing teacups, and at last came to a stop. Before me was a sandy silver track describing a convoluted circuit, uphill from the platform immediately into a series of three camel backs, then a swooping corkscrew that fell into a short plateau, another camel back twisting into a tight double curve, and another, even tighter, single twist descending into the brake run directly before the platform.

Keltic Knot is the most compact roller coaster in the Northeastern United States, according to Fun Country's tourist brochure. It might be that's so; I haven't done an inventory of mini-coasters. I do know for a fact that the Knot is one of the scarier rides I've ever had—and I've had some *very* scary rides.

The lead car is shaped like the powerful head and shoulders of a mighty red dragon, wings half-furled, black lips curled back from teeth like broadswords. I recognized its shape, shrouded in the ubiquitous blue tarp between the tracks; the rest of the cars—which when attached would make up the dragon's body and her tail—were similarly wrapped and spotted around the enclosure. The whole place had the sad, deserted feel of—oh, of an amusement park in off-Season.

Still, appearances can be deceiving.

"Mr. Ignatious?" I called, leaning on the rail and craning toward the platform. The trapdoor was down and padlocked; the control panel was lavishly swathed in plastic, held in place by half a roll or more of silver duct tape.

"Mr. Ignat'?" I called, louder this time, though I was pretty certain now that he wasn't around. "It's Kate."

The wind gusted in and snatched at the tarp around the dragon, making it shake and snap.

"God *damn* it." I bent my head, gloved hands gripping the rail hard. Mr. Ignatious—I'd never known where he lived, or which patch of land, piece of marsh, or stand of trees he called his own. Hell, I wasn't even one hundred percent certain he was *trenvay*. He could just as easily be somebody like Henry—sensitive, accepting, and all too human. Whatever he was, there wasn't any way to conjure him out of the empty ride—at least that much was certain.

Sick to my stomach, I turned away, walking between the Knot and the teacups, the wind tangling chilly fingers in my hair. What the *hell* was I going to do—no, wrong question. The question I ought to be asking—that I ought to've been asking all along—was—where in Archers Beach could Gran have gone that she couldn't come home from?

The answer to that was—nowhere.

Therefore, she was deliberately withholding herself, knowing the terrible danger she courted by so doing.

Which made the next question I should be asking—*Why?*

I was chewing on that one so hard that I didn't notice anything amiss until a slim figure danced out of the lee side of the ticket booth, and slammed me into the Plexiglas wall, knife slashing toward my face.

TWELVE

Friday, April 21
Low Tide 11:42 A.M.
Sunset 7:32 P.M. EDT

The air went out of my lungs in a weak yell, and my head whapped the plastic a good one; the hard shine of the knife breaking into silver spangles. Fire scored my cheek and fingers twisted into my hair, hauling my head back.

"Look at me, bitch!" The voice wasn't familiar; the face, when my sight cleared, was the same.

Curly brown hair; smooth skin, square jaw, thin lips, a diamond chip glittering in the left nostril, clear blue eyes framed by ridiculously long, thick lashes.

His lips bent when he saw I was tracking. It might have been meant for a smile, but the rest of his face wasn't participating. I concentrated on breathing, meeting those wonderfully clear eyes.

"Good girl." He brought the knife up until I could see it at the edge of my vision. "In a minute, I'm going to cut you again," he said calmly, just letting me know how it was going to be. "But first, I got a message for you from Mr. Nemeier. You know who that is?"

"Man with no regard for property lines," I gasped, and he twisted my hair until it felt like he was going to take my scalp off. Tears started, running from the corners of my eyes.

"Bitchy little girls oughta have more respect for guys who can rearrange their faces for them," he said, sounding genuinely disappointed in me. This boy was good; could've made a real name for himself in the Office of the Question.

My chest was on fire; I took a deep breath to cool it, never moving my eyes from his, and kept my muscles loose, mindful that there was something more than tears dampening my face.

"Now," my captor said, giving my head a gentle shake, while the roots of my hair screamed, "it's a good thing you aren't a pretty girl, but you're still not going to like being cut, are you? And what's more, you probably don't have the insurance or the savings for plastic surgery, to fix what I'm going to do to you. That means you'll have a nice reminder every time you look in a mirror. You just bear in mind that it's not the *worst* I can do to you, all right? And be sensible. Mr. Nemeier doesn't hold with having his grass witched. He says, after you get out of the emergency room, before the pain killers wear off—you go on up to the hill and fix what you broke. If you don't, you'll be seeing me again, and it won't just be your face I'll cut then." Another shake. "Are you going to remember that, Kate? Or should I send somebody along to the emergency room to remind you?"

"I'll remember it," I told him, voice quavering—which was fine. There's no shame in being scared when you're facing an enemy—that might be the one thing Aeronymous and Gran could've agreed on. And both of them had made sure I'd known it.

"Good," said the man with the knife. "Now—"

The blade moved, and so did I, kicking out hard.

My technique was still good. He gurgled, sort of, as the shock took him, the knife faltered, and his fingers loosened—enough. I dropped to my knees, not giving a damn if I'd left hair and scalp behind, threw myself sideways, and rolled to my feet, screaming at the top of my lungs, running the instant I was upright, heading for Dodge City.

Unfortunately, I wasn't running fast enough. He grabbed my jacket and yanked me around to face him, knife flashing. I dodged and threw my hand up into the blade—reaction, and a stupid one. That move only works when you're wearing battle gauntlets or an invincibility spell. Preferably both. Otherwise, you're talking a crippling injury, even in the Land of the Flowers.

The tough canvas work glove took the edge instead of my

palm; my fingers closed automatically, completing the sequence, and I twisted, hard.

My late captor let his weapon go—another surprise; I thought he was tougher than that—and stood gaping at me.

I flipped the knife from my right hand to my left and dropped into the stance I'd been drilled in until my muscles *still* remembered it. It must've looked convincing, because he turned tail and ran.

My knees hit the tarmac hard, and I knelt there, the world gone to milky shadows, desperately gasping for air—

"Kate!" Millie's voice reached me, and the sound of pounding feet. She panted up to me, a wrench the size of Oklahoma in one hand, Brand not two steps behind, baseball bat gripped in a freckled fist.

"You okay?" Millie bent down. "At least he run—oh, God, Kate. Your face."

The instant she mentioned it, it started hurting like a sonofagun; the whole side of my face on fire. I raised a hand to explore the damage, and Brand caught my wrist, yanking a wad of tissue out of his pocket and forcing them into my hand.

"Hold that to the cut," he said, businesslike. "Can you walk? Tony's got a first aid kit behind the counter."

"Going to need stitches," Tony said, when Anna had gotten the cut cleaned up and the damage could be seen. "Better go to the emergency room."

"No," I gasped, remembering all too clearly the threat of another interested party getting involved. "Butterfly stitches, Anna."

"Kate, it'll scar," she said softly. "I'll drive you—"

"No!" I said, sharper, and bit my lip, more for snapping at Anna than because her ministrations had hurt me. "Listen, he knew who I am and he said there'd be somebody waiting for me at the emergency room."

"Ah." I felt rather than saw Tony and Anna exchange a look. "So, did you recognize that guy?"

"No, but he said he worked for Joe Nemeier."

Silence, then—

"Butterfly stitches," Anna said, and sighed. "If it gets infected, you'll go to the hospital, Kate. Promise me."

"I promise," I said, and meant it.

Tony bent over, briefly entering my field of vision, and picked up the knife, turning it over in knowledgeable hands.

"You're lucky you didn't lose fingers," he commented.

I held up my hands, still encased in the battered work gloves. "What can I say? They're spun out of titanium."

"They must be," he retorted. "This is a very well-kept weapon."

"Yeah, well, he's a pro." I winced as Anna pushed the cut together and set the first elastic strip. When I got my breath back, I moved a hand. "Tony, how bad is it around here?"

He hunkered down, putting his face level with mine, black eyes serious.

"Not so bad. Nemeier's a dangerous man, but he's smart. He stays low, doesn't involve himself in local disputes. This..." He raised the knife, frowning. "This isn't like him. You must've hit him where he lives. And even then—" He shook his head.

"Even then, he should've just made it so I had an accident," I finished. "I guess I got under his skin—ow!"

"Stay *still*," Anna hissed, and so I stayed still. Tony put the knife on the table by my elbow and moved toward the back. "Coffee, Kate?"

"Coffee'd be great," I said.

He went to the back, reappearing two butterfly stitches later with a Styrofoam cup in one hand and a leather sheath in the other.

"This ought to take your knife," he said, putting it on the table, and handing me the cup. "Careful with that," he cautioned. "It's hot."

Not only was it hot, it was liberally laced with brandy. I sipped it respectfully. My face hurt like hell, my scalp was sore, my chest tender; I felt like I'd been up for days, and my thoughts were a little drifty. Other than that, I was fine.

And very, very lucky.

Nancy appeared just as Anna finished patching me up, alerted by Brand.

"He tried to get Marilyn to call the cops," Nancy reported, sitting on the stool across from me. "According to her, it wasn't no sense to it, now he run off; and she don't need Fun Country in the cop log."

"That's Marilyn," I agreed and gingerly sipped my augmented coffee.

"The mechanicals are tip-top," Nancy said after a pause. "Planning on starting with the brass directly after lunch."

Right on cue, Anna smacked two paper plates of pork fried

rice down in front of us, with an undoctored coffee for Nancy, and leaned against the counter facing us, her arms folded over her chest. I took the work gloves off and shoved them into the pockets of my jacket before using the plastic fork to scoop up a small mountain of rice.

"Kate needs to rest," she said, and gave me a look that she meant to be stern.

I shook my head. "Kate needs to get her butt across the way and make progress on refurbing those animals," I contradicted, and waved my fork. "Immediately after lunch. Which is, by the way, delicious. If you were anybody else, I'd make a serious effort to seduce Tony."

"Kate—"

"Nope, not negotiable," I interrupted. "Wednesday's not getting any further away, last I looked."

Silence. I ate, and Nancy did. After a minute or two, Anna went into the back. I could hear her talking with Tony over the various noises of frying, boiling, and steaming while Nancy and I cleaned our plates, and she finished her coffee. I set mine aside; I'd had enough brandy to make the pain bearable, and it wouldn't do to go tipsy to the horses.

Or maybe it was just what I needed.

"You're looking a little rocky," Nancy commented. "Might be it's good sense to call it a day? Nasty shock to the system, getting sliced like that."

She sounded like somebody with experience; on the other hand, I wasn't without experience of my own.

"I'll be okay," I said, and she nodded. It was my business, after all.

"Well." I pushed my stool back, carefully, and made sure of my balance before committing my full weight to my feet. My head swam a second, then I steadied. Good to go, yessir. I slid the sheathed knife carefully into the pocket of my jacket. If Nancy saw, she didn't comment about that, either—and, really, why shouldn't I take it? It *was* a good knife. You never knew when you were going to need a good knife.

"After you," I said to Nancy. She turned—and checked as Anna came out of the back, throwing a sweater around her shoulders.

"Good!" she exclaimed. "We'll go together."

I eyed her. "Go where?"

"To the merry-go-round," she said blithely. "I'm going to help you paint the animals."

I'd been afraid of that. "No," I said, firmly. "Absolutely not."

Anna frowned, which made her look cute as a bug, and about as threatening. "You think I can't paint?"

"I think you can paint great." I held up my hands. "Look, Anna, I appreciate you wanting to help, but—" I faltered, scrambling for something to tell her that would make sense, without partaking of magic, High Magic, and what the Wise hoped to accomplish by incarcerating six deadly criminals in the Changing Land.

"Them animals," Nancy said unexpectedly from beside me. "They ain't exactly comfortable."

Anna laughed. "I know *that!*"

"Oh. You do." I very carefully didn't look at Nancy.

"Yes, I *do!*" Anna stuck her tongue out. "Your grandmother explained the whole thing to me, about how some of the animals are magical creatures from far off lands." She held out her left fist, and opened the fingers, showing me a bit of rock caught inside a silver wire cage and hung on a chain. "She even gave me a charm against them, see? So I'm perfectly safe."

I held my hand out. "May I see that, please?"

Trustingly, she dropped the charm into my palm. Cut off from the land, and blind as I was, I could only do an ordinary visual scan, but damn me if it didn't look like a chip from the sentinel rock where Nerazi held court. If Gran had given it—and there wasn't any reason for Anna to lie about that, if Anna knew how to lie—then it might actually *be* a charm.

"Tell me," I said.

She shrugged. "Two Seasons ago, there was a problem. I don't know precisely what it was, but—Nancy, you might know; you worked for her that Season."

Nancy moved her thin shoulders in that not-quite shrug of hers. "There was some kind of trouble, but I never heard what," she said, and turned to me. "Anna did help out that year. Went fine."

Well. I handed the charm back to Anna. "*Wear* it, okay?"

"Sure." She dropped the chain around her neck, tucked the smooth chip of rock in its silver cage inside the collar of her shirt, and gave us each a sunny smile.

"Ready?" she chirped.

THIRTEEN

—⚘—

Saturday, April 22
Low Tide 12:47 P.M.
Sunrise 5:48 A.M. EDT

The room was filled with thick yellow light, sort of like an over-full tub of margarine. I turned my head an inch or so on the pillow and focused on the bedside clock. Nine-thirty. I closed my eyes again.

I felt, not to put too fine a point on it, rotten. My head hurt, my face hurt, my knees and stomach—oh, the hell with it. Let's just say that, if my left little finger hurt, it was keeping quiet about it.

This was what came of not keeping up with my combat lessons, and I didn't even have the luxury of pretending that my grandfather's arms master hadn't told me as much.

She'd also claimed that the best cure for sore muscles and bruises was to rise from one's bed of leisure, take up one's sword, and have at it again. Hair of the dog, only considerably more violent.

Well, I could at least take comfort from the fact that she wasn't likely to come leaping into my room, sword at ready and a gleam of sheer deviltry in her eye. Not when she'd been among the first of those who had fallen protecting the House.

My stomach twisted. I breathed, deliberately forcing the air all the way down to the bottom of my lungs, until my chest ached with it. For the count of three, I held it, then exhaled, and lay beneath the blanket as limp as a dishrag—a bruised and contused dishrag.

I am going back to sleep, I told myself, but there was something not quite right about—abruptly, my brain came back on line, and I remembered.

I was supposed to have met Nancy and Anna at the carousel at eight.

"Damn," I said, my voice sounding frayed and bleached. "Get up, Kate."

The mind might have been willing, but the body was inert. I bit my lip, concentrated; sat up, and waited for the room to stop spinning.

Oh, this was going to be a treat. Maybe I really ought to just stay in—

"Get *up,*" I told myself firmly, and pitched the covers back. I was still wearing my shirt and jeans, though I'd managed to get my shoes off before collapsing. Go me.

I got my legs over the side of the bed, stood, and didn't fall down—which had to be counted as a good thing. I hate to fall down.

When the room steadied, I mooched around it, gathering clean clothes. I'd set the alarm last night, in an excess of enthusiasm, but I'd apparently slept right through it, so my opportunity to speak with Nerazi about the leakage from the Land of the Flowers was gone for another day.

"Third time's the charm," I muttered, and hobbled downstairs.

A hot shower melted the worst of the soreness out of my muscles, and I managed, for a wonder, to keep the dressing on my face dry. I toweled off and peered in the mirror, noting how the purple half-moons under my eyes made my skin seem even paler than it actually was.

At least, I hoped that was the case; I'd gotten into the habit of avoiding mirrors, this last decade or so. Be that as it was, according to today's reflection I looked sick and wretched and like I *belonged* in bed.

"And that," I told myself sternly, "is enough whining out of *you* for one day."

I pulled on jeans and a Firefox T-shirt, swallowed a couple of super-strength aspirin, and twisted my wet hair into a knot at the back of my head.

"As ready as you'll ever be," I said to my wan reflection, and headed for the kitchen.

The message-waiting light was blinking on the answering machine. I touched the play button.

"Kate? Henry. Sorry I missed you. Mr. Nemeier's lawyer and I are playing telephone tag. I'm afraid I'll need to resort to old-fashioned methods and send him a letter. If you have any questions, or if you'd like to see a draft, give me a call. I'll be out tomorrow morning, but will be in the office all afternoon."

No need for me to see the draft; Henry knew his business. I dialed the office and told his answering machine so, hung up, closed my eyes briefly, and dialed Tony Lee's Chinese Kitchen.

"Hey, Kate," Tony said. The wonders of caller ID.

"Hey, yourself," I answered "Listen, will you let Anna and Nancy know that I overslept, but I'm on my way? Feed Nancy breakfast and I'll settle up with you later."

"Like hell you will," he said cheerfully. "Anna said to tell you to take your time when you called. The two of them are already working. You might consider taking Anna on full time," he continued, chattily. "She's wasted over here."

"They're already working?" I repeated, my brain having gotten stuck on that. "How—"

There was a pause. "Anna said you'd given her the key."

I'd done *what*? I thought around a surge of horror. I'd given Anna the *key*? With the animals unbound and the wards so much soggy tissue? Was I an idiot?

"Kate?" Tony asked, sounding worried now. "How're you doing this morning? They can handle it, if you just want to play boss and take the day off."

"I'm okay," I said numbly. "I'll be down in a couple." I hung up the phone, and limped over to the kitchen table, where my pocket things sat in an untidy jumble. Cell, wallet, Gran's ring with three keys on it . . . I picked it up, and shook my head. The key to the carousel was gone.

I remembered, like it had happened years ago—I remembered talking with Anna as we put away our paints. In hindsight, I probably had been a little off my head with shock, loss of blood, and Tony's brandy—just like they'd all tried to tell me. It was going to be interesting to see the job I'd done on the painting. . . .

Anyhow, I remembered agreeing that the afternoon had gone

just fine, that we'd gotten a lot of work done, and not one sign of trouble from the magicked animals, the existence of which Anna seemed to take with a half-shaker of salt. I'd agreed that I should go home and get some rest. I remembered telling Nancy goodnight, and I remembered getting into Brand's Jeep for the five block ride back to Tupelo House. Hell, I even remembered waving to him from the porch, as he chivalrously waited until I gotten the door open.

But actually giving Anna the key...

It gave me chills just thinking about it.

My aches eclipsed by horror, I grabbed my jacket off the hook and slammed out the door. My sneakers skidded on the damp wood and I slipped, the concrete blocks at the foot of the flight achingly clear as I tottered on the thin edge of the top step, gravity pulling my shoulders—

I snatched at the rail, pivoted until my stomach was against it, and hung there, shaking, spangles of light obscuring my vision.

When the shakes had eased off and I felt like I had my balance back, I lowered myself—keeping a good grip on the rail—to the top step, waiting for my heartbeat to drop back out of panic mode.

It *had* been okay yesterday, I told myself. The animals had been remarkably well-behaved, which had given me a lot of respect for Anna's charm. Gran must've settled a ward into the silver before she wove it around the stone. Whatever—it had certainly done the trick, and the three of us had put in a prodigious amount of work before Tony and Brand came in at six and insisted that we call it a day.

"It was *fine*," I whispered, like Gran soothing away one of my numerous nightmares, when I'd been a kid. "Everything's fine."

With the possible exception of myself.

Business as usual.

Carefully, I stood up and went down the stairs, slowly and respectfully. Once I was standing on the concrete blocks, I put on my jacket and gloves, grimacing when my fingers brushed the knife in my right pocket.

Jacket buttoned, I headed for Fun Country, only limping a little.

Tony had customers when I came into the park—two gray-haired ladies in determinedly casual slacks and fitted pink sweatshirts. He waved at me over their heads, and I waved back, angling toward the carousel.

The walk from Tupelo House had done me good; the limp had worked out, and my other aches were less intrusive. Of course, that could've been the aspirin. In either case, I was feeling slightly more sanguine about my ability to actually get some work done today.

I was two paces from the open hatch when I heard Anna shout. Heart in mouth, I ran into the enclosure—and knew we'd been set up.

It had taken the pooled resources of all six prisoners to get one of them free and moving, with nothing left over for wards or illusion—that was the good news.

The bad news—they'd chosen the unicorn as their champion.

Anna was on the far side of the carousel, slowly backing away, sweater slipping from her shoulders, a paintbrush held before her like a sword. The unicorn danced forward, light and malicious on little goat feet, and dipped its head, horn flashing. There was a scream of tearing cloth, and a howl of feline rage. The unicorn reared as a calico cat landed four-square, all claws extended, on its tender rump. Anna stumbled, feet tangling in the trailing sweater. She went down, and rolled, smart girl, as cloven hooves hit the floor where her head had been.

The unicorn bucked, snorting. Unbelievably, the cat held on, wailing like a fire engine, and I was running, onto the platform and across, giving the batwing horse the back of my gloved hand when it slashed at me, and jumped.

I landed in front of the unicorn the same instant the cat went flying. I heard a dull thud as it hit the metal storm wall and winced, then I was the center of attention, more fool I.

Well met, Keeper, a golden voice sang inside my head.

"Get back where you belong," I told it, and was pleased to hear that my voice was firm and clear. "Do it now."

Will you impel me, little Ozali? it asked, amusement rippling along its thought. I didn't answer, and it snorted.

I didn't think so.

It lunged. I danced back and to the left, the horn narrowly missing my belly, spun to the right—and the horn caught my jacket, slicing it from waist to armpit. The unicorn snorted; it sounded like laughter.

How long will you dance?

"As long as it takes," I answered, though that was naked bravado. My chest was already tight, my eyesight graying at the edges. This was going to have to end fast, or it was going to end badly. I snatched at my pocket.

The knife felt good in my hand: well balanced and clean. The unicorn lunged; I parried, cold iron turning ivory, and inside my head, it was the unicorn who screamed.

"Anna!" I yelled. "Run—and lock the door behind you!"

Doors will not hold me, nor the words of a dead woman bind me! My head rang with the unicorn's shout, and I dodged the next thrust more by luck than any half-remembered battle skill.

The unicorn whirled, supernaturally fast, leading with its horn. I got the knife up, engaged, turning the horn like an opponent's sword, and followed through in a pretty damn good riposte, slashing the tender nose. The unicorn screamed and slammed its head sideways into my arm. It was an awkward blow and not up to its full potential, but it was good enough to do the job. The knife flew out of my hand; I twisted, lost my footing and and fell, scrabbling across the floor on hands and knees.

The unicorn screamed audibly, stamped, and blew, blood spattering the concrete floor.

"Stop!" Anna cried, and stepped between me and certain destruction, the stone charm swinging on its silver chain from her fist. "I command you—"

The unicorn lunged. The charm spun away to the right, Anna to the left. She fell to the floor, boneless, red spattering her shirt.

"No!" The scream tore my throat, and I reached—reached as I'd sworn never to do again. Reached for the land.

Please...

I expanded, the sea roared in my ears, gulls laughed, and plovers ran. I felt the caress of the waves upon me, and the prick of the roses on the dunes. I was ancient, I was epic.

And I was pissed.

I surged off my knees and lunged, weaponless. The unicorn whirled to meet me and I grabbed its horn in my gloved right hand, tangling the fingers of my left hard in its golden mane.

"Yield," I said, and the whole power of the land rang in my voice. "Or I destroy you now."

It jerked its head, testing me, but I held like a barnacle on the side of Googin Rock.

"Unmade," I crooned. "Returned in disgrace to the element that gave you birth, your deeds undone, unsung, and unrecalled..."

I yield, Keeper. The golden voice was scarcely a whisper.

"Back in place," I said, and walked it onto the carousel, keeping my grip firm, which was no small task, with the myriad voices of the land running riot inside my head.

The unicorn took its place meekly, shook its mane into order, raised its off front foot, and froze, a mere tupelo wood carving, somewhat in need of paint.

I spun and jumped to the floor, running to where Anna lay, too still on the blood-spattered floor.

Oh God, oh God, oh God . . .

"Anna?" I dropped to my knees by her side and touched her pale lips. From the land came a damage report: trauma to the chest, broken neck, shattered pelvis . . .

"She's breathing," I whispered, and I gathered her into my arms, closing my eyes while the essence of the land rose within me.

"Anna!" Tony's voice echoed off the metal walls; his rapid footsteps loud and gritty. I got my eyes open as he went to his knees beside us on the floor, and extended a hand, not quite touching her still face.

"Is she—"

"Out cold," I said, unsteadily, cuddling her slowly warming body against me, her head resting on my shoulder, and thankful that Tony couldn't see me shaking. Close. *So* close. Even the land can't raise the dead.

"We had a scare," I murmured. "She took a bad tumble. Might be a little confused when she comes around." I looked at him, seeing the fear ebbing in his eyes as he touched her hair. "You want to call the Rescue? My cell's kinda inaccessible." Under Anna, in the pocket of my jeans. If it had survived the attempted prison break.

Tony flipped open his phone and made the call. Give them credit, the Rescue was there in minutes, EMTs, stretcher, oxygen— the works. They took my story of a fall off the machine, a head coming into forcible contact with concrete, and spilled paint with professional nods, got her onto the stretcher and wheeled her off, Tony walking beside her, already on the phone to one of the numerous Lee cousins, who would come down to mind the Kitchen while he was gone.

I followed the stretcher at a decent remove, and waited while they loaded it, Tony climbing in without a backward glance. The two tourist ladies in their pretty sweatshirts hovered near the base of Summer's Wheel, their eyes wide.

"What happened?" asked the one wearing the kitten and butterfly appliqué.

"She fell off the machine," I said, hating the lie that shortchanged Anna's valor. "Forgot where she was and took a bad step. Knocked her head. She'll be fine."

"Goodness, I certainly hope so!" the other lady exclaimed. "Of all the rides—I always thought the merry-go-round was the safest!"

The ambulance pulled out then, lights flashing and siren screaming, and the two ladies retreated down the plaza. Me, I watched until it had turned the corner onto Grand, siren blaring as the driver gunned it, heading for Saco and Southern Maine Medical Center.

When the siren's echo had faded, I went to look for the calico cat.

It wasn't with any particular surprise that I found Nancy Vois sitting on the floor next to the utility shed, shaking her head kind of slow and careful, and running her fingers through her wispy, rust-colored hair.

"Pretty brave," I said, sitting cross legged on the floor across from her. "Taking on something ten times your size."

She settled her cap and slanted amber eyes at me from beneath the shelter of the brim. "Your gran didn't mind it," she said defensively.

"I don't mind it, either," I said. "Good God, woman—do you know what *I* am? You think I'm going to shun an honest shapeshifter?"

Another sheltered glance. "Anna all right?"

"She's fine. Likely to be a little scrambled in the memory department, maybe dream about unicorns coming off the merry-go-round or some such bad-knock-in-the-head nonsense. Other than that, there shouldn't be any problems."

Nancy's mouth twitched. "Good. You got 'em nailed down now?"

That was a good question, and not her fault that I didn't exactly have a good answer.

"They're nailed as good as I can nail 'em," I said, which was true. "I'm going to have to study on what else I can do, to make sure we don't get any more accidents." Also true. Go me. "How about you? Everything okay?" I asked. "No broken bones, contusions, cuts, scrapes?"

"I'm fine." She moved her shoulders, grimacing. "Gonna be stiff, later."

I nodded. "Why don't we call it a day? If, after a good night's sleep, you still want to work for me, I'll be here at eight o'clock tomorrow morning. Deal?"

Nancy outright grinned. "Deal."

I observed her closely as she climbed to her feet, but she seemed as fine as she claimed. I got up, noticing a little stiffness, myself, and walked with her to the door.

"Anna left the key on the fuse box," she said, and slipped out into the bright, breezy day. "See you."

"See you," I answered, and watched her walk away, taking the left, deeper into Fun Country. Across from me, Billie Lee waved from behind the counter. I nodded and raised a hand.

Then, I stepped inside the storm gate and shut the hatch behind me.

FOURTEEN

Saturday, April 22

It was quiet inside the storm gates. The animals—those that were something more than mere wooden carvings—were keeping very still. Waiting to see what I'd do next.

Something I wished I knew, myself.

I took a slow tour of the premises, trying to accommodate myself to senses I'd gone long years without. The land was like a child whose favorite aunt has just come to visit. It kept snatching at my attention, wanting to tell me, show me, touch me. I could feel myself being pulled in a treacherous emotional undertow, and fought for equilibrium.

The land doesn't know any moderation, and if a Guardian isn't strong, adamant, and downright bloody-minded, they'll get swallowed up by it, which doesn't do the land or the Guardian one damn' bit of good.

So I made my circuit, and I struggled, and I finally managed to convey the fact that I was *busy* just now and needed some space. The immediacy of the roses, the surf, the rocks; the health, wealth, and worries of Archers Beach faded from the cacophony of a bagpipe band standing directly inside my ear to something like a symphony played—quietly—by a full orchestra in a small room, and I was able to concentrate on my other problem.

A sense of danger, of edges and of bloody intent caught my attention. I looked around, took two steps toward the wall and plucked my knife out of the shadows. Inspection proved the edge still true, no nicks or other damage evident. I swiped the blade clean on my sleeve as I continued my perambulations, sheathed it, and slipped it between my belt and my jeans, at the small of my back.

The wards—that is to say, Gran's wards—were gone, completely dissipated. It may have been that the last few rags had been utilized in the magical action that had freed the unicorn and had him threatening ordinary citizens in broad daylight. Or not.

My foot sent something skittering across the floor, and I looked down, seeing what had been bright, spattered blood, now blots of brown paint; and Anna's charm, glowing gently. I picked it up and slipped the silver chain over my head, wondering why Gran had given the thing to her at all.

Another question to ask, when I caught up with her. Which was going to be *today*, if I had any say in the matter at all.

First things, though, came first.

I climbed onto the carousel.

What vengeance, Keeper? the batwing snarled inside my head.

"You know the terms of your binding," I said, sourly. "Believe me, if I had my druthers, I'd smash the lot of you into toothpicks."

Well, then, it persisted, *what action, as you choose to honor the word of the so-called Wise?*

"Why, I'll bind you, silly creature," I said, and reached out again to the land, shaping my request in painstaking detail. For a moment, nothing happened, then the shadows at the base of the batwing's hooves began to twist, take form and grow.

Up they came, from left and from right, from back and from front: Vines, thick with sea roses and with thorns. In a trice, the six were secured. The batwing shifted, heedless of the thorns, snapped uselessly at its restraints, and subsided.

Very well for now, with no one to see. But not so good in the long term, eh, Keeper? What will you do tomorrow?

"Worry about that for me, will you?" I said. "I've got some errands to run."

I stepped off the carousel and headed for the hatch.

❋   ❋   ❋

*Some*body had been working on Keltic Knot. The leader was unwrapped and seated on the rails. The tarp was loose on a couple of the cars, the padlock was off the trapdoor, and the controls were completely tarp-free.

But of Mr. Ignatious, there was no sign.

"Mr. Ignat'!" I called, leaning over the guard rail. A gull shouted overhead in mimicry, laughed loudly at its own cleverness, and sped away.

"Mr. Ignat'!" I yelled again. "It's Kate!"

Not even a gull answered this time. The land helpfully fed me an image of black and empty tarmac, which could've meant anything. Fine. I swung a leg over the rail and dropped into the enclosure.

I checked the shed at the back of the lot first. No Mr. Ignat'. Skinny as he was, there wouldn't have been room for him among the tools and whatnots, all ordered and hung up so neat it made Gran's housekeeping look positively slipshod.

Outside, I raised the trap, and peered down into the dark.

"Mr. Ignatious?" I called. The darkness swallowed my words, and gave nothing back.

Sighing, I lowered the trap and climbed the stairs to the platform, where there were more signs of work going forth. A can of WD-40 and a screwdriver sat on the deck next to the controls, and the go-stick was locked up tight. Frustrated, I spun on my heel, catching a flicker of reflection in the rear view mirror.

Most single-operator rides have a rear view mirror on a flexible neck at the control station. That's so the operator can see if anybody's coming up behind them, or if maybe somebody'd jumped the exit gate to get themselves a free ride.

Keltic Knot's mirror was in winter position, facing the operator's usual position, and bent slightly down. I looked again, expecting to see disjointed reflections in a foggy glass.

What I did see was myself. My hair had half come loose from its knot and was flying in black tendrils around my face, which was pale, but by no means paper-white, smooth and unmarred.

I blinked, and touched gloved fingers to my cheek, where Anna's butterfly stitches had been only this morning. The dressing must have come off during the fight with the unicorn, though I hadn't seen it when I made my sweep. And the land—the land had healed my hurts, too.

I took a breath, noting that my eyesight was perfectly clear. My chest was pain free and I wasn't gasping for breath, though I'd jogged the whole distance from the carousel.

I sat down on the top step, hard, as the reality of what I'd done punched me in the stomach.

"Oh, no . . ." I heard myself whisper, hearing the land singing contentedly in the back of my head.

The relationship between the Guardian and the land is fluid. By which I mean that each partner is informed by the essence and the nature of the other. While a Guardian must resist the lure of becoming one with the land, *caring for* the land falls squarely inside her duty. It's a delicate dance, and the choices aren't always easy.

Say, for instance, that a Guardian realizes that her essence is horribly flawed, and that the flaw will inevitably infect the land. It's no less and no more than that Guardian's duty to remove herself from the partnership.

Or so I had reasoned a decade ago, choosing my own death rather than poison the land further. I'd sworn then that I'd never renew the bond, and took myself far away to insure it.

And now I'd—I'd . . . and dammit, it'd been so *easy*. I'd barely registered the renewal of the bond until—

I swallowed and stiffened my spine, there on the stair, and shook my hair out of my eyes.

"This can't continue," I said aloud, though there really wasn't any need. "I was wrong to renew the—"

Rejection blared through my head, so hard and loud that I saw stars.

"Hey!"

In the back of my head, the land giggled and strutted, like a kindergarten class that had gotten the better of the teacher. I drew a breath and the kindergartners morphed into a full marching band, complete with trombones, ticker tape, and a jet plane fly-by.

I lost myself briefly in the confusion, and by the time I'd struggled back into my head, I was pretty well steeped in how very glad the land was to have me back.

Along with the music, images fluttered through my head: Anna's healing, the rose ropes binding the prisoners, my own unmarred face in the mirror... The land demonstrating how useful the bond was to me.

And I had to admit it was right. Land magic is by no means *jikinap*, but it is something very much better than a poke in the eye with a sharp stick. And it wasn't like I didn't need all the help I could get.

In fact... I blinked as the idea came fully fledged into my mind.

Gran was a dryad; a creature of the land. That meant, among other things, that she couldn't hide from it. If I melded with the land and searched for her...

I chewed my lip, thinking.

Upside: The search would be efficient and, I hoped, quick.

Downside: Completely melding with the land was—all right, it was dangerous. Definitely not something even I was willing to try on my own.

But. If I had somebody to spot me while I went in, who could pull me out if I got lost, then the operation went from insanely dangerous to not much more dangerous than crossing Grand Avenue at the height of tourist season.

For the somebody, I needed a middling good magic worker, like Gran; or a powerful *trenvay*, like Nerazi.

Or, if he was to be believed, and I had no reason to doubt him on this particular point—Borgan.

If Gran had been within reach, I wouldn't have been doing these calculations, and Nerazi... In my completely biased opinion, the mission to find Gran was now on Code Red. If I had a choice, I'd rather not wait until the wee hours, when I might or might not find Nerazi, who might or might not be willing to help me.

Which left Borgan, whom I'd insulted and walked out on.

Just... peachy.

Kate, you haven't lost your touch, have you?

I took my gloves off and stuffed them in my pockets, fished my cell out of my jeans and checked the time. Going on for one o'clock.

Well, I thought, swinging myself over the rail and dropping lightly onto the entrance ramp. *I haven't had a good helping of crow for quite a while.*

The Kinney Harbor Seafood Exchange was bustling, noisy with the shouts of fishermen, buyers, and the unremitting hilarity of gulls. Not wanting to get knocked in the head with a net, or splashed all over with a fresh haul, I leaned up against a post at the landside entrance, and scanned the crowd.

It isn't as easy as you might suppose to spot one particular fisherman on a pier full of jeans, work sweaters, and cuss words—even a fisherman the size of a small mountain. In fact, I wasn't having any luck at all identifying my man when one of the buyers took pity on me.

"Lookin' for something particular, missy?"

"I wonder if Captain Borgan's brought his haul in yet."

"Seen him not too long ago . . ." He looked over his shoulder. "Andre!" he bellowed. "Ya got some goods down here if ya want 'em!"

The racket died down as all eyes turned toward the door, then surged again in a chorus of ribald jokes. My benefactor gave me a grin. "He'll be along shortly, missy. Just you rest there."

Rest there I did, not having any choice, until there came a movement from the far end of the pier, and there was Borgan, moving slowly but steadily toward my position, trading laughter and shoulder punches, a grin on his face until he broke free of the crowd and saw me.

I swallowed, stood up straight, and looked him square in the eye, waiting.

The right corner of his mouth twitched—whether it was anger, humor, or resignation, I couldn't tell—but he gave me the grace of a stiff, formal nod.

"Kate," he said, entirely noncommittal.

"Borgan," I answered hoarsely, and cleared my throat. He was barefoot, his jeans rolled, the sleeves of his work sweater pushed up on his arms; he smelled like fish, and sweat and salt. Not precisely a figure to inspire either delight or desire. Despite which, the land shouted both, loud enough that it set my knees to shaking.

"I'd like that cup of coffee," I said, pleased that I sounded four hundred percent calmer than I felt, "if it's still on offer."

Silence, while he measured me out of bland black eyes, and finally gave me a curt nod.

"I've gotta finish up here. Meet me at the dock in half an hour."

"Sure." I hesitated. "Thanks."

"See you," he answered, and went back the way he'd come. I stood and watched until I lost him in the general confusion, then turned and walked down the ramp, hands fisted in my pockets to still the shaking.

FIFTEEN

Saturday, April 22

Forty-five minutes later, I was on the dock, elbows on the rail, and the beginnings of a good seethe brewing.

I'd taken the long way around, not having any desire to be on display for the local guys when they moored their boats and rode their dinghies in to dock. *That's the girl came for Andre Borgan at the 'change,* they'd tell each other, and give a knowing grin in my direction.

Nope, didn't need that.

'Course, I very much didn't need to be stood up, either, though it looked like I was going to be.

Overhead, the gulls circled and screamed off-color jokes at each other. Out in the center of the harbor, the Tancook Schooner danced at her mooring, as if she were impatient for a sail.

There was a stir of shadow on the schooner's deck, and Borgan came topside, swung over the rail and dropped lightly into his dinghy. He cast off, plying the oars with calm power, and was tying up at the base of the dock in no time at all.

I kept leaning, trying to look casual and hanging on to my seethe with both hands while the land turned cartwheels inside my head in an excess of pleasure.

Borgan vaulted to the dock, glanced 'round, and walked in my direction, boot heels firm against the weathered boards.

"Sorry I'm late," he said when he was in easy talking distance. "I thought maybe you'd appreciate it if I took a shower first."

His jeans were faded and soft-looking, his shirt black, open at the throat under the leather jacket. He leaned on the rail next to me and looked out over the harbor. Electricity crackled along my nerves, and the land fair quivered with delight.

"Andre?" I asked, testing whether I still had control of my vocal cords.

He shook his head. "That's for licenses and suchlike. You call me Borgan." He shifted his elbows on the rail, settling himself.

"You sure did make a noise this morning," he said conversationally. "Land shouted so loud, it scared the fish. What made you change your mind?"

I took a deep breath, watching the Tancook Schooner dance, my bad temper draining away like sand through my fingers.

"You know Anna Lee?"

He nodded. "Nice lady. Got a big heart."

I flicked a glance at the side of his face, suspecting sarcasm. He turned his head, braid swinging, and met my eyes.

"Seriously," he said.

I nodded, jerkily, and went back to overlooking the harbor.

"Anna broke her neck this morning," I said quietly. "I— She's a good person. What you said—a big heart. The world's better with Anna in it. I couldn't just let her—" My voice broke.

"Die," Borgan finished for me. I caught his nod out of the corner of my eye. "I can see that. She gonna be okay?"

"Yeah. Tony called the Rescue. I told them she fell off the carousel and hit her head. If they didn't buy it, they were polite enough not to say."

"Hmm." He turned his head to look at me. "What actually did happen, if you don't mind saying?"

I hesitated, then pushed upright and turned to face him.

"Do you know about the carousel?"

He raised an eyebrow. "You mean about there being half a dozen desperate criminals, stripped of their names and their memories, bound into six of the animals by the Wise, who want to see if and how the Changing Land'll change them for the better?" He snorted. "Yeah, I know about the merry-go-round, Kate."

"Okay." I sighed. "What *actually* happened is that the wards got 'way too thin—my fault—and the unicorn broke loose. It went after Anna. I tried to turn it with the knife I got off Mr. Nemeier's hired hand yesterday, but my fencing's rusty, and it knocked me down. Whereupon Anna, who thought the charm Gran had given her awhile back protected her from exactly such dangers, jumped between us—"

"And got herself all kinds of broke." Borgan shook his head. "Most people, they see a unicorn come strolling off a merry-go-round? They either scream and run, or check themselves into Detox."

I felt my lips twitch toward a smile. "Anna's not most people."

"That's so," Borgan murmured, and again, "that's so." He pushed out of his lean, hitched a hip onto the rail, and looked down at me, his eyes dark and ironical.

"You got a real gift for storytelling, by the way. Every tale you give out hints at six you haven't. Makes it hard for a man to know where to start asking his questions." He looked over my head and was silent for the beat of five, apparently considering his options, then nodded and looked back to me.

"The knife from Nemeier's crewman," he said. "I'm taking it that the lawyers weren't able to settle everything out all nice and polite?"

"Henry can't get the Boston lawyer on the phone. The message I got yesterday was that Mr. Nemeier wants me to fix the damage to his grass." I touched my cheek, the skin smooth under my fingertips. "He cut me, as a reminder, and a promise of worse things to come, if I didn't do what I was told."

Borgan looked at me. Before I knew what he was about, he had his hand under my chin, tipping my face up to his. My heart slammed into overtime; I swallowed, and Borgan let me go.

"Seems to have healed clean," he said.

"The land," I managed, and he nodded.

"Can I take a look at that knife?"

"Sure." I reached under my jacket and slipped it out of its nestle against my backbone, offering it to Borgan across my palm, like I'd been taught, hilt toward him.

He gave me a formal nod and picked it up, holding it like he knew what he was doing, which he probably did.

I watched as he sighted down the edge, and then weighed it in his hand, eyes half-closed.

"Turned unicorn horn with this, did you?" he asked eventually.
I nodded. "It's a good knife."

"So it is. How did you say you got it off him?"

"I didn't. But if you must know, I kicked him in the balls."

Borgan grinned, black eyes glinting. "Did you now? And what happened to him after?"

"He ran off."

"That's too bad." He flipped the blade neatly and offered it to me, hilt first. "Keep it by. You never know when you might need a good knife."

Right. I slipped it away into its sheath, and stood looking up at him.

"Borgan—"

He raised a hand and I stopped, waiting.

"Tell me," he said, "about Tarva."

I blinked, surprised. "Tarva? I told you, he was my friend."

Borgan nodded, and moved his hand, silently inviting me to expand on that bare fact.

I shrugged. "When I was new here, Tarva showed me how things worked. Everything was a joke, but a *friendly* joke. I didn't have to be on guard every second in case somebody wanted to kill me, or..." In fact, Tarva had shown me that it was still possible to have fun, to laugh, and...to care in spite of everything that had happened.

"He taught me to swim," I told Borgan.

He looked startled, and I threw my hands up in exasperation. Everybody—Gran, Nerazi, Mr. Ignat', and, yes, Tarva—had been astonished and amused to find out that I hadn't known a doggy paddle from a dalmatian when I arrived in Archers Beach.

"Yes, I was born into a House of the Sea, but I never learned how to swim, all right? There wasn't any need for me to learn how to swim. No sea in the Land of the Flowers would have hurt Princess Kaederon, for fear of what Aeronymous—my grandfather—would do if they had." I looked out over Kinney Harbor, then back to Borgan.

"The Atlantic Ocean, on the other hand, doesn't give a damn if I live or I die. I've always liked that about it."

Borgan tipped his head. "I think you'll find the sea cares more than you suppose," he said quietly. "Why did you kill him?"

My temper flared, and I embraced it, giving him the best glare I had in me.

"I don't think that's any of your business."

"I think it is," he returned placidly, and crossed his arms over his chest. Waiting.

My first impulse was to let him wait until the ocean froze, but, dammit, I needed his help. Today.

"Just an overview'd be fine," Borgan murmured.

I shook my head, lifted my hands and let them fall, defeated.

"Sure—an overview. Tarva used to think it was a barrel of giggles to steal fish out of nets. One guy—Dan Bentley, his name was. Dan, in particular, took the joke bad—real bad—which, y'know, only added to the spice, as far as Tarva was concerned. He was having so much fun with the man, he'd shift and go up to Neptune's at the end of the day just to ask him how many fish he'd caught for the seal..."

I let it drift off, remembering how I'd tried to talk him into cutting the guy some slack. But Tarva only laughed at me, and the other guys started to take up the joke, while Dan got madder and madder until even the land took note, which was when—

"I decided the best thing to do was to force Tarva to leave the guy alone, so I—" My voice squeezed out. I swallowed and took a breath. Borgan waited, calm and relaxed against the rail.

"It didn't do any good to talk to him," I whispered. "So, I used High Magic to override his will, and—and set him under a geas not to hurt Dan Bentley, which stealing his fish surely did." I shook my head.

"Trouble was, that didn't stop Dan Bentley from hurting Tarva. He came into Neptune's one night, already drunk, and madder'n hell. The fish hadn't come to his net that day, or the day before, and he was feeling the bite. Tarva didn't say anything to him—not that night. He couldn't. But he was there, and all it took was Dan seeing him. He pulled a knife, and Tarva—" I swallowed. "Tarva couldn't fight back. Because of me, of what I'd forced on him. He was dead when the other guys pulled Dan off him." I looked out over the harbor; the schooner was quiet at her mooring now, as if dancing had tired her out.

"Hmm," said Borgan. "And that was your fault, was it? Your death?"

"It is," I said, still watching the boat. "And worse. I know what it feels like to be under someone else's will—to watch my hand move, and not be able to stop it, or change its intent. I—I swore

I'd never do that to anyone, and my friend—" I shook my head. "It's proof that black blood will tell, no matter that I'd learned better. Proof that the land—and the people I cared about—would be better off without me."

"And so you cut yourself off from Archers Beach and went out to the dry lands to die," Borgan said, his voice shockingly matter-of-fact.

"That's right. And I almost made it, too." I turned my head to look up into his face, which was politely noncommittal. "Then Gran went missing and I had to come back, and there's a decade's worth of dying all gone to waste."

Borgan's lips twitched—a smile, I was pretty sure. "So, what is it you want from me, besides a cup of coffee?"

"I want you to act as my safety line, while I meld with the land and look for my grandmother."

He looked over my head. "That's a lot," he said, softly. "A lot to ask, Kate."

"I know it is. But it has to be done soonest and you're—" I closed my mouth before *what's available* escaped.

Borgan snorted lightly, as if he'd heard what I hadn't said, and it amused him.

"So," he said, still looking out to sea, "what do you know about me?"

"I know you're *trenvay*," I said slowly. "That you're powerful. And old." The last one was a surprise, then wasn't, as I thought about it.

"How d'you figure old?" he asked.

"I didn't," I told him truthfully. "The land knew."

"Hmm. And powerful?"

"You ranked yourself with Nerazi, and that's plenty powerful for me."

"I did say that, didn't I?" He looked down into my face. "Any idea *what* I am?"

"What—" I blinked, and waited, but this time the land had nothing to tell me, aside that it was beyond delighted with its good friend Borgan. I fielded my best guess.

"A selkie." I put light fingers on his leather sleeve, snatching them away almost immediately, heart racing.

If Borgan felt a reciprocal jolt, I couldn't tell it from his face.

"That's a good guess," he said and pushed out of his lean to stand tall before me. "Kate."

I looked up into his eyes, and even the land quietened for a second or two.

"Understand what you're taking on. You'll have to trust me. Maybe as hard, or harder—you'll have to trust *you*. Now's the time to ask yourself, *Can I do this?*"

"I have to do it," I said, and felt the land bolstering my resolve. "It's not going to be pretty if those animals get loose. I don't have enough *jikinap* left to light a cigarette—hell, frying a strip of grass almost finished me. If I don't find Gran *now*, I'll have to try to pull in an Ozali from another of the Six Worlds, which is *not* optimum, or I'll need to ask Nerazi to call on the Wise, which is so much less than optimum that words pale."

Borgan grinned. "Got a real respect for authority, don't you?"

"The trouble with the Wise is that you never know what they're going to do, or if they'll unilaterally decide that there wouldn't *be* a problem if they just remove the person who called them in from the equation."

"They are a thought whimsical," Borgan agreed, and shrugged. "All right, Kate, I'll stand watch for you. Choose the ground."

I nodded, having previously thought of this.

"It's up in the middle of town," I said, apologetically.

"That's all right. I can use some exercise." He waved me ahead of him. "Lead on, pretty lady."

SIXTEEN

Saturday, April 22

Up in the more or less middle of town, there's a park—a couple benches, a sundial, a few maples with daffodils planted 'round their feet. It's the site of the old Archer homestead. There used to be a plaque there saying so, but it vanished years ago, and the town never bothered to replace it. The Garden Club takes care of mowing the lawn and seeing to the flowers, and it used to be that the guy across the street would rake the leaves in the fall. Maybe he still does.

With a good four blocks of buildings to keep the sea breeze at bay, it was positively warm on the old home land. I took off my jacket—and Borgan sucked his breath in through his teeth.

I threw him a glance over my shoulder.

"Problem?"

Wordlessly, he opened his fingers, and I obediently spread the jacket out between my two hands. The drape was a little off, what with the unicorn's mods. Borgan shook his head.

"Came within a quarter inch of being skewered," he said. "You didn't think to mention that?"

"I told you my fencing's rusty," I said defensively, "and besides, it missed."

"It's an inch that's as good as a mile, Kate. You start dealing in fractions and the odds get jittery."

"It wasn't my idea of a good time," I snapped. "And I suppose *you* never took a risk in your life."

"There's a fine thing to suppose about the man you just asked to keep you from doing something hugely stupid," he retorted, and I laughed, turning away to drop the ruins of my jacket at the base of the sundial.

Three o'clock, according to the pointer—the sundial doesn't do daylight savings time. I bent down and brushed the grit from the brass face, my fingers tracing the cast letters:

There's always time for magic.

Right.

Sighing, I folded my legs and sat on the damp grass, squinting up at Borgan, standing above me with the sun over his shoulder.

"Ready?" I asked.

"That's me should be asking you." He sighed and sat across from me, effortlessly cross-legged, jacket on his knee, and extended his hands, palms up. I put my hands on his, and yanked back, breath hissing, the land yammering and jumping, pulling at my attention like a kitchen full of puppies.

"Kate?"

I pushed the land *down* and told it to sit, and took a second to sort myself out before looking into Borgan's eyes.

"Could you turn it off, please?" I asked politely.

"It?"

"The glamor. I'm not going to be able to do this at all if I'm thinking about how nice it would be to kiss you." Borgan lifted an eyebrow, and I added a hasty, "For instance."

"Hadn't thought of that," he said. "Though I think it would be nice to kiss you, too. Time and a place for everything, I guess. Let's see what I can do..." He closed his eyes, and I had a sudden sense of *departure* from the land, as if the rather substantial person sitting on the grass before me was nothing more than a shell.

For the space of three long breaths, he sat perfectly still, and as far as the land was concerned, absent. Then he sighed, opened his eyes, and held his hands out once more.

"Try now," he said.

Tentatively, I extended my hands.

There was a tiny frisson of energy just before our palms touched, then only warmth, skin to skin.

I closed my eyes, and the land snatched at me, overloading my senses with color, taste, smell; I saw Archers Beach laid out beneath me, gull's eye view; felt the satisfaction of a rose in the sun, the simple contentment of wind-brushed grass—

Gasping, drowning in sensation, I pulled back, struggling into my own head, opened my eyes—and saw Borgan watching me, a frown on his broad face.

"Might be time to ask that question again," he said quietly. "Can you do this?"

I took a deep breath, tasting grass, salt, and leaf. "I *have* to do this," I said, as firmly as I could. Borgan shook his head.

"*Have to* isn't *can*," he said.

Which was true enough. But—

"I'm out of practice, that's all. The land took my pledge when I was a *kid*, with a serious amount of magical education in my immediate past. I didn't even have to think about how to handle the bond. Just give me a minute to get the hang of it again."

"All the minutes you want," he said calmly, and tipped his head. "If you'll take advice, it might be reasonable to just go with the flow. Remember, I'm holding you, and I won't let you get lost."

It was an absurd thing to say, and absurdly comforting to hear. I gave him a smile and took a breath.

"Once more," I whispered, "into the breach."

The greeting was more restrained this time, as if the land had understood the need for a little moderation. I went slowly, like wading into the surf until the undertow takes you, and sweeps you out to sea.

I couldn't have isolated the moment when it happened. Suddenly, I wasn't aware of the land's presence as a separate component inside my head, that was all. I was vast, and green, and limitless. I was marsh and rock. I was all of the trees on Heath Hill and every crumb of thin, sandy soil. Leaves and trash tumbled across my back and the wind combed the grasses of my hair.

There were voices all about me, the voices of those who were sustained by the land. I held myself as still as I might, listening for one voice, particular and unmistakeable . . . and not hearing it.

What I did hear, though, was—static, call it, like when you put the car radio on "search" and the scan hits a spot where there ought to be a station, but it's out of range. There was, now that I was in a position to hear it, a lot of static.

A *lot* of static.

The last time I had melded with the land, years ago, there had been two spots that were off the air: The Boundary Stone, that divided Surfside and Archers Beach.

And Googin Rock.

I concentrated, trying to isolate each empty band; to count— one...three...five...

Nine.

Just above the fizz of static, I heard something else. A wailing and a crying, hopeless and maybe not completely mad. And I was wrong—the static was there, too, fizzing along the far edges of agony.

I focused—and performed the analog of opening my eyes.

My attention was immediately drawn toward the northern salt marsh. I went willingly, struggling to see in a black-and-gray mist—a sort of visual static—tasting mud, foul and thick. I moved closer yet, the marsh's pain dinning in my ears. Black tendrils whipped out of the mist, wrapped around my essence, pulling me down into itself, as if—

I snapped to a halt, with a sensation like a rope tightening around the waist of my simple human body. The black tendrils fell away, wailing, and I rose into the melding of place and spirit that was Archers Beach.

This time, I did my utmost to ignore the static, annoying as it was, bringing every bit of my concentration to the task of isolating—of locating—one single, familiar, and beloved voice.

After a time that seemed good to me—realizing that time within a meld has no relation, really, to the time the sun told along the brass dial in the park where Borgan sat with my body—I reassigned my concentration to Heath Hill.

The trees there murmured and caressed me as I flowed among them, to the Center, and the tree itself, the ancient tupelo. I extended myself to encompass it—and reeled back, retching, horror shredding my concentration. Borgan's lifeline tightened cruelly around me and I was jerked up and outward—gasping and coughing like a fish out of water.

"Kate!" Hard hands on my shoulders, shaking me, pulling me

completely out of the land and into the world of men. I took a calmer breath, and opened my eyes to dusk, and the long glow of sundown over the sea.

"Kate?" Borgan's hands were gentler now. "Did you find your gran?"

"No," I said, blinking up at him. "She's not on the land." His eyebrows went up, and his lips parted—but he held his peace when I raised my hand.

"She's not on the land," I repeated. "Worse, there's a blight on her tree."

"A blight," he repeated. "How bad?"

I sighed, seeing it again in my mind's eye. "From this perspective, hardly bad at all. Just a blot, really; an ink splotch. Nothing she couldn't put right in half a second. But she's not in her tree. She's not—*anywhere*."

Borgan frowned. "Everybody's got to be somewhere," he pointed out.

"And a *trenvay* more than most." I scraped my hair back off my face with fingers that weren't quite steady, took a deep breath and gave him a nod.

"Thank you."

"What you asked me to do," he said, with a half-shrug. "Now, if your gran's—damn it, she's got to be here! The woman's tied to her tree!"

I nodded in sympathy. "I know. But, trust me, she's not. Here, that is. I hope she still *is* tied to the tree," *somehow,* "or else we've got *bad* problems."

"I thought we already had bad problems."

"Not 'til tomorrow," I said tiredly.

"Anything might happen by then," Borgan agreed. "What'll you do now, Kate?"

I sighed. "Go see Nerazi. Cut out my liver in exchange for a straight answer, or a—" I looked at him, sharp. "There's snallygasters, Black Dogs, and willie wisps on the beach, so the heeterskyte tells me."

He nodded. "I've heard the same. Haven't seen any, though, and to tell the truth, I'm more worried about those smugglers we talked about."

"Maybe we'll get lucky and the Black Dogs'll do the smugglers." I levered myself upright, only staggering a little, and managed not to glare as Borgan came to his feet as light as a feather. He reached into his pocket and pulled out his cell.

"Beam me your number?" he asked, and I laughed, relieved at the everyday-ness of it, and pulled out mine. "Exchange of hostages."

"Done."

I slid the phone away, and bent to retrieve my ruined jacket, straightening slowly.

"Thanks," I said again, and held out my hand.

He took it, and before I could blink, bent and placed a lingering kiss on the back.

"There," he said, straightening and giving me the devil's own grin. "That was nice, now wasn't it?"

"Get out of here," I snapped, heart pounding with, I told myself, anger.

"All right," he said equitably. "See you around, Kate. Give a call if you need me." He slung his jacket over his shoulder, and turned away.

"Borgan," I said, hearing the fizz of static in memory.

He turned back.

"Kate?"

"There's—" I cleared my throat. "I felt like there're a number of sections of the Beach not . . . not reporting in. No voice, no— just static."

He didn't say anything, just stood there waiting, like he expected me to go on.

"I just wonder," I said lamely, "if you know what happened."

He blew out an exasperated breath.

"Didn't they teach you anything over there in Flowerland, Kate? As above, so below? Sound familiar? Or did you think you could die alone?"

I was still gaping, speechless, when he gave up on an answer, and strolled out of the park, across the street, heading downhill.

Toward the sea.

SEVENTEEN

"Princess Kaederon." The voice was smoky and rich, like dark chocolate laced with ginger. I hated it; hated what it could make me do. Hated myself for not being strong enough to resist it.

"Princess Kaederon," Ramendysis said again, caressingly. I concentrated on my handwork—stitching the binding spells into the sable pennants, and did not dare look up.

"Will you play the coquette, then?" he murmured, I felt it, the hated crawl of his power over my skin. He was going to force me to do it again. I was a coward, a fool, and a weakling. At least I'd managed to hide my shame from my mother.

"How she teases me," Ramendysis said regretfully. "And yet, my lady, you will shortly see the fullness of her affection."

My heart froze.

"The child grows comely," he continued. "And increasingly skilled."

"Indeed, sir," my mother said steadily, "she honors my husband in her face."

"Why, so she does!" he exclaimed, and I felt his shadow shift behind me. "That must be the reason I love her so well. For you know, dear Lady Nessa, how fond I was of your husband. It quite distressed me to unmake him. To find that he lives again—ah, that would be delight, indeed!"

"Princess Kaederon," he said for the third time, and the binding thread stuck to fingers suddenly damp. "Rise, and show your mother how you return my regard."

His will moved my limbs. I fought to stay seated—fought my own muscles—gripping the embroidery frame, deliberately driving the needle deep into my finger. The pain helped, a little, though I was shaking like a leaf in a storm wind with the effort to resist him.

"She grows," Ramendysis remarked, amusement lacing his rich voice. "But perhaps not as much as we feared. Kaederon. Your little game grows tiresome. Come to me here."

His will struck me like a lash. My fingers snapped open and the embroidery frame fell with a clatter, silks spilling like jewels across the floor. I felt my body rise, and turn smoothly on a heel. As always, he imposed a smooth, gliding walk upon a body more accustomed to striding, my back forced straight to the point of agony.

He was lounging on his favorite piece of furniture in this room that had once been my private parlor; the chaise where he had compelled me to sit and watch while he broke each of my servants in turn, absorbed their *jikinap*, and rendered their bodies into dust.

Beside him stood my mother, grave and calm in her sea-green dress, her hair loose around her shoulders. She smiled at me as I glided across the floor, and my frozen heart broke into a thousand pieces.

Ramendysis also smiled, and extended his long, white hand. "Come," he whispered, and my traitor body continued onward, resistless, just as it would very soon pull the gown from its own shoulders, pinch and massage its own budding breasts, kneel down and part my lord's robe for him, so that—

No.

Six paces out from doom, between one unnatural step and the next, I stopped.

Ramendysis frowned, his power oozing over me like honey. My skin began to burn, or so it seemed. I dared not break my concentration by looking down at myself. *Better to burn,* I thought. *Far better to burn.*

"Well," Ramendysis said softly, and brought himself up on an elbow, storm gray curls swirling about his head.

I felt his will increase; the weight of his regard all but unbearable. But those other things—the horror of doing those things ever again, of watching my body move in response to another's desire... My will was set in utter opposition to his, and I held my ground.

Unfortunately, holding my ground was all I could do, resistance my only weapon. I could neither retreat nor disengage.

"Sir." My mother's voice was coolly amused. "This is unworthy of you."

Ramendysis turned to look at her, and the weight of his will eased by a fraction.

"Unworthy? Conquest is always worthy, madam." He flung up a white hand, amused. "But, there. You were not born to this land. Our customs must be forever strange to you."

My mother laughed, a light, cruel sound that I had never heard before. "Fie, sir! What is the conquest of a quarter-bred child to one of your stature?" She tipped her head, her hair flowing like water over her bare brown shoulder. "What you want, I feel, is a powerful and fully capable woman, one who will increase your stature a hundredfold, whether you choose to drain her, or to use her." She smiled, and moved forward in a glide eerily like that which Ramendysis had imposed on me, placing herself between us.

"Acknowledge your true desire, my lord—you want a woman of *voysin*. You hunger for that which is rare in this land, and which is the greatest treasure of mine."

There she stood, her hair loose down her back, glowing like a star with the seductive power of her *voysin*. I felt a tremble of desire—and if I, quarter-bred and a child, was so moved, who can doubt that Ramendysis, warrior, philosopher, and mage, was moved even more and on levels that I could scarcely guess at? Who, indeed, among the good folk of the Land of the Flowers could have looked upon that *voysin*, the fire of her soul, and not desired to possess it?

Ramendysis tipped his head, with a show of thoughtfulness. "I understand that you offer yourself to me—willingly," he said, his voice perhaps not as nonchalant as he wished it to be.

Nessa, my mother, shook her head, slow and seductive, raised a hand and brushed the back along her cheek. She must have been smiling at him, and it sickened me to know it.

"My Lord Ramendysis is not a child. He knows that there is a price for everything worth owning."

"And your price would be?" As if he were compelled, which was impossible, Ramendysis rose from the chaise, and looked upon her, his face avid, his attention wholly on her, but his will—enough of it—still on me.

"My price is this. Have my child conveyed immediately to the Changing Land and placed into the care of my mother, Ebony Pepperidge, severing all her ties and duties to this House and Land. Let the Ozali Zephyr be the one who transports her."

I saw the ebony lace move over his breast as he took a breath. "And that is your price?"

"It is."

"And what do I gain, in return for depriving myself of an amusing toy?"

My mother leaned forward, and set a languid hand over her breast. "You gain my soul, put willingly into your care." He said nothing, and she straightened, head tipped to one side.

"But perhaps my lord feels that resistance lends spice?"

"When other attributes are absent—yes," he said, breathlessly. "However, you propose to place yourself and your *voysin* entirely into my keeping..."

"Yes..." she whispered, and took one single step backward. "But none of it until the child is safe away from here."

He stared at her. "Do you suppose that I can't force you as you stand here?"

She laughed.

He spun, his will leaving me so suddenly I fell to my knees, and clapped his hands.

A messenger coalesced out of the air, silver wings glittering.

"Go to the Ozali Zephyr," Ramendysis said, the rich voice strained, "and beg her to attend me here. I have a boon to ask of her."

"No," I whispered, and thrust myself upward, collapsing again when my abused muscles refused to hold me. "Mother, no..."

Her hand fell on my hair. "Hush," she said gently, and my throat closed.

But that didn't stop me from screaming.

EIGHTEEN

Sunday, April 23
Low Tide 1:09 A.M.
Moonrise 3:47 A.M. EDT, Waning Crescent

One good thing about screaming yourself out of a nightmare is that you're full awake and ready for any pre-dawn rendezvous you might happen to have.

I left early for my hopeful date, the dream driving me to seek clean air, unburdened by any scent other than salt and sea.

For of course it hadn't been a dream, but a memory. The replaying of the hellish bargain my mother had made to save me from the attentions of our just overlord, the murderer of Aeronymous, Nathan, and all of our House. My mother had been spared, as I had come to believe, because she possessed the brilliant, seductive *voysin* which is the birthright of those born to the Changing Land. I think that Ramendysis had always meant to consume her—I had only been the means to ensure her acceptance of his will; her total surrender. Not that he hadn't tried to renege on the agreed terms: I'd shown some spark, after all; there might conceivably be a swallow of *jikinap* to be had from me. Zephyr had been too canny for him, though.

Now and then, I still wonder what happened to her.

The wind blasted me as I left the dune walk and came out onto the beach. I was wearing the trusty Google sweatshirt over

Gran's sweater and a long-sleeved denim shirt, which turned out to be a warmer solution than my now-air-conditioned jacket; and the work gloves were keeping my fingers toasty. The knife I'd taken from Joe Nemeier's messenger boy was thrust like the afterthought it had been between belt and jeans at the small of my back. Not much protection against either Borgan's smugglers or the heeterskyte's bogies—but something more than a pure heart.

The tide was out—'way out; soon to be dead low—and three Subarus could have raced abreast down the strip of firm sand. Me, I walked, the sense of the land a quiet, comforting murmur at the back of my head, no louder than the distant plash of water against shore.

Up in the dry sand, I could hear the plovers trading the day's news among themselves. Now and then, I would see a flicker of wings in my averted vision, but no heeterskyte called welcome, or came nigh to pass the time.

Just as well. My thoughts were shadowed by my memories, and I doubt I was good company.

The boundary rock came into sight, and I angled toward it, taking it easy. At a conservative guess, I was an hour ahead of the time I could reasonably expect to see Nerazi, though she had been known to stop by the rock early.

And sometimes, she didn't stop at all.

At the back of my head, the land continued its contented murmur. The wind puffed a petulant gust from up Surfside way, flinging a thimble's worth of dry sand into my face as I ducked 'round to the protected side of the rock.

It was crouched in the deep shadows where stone met sand, pulled in tight on itself, hidden even from the land, waiting for its moment—

The tentacle whistled as it cut the air, and old, old reflexes pitched me forward and down, rolling in a spray of dry sand, the land blaring alarm at the unnatural thing that skittered out of the shadow on caterpillar feet, two sets of tentacles flailing.

I twisted and got my feet under me, coincidentally kicking sand into its great eye, and snatched the knife free from its nestle against my spine. The blade gleamed like rune-steel in the darkness, and the snallygaster hissed, tentacles whipping in earnest now.

I caught the first in my gloved left hand, slashed at the second with the knife, and stamped on the third.

The fourth, unfortunately, got a grip on my ankle. I slashed again, severing the sensitive tip of the wounded tentacle. The snallygaster screamed, and tried to yank the other out of my grip. I held on like it was a lifeline, feeling the pressure around my ankle tighten. If I didn't end it fast, I'd take crushed bones away from this encounter.

Twisting, I used the knife on the appendage I had in hand. The blade cut the rubbery flesh like going through hot butter, black blood spurted, and a stench like rotting flesh tainted the clean sea air. The snallygaster's cries of pain and outrage disappeared into the ultrasonic, and I went down like a ten pound sack of taters, a second tentacle tight around my thigh.

I slashed down—stupid, but the only move I had. The knife cut 'gaster-flesh, severing the tentacle two-thirds of the way through. Good enough for rock 'n roll. I twisted, the flailing stump hit me in the head, and blood like hot pitch spattered my shoulders. I slashed again, at a bad angle. The 'gaster was convulsing, slamming me against the sand, grit in my eyes, ears, nose, mouth. I jacknifed, ignoring the shriek of agony from my abused ankle, and brought the knife down, blind.

The tentacle parted, and I was rolling, away, away.

A noise like a locomotive running at me across the beach, steam whistle wide, screaming death, destruction, and—

Silence.

I lay face down in the sand and whimpered, the land dancing manic in my head.

Eventually, the land quietened, my heart rate came down to within shouting distance of normal, and I pushed myself up, sitting half-curled in the sand to take stock.

I reeked. My clothes, hair, and face were sticky with black blood, and there was something unfortunate going on with that ankle. I started to roll my jeans, the land leaning over my shoulder—when I heard the howl.

"Oh, no . . ." I breathed, and as if in answer, a second howl answered the first.

No dog born to the Changing Land could produce such a sound—mournful, savage, and insatiable. Snallygasters hunt alone. Black Dogs run in pairs.

A third howl, closer now; inside my head, I felt the pounding of huge feet upon the sand. Around me, the night air thickened and the blood chilled in my veins.

Carefully, favoring the wounded ankle, I got to my feet, my back against the rock. The blade in my hand blazed like a lantern, and I spared a wonder for where Joe Nemeier's boy had gotten such a weapon while I fished my cellphone out of my pocket.

I found Borgan's number and hit "send." Another howl scarred the night; the land's awareness flickered and for an instant I saw them, running shoulder to shoulder down the beach, red tongues like flame, iron nails for teeth, then the cell connected and his voice was in my ear, tiny and too far away.

"Borgan," I gasped, but he overrode me—

"...voice mail box for Andre Borgan. Please leave a message and I'll get back to you just as soon as I can."

Fuck.

"Never mind," I said, and thumbed the phone off.

All right, Kate, I said to myself, shoving the cell into my pocket, *think. The cavalry is not going to arrive—what're you going to do?*

Good question.

The sand at my feet stirred, swirling, struggling, shapeless— collapsing. I stared—and gasped a laugh. *Well, why not?*

It wasn't as if I had a better idea.

The sand stirred again, and a form took shape in a fog of swirling particles.

Half a dozen steps ahead of my position against the rock, a White Dog stood, with a wolfhound's sharp muzzle and long fragile legs, ears pricked to attention, tail down and held close.

It wouldn't last long, right here on the boundary, where the land's power was weak. But it might last long enough.

The Black Dogs howled—two strides from the far side of the rock, no further—and I heard the White Dog growl.

"Good girl," I murmured, and braced myself against the stone, knife held at ready. If the White Dog could take one, I might be able to take the other, though even with help it was going to be nip and—

They came 'round the rock silent and fleet, their great paws throwing up gouts of sand. Ears flat, the White Dog crouched, all but invisible. She let the first one by, and leapt for the throat of the second.

I held my ground, though what I wanted to do was shrink back into and become one with the rock. Black Dogs are only a simpering shadow of the great hunting hounds of the Land of the Flowers. I reminded myself of that, swallowed and waited for my moment while the Dog displayed its teeth in a snarl.

Behind it, the White Dog and the Black were locked in mortal combat, eerily silent, now it was come down. As I watched, they broke, rolling to their feet, and backed away from each other. The Black Dog was bleeding from a dozen superficial wounds. The White Dog...was diminished, melting as I watched, crumbling into bits of sand...

My particular Dog leapt, teeth flashing. I met it with the knife, scoring a glancing hit on a broad shoulder, and the Dog fell back, tongue lolling.

I felt heavy where I stood, unbearably sleepy and slow. What was I doing here, out in the cold night, wounded and stupid, standing against a creature I had no hope of defeating? Best to just put the knife down, submit—

The land screamed at the back of my head and I snarled, my fingers tightening on the knife I had almost dropped. The Black Dog saw my snarl and raised it a long, belling howl. My heart shriveled up inside me.

In spite of it, I held onto the knife, and kept my back firm against the rock.

"You want me," I panted through a miasma of despair. "Come get me."

Behind its shoulder, the White Dog was little more than a sluggishly moving pile of sand. Its opponent raised a leg and peed on it, washing the sand back into the beach, and turned its lantern eyes on me.

Not good. Oh, so very not good, with my blood like molasses in my veins and my head heavy and thick. What was I trying to prove here, anyway? The nearest Dog inched forward, stiff-legged; the second went out to the left, moving to box me in.

The nearest Dog growled, low in its heavy throat. I hefted the knife, and got myself firm on my good leg, while despair clawed my spirit.

"Not without a fight," I told the Dogs, my voice cracked and shaking. I lunged.

The ankle screamed blue murder. I ignored it and pitched forward into a maw full of fearful, rusty teeth, got an arm around that broad, loathsome neck and plunged the knife down. The

Dog screamed, pain and plunder filled the world, and the land showed me the second Dog, leaping for my back, jaws gaping...

I wrenched my knife free—and went flying as my Dog shook me off. The sand cushioned my landing, and I rolled to my knees, foreknowing my doom—

A scarecrow figure in a swirling black overcoat, pale hair fogging the air, crouched between me and the Dogs, arms spread, holding two at bay with nothing more than his naked fingers.

I tried to get up; the ankle folded on me, and I went down again. My benefactor kicked sand at one of the Dogs, simultaneously lunging at the second, starlight finding an edge in his hand in the instant he struck. The Dog backed up, stunned, wavering... pointed its nose to the darkling sky and howled to curdle the blood of the damned.

Its mate launched itself at the man's unshielded back.

I flipped my knife, caught it by the tip and threw—which was stupid and useless and lost me my only weapon. Glooskap, or St. Jude, or some other Higher Power that loves idiots guided the steel; it sunk into the leaper's throat. The Dog's dead weight hit the man, knocking him to his knees, but it was already dissipating by then, the other Dog curling like black smoke into the night sky.

The man came to his feet slowly, as would someone who had to mind his knees, plucked my blade from the sand and walked over to where I lay. He hunkered down and pushed the limp fedora back off his forehead with the tip of the knife. His face was long and bony, his mustaches drooping and pale, his eyes light blue and as candid as a child's.

"Good morning, Katie dear," he said in the warm, comfy voice that had soothed away many a childhood terror. "How's my favorite black-hearted pirate?"

Despite pain and the creeping horrors, my lips twitched toward a smile.

"Mr. Ignat," I said, shakily. "What're you doing here?"

NINETEEN

Sunday, April 23

"Taking a walk in the fair morning, the same as you, yourself," Mr. Ignatious answered, and waggled his shaggy brows conspiratorially. "No other reason to be out on the beach at such an hour, now is there?"

I giggled, distantly registering it as too high. "No other reason that I know of," I agreed unsteadily, and pushed myself into a sitting position, gasping when the ankle sued for damages, tears starting to my eyes.

"Say!" Mr. Ignatious put a cool, dry hand under my chin and raised my face like I was twelve years old, and I let him do it, sitting still and soothed under his pale, dreamy gaze. He smiled slightly and took his hand away, patting me lightly on the cheek.

"You don't look so good, Katie. Bad night?"

I felt my mouth waver into a grin. "You could say."

"Well, then, I've just the thing!" He raised his left hand dramatically, plunged it into the copious pocket of his overcoat, and with a stage magician's flourish pulled out a flask, silver flashing in the starlight.

"Hair of the dog," he said, with a solemn wink. I felt laughter bubbling, and bit the inside of my cheek, hard.

125

Mr. Ignatious shifted to his knees in the sand, blinked at the knife in his right hand, and blinked at me.

"Is this yours, Katie?"

"Is now," I said. "I took it off somebody who didn't appreciate it."

"And its name?"

Name?

I looked it, held with careless grace between long bony fingers. The blade gleamed—no, it *glowed,* gently—and it was absolutely clean, no stain of ichor or blot of blood marring the smooth surface.

Where had Joe Nemeier's boy gotten such a thing?

"Mam'selle," I said, the name sweet on my tongue.

Mr. Ignat inclined his head, and offered her to me, hilt first, across his forearm.

"A blade any buccaneer should be proud to wear!" he proclaimed. "She becomes you, Katie."

I took Mam'selle solemnly, and touched her hilt to my chest, above my heart. "My thanks for the return of my weapon, sir," I said, hamming it. "I'll let you live."

"Well, now, that's spoken like a gentle pirate indeed," he allowed.

Back when I was a kid, telling tales out of the fire, Mr. Ignatious had gotten to calling me Kate the Pirate, in honor, so he'd said, of my black, wicked heart. It should've stung, but such was Mr. Ignat's charm that it only made me smile, even then, when my smile was as rare as snowfall in August—and it somehow made being part of a race that pillaged and robbed as a way of life...easier to bear.

I looked down at...my...knife, saw the shadow of my own face in the glowing blade. A gentle lady, I thought, and not one to bite the hand that held her. As she had demonstrated amply during the late hostilities.

I inclined my head—courtesy to an ally—and slipped her away into the sheath at the small of my back.

When I looked up, Mr. Ignat' had the flask uncorked.

"Hair of the dog," he said again, pressing it into my hand. "Drink up, matey; this draught'll make a man of ye!"

I laughed, shakily. "Could be that's just what I need." I knocked back a good swallow, expecting the fire of cheap whiskey. Instead, I got a smooth, butterscotch-y flavor that warmed the throat gently and only ignited when it struck the heart.

"Wow," I said reverently, and passed the flask back.

While Mr. Ignat' was having his dram, I sat myself up, teeth grit as I straightened the wounded ankle, and reached to the land again. Immediately, the pain lessened, and it seemed to me I could feel the bones being re-knit.

I sighed, looked up and found the flask being offered again.

"Hair of the dog," Mr. Ignatious murmured, shaking it temptingly. "Just what a weary warrior needs, black-hearted pirate though she be."

I took the flask and had another hit. The stuff tasted even better this time, burning away the creeping horrors and the chill of sitting on damp sand in the cool pre-dawn.

"Ah!" Mr. Ignatious smiled beatifically. "Just the thing, just the thing!" He slipped the flask out of my gloved fingers and had himself another swallow.

"What *is* that?" I asked.

"A shy little home brew your grandmother and I concocted. I'll tell you, Katie, it's a crying shame what they're selling for strong drink in the stores today."

"Hope it's not too strong," I said, accepting the flask when he passed it to me again. "I'm going to have to walk home, eventually."

"Now, now. A medicinal dose, only."

Another sip. There couldn't be that much more left, I thought, but my sip turned into two and there was still liquid sloshing in the flask when I handed it back.

"Mr. Ignat'."

He looked at me from beneath shaggy golden eyebrows. "Katie-my-love?"

"Where's Gran?"

Pale blue eyes blinked. "Gone away on a spot of business, dear. That's what she told me."

"It's what she told Nerazi, too. And the letter she left said if I was reading it, she'd been away too long and it was all gone to hell. Whatever that means." I touched his hand, lightly. "If you know where she went, please tell me, Mr. Ignat'. I've got—I've got some trouble only she can help me with."

"Hmm." He had himself a good, long swallow from the flask before passing it to me again.

"Katie, you know your gran doesn't confide her deep secrets to old Ignat'," he said, as serious and as sensible as I'd ever in my life heard him speak. He sighed and nodded at the flask.

"Drink up, Katie. It's a shame to keep good whiskey waiting."

Obediently, I drank, the liquid sweet and seductive in my mouth; and sat holding the flask in my hand. It was no lighter now than it had been when I'd taken my first draught.

"Mr. Ignat'—"

He shook his head. "I don't know where she's gone, dear. I wish I did—or I think that. Maybe it's best I don't know—seems Bonny believed so." He shrugged, a rumple of thin shoulders beneath the overlarge coat. "She's gone away before, and she's always come back. That'll have to do for the likes of us, tipsy, black-hearted knaves that we be."

He nodded at the flask. "Have another sip, then it's up with the pair of us and back to town."

I shook my head, holding the flask against my thigh. "Can't. I've got to see Nerazi."

"Not tonight, Katie dear. She'll wait 'til the sea has cleaned the sand."

I looked around, seeing the dark blotches of 'gaster blood, and the churned, gouged sand. It occurred to me to wonder what might have happened, if I hadn't come along and disturbed the peace. The snallygaster, at least, had been waiting for—someone...

"I don't mean to be rude, Katie, but there are some of us here who are thirsty."

"Sorry." I raised the flask and drank, this draught sweeter than the first, and passed the flask back. He drank while I gave attention to my ankle. Good to go, I decided. Beside me, Mr. Ignat' stowed the flask and rose in a billow of coattails, holding his hands down to me.

I wrapped my fingers 'round his wrists, and he pulled me up, then stood looking down at my hands.

"Nice gloves, Katie. Worthy of your station."

"Funny, that's what Nerazi said."

"Now, there's a woman both wise and deep," Mr. Ignat' said. "If I had any secrets to hide, and your grandmother not to hand, I'd give them to Nerazi for keeping." He stepped back, and I let go his wrists, taking an experimental step forward.

Good, but not great. It was going to be a long walk home.

Mr. Ignat' offered his arm, the wind making free with his coattails.

"Lean on me, Katie, and we'll go together. It's a splendid morning for a walk."

TWENTY

Sunday, April 23
High Tide 7:30 A.M.
Sunrise 5:46 A.M. EDT

"Sure you don't want to come in?" I asked Mr. Ignat'.

He smiled, sweet and vague, and shook his head. "It's a fine, pleasant morning. Now that you're safe home, I believe I'll continue my walk."

I hesitated, not particularly liking that, not with there being a couple hours still until dawn, and the critters from across the Wall apparently having a field trip . . .

"I'll be careful, Katie." He raised a hand to trace an extravagant cross over his heart. "Pirate's honor."

It's hard to argue with pirate's honor, and what was I going to do, anyway? Hit him over the head and drag him inside?

"All right, then," I said reluctantly. "Remember what I told you about Marilyn wanting the Knot ready by Wednesday."

"I remember everything you tell me, Katie," he replied gallantly. "Go now and take your rest." He smiled again and went down the stairs, soft-footed on the old wood, turned right at the bottom and headed for the dune path, coattails flapping.

I sighed, opened the door, and went inside.

❋   ❋   ❋

My clothes were a loss. If there's any stain remover in the Changing Land capable of removing 'gaster blood, I've never heard of it, and it was with a certain feeling of ill-use that I shoved the Google sweatshirt, my jeans, Gran's sweater, my favorite denim shirt, and much-abused sneakers into a black plastic trash bag and tied it shut. Half my wardrobe destroyed inside of a day. Not that it was all that much of a wardrobe, but dammit, I'd *liked* that shirt, and jeans don't exactly grow on trees.

At least the cell phone had survived. A damp paper towel took most of the blood off the plastic clamshell; and the screen was untouched. A thorough inspection of Mam'selle the knife found her edge intact, which pleased me more than it maybe should have.

Grumbling, I stepped into the shower, turned on the water as hot as I dared, and stood under the moderate deluge, eyes closed, thoughts chasing each other inside my head like a team of particularly energetic gerbils.

Eyes still closed, I reached out and grabbed the soap. Despite tonight's—*last night's*—unscheduled adventure, I was no closer than I had been to locating my grandmother. The prisoners were bound precariously at best; the Wall between the Worlds had apparently thinned to the thickness of Kleenex; Gran's tree was sickening—oh, and a megalomaniac with a lawn fixation wanted me maimed.

I might just as well have stayed in Albuquerque, for all I'd accomplished here.

Oh, cut yourself some slack, Kate, I thought as I lathered shampoo through my hair for the second time. *If you hadn't come back, Anna wouldn't have been attacked by the unicorn and gotten 'way too close to dead.*

And if I didn't figure out a way to bind those six desperados *right now,* there was more, and worse, mayhem in the Beach's very near future.

Dammit, Gran, what were you thinking?

The water was getting cold. I turned it off, wrung out my hair, and reached for a towel.

Some minutes later, nattily attired in my last, and rattiest, pair of jeans, a Miskatonic University T-shirt, and cowboy boots that had seen better days, I dumped water into the coffeemaker's reservoir, shoved the pot onto the hotplate and punched the "brew" button.

It was four-fifteen in the morning, according to the clock on the stove. No sense going to sleep for a couple hours, supposing I *could* sleep, which I doubted. Better just to caffeinate and move on.

While the coffee brewed, I built myself a Swiss cheese sandwich on whole wheat, with butter and a sprinkle of salt, and ate it standing up, staring at nothing in particular while the gerbils ran 'round and 'round inside my head.

Dammit, the woman left a letter. Why couldn't she have said something useful, while she was going to the trouble?

I stopped in mid-chew, blinking.

Who was to say, I thought, carefully, *that she hadn't said something useful, and granddaughter Kate was just too blockheaded to understand?*

I put the half-eaten sandwich down on the counter and went into the living room.

The manila envelope was on the coffee table, half hidden under the laptop. I carried it back to the kitchen, opened it, and pulled the contents out in a handful, dropping them to the tabletop.

I pushed the deeds and the bank book aside, took up the folded piece of stationary, and flipped it open. The leaf that had been pressed between the folds fluttered to the floor.

Sighing, I bent over to pick it up—you don't live with a dryad without learning a respect for leaves—and went to one knee, one hand gripping the edge of the table, the other cupping the leaf against my chest.

I was seized with a longing so intense, it near melted my bones, and in my mind's eye I saw Heath Hill with aching clarity. Wind tousled my hair, and I heard the high clatter of merrybells, beneath them, a frail, tuneless singing, "Who'll fetch me home to the hills so green..."

Oh. My. God.

I pulled myself to my feet and put the leaf on the table as if it were a priceless jewel. Which, in a way, it was.

Unless I was completely out of my mind, Gran had left me proof that Nessa, her daughter, and my mother, was still alive.

And now I knew where Gran had gone.

I don't know how long I stood, staring at the small, perfect leaf that looked as green and as moist as if it had been plucked from its tree only a moment ago. It was an awful and precious thing, that leaf. Even the land was subdued.

Finally, I took a breath, shook myself, walked over to the coffeepot and poured myself a mug full. I rummaged in the fridge for the milk, added a dollop, and sipped, carefully not looking at the leaf glowing faintly atop Gran's kitchen table.

"Question it, Kate," I said out loud. "You know better than to just go jumping to conclusions."

Well, I did, at that. So, then, first question: I'd seen and handled the leaf the day I'd arrived; why hadn't it stood up and saluted then?

That one was easy: I'd been dying and had yet to reunite with the land.

Next question: Where the hell had Gran gotten the leaf?

Ooh, stumper. I sipped my coffee. The leaf couldn't have crossed the Wall by itself, and it wasn't likely to have come across via snallygaster or Black Dog. Which left—what, exactly?

Your gran, she didn't much care for him, Nancy Vois said from memory. *Looked like a bill collector to me.*

Bill collector? And not only had Gran not particularly liked the guy, but the batwing horse had nipped him.

"Right," I said, and put the coffee mug on the counter next to the half-eaten sandwich.

At the kitchen table, I slipped the leaf into Gran's letter, folded it, carefully, into quarters, and slid it flat into the back pocket of my jeans. Mam'selle in her sheath went through my belt at the small of my back, cell phone into front jeans pocket. I pulled on my remaining piece of whole outerwear, a white hoodie bearing the legend "Tux Rules" next to a graphic of the Linux penguin, and was ready to rumble. The land sat alert at the back of my head, ears pricked with interest, neither boisterous nor bouncing.

I had my hand on the doorknob when my cell phone warbled; I flipped it open before the second warble was quite finished, took in the number displayed on the screen, and said, "Borgan?"

"Wonderful thing, technology," he said affably. "Sorry I missed your call earlier, Kate. Everything okay?"

I leaned my back against the door.

"If you consider pitched battle with a snallygaster and two Black Dogs okay, I'm in the pink," I told him, unable to resist sarcasm.

"You walk away to tell the tale?" he asked, static crackling around his voice.

"I'm telling it to you, aren't I?"

"That you are. And I'm looking forward to hearing it again when you're done polishing it up."

I snorted, halfway between irritation and amusement, then thought of something.

"Borgan—that ambush I'm telling you about, it happened right at the Boundary Stone—Nerazi's rock. The 'gaster was waiting right there, inside the shadows. I was ahead of her usual time, but—"

"I'll check to be sure she's all right," he promised. "Anything else?"

"No—yeah." I bit my lip, then said slowly. "Let me bounce this off you: What if Gran went across the World Wall and into the Land of the Flowers?"

Static crackled, then Borgan said, "Why would she do that?"

"What if she had what appeared to be compelling proof that someone—someone dear—who she'd supposed was dead, was in fact alive and aching to come home?"

"That'd do it," he acknowledged. "Did she? Have proof, that is."

"It looks like she did. I'm on my way to see if I can get confirmation from an independent source."

"Be careful with that independent source," he said, voice fading in a storm of interference. "I'll check on Nerazi for you."

"Thanks," I said.

"No problem. I'll see you later, Kate." He ended the call.

I flipped my cell closed and slipped it away. Three minutes later, I was jogging through the misty streets, heading for Fun Country.

Inside the storm walls, the carousel glowed, bathing the metal walls in an oily, pearlescent shine, like the inside of an oyster shell. I locked the hatch behind me and walked forward, not bothering with the electric light.

Greetings, Keeper, the batwing's voice rang nastily inside my head. *My, how the child has grown.*

I mounted the deck and looked down at it, standing secure in its binding of roses. One baleful eye rolled; nostrils flaring red.

"Two Seasons ago, a man came here to talk to my grandmother," I said, without preamble. "He came up onto the carousel, and you bit him. Nancy Vois saw it happen. I'll thank you to tell me what transpired between the two of them."

Horrible laughter echoed inside my head.

What reward should I do so, Keeper? What punishment if I do not? You have no carrot and I am stuck. Until such time as the so-called Wise see fit to liberate me.

"Reward? My thanks, as I said. Punishment? The Wall between the Worlds is breached. Black Dogs and other vermin are crossing over from the Land of the Flowers. It'll get worse, unless you give me the information I need to mend things. I know you have an intense fondness for the Dogs, and I can make sure they know where to find you."

Silence. Then, *Well. The Keeper has both a carrot and a stick. Your thanks I spit upon. The Black Dogs, however . . .* Its thought faded. I leaned against a brass rail, arms crossed over my chest, and waited.

I fear you will be disappointed in the small tale I have to tell, and will set the Dogs upon me in your dismay.

"If you spit on my thanks, I can only imagine what you'd do to my assurance that I'll meet truth with honor," I said, nasty in my turn.

Swear on the land, the batwing said, *that you will not give me to the Dogs.*

I considered it. "And what reward, should I do so? What punishment if I do not?"

I swear, upon my essence which is bound into this object, that what I will relate to you is factual. If I should lie, then I submit forever to the wood, and this world.

I blinked. "That's pretty damn' potent."

As you note, the Black Dogs are no friends of mine.

I nodded, and came out of my lean, reaching for the land, feeling it leap to my touch.

"I swear upon this land of which I am Guardian that I will not give you to the Black Dogs nor lead them to the place where you are bound, if you tell me the truth as you have sworn."

My words swelled, filling the pearlescent space, and vanished, swallowed and sealed by the land.

There was a moment of silence, then a small noise inside my head, as if the batwing horse had cleared its throat.

Very well, it said. *There was an Ozali who came. Who, I cannot tell you. He had woven a glamor about himself, but he could not mask the odor of High Magic, and did not care to conceal his contempt for this place or for the Old Woman.*

"So far, so good," I said, tentatively pleased that my guess and fact agreed. "What did he want?"

Now, there stands a puzzle. It seemed that he wished to speak of gardens and growing things, and the phenomenon of spring in this Land, so unlike the constant summer of his own.

My heartbeat quickened, and the sense of interested attention from the land increased. "Gardens?"

It was the substance of his early conversation—perhaps a pleasantry; an acknowledgment of the Old Woman's antecedents. Though given his tone and bearing, it seemed more insult. In any case, he eventually came to speak of an item which he had . . . lost, or which perhaps had been taken from him, that he sorely missed, and of which he had reason to believe the Old Woman held knowledge. He offered a fair and equal trade—this item for a singular plant, to be found only in his personal garden, and which, unlike all the rest of the plants in his native Land, hovered between winter and spring. He offered her a leaf, which he said had come from this plant, that she might judge its uniqueness for herself.

Eureka.

"And my grandmother?" I murmured. "Did she accept the trade?"

It appeared the Old Woman was wholly disinterested in the proposed transaction. She said to the Ozali that transplanting is a risky enterprise, and that some things are well enough lost. That was essentially the end of it, though the Ozali continued to importune her for some time. At the last, he descended to demands, but never spoke more plainly. Indeed, Keeper, the two of them seemed to understand each other very well, but the Old Woman simply did not wish to do business.

"I . . . see," I said, damn' near deafened by my own heartbeat. "And you bit him because he was importuning the Keeper."

Laughter, sweet and terrible.

Nay. I bit him because the Old Woman had let me slip a mite from her regard, and it was possible to do so. What care I for the dignity of my jailers? It paused, then added, *That she let her regard waver—that would seem to betray more interest in the business than she cared to acknowledge.*

"It would, wouldn't it?" I was finding the batwing's little story charming, but a bit thin of certain pressing details.

"Can you think of anything that was said which might give me a clue to who this particular Ozali was, or what exactly he wanted in return for that plant?"

He was oblique, Keeper, and careful even of the ears of the damned. It pleased him to note that his arm was long and his touch potent. The Old Woman seemed to find this . . . amusing.

"Well, then." I chewed my lower lip. "Thank you for your information." I turned to go.

There was one other thing said by this Ozali which may be of interest, the batwing murmured between my ears.

I paused, one hand on the pole. "And that was?" I asked, not bothering to turn my head.

Why, only that he would be back, Keeper, if his lost treasure was not returned to him, whether or not the Old Woman cared to accept the exchange.

TWENTY-ONE

Sunday, April 23

Fun Country wears an air of sleepy menace in the hour just before dawn. The drowsing rides rise out of the mist like the monoliths of lost R'lyeh; the shuttered shops and games are transformed into the secret resting places of the patient Elders.

For those who are underwhelmed by the antics of Shub-Niggurath and that lot, the park offers shadows, silence and a geography made uncertain by sea mist.

Unsettling, at the least.

Since I was already plenty unsettled, and deep in my own worries, both efforts were lost on me.

While it was nice that the batwing's story jibed with my pet theory and the existence of the leaf, it left 'way too many questions unanswered for my peace of mind.

An Ozali from the Land of the Flowers—the only one of the Six Worlds that resides in eternal summer. It would have been nice if he'd given his name, Ozali being pretty thick on the ground in that Land. As it was, my stomach hurt, and my back brain was revving up for a full-fledged panic attack.

Ramendysis had been the last owner of my mother's soul—*but surely*, I thought, taking a deep breath of misty air—*surely*

Ramendysis had long ago returned to the elements which had given him life, destroyed by his own power? He'd been something of a prodigy, granted, cutting a swath through Ozali in his World and, according to rumor, in others, as well. No one before him had managed to contain and control so much *jikinap*, but he *must* have overreached himself by now.

I took another breath, moving through eddying swirls of mist.

Stipulate, I told myself, *that the Ozali who visited Gran is somebody other than Ramendysis.* My back brain dropped from red alert to orange, which was something, though my stomach still hurt. Whatever.

That stipulated, I continued, forcing myself to think linearly. *What is the nature of his lost-or-stolen treasure? More importantly, has he already returned, been satisfied and departed, or is that still in the future?*

For that matter, *was* the leaf the proof that I—and I was per-suaded, Gran—believed it to be? My mother was dead, her *voysin* drained, her *jikinap* taken. And the dead don't come back to life, even in the Land of the Flowers.

Did you, I asked myself carefully, *see the body?*

I paused by the kiddie railway, one hand braced on Tom Thumb's engine, and stared up at the Galaxi, the bottom half of its metal frame shrouded in misty shadow, the top half seeming to hover, unconnected to the ground.

In cold and sober fact, no; I hadn't seen my mother's body. Zephyr had managed to break us both out of house arrest before Nessa's death freed Ramendysis from the letter of his promise to her.

What I *had* seen—I'd seen her in her last decline, her eyes dead, partner to any atrocity Ramendysis cared to commit; accomplice to every murder; his sins eroding her soul...

I gagged, shaking my head. If she wasn't dead, she would have wanted to be, of that I was certain. And Ramendysis had looked to be well on his way to granting her the final grace at the end of her torment.

But what if... What if he had managed to keep himself from taking the final, annihilating sip of her essence; the last, seductive swallow of her power? What if he had... What if he had given her soul *back*, what was left of it—and then watched to see what she would do?

It would have been cruel, which certainly fit Ramendysis as I'd known him. Also, it would have given him a lever, in case he should ever need one, to use on one of the few Ozali native to the Changing Land, a notion not incompatible with Ramendysis' thought processes.

And, then, when his head exploded, or he was taken at last at duel or in ambush, someone else had come into possession of his gardens, noticed the unusual plant, did a little research, and, when his treasure went missing, decided to indulge in a spot of blackmail.

Which brought us right back around to *Treasure, Nature of*, and no answers in sight.

Life, I thought, and theory, were getting 'way too complicated.

I went to the left, passed the Whale's Tail, and in due time found myself at Keltic Knot.

The dragon was asleep beneath a blanket of sea mist. I leaned against the fence, the damp metal cold against my palms.

Mr. Ignat', I thought, should at least hear the batwing's story and my theory. Touch the leaf, too, in case it would do him any good. Problem was, I needed somebody to talk to—and it was just barely possible that Gran had mentioned the Ozali's visit, or the existence of the so-called treasure.

I touched the land, smiling at the eagerness of its response, and formed my request, shaping the image of Mr. Ignat' with care.

The land accepted the commission. I felt its attention shift, leaving me—not alone, exactly, but momentarily out of the center of attention.

The breeze danced in from the ocean to play with the mist, and I shivered. The Tux hoodie wasn't as warm or as thick as the late, lamented Google sweatshirt. I pushed away from the railing, passed between the Knot and the Scrambler, and stepped out onto the beach.

Far away and hidden in the mist, the ocean whispered secrets to the shore. I raised my hands and ran them into my mist-dampened hair, wincing when my fingers pulled knots.

The land was still searching, which might mean that Mr. Ignat' had crossed the boundary of Archers Beach, or only that he was being hard to pin down. I sighed, twisted my hair into a loose knot at the back of my neck, pulled the hood up, and stood working my cold fingers until I realized what I was doing and yanked the work gloves out of the kangaroo pocket. Absently, I pulled them on, my mind still chasing its own tail.

At least Gran hadn't—according to the batwing—accepted the Ozali's proposed trade. That was a mug's game, and she knew it. You just didn't *do* deals with Ozali in general and Ozali from the Land of the Flowers most especially. It was stupid, almost always painful, and 'way too often fatal. *Trenvay* will trick the unwary for the sheer joy of the game. But Ozali don't care who or what they hurt in pursuit of their heart's desire.

The tragedy of the Land of the Flowers is that it produces so *many* mages. Even those who might otherwise rather not accumulate *jikinap* seek it out, rather than live their lives as prey to those with more—especially the ruling class of Ozali. And the Ozali themselves—contention at the top means there's no stability; it's every lord and lady for themselves, though there is the pretty fiction of a council of equals...

So, anyway. Gran had turned the deal down cold, playing at being disinterested in the possibility of her daughter's continued existence. Thwarted, at least for the time being, the Ozali descended to threats, followed by a grand exit.

Whereupon Gran went into action.

The steps she'd taken had been desperate, but I could see her reasoning. It was one thing to have lost a daughter in the on-going war zone that was the Land of the Flowers, and quite another to have news that your daughter's essence was still green, and might yet be recovered, nurtured and regrown.

So, Gran had sung herself through the World Wall, thinking to do a snatch and run...

Dear Kate, If you're reading this, things have not gone as I had hoped and expected that they would.

Uh-huh. Time moved different in the Land of the Flowers. The geography, the culture, the people—none of that was going to be either comfortable or comforting to someone rooted in the Changing Land. Not to mention that the place was crawling with *jikinap*-crazed Ozali, who wouldn't hesitate half a heartbeat before snacking down a minor Ozali from a useless and annoying Land.

Gran, why didn't you call me?

I sighed. Yeah, right. What good would I have done her, failing and blind as I'd been? I would have only slowed her down.

The land entered my consciousness with a self-important bound. Images rolled before my mind's eye, augmented with sound and taste.

It took me a few minutes to figure out where the land had found Mr. Ignat'—and to believe it, once I had.

Googin Rock.

I'd known Mr. Ignat' was foolish, but I hadn't thought he was suicidal. I queried the land, but it was adamant, replaying the whole sequence over again for my benefit.

I closed my eyes against the mist, and listened to the distant voice of the sea.

Well. Googin Rock. What the heck, I could use some exercise.

I got moving, heading south down the beach in the pre-dawn chill.

Archers Beach hasn't always been a hole-in-the-wall, hardscrabble town with a main drag full of empty storefronts and a run-down amusement park its best and last hope of making a dime.

Back in the 1890s, the Beach had been a sight to see. There were luxury hotels, casinos, and concert halls crammed onto every square foot of the place. First class acts came up from Boston, New York, and Washington, D.C., to entertain the tourists who poured in by the double-dozens. A pier was built out into the ocean, 1800 feet long and twenty feet above high tide. There were fancy restaurants and posh shops and the Sea King Casino, as seductive a den of pleasurable ruination as ever man did see.

That was before The Fire, so fierce it burned the whole place right down to the ground in a single night, and the best they could do was pin the cause on some poor girl who they said had left a hot curling iron too near a lampshade in her hurry to meet her beau.

The truth of the matter is, that girl was innocent. The fire was started by an Ozali from a House of Flame. It wasn't, as Gran always insisted, his fault, exactly, that the place burned down. He'd been running for his life from a posse of Ozali, and didn't have time to be careful.

Be that as it might, the Ozaliflame had a good enough lead on those that wanted him returned to the fire that spawned him that he made it to the Wood on Heath Hill, swore fealty to the Lady, and bound himself to the Changing Land. That should've been the end of the matter, but the posse wanted a life, and failing that, they wanted pain.

The Fire Ozali's life, the Lady would not cede, nor would she release him from his oath. But she and all the *trenvay* she could call upon were no match for a half-dozen angry Ozali, and in the end they got their pain.

The Fire Ozali was allowed to stay in the Changing Land, all right. Bound into Googin Rock.

The incoming tide played 'round the Rock in wicked currents; the waves breaking over its bladed, chancy surface hissed and boiled, mixing steam into the pre-dawn mist, and if Mr. Ignat' was anywhere near the place, he was invisible.

I queried the land again, and got the equivalent of a baffled stare for my answer.

Still...

I stood on the wet sand and watched the balefire flicker and flash, thinking.

The Changing Land is the last and the least of the Six Worlds. There is *nothing* native to the place to entice or interest any resident of its sister worlds, all of which are endowed with far more grace, beauty, and magic than we are. No brag, just fact.

That being so, and the things most considered "treasure" by Ozali being those which can augment their power...

It could be that the imprisoned Ozali was a treasure, indeed, for a mage on the rise and in need of easily-acquired *jikinap*. Also? That particular leap of logic would neatly explain the *other* reason Gran hadn't been interested in the proposed exchange.

Point: It would be a heavy blizzard and six feet of snow covering the smoldering coals in Hell before Gran, in her hat as Lady of the Wood, released the Fire Ozali from his oath, or his sworn service. Put a good deal of stock in oaths, did Gran.

Point: The residents of the Land of the Flowers *do* embrace a code of honor. According to that code, an exchange of hostages must, in order to have force, be equal. In other words, you don't trade a donut for a diamond.

A daughter for an oath-sworn, though...

A lead wave hit Googin Rock, with a crash and a hiss of steam.

It looked to me like the Fire Ozali was still snug in his dungeon, and damned peeved he was about it, too. Which led one, should one be the driver of this particular fraught and faulty logic train, to believe that the Mystery Ozali had not yet returned to claim his prize.

If the prize was, after all, inside Googin Rock.

Well, there was one person, at least, who might know. If he didn't blast me out of time and space for daring to disturb him in his torment.

I walked forward three steps, until I was standing on the narrow, sand slicked apron of stone that was the only part of Googin Rock that stood above the incoming tide. *Jikinap* starved as I was, I expected to see nothing more than what I already saw.

Color me surprised.

It was like walking through the sea mist curtain that hung between my grandfather's private chamber and his Law Room. The woven energies comprising the fabric of the curtain parted, and suddenly one could see clearly, in all directions and upon all levels.

Googin Rock lay before me etched in dreadful clarity, flames of red and blue, yellow and green flickering hungrily beneath the black, bladed surface. Over and about it, confining both flame and hunger, stretched a dense and complex knotwork of forces; living *jikinap* twined and twisted with homey *trenvay* magic to produce a seamless and shimmering silver covering, like the finest and strongest mail in my grandfather's armory.

I extended my thought to touch the land, and with that brace and anchor, dared to try my will against those pulsing strands of power.

It was an idiotic thing to do and I could well have been fried. Happily, the only thing that happened was that my will slid off the binding, like a prince off a glass mountain, leaving me breathless and annoyed, but basically unharmed.

All right, I thought. *There's more than one road to Amber.*

Carefully, I shaped my request. The land accepted the commission and vanished from my consciousness—reappearing not a heartbeat later, with a wail and a bump.

So much for an impromptu social call. If I wanted in, I'd need the help of at least one *trenvay* of Nerazi's status, and an Ozali skilled in spellweaving, always remembering that there wasn't any guarantee that the Ozaliflame wouldn't seize the opportunity to torch us all.

Not that I thought the bound mage was a bad guy, necessarily—in the stories, Gran always claimed he was honorable, if a trifle rash. However, a hundred years chained inside a rock and drowned every twelve hours is bound to take its toll on a man's sanity, Ozali or not.

I went backward three steps; the curtain of energies parted and fell closed just beyond the tip of my nose. Googin Rock lay as it always had, bladed, black, and chancy, hissing as the waves broke over its surface, the fell-fire above it mixing uneasily with the mist.

Shaking my head, I turned and stepped from the apron of rock to the sand.

Inside my head, the land screamed.

The air was heavy with despair and dismay; a miasma arose from the waves, slowing my thoughts, my heart, and my feet. I shuddered; the land screamed again, and I heard the pounding of paws upon the sand.

"Dammit!" I spun, and there they were, two blots of hopeless darkness against the purity of pre-dawn, tongues lolling and iron teeth bared, slavering to destroy hope and beauty and love.

"I have had enough!" I yelled, and raised my hand, pointing. "Begone!"

Heat rushed through me, and a tang of butterscotch, reminiscent of Mr. Ignat's home brew.

The lead Dog vanished with a small *pop!* of displaced air.

The second Dog plowed to a halt, sand spraying. It whined, sat, and raised a paw, head tipped to one side in doggy dismay.

I glared at it. "You deaf? I said *begone!*" I stamped my foot, not very impressive in sand, and for good measure added, "Go home!"

It licked its jowls, sighed—and blinked out of existence.

I sat down, hard. The land nuzzled me worriedly, but I was staring at the huge paw prints in the sand, remembering with sudden and sinking clarity the flask that never got any lighter, no matter how much we drank, and cursing myself for a complete and total idiot.

Because of course, as any child can tell you, there are three ways for a mage to gain *jikinap*: steal it, earn it—or accept it as a gift.

Hair of the dog, indeed.

I exhaled and looked at the sky. Not dawn yet. Still, it might've been a fluke. Black Dogs aren't particularly known for having a sense of humor, but this pair might've decided it would be fun to play with me—vanish and then sneak on back...

One more test, then, and here's hoping I was wrong.

I scooped a hasty circle in the sand; sat back on my heels, hands on my thighs, and concentrated.

One of the more amusing features of modern fantasy books is how the author always makes it seem that making a fire by will alone is, y'know—*easy*. Like any old Assistant Pigkeeper can touch off a nice, polite little flame first try out of the box.

Take it from me, willing a contained fire into existence is not something the hopeful, untutored mage should try at home. Technically, it wasn't something *I* should be trying, years out of the schoolroom as I was—and to hear him tell it, not my tutor's most apt student ever—but I'm nothing if not imprudent.

Carefully, keeping a close eye on the details, I built the thing in my head: a beach fire at the end of a long, joyous night, just a few pale flamelets dancing tiredly among red embers.

I felt a tickle of heat around my heart, and a shy warming of my blood. Good, good. I concentrated on the shallow, scooped pit and pictured my weary little fire there.

Heat flared; there was a white whoosh and a silent explosion, knocking me flat on my back. I lay there, staring up at the towering orange column, hastily extended my will, connected with the inferno and—breathed in.

The fire seared, but I kept myself centered, sucking it down, down...until there was nothing in my little sand pit but those few, intended chunks of mostly burned driftwood, glowing warmly red, a few homely flames flickering across the spent surface.

"Gah." I closed my eyes, and lay there. Inside my head, the land gave the equivalent of an exasperated sigh and settled down to wait.

Well, I thought, *I can bind the prisoners now.*

That's what you call your silver lining.

I don't know how long I lay there, brooding. Eventually, the land nudged me and I sat up, blinking at a gold and pink sky. I extended my hand and put the embers out, taking the power back into myself. Then I stood, brushed the sand off me as best I could, and started back to Fun Country.

TWENTY-TWO

⟨⟩

Sunday, April 23
Low Tide 1:50 P.M. EDT

She returns.
  Her sword and her shield shineth ere the sun.
  She is like unto a goddess, her glance to slay; her touch to heal...
I sighed, and crossed to the fuse box. "Everybody's a comedian."

The electric light came on with a snap. I maybe closed the hatch a little harder than was strictly necessary, and turned to face the carousel; in particular, the six rose-bound figures.

"So!" I said brightly. "Who wants to be first?"

Silence so thick you could pour it on pancakes and have it for breakfast.

"All righty, then!" I stepped forward, pushing up the sleeves of my hoodie, swung up onto the deck, and walked 'round, 'til I stood in front of the unicorn.

"You first, I think," I said, and before it could react, or even answer, I extended my will and spun a halter of pure energy, binding essence to wood, and sealing both to the carousel. I did it as fast as I could—Gran had always said that quickness was a mercy—feeling the imprisoned spirit become listless and compliant. Maybe I waited a bit too long; maybe testing my work three times was excessive. I was a long time out of practice and

147

I'd never possessed *jikinap* on this level. I distrusted it, doubted my ability—and I couldn't afford any mistakes.

Satisfied at last that the bonds would hold, I moved on to the hippocampus, and 'round in order until I had bound five and only one remained.

A boon, Keeper, the batwing whispered loathsomely between my ears.

"A *boon?*" I repeated incredulously, the binding spell warm as honey on the back of my tongue. "What *boon?*"

Bind me lightly, it urged. *Protect those you deem innocent, but do not tie me to oblivion.*

"Why not?" I asked.

Why, because I am Changed, Keeper. Is that not the outcome desired by the Wise?

"Being a smartass isn't likely to get you what you want," I pointed out, and before it could answer, added what I had always been taught. "We bind you as we do as a mercy, to ease your suffering under the geas laid on you by the Wise."

I know it is thought such, and in days past I have embraced the gift. However, I have dreamed and truly . . .

I paused. My grandmother had taught me to be respectful of dreams.

"Can I get any details, here?"

Keeper, I have little enough. The wind belling my wings, and the sweet bloom of power in my blood.

"A memory, then," I suggested.

I . . . think not, the batwing murmured. *Within the memory I am granted—which is that of my imprisonment—I have never flown. If I had power, I am now bereft. This wheel stands beyond the range of the everyday sea, yet I felt spray on my flanks. Small as it is, I believe it to be a True Dreaming, Keeper, and yet to be fulfilled. I would, by your grace, stand ready to meet what may come.*

Sarcastic and bitter as it was, the batwing rarely outright *lied*. And—perversity being my middle name—I was more inclined to believe the small dream described than I would a detailed and grandiose saga.

It was true that the added kick of oblivion wasn't necessary to the binding spell. But—

"I don't want to be hearing snarky comments out of you all Season."

I will be as still as the wood from which my prison is carved. I so swear upon my name, which was taken from me.

I'm not sure, myself, if it was that particular reminder of the cruelty of the Wise, or the batwing horse's refusal to invent a dream of glorious destiny for itself, despite the stakes, that convinced me. In the end, though, I bound it as lightly as conscience would allow, and hoped I'd have no reason to be sorry for it.

You will not regret, Keeper, it whispered between my ears when I was done. I snorted, stepped off the carousel, and went to fetch my paints and brushes.

By the time Nancy arrived, about ten minutes before eight, I'd finished touching up the otter and the bucking bronc, and was rubbing cleaner on the loon.

"Mornin'," she said, nodding, and I gave her a nod back.

"Glad to see you decided to stay on. Feeling all right today?"

"Fine as frog hair." She took off her cap and re-settled it. "There's tourists all over this town," she said. "Looks like Early Season out there."

"They all here for that contest?" I asked, but Nancy only shrugged and moved on toward the back. She was back in two shakes, armed with rags and Brasso.

"Got everybody settled, I see," she said, giving me a wise glance out of ale-colored eyes.

"Yup," I answered.

She nodded like she hadn't expected anything else, and got down to brass tacks.

Around about 9:30, I stood, and stretched and looked over to Nancy. "I'm for some coffee, how 'bout you?"

"Good idea."

She sealed up the Brasso, I set my brushes to soak, and the two of us ambled out into the day. I blinked as we came into the sunlight—and again at the number of pressed jeans, casual khakis, new sneakers, and pastel sweatshirts on the midway.

"What on earth do they think there is to see?" I asked rhetorically.

Nancy shrugged. "Maybe it's a church group or something—folks up from Portsmouth on a day trip."

"As likely as anything, I guess," I said as we crossed over to Tony Lee's. We waited in line behind a plump guy wearing a sweater that exactly matched the pink of his scalp, his stick-thin wife bundled up in fleece jacket, watch cap, and scarf. She received her Styrofoam cup in both hands, like it was the Grail, and bent her face into the steam.

"Hi, there," I said to Anna when it was our turn. "Didn't the doctors at least give you a day off?"

She wrinkled her nose and put a handful of creamers on the counter. "I was supposed to stay home and 'rest,' but there are so many tourists, Tony needed help and Billie had other business today. Besides, I feel fine."

"That's good to hear," I said, and meant it with all my heart. She smiled and stepped into the back, reappearing a moment later with two rice paper packets. She put them on the counter next to our creamers.

"Breakfast," she said, and turned away to draw our coffee.

The egg rolls smelled wonderful, prompting my stomach to note that it had been a good long time and numerous adventures since my last meal.

"I—" I began, and Anna raised a stern hand.

"You *will not* pay, and you *will not* offer to pay," she stated, and I grinned before I reached beneath my hoodie, found the chain and drew it over my head.

"I was only going to say—I've got your lucky piece," I said, holding it out. The stone fragment spun in the busy air.

Anna took it, reluctantly, to my eye, and held it at arm's length, watching it twirl at the end of its chain.

"It—it didn't do any good, this lucky piece," she said slowly. "I still fell and hit my head."

"It worked just fine," I said, firmly. "You could've been hurt a lot worse."

"Could've broke your neck," Nancy added, while she peeled little plastic buckets and dumped creamer into her coffee. "That was a nasty tumble, no mistake."

"Oh." Anna considered the fragment for another long moment, then smiled crookedly and slipped it over her head. "I guess you're right; it could've been lots worse."

"Absolutely," I said forcefully, and looked over my shoulder. A crowd of six tourists was headed our way. I gathered up coffee, creamers, and egg roll, and gave Anna a smile.

"I'll just let the paying customers through," I said. "Thanks, Anna!"

"For dinner, we have dumplings," she called, and I heard Nancy groan beside me as we headed back toward the carousel.

"I'm going to weigh double, if I keep working here," she said.

"Don't worry about it. Chinese food isn't fattening."

It got progressively warmer as the day and the work went forth. Nancy and I both stripped to T-shirts—hers showed a leather-clad teddy bear astride a Harley, and bore the fading legend "2002 Toy Run"—and a little while later, I left off painting to push open the ocean-side wall and let the breeze through.

This turned out to be a mistake. More than one—hell, more than a dozen—early tourists poked their heads and sometimes their whole selves inside the storm doors, exclaiming over the fact of a merry-go-round. Nancy and I took turns telling them that we weren't open yet, a hint that most took. One guy stood watching us for twenty minutes, drawing on a pipe that looked dead cold to me, then pocketed the thing and left the way he had come.

"I love work," Nancy muttered. "I could watch it all day."

"Now, now. Paying customers."

"Not yet they aren't."

"Point."

We worked on, the air spicy with the mingled scents of turpentine, brass cleaner, and ocean. I finished painting the seal and stood, stretching the kinks out of my back while I looked around and took note of what still needed to be done. Wednesday evening, huh? Might be we could make it.

A shadow moved at the door to the midway. I sighed and called out, "Sorry, we're closed! Come back Wednesday after six!"

"Actually..." The shadow moved, and Marilyn Michaud hove into sight, looking, if you'd like to believe it, just a tiny bit abashed.

"Actually, Kate," she said, "that's what I've come to talk to you about."

I eyed her, wondering if this meant that the Wednesday opening was a wash, the supposed prize a mirage—latest in a long line of mirages and mistakes for Archers Beach.

"We're not having a Super Early Season after all?" I tried to keep my voice mild, but either I didn't succeed or Marilyn had a guilty conscience. She started, then raised her hands.

"No, no, of *course* we are! The thing is, the company wants to know if you could open...earlier."

I took a careful breath. "How much earlier?"

"Monday?" she said in a small voice.

"Monday! We're already busting our humps getting this ride ready for Wednesday, and now you want us to open tomorrow?" I threw my hands out, showing her the state of not-readiness. "Does this ride look like it's ready to open to you?"

"Kate—"

"Dammit, Marilyn!" I overrode her. "We're already pulling a rabbit out of a hat here, and now you've got the goddamn nerve to ask for a kangaroo?"

"Kate, I know it's an inconvenience. The company regrets—"

"Screw the company," I said succinctly, and supposing that she didn't already.

Marilyn took a hard breath. "The company—and the Chamber— did miscalculate. I admit that. We didn't think we'd start seeing the advance wave until Tuesday afternoon. But they've been coming in since Friday evening, and now we've got a couple hundred people here, three days ahead of the advertised opening. If we don't do something to make them welcome, we'll lose their trust—"

Meaning, they'd go away without leaving any cash in Archers Beach. Okay, I wasn't so pissed off that I couldn't see *that* was a no-win situation. But have the ride ready by tomorrow night? No way, no how, no sir.

"Marilyn, look," I said, trying to moderate my tone. "I'm sorry if I sounded harsh. I appreciate that we've got people here, and I know it's in our best interests to make them feel at home. But we're not ready, and I'm not seeing how—"

"We can do it," a firm voice interrupted. I blinked and turned to stare at Nancy Vois, but she looked the same as always, with nothing overt to show that she'd suddenly snapped.

"You think?" I asked her, waving a hand to include the sum of our unfinished business.

Nancy nodded. "Sure. Brass is almost done. Painting's almost done. We string the lights, polish the mirrors—tourists won't know we haven't done the final wax or touched up the rounding boards. It'll glitter, the animals'll look sharp, the organ'll be loud, they'll see their reflections havin' fun in the glass—that's what they want. They'll see what's supposed to be here. All we got to do is give 'em a little help."

So said the woman whose secondary shape was a calico cat.

And, I admitted to myself, she was right, too. People *would* see what they wanted to see, just like they always did—and they'd see the carousel in all its glory, if we hit the proper grace notes and didn't let on that there was anything more to want.

"Well, if you've got it figured..." I gave Marilyn another glare, just to show that I still wasn't thrilled with this.

"We'll give it our best shot," I told her.

She forced a smile, and gave Nancy a grateful nod. "That's all we can ask."

We went into overdrive as soon as Marilyn left. I painted like a madwoman while Nancy hurried the brass along, then got busy with the lights, the two of us working in easy silence, until there came a rustle at the hatch, and Tony Lee called out, "Anna said to tell you it's five o'clock and there's dumplings with your names on it in the kitchen!"

"Dim sum!" Nancy said. "I'll be right over!"

"Five?" I blinked, then jumped to my feet, pausing only to thrust my brushes into turpentine and smack the lids down on the paints.

"Tony, I'm sorry—gotta see somebody."

"Stop over after," he said as I jumped off the carousel and grabbed my hoodie. "Otherwise, Anna will be angry."

I paused with the hoodie half up my arms, and stared at him, round-eyed.

"I'm trying to picture this," I told him earnestly.

He laughed.

"Come by when you can," he said, and headed for the hatch.

TWENTY-THREE

※

Sunday, April 23
High Tide 8:15 P.M.
Sunset 7:34 P.M. EDT

Baxter Avenue was a zoo. There were tourists going and tourists coming and tourists standing around in big, sloppy groups, talking and laughing. Two teenagers in black T-shirts and black jeans were getting the lobster pitch set up, and lights were on around the fortune-teller's store front. From somewhere to the right I heard the hiss of an air tank, which meant that the dart game was getting ready for customers.

I threaded my way through the noise and bustle, grumbling to myself. Crowds are no fun when you're on the short side of average. Gran would just glide through a mob like this; people would look up, see her coming and automatically step out of the way. Me, they didn't see at all, unless I banged an elbow into a knee as I tunneled by.

Eventually I made it to the service alley, where I paused in the shadow of a police call box to catch my breath and wait for a break in the steady flow of happy pedestrians.

To the right of my position was Katahdin Street, which was even more crowded than Baxter. The stage where local bands sometimes played during the Season had been opened, and a couple guys in Fun Country Maintenance uniforms were tinkering with the mike and the lights. The speakers crackled, spat, and a guy's voice boomed across the park, asking, "Is it on now, Morris?"

Strung over the plaza, low enough that Borgan would have had to duck to get under it, was a brand new white banner, red letters shouting out: ARCHERS BEACH WELCOMES SENIOR FUN LOVERS!

Well, at least now I knew which group was giving the prize, I thought, and spied the hoped-for break in the crowd. I darted across the alley, ducking to the inside of the walk, close by the log flume, and proceeded at a reasonably good pace, hugging the Plexiglas splash guard.

I slipped 'round the corner, relieved to find the side street almost deserted.

To the left, back against the beach, the red and gold lights were on at Keltic Knot. Nearer to hand, the Scrambler was running, slightly squeaky at half-speed. A black haired girl with multiple piercings stood behind the controls, her attention on a guy who might've been her father, who was studying the movement of the cars. He raised a hand and brought it down, and the girl obediently pushed the stick. The guy was walking into the center of the pattern before the cars had completely stopped, a can of WD-40 in his hand.

I jogged down to the Knot, and looked over the fence.

All of the cars were on the track and the track itself had been greased until it shone like true silver. Up on the platform, a purple boom box that had seen better centuries was precariously wedged between the stick and the control box, something Big Band-ish blaring tinnily from its dented speaker.

The owner-operator, however, was not immediately in evidence.

"Mr. Ignat'?" I called. "It's Kate."

When I had counted to fifty and still hadn't gotten an answer to my hail, I swung over the fence.

There were numerous signs of busyness around the ride and its enclosure, but the author of these projects was nowhere to be seen. I stood in the middle of the track, spinning bemusedly on a heel.

You should've remembered to get his cell number, Kate, I told myself wryly.

Inside my head, the land bounced once, and images began to appear behind my eyes. This time, the geography was easier to figure; either the land was getting better at presentation or I was getting better at deciphering. But—

"What the hell's he doing at the Boundary Stone?" I asked the lead dragon. She, of course, maintained an inscrutable silence; overhead, a gull shrieked an obscenity.

Well, I certainly wasn't going to go walking all the way down to the other end of town, only to find when I got there that Mr. Ignat' had moved on, which the smart money said he would've done. And I was getting tired of playing hide 'n' seek.

Irritated, I turned and marched back to the tool shed.

The clipboard was hanging on its hook just inside the door, exactly where it had always been, the stub of a yellow pencil dangling from a string held to the back with a strip of duct tape.

I hauled it down and wrote a short note, including my cell number and the phone number at the house, which he should have by heart, but with Mr. Ignat' it's better to err on the side of multiple repetitions.

Message composed, I pulled the sheet out from under the clip, hung the board back where it belonged and stepped outside. Mr. Ignat' hadn't reappeared; the land, when queried, replayed the footage featuring the Boundary Stone. Great.

I carried the note up to the platform and anchored it under the purple boom box. If Mr. Ignat' didn't see the paper flapping when he got back, he'd definitely see it when he went up to turn the music off for the night. That was the best I could do.

My temper no better for having done it, I swung over the rail and headed for Tony Lee's.

I hit gridlock at the service alley—a solid wall of bodies there was no getting through or around. The two burly guys directly in front of me were wearing shorts and T-shirts, in outright defiance of the weather. The group of three elder ladies coming in from the left were bundled up in fleece jackets, brightly colored scarves tied over white hair. A couple of gray-haired guys came up on my right, one in a polo shirt and khakis, his buddy sporting a denim shirt and jeans.

Should've gone around by the beach, I scolded myself. In fact, I thought, as another bunch filled in behind me, I'd better go back the way I'd come *now,* before I became an inextricable part of the problem.

I'd just turned 'round when the guy in denim raised his arm and swung half a step back, bumping me hard. I staggered, felt the land scramble, and, simultaneously, big hands around my waist, lifting me effortlessly.

"'Evening, Kate," Borgan said. "You're looking good. Much better than a couple days ago. Land hereabouts must agree with you."

I looked down into his face, a novel perspective, noting the glint of mischief in the night-black eyes, and the quirk of a smile at the corner of his mouth. It was tempting—'way too tempting—to bend my head and kiss that quirking corner. I sucked air in a not-entirely-successful attempt to put such foolishness at a distance, and gave him a neighborly nod.

"Borgan," I said calmly. "Put me down, please."

"Sure," he said, matching my tone with wicked accuracy. He spun and set me gently on my feet atop a sawhorse that had been shoved in front of the ticket stand. Not the most stable perch in the world, though it had the benefit of putting me on a higher level than my rescuer—another novelty. I put a hand on his shoulder to keep from tottering over backward, and tried some more deep breathing, though to tell the truth, the ocean air wasn't helping me out as much as I had hoped.

"Thought you'd be interested to know that I had a word with Nerazi," Borgan said, turning slightly so that his other shoulder nestled against my hip, bracing me where I stood. "She's fine. Never came in to the mainland at all last night, as it happened; there was some business on the Islands that kept her."

"Good," I said, sounding slightly breathless in my own ears. "That's good."

With his shoulder for support, I could move the hand I was using as a brace, I thought, and did just that.

His braid was heavy and warm against my fingers, the beads smooth and cool; the whole thing 'way too pleasing.

Borgan raised his head and smiled up at me, slow and unexpectedly sweet.

"That's nice," he murmured.

"Yes," I managed to say calmly, "it is." I moved my hand with an effort and tucked it into the hoodie's kangaroo pocket. "But it's only glamor."

"What if it's not?" he asked, sounding genuinely curious.

"Then I'll be very surprised," I told him tartly.

He laughed.

"Good evening!" A hugely amplified voice broke over the crowd, and the voices around us quieted. "I'm Dan Poirier, the president of the local Chamber of Commerce, and I want to say, on behalf of the residents and the businesses of Archers Beach—WELCOME! We've heard that you're a fun loving bunch—"

Hoots and shouts and loud applause from the crowd. Dan Poirier yelled "Yes!" into the mic, which loosed another round of cheering. Borgan leaned in a little closer, thereby placing my peace of mind in mortal peril.

"Cut it *out*," I whispered in his near ear, and felt the laugh rumble through him.

"It's not nice?" he whispered back.

"Turn the glamor off and we'll see how nice it is," I said sternly, and he laughed again.

"Is off," he said, while the crowd indulged in a third round of cheering. "Never been on."

I turned my head to stare at him, lips parted to say who knew what. Happily, Dan Poirier chose that moment to get back to speechifying.

"Yessir, we've heard all about you folks! And we have got some SERIOUS fun lined up for you!"

More cheering, then Dan's voice again.

"Tonight, we're going to kick things off with an old-fashioned street party, finishing up with fireworks on the beach! And tomorrow—" He paused until the hoots of delight settled down.

"Tomorrow at NOON Fun Country's famous Name Rides and the most challenging games of skill and chance on the eastern seaboard will be open non-stop 'til TEN P.M.! But that's not all! The WORLD FAMOUS Archers Beach PIER will open tomorrow at eleven A.M.! Neptune's Retreat will be serving your favorite beverages and local Maine microbrews—"

Cheers and hoots.

"AND! Tomorrow night at eight—ESPECIALLY FOR YOU— Portland's own Ms. Lori Kennet will be LIVE at the Sea Change Casino and Lounge, bringing you Maine's best blues. NOW DOES THAT SOUND LIKE SERIOUS FUN OR WHAT?"

The crowd roared. On top of the sawhorse, I tottered and was secretly glad for Borgan's continued support.

"ALL RIGHT THEN!" Dan Poirier screamed into the mic. "LET'S BOOGIE!"

There was half a minute of dead air before the sound system

delivered "Twist and Shout" at a volume that was likely heard on Wood Isle.

"Time for me to get the hell outta here," I yelled into Borgan's ear.

He nodded. "I'll walk with you," he said, and stepped back. I felt a pang at his withdrawal, though I was damned if I was going to let him know that. He smiled as if he knew anyway, and held his hands out to me. Sighing, I took the offered assist and dropped lightly to the ground.

"Lead on," he said, slightly louder. I shook my head.

"*You* lead on!" I yelled. "Tall's good for something, isn't it?"

He might have laughed; it seemed so. Then he took my hand and moved to the left, drawing me after him.

As I had suspected, once people got an eyeful of large Indian heading in their direction, they melted out of the way. There was still some tacking and backtracking involved, imposed by the sheer number of happy dancers, but we were making good progress toward the beach side of the park. In fact, we were under the Galaxi, Borgan tacking left against the current, when "Twist and Shout" ended, and "Hokie Pokie" began.

It's a fact well-known among the organizers of street parties, class reunions, and pre-school birthday parties that *everyone* will dance the Hokie Pokie. Worse, they'll expect *you* to dance the Hokie Pokie, too, even if you happen to be one of the seventeen people on the face of the earth who are utterly immune to the charms of the thing.

A woman in a purple exercise suit and a red hat decorated with numerous scarves and flowers, grabbed Borgan's free hand. A man wearing a toupee and a plain white shirt tucked into neat khakis grabbed my hand. It was either join the circle or get seriously ugly—and damn if Borgan didn't already have his left foot in.

We were at the point of putting our right arms in, and I was hoping with all I had in me that we were only fated to do one round, when the circle we were in staggered—and came to a complete stop.

The woman in the red hat was standing soft and tentative, like a dreamer, blinking at something halfway between Tom Thumb and forever. On her far side, a man wearing a brown pullover was looking vaguely around, as if he knew he'd lost *something*, but wasn't exactly sure what. The rest of us were staring at them, apprehension on quite a few faces, and—in my case, at least—with a creepy little twitter along nerves I'd almost forgotten I had.

Slowly, I turned around—and looked up.

Perched midway up the Galaxi's blue-and-pink girders, raining sullen orange sparks like a Roman candle gone very, *very* bad, was a willie wisp.

"Kate?" Borgan was beside me. I pointed and he followed my line of sight.

"Damn it," he said conversationally.

"Won't do a bit of good." I looked around, just in time to see another one of our dance partners go kind of soft-faced and puzzled.

"Ah, shit," I muttered, around a sinking feeling in my stomach. I turned back to stare at the willie.

In the Land of the Flowers, willie wisps scavenge elemental fragments, and they're extremely shy of people, the least powerful of whom can shred them with a Word.

In the Changing Land, willie wisps feed on memories, and they're positively brazen. And this particular willie wisp had happened on the mother lode.

"What's that?" a woman asked somewhere behind me, and I swallowed another curse. All the situation had needed was somebody with half-Sight picking out the willie. And once one saw it, in the way of things, they all—

"Light show," a man said, sounding calm and factual. "Guess we're about to have us some entertainment."

Right. I took a breath, feeling a Word building at the back of my tongue. The willie sputtered, expanded, and threw out a wet handful of puke-green sparks. Sort of the willie wisp version of a raspberry.

The Word was filling my mouth, crowding my tongue, making it hard to breathe—and there was only one thing to do about that. I raised my hand, pointed straight at the willie, and Spoke.

The instant it left my mouth, I knew it was far, far too wide and deep a Word for conditions. For one scary moment, the Galaxi's steel gridwork shimmered, waves of heat rising from the girders, molten metal trembling on the edge of dripping onto the watching crowd. Then—it solidified and returned to normal. Well, except for the willie wisp which, unharmed, bounced around like a demented and deeply wrong Super Ball, phasing from orange to yellow to red-purple-blue-green. A couple of the watchers clapped half-heartedly.

"Need a bigger gun?" Borgan asked quietly. I shook my head.

"That Word was almost too much. If I go that road again, we'll end up with a smoking crater where the Galaxi used to be," I said. And the willie wisp probably wouldn't be discommoded in the least. I bit my lip, not liking my options, but hating the consequences if I didn't get rid of that nasty critter—and fast.

"I've gotta get closer," I told Borgan. "Throw me."

He looked down into my face. "*Throw* you?"

"C'mon, I don't weigh that much! A big guy like you shouldn't have any trouble at all hoisting me up to that girder."

"Kate—"

I held up a hand. "You've got a better idea?"

He frowned, glanced around—six folks now looking a bit gone at the edges—and back to me, mouth hard. "No."

"Right. Throw me."

He gave a stiff nod, and walked forward, a tough-guy roll to his hips.

I hauled the work gloves out of the hoodie's kangaroo pocket and pulled them on.

Two feet out from the Galaxi's base, Borgan turned and dropped to one knee with heart-stopping grace, his hands linked low before him.

I glanced up to make sure the willie was still there, swallowed, and before I could overthink it, threw myself into a run.

My right foot went into the cup of Borgan's hands, there was a moment of lift, and I was hurtling through the air, the land wailing inside my head, straight for the woven metal frame. Live, as they say, without a net.

Heart in mouth, I grabbed with gloved hands, held on, and did one revolution around the girder of my choice before swinging a leg over and sitting it astride. Below me, I heard whoops, yells, and applause, but I didn't dare look down. Instead, I held on to the girder with both hands, took three deep breaths—and looked up.

Two levels above and one over, the willie wisp spat a line of nasty puce sparks.

"Don't give me attitude," I muttered. The land darted back and forth inside my head like a worried hound, then was gone, leaving behind an impression remarkably like a feather bed. Nice to know I'd have something soft to land on when I fell.

Carefully, not rushing it, I got one foot braced on my girder, pushed, and rose shakily, snatching at a strut the instant it came within reach, and rested, swaying a little, the wind off the ocean blowing my hair into my eyes. I was pleased to find that the old work gloves were nice and grippy; the leather-soled boots, though—not so much.

Well, a warrior doesn't always find a level field for battle, as my fencing teacher used to say, usually right before she whipped my sorry ass from one side of the orchard to the other in the naive belief that I was learning something from the exercise.

Wobbling a little on my chancy footing, I tried to empty my mind of everything except the willie wisp—not easy, under present circumstances. The willie, possibly believing that it was about to witness a new and exciting form of suicide, dropped down one level and spun closer.

I breathed in, forcing the air down to the very bottom of my lungs, and focused grimly on the willie. The temptation was just to blast the damn thing out of existence, but my two recent experiences with elevated levels of *jikinap* made me more cautious. I couldn't afford to blitz the roller coaster, or risk hurting any of the innocents below. What I needed was a pin-laser, not an H-bomb.

Slowly, shaking with the effort to control it, I allowed the *jikinap* to rise in my blood. Slowly, a Word took shape inside my mouth; a small Word, and a hard Word, tasting of smoke and—

The willie wisp drew in on itself, becoming a dense green-and-orange ball, my lips parted—and the willie spat, sparks striking my face, burning...

Low on my horse's neck, I followed Zephyr as we tore breakneck through unmapped woodland. She'd said it was madness to go by the road; but surely this route was no saner. Branches whipped overhead, leaves clashed and broke, showering me with dusted crystal. My horse—bold Sinbar—wove between the trees under his own judgment, reins loose on his neck. My care was to stay seated, and to pray that he stumbled on no unseen object, slowing us, or—Elements avert!—breaking a leg.

I was breathing hard, my heart pounding louder than Sinbar's hoof beats. Ahead, the trail curved, dark between the trees.

Zephyr's wind stallion flowed 'round the curve and was gone. Before we could follow, a rider came out from the trees, enclosed in a nimbus of power, and stopped in the center of the path.

Sinbar skidded and reared, almost unseating me. The figure before us flicked her fingers, and he dropped to four feet, held motionless against his will. I was under no such compulsion, but I sat just as frozen.

My mother raised her hand, slowly—painfully slowly. I blinked, and looked to her face, saw the tears and knew that she was compelled by the one who held her soul. Compelled . . .

Power swirled, the slim brown hand continued to rise, and I saw my doom boiling at her fingertips.

I screamed—and screamed again as the memory shattered about me, and I was once again precariously balanced on the slick steel girder, a hint of butterscotch on my tongue and the echo of a Word in the wind.

Above me, the willie wisp swelled, shrank—and exploded—orange and green and red and violet streamers escaping in all directions.

A streamer whipped across my cheek, burning. I jerked sideways, twisting after balance, but there was no stopping my feet in their slick-soled boots from sliding off the steel.

From below came a shout, a scream, and a scattering of applause. Above me, the last glowering sparks of what had been a willie wisp sparkled, turned, and faded into the dusky air.

I bit my lip, laboriously pulling myself back up onto the girder. Arms trembling, I turned, exquisitely careful, to look out—and down.

"You didn't think this through, Kate," I muttered, wondering how soft a landing zone might be waiting for me, after all, and if the land could do anything with tarmac.

"Kate!" a big voice called. I looked down again, and there he was, arms extended, looking as solid, reliable, and welcome as Cape Elizabeth Light in a storm.

I jumped.

TWENTY-FOUR

Sunday, April 23

"What happened up there?" Borgan asked some time later, after we'd taken our bows before an appreciative audience and exited far more coolly than I at least felt, stage right.

"It looked like you had it all wrapped up, and the next thing I see, you're sliding off the beam and about to put the land to some trouble."

I sighed and leaned against the back side of the Whale's Tail, while I pulled off the work gloves and stowed them.

"Willie grabbed out a bad memory and threw it in my face," I said, shivering. All the bad memories I carried and it had to have been *that* one. But, of course, willie wisps have a feel for such things.

"My own damn' fault," I continued, trying for calm. "I was too careful with the *jikinap.*"

Scared of your own power, I thought. Not *a plan for long-term survival, Kate.*

"About which..." Borgan said after a moment. "Rumor was you didn't have enough wattage to light a match." He squatted down on his heels in the sand and looked up at me. "That changed, did it?"

I laughed. "Oh, yeah. That changed. You know Mr. Ignat'?"

"Sweetest man in the world. Not a breath of sense in him, but don't let that bother you."

"I never have," I said. "Mr. Ignat' had almost as much to do with raising me as Gran did. He introduced me to grilled blueberry muffins, and fiddleheads; watched Saturday morning cartoons with me, and just—" *loved me, without question or censure,* "made me feel safe." I sent Borgan a sharp look, daring him to laugh, but he only nodded.

"Also, he's not . . . always . . . simple. Sometimes, he's downright complex. Last night—this morning—being a case in point. He showed up just when the Black Dogs had a two-to-one lead, sent them packing, then offered me his flask." I paused, but Borgan didn't have anything to say. I shrugged.

"So, I had me a good slug of the smoothest liquor I've tasted in . . . a really long time. He said that Gran and him had brewed it together. Between the two of us, we drank what should've been the whole flask, only the damn' thing never did get empty, and I was too jazzed on adrenaline to care." I sighed.

"The upshot being that I now have more than enough *jikinap* to light a match. If I'm not careful, I get the sense that I could burn down the whole town."

"Blame that on the whiskey, do you?" Borgan asked after a while.

"Yup. Also? I can't find Mr. Ignat'. I've been by the Knot twice to see if he's okay and to tell him where I think Gran's gone. I can see he's been working on it, but he himself I haven't seen since early morning—and not for lack of looking."

Borgan nodded, glanced down at his hands, then back to me. "What did happen to your gran? You were thinking she sang herself across, when we talked this morning, and were on your way to a second opinion."

"Right." I sighed. "I got the second opinion, and everything jibes. Listen . . ."

I told the tale as quick as I could without leaving anything vital out. At the end of it, Borgan sighed and came to his feet. "You still got that leaf?"

"Yeah." I pulled the folded letter out of my back pocket and handed it over. "See what you make of it, will you?"

He nodded, unfolded the paper carefully, slipped the leaf into his palm—and gasped, face tight with pain.

"Damn," he whispered, and folded the leaf reverently into

Gran's letter before passing it to me. I slipped it away into my back pocket.

"So," I said. "It's the real thing?"

Borgan sighed. "It's *a* real thing. Whether it's your mother or not..." He shook his head.

"Yeah. But Gran would've known."

"Or she went on hope," he said. "But I think you're right that she went. She couldn't have done anything else, not the Bonny Pepperidge I know."

"Not the one I know, either," I admitted.

"Well," Borgan said after a moment or two of dead air. "You've had some kind of a day. What about dinner?"

Reminded, my stomach informed me, loudly, that it had been some hours since my breakfast egg roll, and while the land would nourish me, it just wasn't the same as—

"Oh, hell!" I said, pushing away from the wall.

Borgan's eyebrows went up. "Is that a no?"

"Actually, it's an Anna-is-expecting-me-for-dinner-sometime-this-century-and-I-totally-forgot-until-right-now." I took a breath. "And Tony said if I didn't make it, she'd be mad as fire at me."

"This, I've got to see."

"C'mon, then," I said, and headed up the beach at a trot.

Baxter Avenue still being impassable due to street-partyers, we went 'round to the back of Tony Lee's and knocked on the service door. It popped open in a shorter time than I would've predicted, and Anna grabbed my arm, pulling me inside. Borgan followed on his own.

"Kate, you must be starving, come in here and—Andre! What a surprise!"

It was, to judge by her smile, a surprise of the pleasant variety. For his part, Borgan gave her a respectful nod, and a sideways glance out of mischievous black eyes.

"Now, Anna, you know I can't go for long without seeing you. Too bad you're married to such a nice guy, or I'd carry you off for sure."

Anna laughed and closed the door, snapping the lock shut.

"Kate's already threatened to steal Tony," she said, sidling between the Number Two stove and the prep table.

"That so?" Borgan said, and gave me a grin. "Might be less trouble for everybody, then, if Kate and me just called it a match."

I gave him a glare, but he was watching Anna.

"I think that would work out just fine," she said composedly. "Sit down, both of you! Andre, you're having dumplings?"

"Yes, ma'am."

We got ourselves situated on the out of the way side of the prep table. No sooner had we pulled out the stools than the promised dumplings arrived on paper plates, plastic utensils on the side.

"Coffee's coming," Anna said. "Kate, Nancy asked me to tell you that she's got to leave for home at eight. She'll close the storm walls before she goes, but she doesn't have a key to lock up."

"Right," I said, digging in. "I'll get Nancy a key—tomorrow, I guess. And I've gotta get some clothes..."

"Dynamite opened today," Anna said, bringing two Styrofoam cups of coffee to the table, and heading back to the stove. "Mr. Kristanos said they were going to stay open 'til ten."

"Anna!" Tony called from the front. "We need more egg rolls!"

Borgan rose, moved over to the warming counter and picked up a tray. "I've got 'em," he told Anna. She flashed him a smile over her shoulder.

"Thanks, Andre."

"No problem," he assured her, and went up to the front. I heard the rumble of his voice, and Tony's laughter; and sipped my coffee, thinking. Borgan was obviously welcome here—not only welcome, but at home. Before I could decide if that bothered me or pleased me, he was back and picking up his fork.

"Who could have thought it would be so busy?" Anna said from the stove-side counter. She sounded delighted, and not tired in the least. "I bet the Chamber's pleased."

"Ought to be," I said, finishing up the last of the meal and putting my fork down with a sigh of pure contentment. "Anna, those dumplings have got to be illegal. Thank you."

"There's more if you want them," she said, and rushed on. "Marilyn says if we win the competition, then we'll have a Super Early Season next year, too."

I looked at her, but her attention was on her work. "Same group?"

"I'm not sure—Marilyn would know, I guess."

"I guess." I drank coffee. Beside me, Borgan finished his dinner, picked up his plate and mine and went over to put them in the trash can. That done, he stepped to Anna's side.

"Anything you need done on the town? Errands run?"

She flashed him a smile. "We're fine, Andre. As soon as we heard there were going to be fireworks, Tony called in a second order."

I slid off my stool, and deposited my empty cup in the trash. "You're staying open for the fireworks?"

"Until *after* the fireworks," she corrected, and threw me a grin. "Make egg rolls while the sun shines."

I laughed.

"I'm sorry I was late for dinner. We—got caught up in some things."

"It's no problem at all, Kate. We're opening tomorrow at eleven. We'll send lunch over around two." She gave me what she probably thought was a fierce frown. "Do you understand me, young lady?"

I raised my hands in surrender. "Yes, ma'am. I do."

"Good. Now, you'd better go lock up. Andre?"

"Pretty Anna?"

"You help Kate carry her packages home from Dynamite, all right? And see she gets in safe. Somebody hurt her right here in the park a couple days ago—the cut's healed now, but—"

"She told me about it," Borgan interrupted. "I'll take good care of her, Anna, don't worry."

She smiled. "I won't, then."

True to her word, Nancy had closed up as best she was able. Borgan followed me inside and stood by the control stand while I made sure the storm walls were tight, and did a tour of the ride. Nancy'd got all the lights in, I saw, polished the brass on the orchestrion and cleaned the glass. Hell, she'd even threaded in a roll of Violano paper. All we'd have to do tomorrow would be push back the walls, turn on the lights and start selling tickets.

"I feel like such a slacker," I said, maybe to Borgan, maybe to myself. "Nancy's put in a day and a half's work while I was goofing off."

"Taking out a willie wisp and preserving the memories of a couple hundred folks who probably value them high," Borgan said quietly. "Trying to check on the old gentleman. Flirting with me."

"I was *not* flirting with you," I said absently, pausing to inspect the bindings on the goat. Still strong and tight. Good.

"Well, now I'm heartbroken," he said, his voice closer at hand. I turned and saw him walking toward me around the carousel.

He checked when he came level with the batwing horse, and frowned down at it.

"This one's awake," he said.

I sighed and went to join him. "It asked to be, had a good reason, and backed it up with an oath, so I agreed."

Borgan nodded, but didn't move, his gaze still on the batwing. "What're you going to do? About your gran, that is."

I shrugged. "I don't know. If I had any friends in the Land of the Flowers—but I don't. I guess I could cross over myself and look for her." *Though I'd rather not,* I thought. And then I thought of the blight on Gran's tree and was ashamed.

"It might be," I said to Borgan, "that's the best thing to do. Now the prisoners are sealed, Nancy can run the ride, though I should get one other—"

"Would that be a little risky?" he asked. "Crossing over."

I stepped off the carousel. "A little," I said. "Yeah."

Forty minutes later, I came out of Dynamite, staggering under the sheer number of bags, and found Borgan leaning against the light pole, hands in pockets, watching the crowd. He straightened when he saw me and stepped forward with a smile.

"You don't have to carry my books home from school," I told him, a little snippier than I had really intended.

"Well, I do," he answered mildly, taking the bags out of my hands. "I promised Anna."

Which was, I had to admit, a point.

We cut across Jerome's parking lot, weaving between parked cars to the other side, turned right and walked down Grand. There were maybe a half-dozen tourists on the stroll, taking in what sights there were.

"I wonder if they know this is the wrong side of town," I said, tucking my hands into the pockets of my new denim jacket.

"Nothing wrong with this side of town," Borgan answered, and glanced up at the sky. "Oughta be sending up the fireworks soon."

Right on cue a single rocket screamed into the sky and exploded in a brilliant flower of light.

"What did you mean," I asked, around the echoes of the explosion, "when you said you'd never used glamor on me?"

Fireworks bloomed overhead—one-two-three—happily, sans explosion. Borgan looked down at me, eyes hidden in shadow.

"Meant what it sounded like," he said, his voice just a shade too earnest. "I'm really sorry, Kate, but it seems you like me for my own self."

"Sure I do."

"Is that so hard? Anna likes me."

I laughed. "Anna likes *me*, which ought to tell you something. She doesn't like everybody, but she does have range."

"Anna liking you does tell me something," Borgan said, and his voice was perfectly serious. "You're too hard on yourself."

I shook my head, and paused to look both ways down the empty street, while pink, blue and white fireworks cascaded down the sky, accompanied by an emphatic *BANG!*

"We can cross here," I said, and stepped out, Borgan at my shoulder.

Bob's was closed when we went by, a sign in the window promising a 5 A.M. opening on the morrow.

The street was quiet, except for the echo of the explosion—and the scream of ungreased hinges, followed by a metallic clang from the alley beside my next-door neighbor's house.

Borgan frowned, put my bags down on the sidewalk, and moved, quick and quiet, toward the sound. I followed, not as quick, but quiet enough that we both scared hell out of Gaby when she turned around, a six pack of empty beer bottles clutched to her chest.

"Eek!" she screamed and fell to her knees, her body bent over the empties.

"Take it easy, Gaby," I said. "It's only Kate."

"There's somebody else!" she squeaked, staying right where she was. I sighed.

"That's right," I said, patiently. "A friend of mine. We heard you open the Dumpster and wanted to make sure it wasn't... somebody trespassing."

"Trespassing!" Gaby cried, raising her head in indignation. "I'm not trespassing—just after the returnables, is all. Nothing for a son of the sea to bother himself about."

"That's right," Borgan said, his voice easy. "I didn't know you were around, is all. You'll want to be a little careful. There's vermin about—human and fey."

Gaby got to her feet. She gave a stiff little nod in Borgan's general direction, not looking at him. "I thank'ee. That's neighborly."

"Welcome," he said, and turned away. "We'll leave you to it, then. Kate?"

"On my way," I said. "'Night, Gaby."

"How'd you find them fiddleheads, missy?"

"Wonderful," I told her truthfully. "I'd forgotten how good they are."

Gaby snorted and rustled around in the shadow of the Dumpster for her bags. "Goodnight to ye, then. There's some of us got work."

I grinned and went back out to the street, where Borgan was waiting, bags in hand.

He followed me up the stairs and waited patiently while I opened the door, then handed me the bags one at a time so I could set them inside.

"Well," I said, a little too brightly. "Thank you—for all your help tonight."

"Didn't do anything except make sure you had room to work," he said. "Kate—" He paused as a small war's worth of explosions echoed down the beach, bouncing off the sides of buildings and waking weird echoes. Grand finale, it must've been; the air felt empty when they were done.

"Kate..." Borgan said again—and stopped.

"Yeah?" I said.

He shook his head. "Don't do anything, will you? About your gran. Sleep on it, at least. I'll talk with Nerazi—see if she's got any ideas, once she hears the tale."

I yawned, belatedly covering my mouth, abruptly and acutely conscious of having been up since just after midnight, and of the day's many adventures. The land had been keeping me vertical, but apparently it had decided that enough was enough.

"Okay, I'll sleep on it," I told Borgan. "And it looks like it better be soon."

He grinned. "Go on in and get your rest, then. Meet me at Neptune's tomorrow—'round seven? Give me a chance to buy you that drink, an' let you know what Nerazi tells me."

I nodded, fighting another yawn. "Sounds good," I mumbled. "See you then."

"'Night," said Borgan as I stepped into the house.

He was still standing there, hands in his pockets and face attentive, when I turned back to close the door.

TWENTY-FIVE

Monday, April 24
High Tide 8:36 A.M.
Sunrise 5:45 A.M. EDT

Sunrise found me at the northern salt marsh, a solid seven hours of sleep under my belt and a stainless steel commuter mug half full of coffee in my hand.

The land was responsible for this display of virtue; waking me before the stars had faded, and dragging me out here. And, truthfully, I should have come sooner. It was my duty to care for the land—and the northern marsh was one sick puppy. I'd felt it when I'd merged with the land to look for Gran—well. If it hadn't been for Borgan, the marsh would've probably killed me.

At first glance, the marsh—Heron Marsh, as it's called on the town maps—looked, well...like a salt marsh: arrow grass, salt hay, cattails and slough grass; native phragmite shaking its feathery plumes in the breeze; water channels; mud.

Second glance caught the sparse and sickly condition of the vegetation, the green scum in the center of the channels, and the water line that was 'way too low for this time of the day, when the tide had been coming in for three hours and more.

I knelt down, pleased that I had the foresight to wear my old jeans; wincing as the broad-leafed weeds crunched beneath me.

Tentatively, I touched the swamp, letting my consciousness float on the scummy surface.

Exhausted, despairing sobs shook me. Carefully, oh-so-very-carefully, recalling my last encounter with the marsh, I allowed myself to sink below the surface.

Thirst. Self-disgust. A feeling of filth and degradation. Longing, for the rise and fall of the cleansing waters. All very well and good, but what I needed was info, not feelings.

I let myself sink one more level down.

Bad idea.

Sticky black tendrils were around me before I sensed anything wrong, pulling me down toward the unwholesome stew at the bottom of the marsh. The wailing and the longing of the marsh were gone, replaced by an acid bath of rage.

I struggled, trying to snatch myself back into my body, but it was like wrestling with the Tar Baby. Everything I did only stuck me tighter, and this time there was no Borgan on hand to pull me free.

Kate, you're an idiot. A dead, enthralled—or both—idiot, if I didn't think of something quick.

I stopped struggling, and forced myself to lie quiescent in my captor's grip.

The descent toward the bottom . . . paused, and a sense of puzzlement reached me through the rage.

I formed a question with exquisite care, projecting calm competence, which was a fabrication worthy of any *trenvay*.

Happily, my captor bought it.

Images and sensations tumbled through me, tearing at my captive essence. Sickness, despair, *anger,* oh my yes. Betrayal. And, like the refrain of a particularly tragic ballad: Thirst. Self-disgust. Degradation, and longing.

I pictured the channels as I had just seen them: the water low and coated with scum; the plants failing. Rage began to boil again from what I was now pretty sure had been—was—the *trenvay* attached to the marsh. Not willing to take another acid bath, I hurried the next set of images, picturing the water level rising, the scum swirling away, the plants rejuvenated.

Rage subsided, usurped by a longing so intense that my too-far-away body probably threw back its head and howled.

You can do this?

God. Coherence.

I can try.

A shimmer of anger, hardly noticeable at all.

Will *you do this?*

Free me to myself and I will do everything in my power to succor you.

I hung in nothingness, waiting for an answer, trying not to think about what would happen if the answer was no. A crazed *trenvay,* poisoned by the sickness consuming his soul-place... The longer the silence stretched, the less hope I had for a rational decision.

The black tentacles of my prison fell away, and I was thrust out of the marsh and into my body with a force that knocked me flat, breath escaping in a gasping, flattened-out scream.

I lay on the damp ground looking up at the silver and blue sky, just... breathing. In the back of my head, the land was calm and attentive, like I hadn't just almost gotten myself zombified.

After a while, I sat up. My coffee cup was lying on the weeds by my knee. I picked it up—and sighed. Empty.

All right, Kate. This is where the Guardian business gets down and dirty.

Right. I looked out over the wounded marsh, fishing for a clue.

Salt marshes need the tide to clean them. Cut off the tide and you choke the marsh, killing everything that depends on it: plants, fish, bugs, birds. Back in the 'way back, men used to fill the marshes, or ditch and drain them—to keep mosquitoes down, or to gain more land to plant. Once various bright, ecologically inclined lads and lasses had noodled out that the marshes were a critical buffer zone between the land and the sea, that kind of thing theoretically went out of vogue.

Except, in some areas, in an effort to protect the works of men at the expense of the marsh, floodgates have been built across the ingress channels. Most of the time, such gates stood open, closed only against double high tides and storm surge.

During my childhood, there hadn't even been *talk* of a flood-gate on Carson Creek, the path the tide rode into Heron Marsh. During my childhood, the rich people from Away hadn't started building condos and expensive summer homes on the edge of the marsh, either.

The smart money said there was a floodgate across the ocean's ingress now, put in place to protect those high-value properties.

Or maybe some developer had hit on a scheme to make profit from the weedy "wasteland."

Only one way to find out, now, isn't there, Kate?

I climbed to my feet, stuffing the stainless steel cup down the front of my jacket, and turned east. Toward the sea.

It was easy to find—a simple sluice gate, meant to be opened and closed by hand. Preferably a hand supported by a strong back, since the wheel that turns the worm drive is typically pretty hard to move.

In the case of the sluice gate across Carson Creek, this had been taken to an extreme: The wheel was locked with rust, the worm drive inoperable. The sea itself knew how long the thing had been locked down. I was guessing a year, minimum, given the state of the marsh and its *trenvay*.

I leaned over the rail of the operator's platform and looked down. The incoming tide was filling the blocked channel. Soon it would overflow into the bank on either side. I could see evidence that this had happened before, many times—grasses and reeds half-buried in silt, the bank itself undercut and on the edge of being unstable.

The damn' gate wasn't only hurting the upper marsh; it was creating a whole different order of havoc downstream.

Just for fun, I pulled on my work gloves and tried the wheel, throwing my whole weight against it. I might as well have tried to pull Googin Rock out of the tide. Panting, I stepped back and considered my next move.

"Should've brought a can of WD-40," I muttered. Though I had a feeling that this wasn't a problem that could be fixed with a couple shots of lubricant.

There was a Public Works plate set into the platform's deck. I'd be within my rights as a concerned citizen to bring this problem to the attention of the superintendent. And, eventually, they'd get around to sending a couple guys down in the town pickup to study the problem and maybe spray the wheel and the screw with WD-40 before trying their best to break the rust's embrace.

After they'd figured out that the problem was bigger than their heads, they'd report back to the boss, who would have to go to the town manager for permission to spend money to get an expert in to give them a repair estimate, and—

By the time all the paperwork and budgeting and discussion was done, the marsh and its *trenvay* would be beyond anyone's help.

The land stirred, reminding me of its presence. Unfortunately, this wasn't a problem that the land's peculiar power could easily address. We might, I supposed, reroute the channel around the sluice gate, but that—while not exactly a project for the ages—would be time consuming, not to say even more destructive of trees and bank.

No, what I needed was a quick fix, something like WD-40, only with more punch, to melt the rust off the wheel and—

I felt a tickle of warmth in my blood, and the breathy hint of a Word along my tongue. *Jikinap,* rising to the challenge.

"Oh, no," I said. "No. Absolutely not." Like *that* did any good.

The more a mage accesses her power, the easier it is to use, and the more she becomes dependent upon it. The more dependent a mage becomes, the less she controls her power, and the more her power controls her. I was already on the bumpy road to hell, what with dismissing Black Dogs, shredding willie wisps, and making mage-fire on the side. I so did not need to be raising *jikinap* to deal with this.

My blood continued to warm, the power eager to express its dominion over mere matter. I concentrated, trying to drive it back down to the base of my spine, and making no noticeable headway.

You promised, Kate. Everything in your power. You said it.

Well, I *had* promised. Though it would have eased my feelings considerably if I'd been certain it was my conscience speaking.

I closed my eyes and took a good, deep breath of salt air, listening to the ocean smacking uselessly against the sluice gate while gulls argued overhead.

It was true, I admitted, that a well-placed magical nudge could do exactly what a six month study and a budget overrun would, less the time and the monetary expense.

It was also true that I was in possession of sufficient power to accomplish the task, as long as I managed not to catch the marsh on fire in the process.

Power rose, tingling in my fingertips. I concentrated on the rust, and the wheel, and the gate, womanfully resisting the temptation to whack the thing a good one with the magical equivalent of a Big Hammer and have done with it. My magic tutor would have scorned such white-livered quailing, and pointed out—quite rightly—that power belonged to the bold.

I've never actually been very bold.

I thought a shape, building it in my head, slow and careful as I knew how. The power was running hot, now, and I was sweating in the cool air. *Not much,* I said to myself. *A tap, not a whack—*

It was then that I noticed the Word sitting quiet at the back of my tongue, waiting.

It was not, as Words of Power go, very large; though heavy, it was not out of proportion with its purpose. There was a sense of abrasion about it, which ought to answer the rust, and a lingering aroma of oil, which should loosen the drive.

I took a breath and let my half-designed magic machine fade. A real Ozali trusts her spellcraft. But a real Ozali would have had many years to study and hone her skill.

All I had was raw power and a couple of half-remembered lessons from the schoolroom. And the Words, which appeared on their own schedule, according to rules I'd never understood, but which had never done me wrong.

I pushed the boiling *jikinap* as far down my spine as I could manage, centered myself and Spoke.

Heat, the memory of butterscotch, and an accelerated high-pitched squeak. The metal platform bucked under my feet, and I grabbed the rail to keep from toppling into the frustrated water battering against the gate.

Except the sluice gate wasn't there. It was open, cranked as high as the rust-free and gleaming worm drive could take it, and the tide was rushing through the opening, exactly as it should.

I leaned over the rail and watched the water move, picturing it flowing into Heron Marsh, picturing the poor, mad *trenvay* dancing in the current. It would take time for the marsh to recover; the sea had its work cut out for it. But at least the vital cleansing cycle had been restarted.

And that, Gran's voice said from memory, *is how a proper Guardian acquits her duty.*

Yeah, well. I rubbed my tingling fingertips together, and fished my cell phone out of my jeans pocket. Eight o'clock.

Time for breakfast.

Unless you're one of those folks who don't care about rules, or trampling endangered plants, and are okay with spooking heron and loon off their nests—and if you are, please don't tell me—there's only one way back to town from the sluice gate at Carson Creek. Walk west on the overgrown-but-marked trail to the intersection with a thinner and even more overgrown path. Turn south at that intersection. The trail thins again and becomes even more unkempt, but keep the faith. Eventually, you'll come to a wooden deck railed around with brown-painted logs, and a Maine Park Service information board with its back to the trail. Duck under or go over the rail and you're back to civilization, only a quarter mile or so out from Bob's Diner, and a good board walk all the way down to Grand Avenue.

I went under the rail to the right of the info board. The land shifted to alert, feeding me the image of a weedy-looking shrub, like a hundred other weedy-looking shrubs at either side of the walk.

I shrugged and quickened my pace, my mind on other things. Specifically, the location and well-being of Mr. Ignat'. Having just lately taken a refresher course in *Jikinap, its seductive dangers*, I was worried all over again. If he'd been a mere human with some Sight, a few hefty swigs of *jikinap*-laced whiskey wouldn't hurt him. At least, I thought not. But if the Battle of the Black Dogs had done nothing else, it had solidly established Mr. Ignat' as *trenvay*. An ordinary human would have seen only shadows while the Dogs chewed their joy and mauled their spirits. Henry, a human with Sight, would have been able to see them, all right, but he couldn't have done a damn thing about them.

Mr. Ignat' had not only *seen* them, he'd *fought* them—and prevailed.

Which meant that there was a hopped-up *trenvay* of slightly less than modest good sense roaming around Archers Beach. And, as I thought back to my several visits to the Knot yesterday, he was avoiding me.

I was trying to decide if I should notch up from "worried" to "panicked" when the weedy-looking shrub to my right rustled noisily, and a woman stepped out onto the walk. She was tall and thin, with flyaway blond hair and narrow brown eyes, wearing blue jeans and a long-sleeved denim shirt—absolutely unmemorable, except for one thing.

She was pointing a gun at my chest.

TWENTY-SIX

～◊～

Monday, April 24

I didn't think, I reacted, and the bolt was on its way to her heart before my brain got with the program.

In the same instant, she fired, in what should have been the last, defiant act of a dead woman.

Except that the high-voltage spear I'd thrown at her—bounced. So did the bullet.

For a moment we just stood there, four feet apart, blinking at each other in mutual bafflement. I'm sorry to say that she found her wits first, jamming the gun into the waistband of her jeans with one hand and pulling a knife with the other.

I dropped back a step, reaching to the small of my back. Mam'selle fair leapt into my hand, and I went back another step, holding her all wrong, and leaving a hole in my defenses you could drive a semi through.

My opponent smiled, and moved in slow and low, a woman who knew her business, and no mistake.

I went half a step to the right and reached for the land.

"Mr. Nemeier's tired of you," the blonde said, and thrust against my non-existent defenses.

The moment she was off-center, the land moved. The boardwalk

181

rippled under her feet and she staggered, flinging her arms out for balance, knife flying from confused fingers. The walkway bucked peevishly, and she pitched forward, caught her shoe in a gap between two boards and went down, hitting her head sharply.

I approached with proper caution, knife at ready—but she was out colder'n a January blizzard.

"That was too close," I said to no one in particular, and sat down next to her on the now perfectly flat and well-behaved boardwalk.

Taking a single deep breath, I stepped Sideways, which was far too easy to do and would've scared hell out of me if I hadn't already been high on adrenaline.

As I had suspected, my napping adversary had a nice, basic invincibility spell knitted around her. Which answered the musical question, *How come Kate's lightning bolt hadn't fried her?* What it didn't answer was the reciprocal question regarding the bullet.

I hadn't been wrapped in protective magic. Contrary to popular fantasy, an invincibility spell isn't something a mage can bring into being with the snap of her fingers. They take work—*hard* work—and a non-trivial application of *jikinap*. That being the case, and my girl's aim steady as it went, the bullet should have hit its mark.

Blink and I was back to normal sight. I looked down at my brand new jacket—and swore again.

There was a ragged hole in the tough blue fabric, and a gleam of silver behind it.

I reached inside the jacket and pulled out the stainless steel commuter mug I'd stashed there hours ago, in the interests of keeping my hands free.

Dented, oh momma. Ruined, without a doubt. But it had stopped the bullet cold, which is more than most people ask from their coffee mugs.

Dammit.

I put the mug on the walk beside me and pulled my cell out. A blow to the head isn't something to take lightly. No matter my personal feelings, I really ought to call Rescue so Miss Geniality could get—

Ice cold flame sparked against my power. I turned my head, right hand already rising in defense—and blinked.

Saving myself and the ruined metal mug, the boardwalk was

empty as far as I could see. Whoever had crafted my recent opponent's invincibility spell had also had the forethought to weave in a comehome. Her lack of motion must've triggered it.

Sighing, I flipped my phone closed, slid Mam'selle away, and rolled to my feet, coffee mug in hand. There was a trash can a few yards further on. I pitched the mug into it as I went past.

It was going on for ten when I pushed through Bob's front door and into the extended version of Edgar Winter's "Frankenstein." The place was deserted this late in the day—except for the man at the booth nearest the kitchen, his back to the door, faded yellow hair hanging in wind-tangles over his collar.

I poured myself a cup of coffee from the pot on the plate and carried it to the back booth.

Mr. Ignat' looked up and smiled, kind and vague as always, when I slid into the seat across from him.

"Good morning, Katie. How's my favorite black-hearted pirate?"

"A little rugged," I said, dosing my coffee liberally with creamer. "I had to open the sluice gate across Carson Creek so Heron Marsh maybe won't choke to death. The *trenvay* there's in pretty bad shape—you know her?"

"Him," Mr. Ignat' murmured, re-addressing the remains of the grilled muffin before him. "Eltenfleur is his name, and truly, Katie, he's always been a trifle mad."

"Well, he's plenty mad now, and with good reason." I had a cautious sip of my coffee, which was terrible, even by Bob's standards.

"Kate!" The man himself put his head through the hatch. "Want anything?"

"The grilled blueberry muffins are quite good. You should try one," Mr. Ignat' said, like he wasn't the one who'd gotten me addicted to the damn' things.

"Grilled blueberry with a side of bacon?" I asked Bob.

"Coming right out."

"So, anyhow," I said, tucking my hands around the mug and watching Mr. Ignat's genteel attack on his muffin, "I straightened out that problem. On the walk back to town, though, one of Joe Nemeier's henchthings shot me. Not only did she put a bullet hole in my brand new jacket, she ruined my favorite coffee mug."

"How aggravating," Mr. Ignat' said sympathetically. "I trust you spoke to her sternly."

"I knocked her out. I was going to call the Rescue for her, but what should she do but disappear."

He looked at me from under shaggy brows. "Disappear, Katie?"

"Right." I leaned forward, *jikinap* enhanced nerves quivering with the proximity of more of itself. "Just vanished into—thanks, Bob."

"No problem," he said, clattering plates and silverware onto the table. "Anything else?"

"I'm good."

He nodded and looked over to Mr. Ignat'. "'Nother muffin for you?" he asked, his voice over-clear and firm, like he was talking to a nine year old. "Maybe something with a little protein? Eggs?"

Mr. Ignat' gave him a beatific smile. "No, thank you."

"Suit yourself," Bob said, sounding cross, but looking worried. He glanced at me, hesitated—then turned and went back to the kitchen without saying anything else.

"The person who ruined your coffee mug just vanished?" Mr. Ignat' said.

I nodded, mouth full of muffin. He pushed his empty plate away and picked up his mug.

"Yeah," I said when I was able. "Seems there's somebody who's providing Joe Nemeier's happy crew with invincibility spells, and probably with don't-touch-mes, too. That would tie in to what Borgan said about nobody being able to lay hands on them."

"Borgan's a nice boy. I like him extremely. I'm glad you're getting to know him, Katie."

I sighed and ate a strip of bacon. Mr. Ignat' drank coffee. The mid-morning DJ on WBLM told everyone within the sound of his voice that the first caller who correctly named the Beatles' drummer before Ringo Starr would win two tickets to the August 18 Steve Miller concert at the Augusta Civic Center.

"Pete Best!" Bob yelled from the kitchen.

"So call in and claim the prize!" I yelled back.

His head popped through the hatch. "Kate, what'm I gonna do with two tickets to a concert in Augusta?" He vanished again before I could answer.

I drank coffee, put the mug down, and leaned across the table.

"Mr. Ignat', where did you get that whiskey you gave me?"

He looked up, pale eyes wide. "I told you, Katie. Bonny and I made it—oh, ages ago."

"Right, you did say that. When did you start drinking it, yourself?"

Shaggy brows pulled together. "I had a sip or two the other night, to keep you company. Bonny didn't mean for old Ignat' to be nipping the emergency rations. Very precise in such matters, is Bonny, as you know yourself."

"I do," I said, my voice suddenly hoarse. I cleared my throat. "I do know that. Mr. Ignat'..."

"Katie?"

I caught his eyes with mine. "Gran went across the World Wall to the Land of the Flowers," I said.

He blinked, and looked down at his mug.

"That's nice, Katie. Did she say when she's coming back?"

"She's overdue," I said quietly. "She expected to be back by Samhain, is how I read it. Nerazi thinks she maybe meant January first. It's a moot point, anyway, since she missed both."

He nodded, not looking at me. I took a deep breath.

"Two Seasons ago, an Ozali visited Gran at the carousel. The batwing horse saw him, and so did Nancy Vois. He wanted Gran to return something of his that's here, in Archers Beach. She refused." Another deep breath, and still he didn't raise his head. I wanted to grab his shoulders and make him look at me, but I didn't dare touch him, for fear my roused and ever-hungry power would cause me to do something terrible. "Mr. Ignat'—do you know who that Ozali was? Did Gran tell you?"

"I don't know who the Ozali was, Katie," he said quietly, and at long last raised his head. His eyes were bright with tears. "If Bonny ever told me, I've forgotten, my dear." He bit his lip, and looked aside. "I'm so very sorry, Katie," he whispered.

I swallowed, not easy with a lump the size of Rhode Island lodged in my throat.

"It's okay," I told him. "Mr. Ignat', listen. It's okay. Just—if you hear something inside your head, telling you—telling you weird, twisted stuff—don't listen to it, all right? I—you should probably see Nerazi and ask her—ask her to draw the poison for you. Promise me you'll do that. Tonight."

He tipped his head. "Will you be doing the same, Katie? Perhaps we should go together."

I opened my mouth—closed it.

"Not... No. I can't tonight. I've got to see somebody."

Mr. Ignat' nodded; lifted his mug, drained it, thumped it to the table, and reached for his hat.

"Wait—" I extended a hand—snatched it back. Mr. Ignat' paused, hat in hand, head tipped attentively to one side.

"I need a way to get hold of you," I said. "A cell phone number, or—"

"Just call me, child," he said, in a tone of quiet authority that I'd never heard from him before. He settled his hat at a rakish angle, and slid out of the booth. "Well, then, Pirate Kate! We two buccaneers best be getting topside, or it'll be a taste of the lash for us!"

I swallowed; but managed to bring up the canon response with just the right amount of faux terror. "Not the lash!"

"Better look lively, then," he advised me. "Now, who's paying for breakfast?"

I had almost finished lining up the sections of the portable safety fence when Nancy arrived.

"Summer Wheel's running," she said, stepping over and pulling the last section straight. "An' Dodge City's got a line down to the lobster toss."

I hooked the guard chain into the eyelet on the side of the control box.

"It's only eleven," I said.

"We're as ready as we're gonna be," she pointed out, as I straightened. Hands on hips, I spun on a heel, nodding at Nancy when I came back 'round again.

"You're right. What say we pull the walls back and see if anybody wants a ride?"

"Sounds like fun to me," she said, with a grin that displayed dainty sharp teeth.

"Masochist."

We opened to a midway as packed as any evening in high summer. The carousel looked good—no. It looked *great*. The brass shone under the lights, the animals glittered, the decking gleamed. The simple brave sight of it made me smile, and when I glanced over at Nancy she was grinning like a fool.

The "Liberty Bell March" boomed out of the orchestrion, and that quick we had a crowd. Blue-haired ladies in pastel exercise suits, bald gentlemen smelling of cigar smoke, determined blonds, couples, singles and groups of ten—they pressed tickets into my hands and mounted the deck, their faces glowing as they swung aboard their chosen mount, some laughing outright as the ride began to turn, the breeze running fond fingers through their hair. The march segued into the "Chit-Chat Polka," and the animals took flight...

A line formed, its various parts waiting patiently, relaxed, smiles on their faces, and not a few toes tapping. There was no pushing or shoving to mount when the first ride was done and the happy riders dismounted.

"A merry-go-round," murmured a plump lady in a lilac work-out set and sneakers so white they hurt my eyes. "God, it's been *years*..."

The Oriental Funhouse opened around 11:30; I could hear the giant samurai inviting passersby to tour the Emperor's Haunted Palace over the music from the orchestrion. Further away, I heard the rumble and roar out of Dodge City, and over it all the sound of voices, laughing, talking, yelling, laughing...

Around one, we had a break in commerce—not a person standing in line—and I waved Nancy over from her station in the pit.

"Everything's running fine," she said, a grin vibrating off her wire thin body. "Not a wobble nor a glitch."

"You do good work," I told her and meant it. "Look, how's your time today? I need to meet somebody up on the Pier at seven—be gone an hour—maybe two—I guess. Can you cover here? I can close the ride, if you can't."

"Jeezum, no!" Nancy was scandalized. "We can't close the ride during prime time! I tell you what, Kate—gimme off now. I'll come back at six-thirty and keep 'er open while you make your meeting."

I looked at her dubiously. "Couple hours," I said again.

She shook her head. "I'll feed Ma dinner before I come back, and set everything up the way she likes it. I can run the ride 'til closing, if your meeting runs late."

I chewed my lip.

"Okay," I told her. "If it'll work for you, it'll work for me. I hope not to be 'til ten, but—hold on." I reached into my pocket and pulled out the duplicate key. "In case you need to lock up—or unlock, for that matter."

She extended a hand, and paused, sending me a wise look from under the rim of her cap.

"Everything all under control now?"

"Said so, didn't I?"

"You did." She took the key and shoved it into her pocket. "I'll be back at six-thirty."

"Perfect." Over her shoulder, I saw a foursome detach itself from the crowded midway and walk toward the carousel.

"Customers on the way," I said, stepping back to the control station. "Thanks, Nancy."

"No problem." She took herself off, giving the approaching customers a friendly nod as they passed.

"Welcome to the Fantasy Menagerie Merry-go-Round," I said, when they offered me their tickets. "The oldest amusement ride in Archers Beach."

The foursome took themselves onto the carousel and chose their mounts—the ladies to the unicorn and the hippocampus; the gentlemen to the charger and the Indian pony. By the time they were settled, there were eight more in line, tickets to hand, and more coming in. People avoided the batwing horse, I noted. One man in a dark suit and owlish glasses did put a hand on its back and made as if to mount, then changed his mind and sat in the chariot instead.

I would, I thought, have to have a word with the batwing horse.

I uphold my side of the bargain, Keeper, the loathsome voice whispered between my ears. *Surely I am not to blame because some of your patrons are more discerning than others?*

"Try to look adorable, all right?" I muttered, as I hit the warning buzzer and started the carousel turning.

After that, the ride was busy all afternoon. At two, a miniature Lee, who gigglingly gave her name as Debbie, brought me a delicious-smelling bag and a large cup of coffee. I snacked on egg rolls and dumplings while the carousel described its circle.

"That smells *wonderful,*" the woman at the head of the line said. "Where can I get some?"

I swallowed and pointed across the midway. "Tony Lee's Chinese Kitchen, right across from here. There will probably be a line. Believe me, it's worth waiting."

"Thank you!" she said, and turned to talk to the folks behind her, all of them pointing in the general direction of Tony's—which was fine by me. If Tony and Anna were intent on making egg rolls while the sun shone, I was glad to steer more custom their way.

The ride glided to a stop. I hit the buzzer, and smiled at the woman heading the line.

"Ticket, please."

There were still people in line when Nancy showed up on the dot of six-thirty.

"How's it going?"

"I don't think I've ever sold this many hotcakes," I told her, rubbing the back of my neck and moving my shoulders to work the kinks out. "Ticket box is full or near enough. I'll take 'em down to the office and do the count."

Nancy shrugged and slipped between the fence into the control station. "Don't forget your meetin'," she cautioned.

"I won't," I promised, thinking that I'd have plenty of time to drop off the tickets and still make Neptune's at seven for my meeting with Borgan.

I knelt down and opened the ticket box. Four seconds, tops, to change out the full bag for the spare, then I closed the box and slid between sections of fence, taking the bag with me.

"See you soon," I said, and headed out.

TWENTY-SEVEN

Monday, April 24
High Tide 9:12 P.M.
Sunset 7:35 P.M. EDT

I should have figured out that I wasn't going to be the only one arriving at the office with a bumper crop of tickets. Of course, there was only Marilyn on at the desk—Fun Country not believing in over staffing—and of course her count didn't match Brand's and of course he insisted on a recount right *now*...

The upshot of the whole thing being that it was closer to seven-thirty than seven by the time I hit the entrance ramp to the Pier.

I probably should have foreseen that the Pier was going to be absolutely packed with tourists in their pretty polyester clothes, some wearing shorts and short-sleeved polo shirts in defiance of the brisk breeze off the water. Others had made a token concession to the April evening and donned windbreakers and khakis; still others had wrapped up like they were on an expedition to the North Pole.

All of them, though, were rubber-necking, strolling nice and slow like they were on vacation or something; stopping dead in the middle of the walkway to chat and point; and crossing from one side to the other as fancy took them.

The Pier had managed to get every shop, game, and food counter along its length open and manned. If some of those doing the manning were underage, overage, or just a wee bit tipsy, it detracted nothing from the sheer organizational guts it had taken to open on, as it were, a goddamn dime. True, the chalkboard outside the Chart House, at the head of the Pier, announced that they were serving only bottled beer, but it didn't seem to be slowing business down any. The tees and sweatshirts on offer at the Sandpiper Emporium were surely left over from last Season, but the little shop had a line out the door. Across the way, a guy selling potato guns had set up a target on a cord over the rail. *That* was good for a traffic jam, made up in equal parts of those who wanted to take the weapon for a test drive and those who wanted to watch.

With all of that, I didn't make very good time back to Neptune's Retreat, the all-purpose dive and live entertainment center at the far end of the Pier, where I'd been supposed to meet Borgan some time back. I considered giving him a buzz, to see if he'd given up on me, which was when I realized I'd left my cell in the pocket of my jacket, hanging from the back of the operator's stool behind the carousel control station.

Honestly, Kate, I scolded myself, much good it did me. *Well, at least Borgan'll be easy to spot.*

There was a small line at the entrance to Neptune's while each person was passed in by the bouncer, a whip-thin black guy in his mid-forties, dressed in biker's leathers, head shaved and oiled, profile perfect, if you didn't mind the slight leftward list to the nose, where it had gotten broken, back when he was a big kid and rolling his youngers for their lunch money. He'd been in his first year of high school and I'd been in seventh grade.

He was running the show for all it was worth.

"IDs, please, deahs," he said to the white-haired couple imme-diately ahead of me. The woman of the pair laughed, pulled a thin black folder out of her jacket pocket and flipped it open.

The bouncer glanced at it, at her face, and shook his head. "You don't get by me like that, missy!" he said, mock-stern. "Your momma know you got her license?"

She laughed again, delighted, and he waved her through before taking a look at her companion's ID and whistling conspiratorially.

"All right," he said, waving the old gentleman through. "But you treat her right now, man, or I'll be taking her away from you!"

The two of them disappeared into the open bar area, and the bouncer turned, his grin fading as he took me in.

"Hi, Domino," I said, calmly, to show that I was willing to let our pasts stay behind us.

He rolled his eyes, and threw a glance over my head at the people waiting behind. "Kate," he said, low-voiced and not particularly cordial. "Anything particular you want here?"

"I'm meeting a friend," I said, and pointed to the packed region at his back. "In there."

"That so?" For a second, I thought he wasn't going to let me by, and maybe he did, too. In the end, though, the need to make nice in front of the tourists carried the day. Or evening. Domino swung back from the gate with a flourish and a bogus grin.

"You don't find your friend, c'mon back and give me a chance!"

As if.

"Thanks." I slipped past before he had a change of heart, dodging into the wide space between the end of the bar and the supply closet. At my back was a motorcycle that I took to be Domino's, facing the ocean over the weathered wooden rail, its saddle bags rich with silver studs.

Standing on my toes, I scanned the crowd, looking for Borgan, and not having one bit of luck. Sighing, I stepped out of the cul-de-sac and mingled with the crowd heading for the serious action at the end of the Pier.

By the time I hit the dance floor, I'd lost most of my company to the seductions of microbrew bottles in tubs of ice, and fresh-made margaritas. Those who hadn't succumbed drifted past me, toward the building at the very end of the Pier—the Sea Change bar and casino. A pale, smoky reflection of the Sea King, the gambling house of the Beach's heyday; still, the few ratty one-armed bandits and tatty blackjack tables held an allure for some. I thought about it, but decided it wasn't likely that Borgan'd be in the casino. It was much more likely that he'd just given up on me and gone elsewhere to find some fun. Still, it wouldn't hurt to be sure, and I looked around me for a vantage point.

The open air dance floor at Neptune's Retreat is not for the faint of heart—or for those who had partaken liberally of the booze on offer. The only thing between the dancers and a dunk in the ocean is a rail made out of a pair of two by fours. Every Season, one or two dancers go over the side in a fit of exuberance and have to be fished out. Back in my day, Neptune's always had a couple staff members trained as life guards on duty, open to close, during the Season.

The stage was empty—Neptune's was depending on piped-in music for this evening's crowd. Nobody seemed to mind; most seemed so intent on their own conversations I was willing to bet they hadn't even noticed that there was music playing. That being the case, it wasn't likely that anybody would notice—or mind—if I took advantage of an extra two feet above the decking to try and spy out—

"Beer, pretty lady?"

I turned. Borgan smiled and offered a bottle, still dripping from the tub, label out: Shipyard Brown Ale. Not precisely beer, but I wasn't about to quibble. I took the bottle with a nod, and a purely ridiculous surge of relief, that I hadn't missed him after all.

"Thanks. Sorry I'm late."

"I did start to think you'd stood me up," he said, twisting the cap off a bottle of Bluefin Stout. "Want me to open that for you?"

"Please." We traded bottles, he did the honors and we traded back, each taking a sip, while the tourists eddied around us.

"Time got away from me," I said. "Every one of our pre-Season guests wanted a ride on the carousel, and some wanted multiple rides. I thought I had plenty of time to take the tickets down to Marilyn—except every other ride in the park had extra tickets in, too."

He nodded and had a swig of ale, which looked like such a good idea that I did the same, savoring the chocolate-y smoothness.

"I did talk to Nerazi," he said. "Told her about your notion that your gran'd gone over the Wall. She didn't say it was impossible, given the stakes, but she was pretty sure Bonny'd have rigged a safety line—something to draw her back, if she was gone too long."

I nodded. "I thought about that, too. And I think she probably counted on her tree to ground her. The trouble is that there's . . . not a good interface between us and the Land of the Flowers. There's so much change here, it affects everything, even magic. That's why we have to keep renewing the damn' bindings on the carousel; change keeps unraveling the spellwork." I took a swallow of my ale. Borgan was watching me with every indication of interest.

"In the Land of the Flowers," I continued, "there's hardly any change at all, and there's magic in everything—like sand in a gear shaft . . ." I drank some more ale, frustrated by the impossibility of explaining exactly how . . . *strange* the Land of the Flowers was.

"So you're saying that your gran might not be able to find her

'way back across the Wall, even with her tree for an anchor?"
Borgan asked.

I sighed. "I think so. I remember my mother saying that when
she first came to the Land of the Flowers, she couldn't locate
north, which she'd always been able to do at home. And then
she found out it was because, in the Land of the Flowers, there
is no north. No south—no directions at all like we understand
direction here. Even if Gran's still in touch with her tree—if the
bond survived her crossing the Wall—she might not be able to
parse the *direction* of home."

Borgan shook his head. "I don't like to say this, Kate, but—
your gran's *trenvay*, and she's been gone off her land for a good
long time now..."

"You're thinking she's dead. But, see, you're not taking into
account the fact that time runs different in the Land of the Flowers. Over there, she might only've been gone since Wednesday."

Borgan closed his eyes.

I grinned in sympathy. "Yeah. It makes my head hurt, too."

"It does go a good way to explaining why such folks as I've
met from Flowerland have been so damn' high-handed."

"No," I said. "They're high-handed because they're from the
Land of the Flowers and you're not. The Changing Land... isn't
held in very high esteem across the Wall. We're kinda the slum
of the Six Worlds."

"That so?"

"Hey, don't take it personal." I drank some more ale, noting
with something like relief that the bottle was almost empty. No
magic brew here, anyway. Which reminded me.

"Borgan—what you said about not being able to lay a hand
on Joe Nemeier's people?"

He looked down into my face, black eyes ironic. "You about
to tell me you had another run-in with the man?"

"No, with another one of his hired-ons. But, listen! I threw
a fire-bolt at her and it bounced. So after I knocked her out, I
stepped Sideways and had a good, close look. She was wearing
an invulnerability spell." I looked at him expectantly.

Borgan didn't say anything, which was disappointing; I thought
he was quicker than that.

I sighed and laid out the pieces for him. "It looks like there's
an Ozali with an interest in Joe Nemeier's business."

"That's what it looks like," he agreed. He took a swig out of his bottle, sighed, and made a long arm, setting the empty down on the corner of the stage. "Kate, if those folks're wearing magic grease and that's why we can't touch 'em, how come you've touched two?"

I stared at him, mouth hanging open like my jaw hinge had broken. Borgan waited. I closed my mouth, opened it, closed, and finally said, "Good question."

"That mean you don't know?"

"Give me a minute. I'm sure there's a perfectly—"

Jikinap sparked along my nerves. Lots of it. And close.

"Kate?"

I looked around—and saw exactly nothing out of the ordinary, of course.

"Somebody just triggered a pretty potent working," I told Borgan. "I can't see it unless I step Sideways, and I don't—"

"Oh," Borgan said softly, "fuck."

I blinked up at him. "Don't you think we should date first?"

"Hey!" a voice came out of the crowd. "Hey, Indian!"

He sighed, took the bottle out of my hand, and put it next to his on the edge of the stage.

"This could get messy. You do what I tell you, Kate, hear it?"

"Oh, yes *sir*, mister—" I closed my mouth in mid-snarl as two T-shirted guys in their twenties eeled their ways through the crowd by the bar.

"We can't touch them," Borgan said quietly. "That don't mean they can't touch us."

He put his hand under my elbow, turning me into the crowd at our left, but not before I'd seen two more T-shirts moving purposefully in our direction. One of them was worn by a thin woman with flyaway blond hair. She was frowning, like maybe her head hurt.

The pressure on my elbow changed, and I moved with it, obediently, shaking as the power rose in my blood, lusting after more of itself.

"This way, I think..." Borgan murmured.

But "this way" was blocked, too, and I glimpsed yet another familiar face when we tried to angle toward the Sea Change.

All around us, hundreds of tourists remained oblivious of our close personal danger—chatting, drinking, taking in the fresh salt air along with the smell of popcorn. Maybe they thought we were all actors, paid to provide a little authentic Maine color.

Or maybe, I thought, beginning to get a clue as my blood heated dangerously, they were under the influence of *jikinap*.

I turned my attention back to our current problem, and counted six of Nemeier's finest; between them they'd cut us off from all the exits.

The boy whose knife was snug against my backbone stepped forward, pushing people out of his way with a hard hand. They moved without turning their heads, their conversations uninterrupted, the boy and his crew obviously invisible to their eyes. Invisibility spell, then—or maybe not. *We* weren't invisible. Were we? And there was damnall I could do about any of it; I had to *see* the spell to counteract—supposing that I could. And in the meantime there was the very visible trouble already moving in our direction, feral eyes bright, making no effort to conceal their weapons.

We dropped back, matching step for step, the tourists moving, unseeing, out of our way. Borgan took his hand off my elbow and stepped in front of me.

The leader stopped and smiled. "Well, now. Two for the price of one." He turned his head. "That's the bitchy witchy Mr. Nemeier wants to talk to, Jimmy," he said to the man on his right, a short, rat-faced guy wearing a leather vest and tattoos. "We'll take care of the Indian. You make sure she stays right there until we're ready to take her home."

The rat-faced guy grinned and stepped forward, and the land, which had been silent ever since I'd hit the Pier, helpfully offered a collage of sensation—edges and explosions being foremost among them. And all around the tourists talked among themselves, entirely uncurious in the face of imminent mayhem, blood and broken bones.

"Run," Borgan muttered, for my ears alone. "Now."

Some times, you just don't argue.

I turned and sprinted, getting a crazy two-sided visual as the land showed Jimmy jumping after me, Borgan throwing a table, the others surging forward—and *still* the tourists paid not one scrap of attention.

Tourists to the left of me, tourists to the right of me; the rail and the ocean ahead. I swerved, more willing to take my chances with the crowd than the sea, felt a bite in my left shoulder. I skidded on beer dampened planks right before the freight train slammed into me, and I pitched over the rail, a strong arm around my waist.

"Deep breath," Borgan said into my ear.

I dragged air down into the bottom of my lungs, saw heaving green water lacy with foam rushing up—

We hit like a cannonball, plunging deep. The water bubbled and hissed, sand and weed obscuring everything, Borgan writhed, the support of his arm abruptly gone, leaving me to tumble for an ageless moment, until a long, sleek body bore up from below, and I flung my arms about it, lungs burning as we broke water, and I gasped for air, flinging the soggy mass of my hair out of my eyes.

We were not, as I had supposed we would be, heading out, toward the islands. Instead, Borgan was swimming strongly for shore, and there were—things, pellets, like hail, striking the surface of the water around us.

"Go *out*! They're shooting at you!" I yelled, but I might've been riding an ordinary harbor seal for all the attention he spared me.

Right into the surf line he swam, caught a wave and rode it to the water's edge. I rolled free, came to my knees and hurled myself Sideways.

A glassy green blob pulsated above the Pier, its structure something like a willie wisp, but instead of sucking *in* memory, it was spinning *out* illusion.

There was no time for finesse. I threw power against power, spending recklessly, not caring if the effort drained me dry. The blob shredded under my attack, and I fell back into the real world.

A line of bewildered faces peered over the edge of the Pier, while bullets continued to sheer through the water, and Borgan was out there, somewhere—

"Seal!" I screamed, dragging power out of the land to be heard above the music and the racket of the surf. "They're shooting at a seal!"

"What!" I heard one of the women yell. "Shooting a—Henry! Those men are shooting at a seal!"

There was movement on the Pier, the bullets stopping abruptly as I craned for a glimpse, a sign—

And saw a seal roll in the green water at the far end of the Pier, under the Sea Change. Heading for the islands.

Finally.

I closed my eyes in relief, then got clumsily to my feet. I was feeling a little lightheaded, which was probably just the adrenaline. Best thing to do would be—

I heard a clatter on the Pier's security stairs and turned my head just in time to see Domino jump the last four steps and race across the wet sand to me, blanket under one arm.

"*Jesus*, Kate! What the *hell* were you trying to pull? You coulda—"

"There're guys up there shooting at a seal!" I yelled back at him. "You need to call the cops!"

He shook his gleaming head. "There're at least three retired cops up there partying. They took care of the situation real slick, and then stood by to protect the suspects from the old ladies who wanted to rip them arm from leg for shooting at 'the dear thing.' Kirsten radioed the cops and they—"

Sirens wailed right on cue—two sets, from the sound of it; one coming down Grand, and the other right out of the cop shop at the top of the hill.

"Right," I said and sighed, shaking my hair back from my face. A third siren tore the air, singing the distinctive song of an ambulance.

I sent a quick glance at Domino. "Somebody get hurt?"

He rolled his eyes. "Woman jumps off the Pier into the ocean to get between bullets and a seal, you think they're gonna send the Rescue down? Just in case?"

I sighed. "I'm fine."

"Sure you are," Domino said. "That's why there's blood leaking out of that hole in your shoulder."

"Hole in—" I raised my hand, touched my left shoulder experimentally. "Ow."

"Ow, she says." He shook out the blanket and draped it around me. "Just take it easy and wait for the Rescue, okay?"

"Okay," I said, suddenly and completely exhausted. I cuddled the blanket to me with one hand, took a step toward the stairs—and pitched face-first into the sand.

TWENTY-EIGHT

Monday, April 24
Southern Maine Medical Center
13 Industrial Park Road
Saco, Maine

The name on the trooper's badge was "C. Poulin" and she was as serious and respectful a law enforcement officer as you could wish for. Not that I *had* wished for her, well-behaved as she was, but apparently when you get shot, a law enforcement officer is what the state of Maine sends by way of a get well present.

"Ms. Archer, did you know the men who were shooting at you?"

We'd already been through the easy questions—name, age, address, employment—and now we were getting to the meat of the matter. I shifted irritably beneath the thin hospital blanket, which made my arm hurt, despite the copious amounts of painkiller I'd been given prior to the doctor digging the bullet out.

"I had a run-in with one of them a couple days ago," I said. "I don't know his name, but he told me he works for Joe Nemeier, who has a house up on Heath Hill, next to the woods."

C. Poulin nodded and made a note. "Now, Ms. Archer, can you tell me the circumstances of your previous meeting with this person?"

The painkillers were making it hard to track. I took a second to work out which "this person" we were talking about, and shifted again. It was too quiet in the curtained off cubicle; I couldn't feel the land, couldn't be sure if the ripples of color at the edges of things were the results of the shock and the drugs, or if the place was dangerously steeped in *jikinap*.

"Ms. Archer?"

I sighed. "Sorry 'bout that. The man I recognized had contacted me previously to register a complaint his employer thought he had with me."

"That would be Mr. Joe Nemeier?" C. Poulin asked, pen poised over her pad.

"Right."

"I see. And the nature of the complaint that Mr. Nemeier... thought he had with you?"

"He's under the impression that I poisoned his grass," I murmured, watching with a sort of detached horror as the privacy curtain shimmered prismatically. That much wild energy on the prowl, *hungry,* like *jikinap* is always hungry...

"Did you?" asked C. Poulin.

With an effort, I pulled my eyes away from the curtains and the fluctuating energy states. "I'm sorry, lost track. Did I what?"

"Did you poison Joe Nemeier's lawn?"

"Not necessarily. Or only sort of." *That* hadn't come out right, at all. I moved my head irritably on the flat pillow. "My lawyer was going to talk to his lawyer."

"I see. And your lawyer is?"

At least that was easy to answer. "Henry Emerson on Grand Avenue in Archers Beach."

Another note, and another question. "Ms. Archer, would you be able to identify the man you say you recognized from a photograph?"

"Sure," I said, and she nodded, made a note, then flipped the pad closed.

She stood up and looked down at me pensively while she stowed the pad and her pen.

"I may need to talk with you again, Ms. Archer. In the meantime, I hope you understand that what you did—jumping into the ocean in order to save a harbor seal—while brave, was also very foolish and dangerous. You might easily have been hurt far worse than you were, while the seal escaped any injury. It's not particularly easy to hit a moving target—and even less easy when the target's medium is also moving. Bullets ricochetting off the water and striking bystanders, however..."

She let it drift off. I shifted again beneath the blanket, and thought about losing my temper, but I was too tired.

"I understand," I said mildly. "It was an impulse. I really do know better."

She nodded, settled her hat, and ducked through that horrifying curtain, releasing neither lightning bolts nor other killing rays. I began to form the hypothesis that the prismatics were an artifact of the painkillers, but the nurse arrived before I'd gone very far down that road, rustling importantly.

"The doctor will be here in a few minutes. After he talks to you, you'll be free to go home. Is there someone here to drive you or would you like us to call a taxi?"

"I'll be taking her home," a deep voice said. The curtain twitched aside and Borgan stepped into the cubicle—black jeans, black boots, black crew neck sweater, hands tucked comfortably in the pockets of his jacket.

"Hi, Kate," he said cordially. "You look like hell."

"And who are you?" the nurse snapped. He shifted his gaze to her.

"Andre Borgan. I'm a friend of Ms. Archer's. I came to give her a ride home, like I said."

"That's right," I said to her questioning glance. She sniffed and departed, and I gave Borgan what I fully intended to be a smile.

"It's good to see you," I said, which was nothing but the unvarnished truth. He shook his head, eyes serious, and sat down in the chair lately occupied by C. Poulin.

"How long're we supposed to wait for this doctor?"

"I don't—"

"Not long at all!" The overly-cheerful voice of my emergency physician announced. He pushed the curtain back with a flourish and stepped inside the cubicle, lab coat flapping. "It's official," he told me. "The hole in your arm was caused by a bullet."

I blinked at him. "Imagine."

He shook his head, pulled two pieces of paper from his clipboard and brandished them under my nose. "Prescriptions. One for painkillers. One for antibiotics." A third piece of paper came off the clipboard and was duly brandished. "A list of terrifying possible symptoms and side effects, and if you display *any* of them, even the teensiest little bit, I want you back in this emergency room *pronto*. Copy that?" He gave me a stern stare, then turned his head to give Borgan a stern stare, too.

He nodded, extended a long arm and twitched the papers out of the doctor's hand. "I'll make sure she does what's needful."

"Good." The doctor turned to go, then turned back. "One other thing you might find interesting, Ms. Archer."

I paused in the act of pushing the blanket back and blinked up at him.

"What's that?"

"That bullet we dug out of your arm at great personal pain to yourself?" he said.

"Yah?" I agreed warily.

He gave me an owlish look.

"It's silver."

"The sea," Borgan said conversationally, while we waited for the red light at the end of Industrial Park Road to go green, "will eat them."

The painkillers were still fogging up my brain, which was working hard to accommodate the fact that Borgan owned a red GMC pickup that was waxed to an inch of its life. The leather passenger seat cuddled me like we were very good friends, and I had a feeling that I'd nodded off for a second there. I shook my head and sat up straight.

"Would that give the sea indigestion?" I asked. "Remember there's an Ozali in the soup."

Borgan flicked an unreadable black glance at me, eased the truck into gear and turned onto Route 1.

"I know you said the woman this morning was wearing a nice, custom-fitted spellcoat, but do we know that it just isn't her?"

"You said none of the *trenvay* can touch any of Nemeier's crew," I reminded him. "Also? You wonder why nobody on the Pier cared that we were about to get shot, stabbed, and stomped on? Big, fat illusion generator right over top. I went Sideways after you dumped me on the beach and got a real good look at it."

"Hmm. What happened to it, by the way?"

I sighed muzzily and leaned my head against the back of the seat. "I ripped it up. Shoulda taken time to study it, but I had to hurry before one of 'em got lucky and shot you."

Borgan steered the truck casually into the night, quiet coming off him so forcibly it was almost a weapon. I closed my eyes and let the upholstery have its way with me.

"Non-resident magery used in the service of mischief and spite," Borgan said eventually, his voice very soft. "Would that be in violation of that Law the Wise like so much?"

"Yeah," I murmured, not bothering to open my eyes. "Oh, baby, is it ever in violation." I sighed.

Borgan didn't say anything. Quiet filled up the cab and settled inside my ears like cotton wool. It was 'way, 'way too quiet—and suddenly not quiet at all, as the land whooped into my consciousness like an exuberant six year old; vitality flowed through me, and I sat up, biting my lip when the wounded arm complained.

"Take it easy," Borgan murmured, his eyes on the road. "A gunshot doesn't heal all at once."

"At least it was a silver bullet," I said, and shook my head. "Honestly. Do I look like a werewolf to you?"

He gave me a considering glance. "Might be the eyes."

"Thanks."

Borgan smiled, and pressed the brake for the stop sign at the top of Archer Avenue.

"Where's good?" he asked.

I waved my right hand sloppily, meaning to indicate the whole of town. "Anyplace'll do."

He nodded. The headlights scraped vacant storefronts as we turned onto Archer Avenue, and then the dark windows of houses as he took the left onto Seavey and pulled in front of the old Archer homestead. He put the truck into park, and turned the key.

I released the seatbelt, and reached for the door handle. "Thanks for the ride."

"Welcome," he said, unsnapping his seatbelt and popping the door. "Wait 'til I'm around there."

"I'm fine," I said, but he'd already closed his door. I sighed sharply, and pulled up on the handle. *Honestly,* I thought crabbily, *you'd think I was an invalid. I'm perfectly fine now that . . .*

Maybe I swung out a little too energetically. Despite that my feet were on the land, my head went light, my eyesight went drifty, my knees turned to rubber, and—

"Do you *ever* do anything sensible?" Borgan asked, swinging me up against his chest.

I put my head on his shoulder and closed my eyes. "I'm fine," I said again, but I didn't even sound convincing to myself. Borgan didn't bother to answer. He carried me into the park and settled me on the rickety bench.

"Now, *stay there*. I'll be back in a sec."

Nice and obedient, I sat on the bench, the land singing hosannas all around town. I was too tired to enforce quiet, and besides, it was sorta comforting.

I looked down the hill. Fun Country's big sign was lit up, and the fence, but the rides were dark and quiet, which meant—

"It's after ten?" I asked Borgan, who was spreading a blanket on the grass near the sundial.

"Little past midnight," he said, coming over to the bench. "Sit with me, eh? We can tell each other stories."

I looked up at him, a big-shouldered silhouette against a spangled sky. "You don't have to stay with me."

"That's right. I don't. You walking or am I carrying you?"

There was a certain temptation to being carried, but a woman has her pride.

"Walk," I said firmly.

"Good enough." He held out a hand. I took it, not too proud to accept help getting up. As soon as our fingers touched, the land quieted, though I could still feel its joy at my return quivering at the back of my head.

I made it over to the blanket without falling on my nose, though I was shivering and soaked with sweat by the time I had gotten myself seated. Borgan shook out another blanket and draped it over my lap, then dropped down lightly beside me.

"You're going to miss the tide," I said, muzzy again. *I should*, I thought, *raise a little bit of power and burn the damn' painkillers out of my system*. The only problem being that I felt like I didn't have a real good handle on "little bit."

"Finn's fishing for me," Borgan said, and lay down on his back, arms under his head. "Pretty night."

"'Morning," I said, just to be contrary, and he laughed quietly.

"'Mornin' to you, too. Who tells the first story?"

I shook my head, looking down the hill at the dark town. "I don't know any stories."

"Woman as gifted with a tale as you are? I don't believe that."

I closed my eyes. "Hey, listen—I figured out how come the tourists could grab onto Joe Nemeier's little crew of merrymakers when the *trenvay* can't."

"How's that?"

I half turned toward him, leaning on my uninjured hand. "The spells're built to repel magic—like that lightning bolt bouncing off my girl this morning."

"Hmm. And why would that make it so I can't touch 'em?"

"Because you're a supernatural being," I said impatiently, "and so's Nerazi and Gaby and Bob and—"

"I take your point," he interrupted, turning his head to look at me. "It's a nice theory, Kate, but it doesn't explain why you don't have any trouble grabbing onto these boys and girls."

I blinked at him. "How do you mean?"

Silence for the beat of three. "Aren't *you* a supernatural being?" he asked.

I sighed, exhausted again, and lay down facing him, my good arm crooked under my head. "I don't know what I am."

"Well." Borgan turned onto his side, head propped on his hand. "Tell me how you came here from your grandad's place."

"Trust me, you don't want to hear that story."

"Actually, I do." He grinned at me. "After all, it's got a happy ending."

TWENTY-NINE

$\smile$

Tuesday, April 25
Low Tide 3:17 A.M.
Moonrise 3:32 A.M. EDT, Waning Crescent

"My mother sold her soul to the Ozali Ramendysis," I said slowly. "The price was—me. I was to be put into the care of the Ozali Zephyr, who'd been my father's friend. Zephyr was supposed to take me to my grandmother in the Changing Land."

Borgan made a soft sound of interest, his eyes on mine. It seemed like he was drawing the story out of me, word by word... but that was probably only the painkillers.

"Ramendysis was a—a great Ozali. He'd been a hero, my grandfather told me, in the war against Daknowyth, and had just oodles of *jikinap*. The problem is that controlling lots of *jikinap* means that you want to control more, so Ramendysis began to challenge other Ozali to duels. He'd win—he always won—and his opponent's power would be added to his..." My voice faded out.

"Which only made him want more," Borgan said softly.

"Right." I cleared my throat. "Came a time when he had so much, he started absorbing whole households. Aeronymous—my grandfather—our House was strong, and our people were rich in power. But Ramendysis broke us like a twig, and he killed everybody, drank their power... everybody... except my mother. And me."

209

I closed my eyes, breaking the contact with Borgan, but the story had its own momentum now, and I knew I couldn't stop.

"Me—I was a toy. He liked to...to subsume my will—but not all the way. No fun in that. He'd let me stay aware, just enough so I could try to fight him while he walked me up to the top of the watchtower. He'd let me think I'd won for a second before he made me jump. He liked the taste of terror, I guess..."

And later, I added silently, he had liked my passionate hope that this time he *would* let me fall and shatter against the rocks at the tower's base. He'd especially liked my self-disgust when he used me to masturbate...

"He didn't really care about me, except as a hold on my mother. My power was...less than insignificant, my *voysin*...uninteresting— being quarter-bred, you see. No, my mother was his prey; he wanted her—her *voysin* and her soul. But he wanted her to give it willingly...."

My voice ran out again. I took a deep breath, seeing the couch, seeing my hands part his robes, caressing him; feeling my body move itself over him; hating myself, hating what I was doing, while he looked into my eyes—and smiled.

"So," Borgan prodded gently, "your mother finally gave him what he wanted?"

I cleared my throat. "A trade, like I said. Her soul, freely given, for my freedom and Zephyr's escort to my grandmother.

"Ramendysis agreed to the terms, and had Zephyr fetched. But he didn't go so far as to actually let us go. We were his *guests,* see, and subject to his...hospitality.

"Finally, Zephyr took...desperate measures. She bribed a guard—bribed him with a gift of her own *jikinap.* We saddled our horses..."

Cold fingers fumbling the straps, and Zephyr's voice hissing out of the darkness, "Quickly, as you love your life! Follow me close, young Kaederon, and whatever happens, keep your seat."

"We rode cross-country," I told Borgan. "It—I'd never ridden like that before. We were at the edge of the country Ramendysis claimed for his own, when a rider—came out of the trees. She let Zephyr go by—and...He'd sent her—my mother, or what was left of her. To destroy me."

I closed my eyes, memory too vivid for words.

"She didn't do it," Borgan said softly. "I'm guessing."

I swallowed, seeing the power swirling between her hands...

"She...I screamed. Not even a Word. How could I? But she—she raised her hand, and the bolt went into the sky, and Sinbar—she let us past..."

I was shaking, chest cramped, my hand fisted under my head...

Borgan put his palm against my cheek. Warmth flowed through me, gracious as the incoming tide; the shaking eased and the pain in my chest faded. I sighed and stared down the rest of my memory.

The road wound out before us. I was flat on Sinbar's neck, as we ran, shoulder to shoulder with Zephyr's wind-footed steed. Behind—not far behind—the Great Hounds bayed. Ramendysis had a backup plan, of course: Hounds, and with them, hunters, armed with elfshot.

A black arrow hissed past my ear, and I ducked to one side, using Sinbar's neck as a living shield. Ahead of us, the Gate shimmered, the Keeper leaping to her post.

More elfshot rained around us. I felt a burning agony in my back...

"Hold on!" Zephyr screamed, as my fingers slipped on the reins. "Kaederon! Hold on!"

Hold on I did, though to this day I don't know how, and we thundered past the gawping Keeper, our horses leaping—up, into the Gate, over and—

...out into Fun Country.

"We outran them," I told Borgan shakily. "Just barely outran them. Zephyr delivered me and the news to Gran. I was elfshot, and even Gran says she doesn't know why I didn't die of it. Sinbar..." I swallowed. "Zephyr went back to the Land of the Flowers. I always wondered what happened to her."

I took a deep breath, and another one, and opened my eyes.

"Happy now?" I asked.

"Happy?" Borgan sighed. "That's a strong story, Kate. It needs a strong woman to bear it."

Borgan got up and went over to the truck. I stayed huddled beneath my blanket, listening to the contented murmur of the land.

"Water?" His voice was hardly any louder than the land's. I opened my eyes and sat up, clumsy because of my arm, which still hurt, dammit, and took the offered bottle.

"Thanks."

"No problem at all." He sat down next to me and had a swig from his own bottle. "What happened to him?" he asked. "Ramendysis?"

I shrugged. "I hope to God his head exploded. He was overdue."

"Hmm."

We drank our water in companionable silence. I looked down the hill, to the ocean, moving lazily under the stars.

Borgan finished his bottle and lay down on his back again, right arm crossed under his head.

"Beautiful morning," he said, softly.

"It is," I agreed. I finished my water, and put the empty bottle on the blanket near my ankle.

"So," I said, still looking down over the ocean. "Your turn for a story."

"It is, isn't it?" he said placidly, and then didn't say anything else for such a long time that I thought he'd gone to sleep.

I was just about ready to curl up and try the sleep thing myself, when I heard the sound of a deep, deliberate breath.

"I come to this place," Borgan said, quiet and slow. I turned and looked down at him, braced on my right arm.

"I come to this place and I see a thing. What is this thing that I see?" He paused, as if peering beyond the stars. "Ah." He sighed. "I'll tell you.

"Jikinap, the First Person, is making Worlds. He's making Cheobaug, the Land of Wave and Water. He's making Daknowyth, the Midnight Land. He's making the Land of the Flowers, Sempeki. He's using all of his power, and Five Worlds are what he makes. He tries to make a Sixth World, but his power is almost all used up."

I took a careful breath, listening to the ritual cadence, watching the still side of his face.

"It's hard work, making Worlds," Borgan told the stars, "and Jikinap's tired. He lies down to sleep in the Place Between the Worlds. When he wakes, there's a man sleeping beside him.

"'Wake up,' says Jikinap, 'and tell me your name.'

"The man wakes. He sits up and he says, 'My name's Glooskap. Glooskap, the Changer.'"

Power moved on the star-breeze, pebbling my skin. I don't dare move, though, for fear of interrupting the story, or the teller.

"Jikinap looks deep inside this Person," Borgan continued. "He looks deep inside this Glooskap, and sees that he carries the seeds of the Sixth World in his belly. Seeds only, because Jikinap's power is almost used up. He didn't have enough power to make the last World, the Sixth World. He only had enough power to make a man.

"'Well,' he says to Glooskap. 'You were supposed to have been a World, to balance out the other Five. But my power's almost gone, so you'll have to make the Sixth World yourself.'

"'All right,' says Glooskap, and a hot wind blows through the Place Between the Worlds, blows right through that place. The wind blows Jikinap away, and scatters what's left of his power through the Five Worlds.

"'Well,' says Glooskap, and he stands up. He's sorry Jikinap is gone, because he's got some questions to ask. But he guesses he'll have to do the best he can.

"First, he looks inside himself. He sees the seeds of the world there, the Sixth World that Jikinap didn't make. The world he has to make himself.

"Then, he looks outside himself. He sees the Five Worlds that Jikinap made, all different.

"Glooskap says to himself, 'To make a world is a very big thing. I'll need world-stuff to work with. But where will I find it? Jikinap's power was all used up, and my only power is Change.'

"Glooskap thinks, and he looks again at those Five Worlds that Jikinap made. Rich worlds they are, and wide. And Glooskap thinks he knows where to get the world-stuff he needs to make the sixth.

"The worlds Jikinap made are big. There are people there. But those worlds are so big Glooskap thinks that the people won't miss a little corner out of each.

"So Glooskap calls out. He calls out for the Wind That Goes Between the Worlds.

"'What do you want?' asks the Wind.

"'I want you to take me on your back. I want you to blow through each of the Five Worlds,' Glooskap says.

"'If you can keep your seat, I'll take you,' says the Wind. 'But if you fall off, don't expect me to stop for you.'

"'All right,' says Glooskap, and he mounts that Wind. He has a firm hold of it with his left hand, and in his right hand is his knife."

I eased closer to Borgan across the blanket, and looked down into his face. His eyes were closed, his breathing soft and regular, like he really was asleep.

"That Wind," he said, taking up his story, "that Wind Between the Worlds, it blows. It blows fast and it blows in all directions at once. Glooskap hangs on with his left hand and with his right hand he uses his knife, and he slices a piece from the Five Worlds that Jikinap made, the same size slice from each.

"Then the Wind blows back through the Place Between the Worlds.

"'Stop!' Glooskap yells, but that Wind, it keeps on blowing. It won't stop. That Wind, it carries the stars on its back. It blows between the Five Worlds that Jikinap made. It won't stop for Glooskap.

"So, Glooskap lets go of the Wind with his left hand, and he falls. He falls a long way, and the knife jumps out of his hand. Still, he falls, until he falls all the way back to the Place Between the Worlds.

"Then Glooskap looks at the world-stuff he gathered, and he looks at the seeds of the Sixth World in his belly. He sees how the worlds that Jikinap made are all different, and he knows that the Sixth World will be different from them all. He thinks. Then he takes those cut-off pieces of the Five Worlds, he rolls them up and he pops them into his mouth.

"He chews, and chews, and chews, until those world pieces are all mixed up together. Then he spits out the wad of mixed up world-stuff, and he spits the seeds of the Sixth World into it.

"And then he waits.

"The seeds begin to grow, nourished by the world-stuff Glooskap stole. Those seeds grow, and grow, until they become this place here. This place where we live.

"This place, our place, is made, not as Jikinap had intended to make it, but by a Person whose only Power is Change. That Power is in the land. That Power is in every plant and every animal. It's in every stone and every person. That Power is in the sea. It makes us what we are. It makes us different from the people of Cheobaug, and the people of Daknowyth. It makes us different from the people of Sempeki. We are the Children of the Changer.

"Each of us is Change. Each of us *can* Change.

"That is our power."

Silence.

Carefully, I reached out and put my hand against his cheek. His chest moved with a deeper breath; he opened his eyes, and smiled at me.

My heart expanded, aching with joy, and I didn't care one jot if it was glamor or if it was not.

"Was that a good story, then?" he asked.

I moved, curling next to him and putting my head on his shoulder. The land heaved a huge sigh, like a dog settling down by the hearth.

"It was a good story," I said and sighed, the land content inside my head. "Thank you."

"Welcome." He shifted slightly. His arm came 'round my waist, and he put his cheek against my hair.

I closed my eyes, listening to the steady drum of his heart.

"'Night, Kate," he said, the words rumbling against my ear.

Eyes closed, I smiled. "Good night, Borgan."

THIRTY

Tuesday, April 25
High Tide 9:36 A.M.
Sunrise 5:43 A.M. EDT

"Kate." My left ear heard it soft-voiced; my right ear heard it as a rumble. I sighed, not willing to give up the feeling of warm and sleepy well-being, and snuggled closer against his chest.

"Kate." A little louder, and accompanied by a touch as light as moth wings at the corner of my eye.

I sighed again, with resignation this time, and said, "What?" without opening my eyes.

"How d'you feel?"

"Are you seriously waking me up to find out how I feel?"

"No," Borgan said, and I felt amusement ripple through him. "I'm waking you up because dawn's nigh and we don't want to risk some early riser calling the cops on the two vagrants asleep in the park."

"Oh," I said. With an effort, I uncurled, and twisted clumsily into a sitting position; opening my eyes to a sky so light that all but the hardiest stars had already faded. "Damn."

Next to me, Borgan sat up. "How d'you feel?" he asked again.

In fact, I felt... "Good," I said positively.

I raised my left arm experimentally, fingers pointing toward the pale stars. "Better than good."

217

"Then it's time for me to take you down to the house," he said. He rose effortlessly, and held a hand down to me. I didn't need the help, but I took it anyway.

We gathered up the blankets and carried them to the truck, stowing them in the box in the back. Then I got in the passenger's side and he got in the driver's side. We strapped in, he turned the key in the ignition and we pulled away from the curb, heading down Seavey Street, to Elm, up Grand to Dube, and so to Tupelo House.

I released the seatbelt, reached for the door—and stopped, turning in my seat to face him.

He looked at me, eyebrows up, black eyes noncommittal.

"The land likes you," I said, slowly.

Borgan's face got still.

"That's right," he said, carefully. "Me and the land, we go 'way back."

I nodded. Selkies can live a long time; many times the life span of a normal seal.

"Thank you," I said. "I can't remember the last time I slept so well." A smile pulled at the side of my mouth. "Or had such a good story."

"We'll do it again sometime," he said. "In the meanwhile, it's time for breakfast—yours and mine. I'm going to be talking over last night with Nerazi; see if she's got anything to add to the big pile of puzzle pieces."

"Come by the merry-go-round, after, and let me know what she says."

"Will do."

"Okay." I hesitated, then popped the door and slid to the ground.

" 'Morning," I said, looking up at him from the ground.

He grinned. " 'Mornin', Kate. I'll see you later."

"Good," I said, meaning it. And closed the door.

Showered and feeling positively bouyant, I carried my second cup of coffee to the summer parlor, leaned my elbows on the rail and looked out to sea. Stafford Island and Blunt shone like marble in the sunlight; the sea sparkled like diamonds. Tide going out. I took a deep breath, suddenly and simply aware that I was glad to be home. I'd missed this view, these smells, this air.

The day was shaping up to be a fine one, according to the guy on the radio. That was good—pretty weather keeps the tourists happy.

If there still were tourists after last night's fun and games on the Pier. Armed men in a crowded bar, shooting at an example of our precious coastal wildlife—*not* the way to make Archers Beach a must-visit vacation resort.

I hoped that none of our rescuers had taken harm from their prompt action against Mr. Nemeier's kiddies. Which brought me around again to the theory the various spells protecting the bunch of them were tuned to ward out magical beings.

Lame on the face of it, Kate. There was no reason for any Ozali to suppose that magical devices commissioned for use in the Changing Land would come into contact with anything—or anyone—remotely magical. Even those of us who work in power aren't all that good at *jikinap*-fed magic and intricate spellcraft. The *trenvay* fell beneath the radar of most Ozali, land-based magic not enjoying a very good reputation throughout the other Five Worlds.

And yet—not only could ordinary human beings, Changing Land style, lay hands on the very folks the *trenvay* couldn't—stipulating there was no invisibility spell in play—but so could the product of the union between a dryad's daughter and the son of a human woman and an Ozali of the Sea.

Who was herself definitely, as Borgan had pointed out, a magical being. Of some sort.

I sipped coffee, and watched the gulls play over the waves.

I'd learned basic spellcraft, of course; that was in the core curriculum for any child of House Aeronymous, and double for Princess Kaederon, first born of Prince Nathan.

You should've taken the time to study those workings, I chided myself, and shook my head at the gulls and the waves. Down on the beach, Gaby was raiding the trash barrel at the head of the dune trail, which had to be slim pickings this early, even with a mob in town.

I sighed, and drank some more coffee. Damn it, *could* it just be that the spells were being altered by the constant assault of change against their structure? Custom work, like the invincibility-and-comehome spell worn by yesterday morning's assailant, were finicky, delicately balanced things. One wrong syllable, too much power—or too little—in the working, and the whole thing went wonky on you.

But, no. The girl's shield had functioned as it should have and so had the umbrella spell over the Pier—

I stood up straight, coffee sloshing in my cup.

"Kate, you're an idiot."

I went back into the house, and spent a couple of perplexed minutes searching for my cell phone before I remembered that it was still in the pocket of my jacket, down at the carousel.

In the kitchen, I put the receiver of Gran's phone against my ear, paused for a moment to visualize the number as it appeared in my cell's phone book, then dialed.

"Bonny?" Borgan sounded startled.

"Kate," I corrected. "You can't always trust technology, wonderful though it is. Take it from a woman who made her living slinging code." I hesitated. "I didn't wake you up, did I?"

"No, I was just sitting here staring off into nothing, thinking." There was a pause, then a *tsk* of distaste. "I owe you. Sat here so long my coffee got cold." There were subtle sounds of movement, and a creak that I recognized as lines moving in the breeze. He was at home, then. I closed my eyes, picturing the Tancook Schooner.

"What's her name?"

He didn't ask me who. "*Gray Lady.*" The singing of the lines faded, and I heard quiet steps. Going down to the galley to get more coffee, most likely.

I nodded like he could see me, and cleared my throat. "The reason I'm calling is I figured out why *trenvay* haven't been able to touch Nemeier's crowd, when ordinary people don't have any trouble."

"So you said last night. I thought we'd agreed that, pretty as she was, she didn't hold water."

"This is a new theory."

There came a series of clinks, and a faint gurgle, like liquid being poured. "Well, then," Borgan said, "throw 'er in and let's see if she floats."

"Okay." I moved over to the sink, which was as far as the cord would let me walk, and looked out the window into the alley behind the house. "Understand that *jikinap* isn't a resource to be wasted. Even Ozali want to leave as little in workings—spells—as possible."

"That's because while the power's tied up doing something else it's not directly available to the mage?"

He was quick. I smiled, pleased. "Right. Also? If you're an up-and-coming drug lord, I'm guessing you need to keep a pretty close eye on your bottom line. It might be fiscally responsible to protect yourself, and the other folks at the top of the organization. The further down the ladder you go, though, the less benefits you can afford to make available."

"Sounds reasonable to me." Steps again, and the sudden nearby laugh of a gull, which probably meant he was back on deck.

"Good," I said. "Then you'd agree that—if you were an up-and-coming drug lord who happens to have an Ozali on retainer—you'd protect somebody who's an asset to the organization by setting her up with her very own custom-made invincibility spell. There's a couple ways to build that kind of thing, but the most energy efficient, from the Ozali's point of view, is going to be a simple spell to repel hostile action. A lightning bolt on course for your heart—it doesn't get any more hostile than that. Tripping over your own feet and hitting your head a good whack, though—"

"Is just damn' clumsy," Borgan finished.

"Bingo."

"All right," he said, slowly. "How does that work out with the rest of it? The business on the Pier last night, with—"

"Umbrella spell," I interrupted.

Silence for the beat of three. "Pardon?"

"Umbrella spell. They cover a lot of variables in one attractive package; they mostly work; they tend to be kinda squishy, like that thing over the Pier last night. And they're cheap, cheap, cheap to build. The downside is they don't have much of a shelf life, but when they dissipate, the *jikinap* returns to the Ozali, and he can build another one just as good, real fast when it's needed, and in the meantime have use of the power."

"Got it. And?"

"And the guys who came after us on the Pier last night were depending on the illusion-spinner protecting them from the crowd. That's *all* they depended on; once it was gone, they got nailed by a couple of retired cops, just like regular thugs."

"Hmm. So you're thinking that the grunts are being given good enough, while the captains have better."

"And the boss has the best—right. And what they used last night is probably the same kind of thing they're using when they bring the drugs in. An umbrella spell over all the crew present. Take the umbrella away, and the *trenvay* ought to be able to pick them up at will. Hell, the *Coast Guard* ought to be able to nab them."

Borgan didn't say anything. I heard the sound of moving water, and gulls again, shouting insults at each other.

"Take me with you the next time you go hunting drug runners," I said. "I'll destroy the umbrella spell and you can have at them."

"Sure of yourself, aren't you? Hang on a sec and let me think."

I watched a couple young guys in shorts and jerseys run up Dube Street and cut through the alley to Brown. Maybe training for the high school track team.

"All right." Borgan was back. "I don't say she isn't pretty, Kate, but you're missing the boy who cut you. I'm here to tell you that kicking a man in the balls is definitely a hostile action."

I grinned. "Who said he was anybody but a low-level flunky sent down to deal with a girl?" I countered. "I can't prove it, but I'm willing to lay good money that he didn't have one speck of *jikinap* on, around or in him."

"Saving the knife," Borgan said.

"Right. I'd like to know where he got her, myself."

"Might be he'll tell you, next time he's by," Borgan said, and lapsed into silence.

"Well," he admitted eventually, "she floats. I'll lay it out for Nerazi when I see her." There was a short pause. "What's she think of your knife, by the way?"

"Mam'selle," I said before I thought, and added, "it's her name. Nerazi hasn't seen her."

"Hmph," said Borgan. I heard the lines creak, and a snap, like a sail in the wind.

"We still on for this afternoon?" he asked.

"Five o'clock at the carousel," I said. "You're buying dinner."

"That sounds fair," he said, calmly.

I laughed, and hung up.

THIRTY-ONE

Tuesday, April 25
Low Tide 3:42 P.M.
Sunset 7:37 P.M. EDT

At 11:30, I was fiddling with the orchestrion, making sure the Violano paper was settled on the spindles. Behind me, I heard the hatch open and close, and looked over my shoulder as Nancy came across the deck.

"Heard there was some trouble on the Pier last night," she said, draping her arm across the black bear's back.

"There was some trouble," I agreed. "Buncha boys thought it'd be fun to shoot at a seal."

"Story I heard was that you jumped over the rail to get between it and live bullets," Nancy persisted. I didn't say anything, hoping she'd had her say, but there was more.

"Domino said you were bleeding pretty free when he got to you. Said you fainted before the paramedics got there."

"Domino's got a big mouth," I observed.

"Been that way from a boy," Nancy agreed placidly. "You sure you should be working today?"

"I'm fine. It looked worse than it was."

Nancy pushed the rim of her cap up, and gave me a bland look out of ale colored eyes. "Your gran used to say that the sea air was a tonic."

"My gran was born on this land," I said, truthfully. "If she's away too long, she sickens." Which, unfortunately, was also true, and brought forward with more clarity than I necessarily wanted by the feel of her tree up on Heath Hill—strong, yet, and vital, but starting, just barely starting, to fail....

I shook myself, and turned to finish up with the orchestrion. Fifteen songs, and a rewind. The touch of a switch and we'd have all the carousel music we could eat.

"Thanks for closing up last night," I said, hopping up onto the deck and heading for the control booth.

"Least I could do," Nancy said, turning to walk with me. "How're we splitting the day?"

"You mind working another night? Five to closing?"

She moved her thin shoulders. "Fine by me. Tuesdays my aunt brings over beans and a six pack, and her and ma sit around talking about Back When. I'm just as happy to have something to do outside tonight. Tomorrow, though, I need the evening off."

I nodded. "That's how we'll split, then. How was the crowd last night?"

"We had one or two people by. Marilyn sent a runner around twice on the evening for the tickets, which was a good thing, else I'd've drowned."

"Impressive," I said, skipping off the decking and onto the floor. "We might actually turn a profit this year."

"Super early Season's good for everybody, is what I'm hearing," Nancy said, her descent to the floor more sedate. She sighed, hands tucked in the pockets of her jeans. "Be a good thing for the Beach if we won this contest. 'Bout time something turned us around."

I looked at her. "It does seem a lot more run down than I remembered."

She shook her head. "It's like the virtue's leached out of the town. I remember when we were doing all right—it was hard, yeah. That's life. But lately, seems like the only luck we got is bad."

Have you taken a look around Archers Beach? Borgan asked me in memory. *You're not the only one dying.*

The Guardian was the nexus of the land's virtue—I'd known that, of course, when I broke my oath. Not only had Gran made sure I'd understood before I'd offered myself to the land, but certain of the *trenvay*—like Bob, and Lillian, in her time—hadn't been completely happy with the idea that an ozali-trained princess from one of the toitier of the hoity-toity Five Worlds was going to be responsible for the land's well-being. They'd thought my *jikinap*-sticky fingers would soil the essence of Archers Beach.

...an opinion I had too late come to agree with.

And since I'd been back? Since the land had accepted my service for a second time?

Mixed luck was better than no luck.

Wasn't it?

I cleared my throat and walked over to the control booth, noting my jacket, right where I'd left it over the back of the stool.

"Maybe," I said, nudging the ticket box like it was important to have it lined up exact. "Maybe the luck's starting to change."

"From your mouth to God's ear," Nancy said, and pulled her cap down. "I'll be back at five, and look to work 'til closing."

"Good. And I'll see if I can't shake some cash out of Marilyn, so the two of us can get paid." The park usually paid out on Sunday. On the other hand, Marilyn might be happy enough with the level of business that she'd agree to an interim payout. And if she didn't there was always the threat of closing the carousel until she did.

Nancy paused at the hatch and looked at me over her shoulder. "We never agreed on a wage."

"You're right. Think about what's fair, willya? Let me know this evening."

She grinned and gave me a nod before she pushed the door open. Outside, I heard the sounds of a crowded midway, and the voice of the giant samurai, inviting the tourists in.

"Well," I said to the still air—went over to open the walls.

At noon, the tail of the line was just three steps into the midway. At two o'clock it was on the sidewalk. I did manage to drink the coffee Debbie Lee brought over at one, but Anna's good chicken and veggie stir fry went stone cold before I even had a chance to taste it.

"Are you *all* from the Senior Fun Lovers?" I asked a plump dark-haired woman in sensible jeans and a thin flannel shirt.

"Hey, I'm only forty!" She grinned and shook her head. "Came down from Portland with a bunch of the neighbors. We heard the park and the Pier were open and thought we'd beat the tourists."

"Fooled you."

"Yeah, but that's okay," she said, while I leaned over to unhook the rope. "I've been here all day and I'm having a blast. The only time I get to go to a carnival anymore is when I'm riding herd on a bunch of kids." She grinned again and handed me her ticket. "Today, *I* get to be a kid."

At two, a teenager in a Fun Country T-shirt came by to collect the tickets, and gave me a blank receipt.

"Somebody from the office'll bring you a copy of the tally sheet," he said, very serious and businesslike. "When they do, you give them the blank. If nobody brings you a tally sheet, stop down and talk to Marilyn."

"Will do," I said, and rang the bell twice, which meant "ride's over."

Marilyn herself came in at three and handed me an envelope. I lifted the flap and saw a gratifying number of nice green bills in denominations of ten and up. And I hadn't even had to resort to threats. I looked up to thank her, but she'd already disappeared into the crowd.

Around four-thirty, it began to rain. The line melted until there were only fifteen or twenty people waiting, patient and dry, under the carousel's roof. At four-forty-five, all of them had gotten their rides and dashed off into the soggy midway, holding jackets and sweatshirts and sweaters over their heads and laughing like children.

I sighed and slumped against the stool for a minute, eyes closed, before leaning to the ticket box, and—

Magic crackled across the air, vivid as a lightning bolt.

I snatched at the land, receiving a clear impression of horrified panic. The ocean breeze faded; the sound of the rain disappeared. I looked around, inclined to panic myself, and saw . . . nothing beyond the boundaries of the carousel—no midway, no people, no rain, no sky.

Nothing.

"Shit."

"Good afternoon, Princess Kaederon," said the voice that still haunted my dreams. "I hope I haven't come at an inconvenient time?"

My stomach contracted violently, and I was suddenly glad that

I hadn't had time to eat lunch. I swallowed, took a breath of still, sterile air, and turned, slowly, around.

He was standing next to the lion on the carousel, which didn't fool me for a second; I'd've *known* if he'd come through the Gate.

For this illicit visit, he'd chosen to take on the seeming of a man of the Changing Land. A man of power, as the Changing Land mostly counts power. Tall and lithe in his tailored gray business suit, power tie as bright as a stream of new blood down the snow-white shirt; hair expensively barbered, and a heavy gold watch around his wrist. The only thing a little out of the ordinary were his eyes; if you looked close, you could see storm clouds swirling in the gray irises.

Looked like a bill collector to me...

I felt something like a million or so ants wearing electric sneakers running over my skin. The air was suddenly too thick to breathe; and my vision stuttered, colors all gone to fog, as if I were caught between the real world and Sideways—

Center yourself, Keeper, or your power will flow to his, to the dismay and destruction of us all. The batwing horse actually sounded concerned. Not only that, it was giving excellent advice.

Panting, I concentrated. There was an exercise. I'd learned it at my tutor's knee, and only after much wailing and despair. I remembered the day I finally got it, standing in the schoolroom, looking down at the children's maze, eyes tracing the path, so clear from the height at which I stood, that led inexorably and inevitably to the center.

Color returned to my immediate vicinity. My breathing smoothed. The ants in their electric sneakers vanished into the ozone-charged air.

From his place next to the lion, Ramendysis smiled.

"Allow me to congratulate you on your achievements, Princess. You will forgive me if I say that I hadn't expected you to survive, much less to take up your birthright."

"I don't forgive you," I said, my words dropping like stones through the thick air. "And I didn't invite you."

He laughed, and strolled forward, the step off the carousel hardly interrupting his stride.

"I fear you've been too long among the natives of this execrable place, Princess. I have no need of invitations. I go where I please."

He was strolling closer, one hand in the pocket of his trousers, looking catlike and elegant. My feet shifted. Body and soul screamed for retreat—but retreat was what he wanted. And, I told myself, I would be damned if I gave him the satisfaction.

Excellent, the batwing horse whispered, and it says everything about my state of mind that I welcomed its voice and took heart from its encouragement.

"What do you want, Ramendysis?" I asked, and at least my voice didn't actually quaver, if it wasn't as crisp or as bold as I had hoped.

He stopped, as if my question had erected a barrier between us and it amused him to honor it, for the moment.

"I want nothing more than that which belongs to me. I had told the old *earth spirit* that I would have it, whether she chose to accept a fair bargain or no. I also told her what would happen if she refused to surrender it."

"You might have done all that," I said, my voice stronger now. "However, my grandmother isn't here, and she didn't leave me any instructions regarding you, or a package with your name on it."

The still air trembled, and I felt the regard of his *jikinap,* raising the hair on my arms and on my head, drawing my heartbeat like a magnet draws a needle.

I grabbed for the vision of the children's maze, and the sensation faded somewhat, though my hair still floated away from my head, like I was underwater.

"You ask me to believe," Ramendysis said, "that you are unaware of the situation."

"I don't," I said with more candor than wisdom, "give a damn what you believe."

He smiled, and I gagged on a scream. "You will very soon come to care, Princess Kaederon." His smile faded. "Hear me. If I am not reunited with that which is mine, I will remove my restrained and temperate hand from over those who wish to pillage and lay waste to this *town* and all who reside in it."

"If I don't know what you're looking for, how can I return it?" I asked, reasonably. Not that reason had been a particularly strong suit of the Ramendysis I'd known.

He lifted an elegant eyebrow.

I shook my head. "To be perfectly frank, I can't imagine Gran keeping something that belonged in the Land of the Flowers here any longer than it took her to call on The Wise and have them remove it." *Deep breath, Kate.* "Are you sure you lost it here?"

Ramendysis took his hand out of his pocket, which panicked me just as much as he doubtless intended it to.

"I did not *lose* it," he said tightly, "it was stolen from me. It must be here. It was here that the thief was apprehended and imprisoned. He had ceded his essence to the old *earth spirit*. What else might he not have given into her keeping?"

"What else, indeed," I answered politely, though if he called Gran an *earth spirit* in that tone of amused distaste one more time, I *was* going to commit mayhem.

Ramendysis fixed me in his eye, as if he were actually trying to weigh the truth of what I'd said.

"You neither know the name of that which I seek, nor where it is kept?"

I sighed in honest exasperation. "That's what I said, wasn't it? You're the one who took leave to doubt it."

Ramendysis pressed his lips together.

"Very well," he said after a moment. "If what you say is so, then we have only one path open to us."

I eyed him. "Call the Wise?"

"Stupid child. What would that gain me? No, what remains is to ask the thief where he has hidden it. Open the Rock and let him stand forward to answer my question."

I gaped at him. "You want me to open Googin Rock and let the Fire Ozali out?" I bit my lip so as not to blurt out the follow-up question: *Are you crazy?*

"Precisely. Release the Ozaliflame from the Rock," Ramendysis said coldly. "He will be diminished by his time imprisoned, and by the leaching effects of this cursed land. I will put the question, he will answer, and he will be returned to his cell."

"Just like that?" I shook my head, an odd sensation with my hair still floating about my head.

"You were at the binding. You know that it took the Lady of the Wood herself, Seal Woman, and a dozen other *trenvay* to lock the Ozaliflame into the Rock—and he went willingly! I'm not the Lady he swore to; he owes me nothing, though I'm guessing he owes you plenty. Also? He's likely to be just a little peeved at a hundred years under water—" *If not actively, and violently, insane.* "—I think he's going to come out of the Rock swinging. Assuming he can be unbound at all."

Ramendysis frowned down at me; I felt his *jikinap* oozing along my senses, its hunger at once repellent and seductive. I clung to the image of the children's maze like a nun clings to her rosary; still I felt its dreadful caress—and worse, the desire to surrender, to merge my power with his, submerge my will and myself...

From the pocket of my jacket, draped over the back of the operator's stool, my cell phone trilled.

I gasped, and jerked back, blinking. The cell gave tongue again, and a third time while the storm clouds swirling in Ramendysis' eyes grew darker and more dangerous—and then the voice mail took it, or the caller hung up. I shrugged and managed what was probably the world's rockiest grin.

"I say we call on the Wise," I said, and didn't like the smile he produced on hearing it.

"And I say that we do not. Shall I summon one of the blind peasants from without and demonstrate how strongly I feel on this matter?"

My stomach churned and I swallowed bile. Just the thought of what something like Ramendysis could do to one of the childlike innocents who existed out there in the vanished world sickened me.

Peacefully, peacefully, little Ozali, the sticky-sweet voice whispered between my ears. *Allow him his whim. You will be the greater for gathering your allies to you. And, as you say, the Ozaliflame may not emerge from his cage as docile as this one imagines.*

Which was damned good advice. Not for the first time, I wondered what the batwing horse had been, in the Land from which it had been exiled.

I inclined my head, taking the batwing's advice; ceding the point, and the round, to Ramendysis.

"All right. It'll take me some time to gather the *trenvay,* and we don't want to risk being seen by the tourists. Next low tide is four-thirteen tomorrow morning. Meet us at the Rock then." I took a hard breath, the gray air like cobwebs in my lungs. "Now get the hell out of here."

"Of course, Princess," Ramendysis purred. He swept a bow, courtly and graceful. Mist swirled—and dispersed.

He is gone, the batwing told me.

I dove for my jacket, dug the cell out and triggered voice mail.

"Kate," Borgan's voice sounded in my ear, "where's the merry-go-round?" Pause for the beat of three. "Kate?" Another pause. "I'm getting Nerazi."

I hit speed-dial, shaking so hard I could barely keep the phone at my ear, and looked around me. The air was beginning to move, unraveling the isolation spell or whatever he'd used, bringing me the scent of brine. The midway reappeared, as if seen through a dirty window, shadows moving here and there.

"Kate." Borgan didn't sound pleased.

"We've got trouble," I said, and burst into tears.

THIRTY-TWO

Wednesday, April 26
Low Tide 4:13 A.M.
Moonrise 3:54 A.M. EDT, Waning Crescent

They came from the wetlands, they came from the dry, from the highlands and the low. Silent and solemn, the *trenvay* gathered and took their places in a loose ring around Googin Rock, fellfire illuminating their features in the absence of the moon.

Some of those present had stood in the circle when the Ozaliflame was bound into Googin Rock, lending their power and their agreement to the act. Nerazi had been there, and Gaby, and Bob. Others who had made up that band had faded—like Lillian. Still others of those gathering in this morning were too young to remember.

"He's not here! He's not coming!" Gaby twittered. I shook my head, wishing I had so much optimism—but it was Borgan who answered.

"Tide's not out yet. We'll have him at dead low."

"Unless he shows up a year or two from now and gets mad 'cause we're not here waiting for him," Bob put in. A match rasped and flared, throwing his face into a mosaic of bright and dark as he lit a cigarette. He drew, and sighed the smoke out. "This is a bad idea," he said to no one in particular.

"Perhaps," Nerazi answered. "Perhaps not."

Bob snorted, smoke coming out of his nose like the memory of dragon-fire. "Business as usual."

"Right," I said, rubbing my palms nervously down my thighs. The work gloves were in the pockets of my jacket. For this night's business, I was going to need a personal touch. Still, I wanted them near—and Mam'selle the knife, too, nestled in her accustomed place against my backbone.

"Right!" I said again, and the land took my words and delivered them to each and every one of those waiting. "We're here to hold our land against harm. If it looks like there's going to be trouble between the two Ozali, *stand back*. Our first and only concern is to preserve the land, the people, the town. Am I heard?"

"Aye, Guardian." "Yes." "I hear you, Kate." The words drifted back to me and I sighed, feeling Borgan stir next to me. I looked up, and followed his gaze to the left, where a thin, scarecrow figure had slipped into place at Nerazi's right hand, pale hair blowing like dandelion fluff beneath the broad-brimmed hat, coattails belling in the breeze.

"Well, that answers that," I thought, and didn't realize I'd spoken aloud until Borgan's voice reached me, under the sound of the wind and the surf.

"Answers what?" he asked.

Before I could answer there came a flash, a *boom*, and a slap of rain against my cheek. I blinked my eyes clear, and turned to my right, where Ramendysis stood in all the pomp and finery of a Lord of the Land of the Flowers. His stormy curls were crowned with tempests; rings of power flashed upon his hands. His robes were pleated with lightning; scented with ozone.

"Princess Kaederon." He bowed, courtly and sweet, his *jikinap* oozing over me like syrup. I went back a step, stomach roiling, and bumped into Borgan.

"Steady, Kate," he murmured.

Steady, I thought. *Right*. I took a hard breath, savoring the tang of salt, and looked up at Ramendysis.

"As Guardian and keepers of this land," I said, hearing my voice being served out to the entire circle, "we require a guarantee from you before we loose what's bound into the Rock."

Ramendysis laughed, genuinely amused, as far as I could tell.

"Have you forgotten that power has precedence? Allow me to remind you."

The wind died; the air grew heavy and dull, as if the very mother of storms was a-building at the door into Saco Bay. I took a breath, gagging on the reek of dead fish, and felt Borgan's hand on my shoulder.

"Nooooo!"

The scream beat against the heavy air. I spun in time to see Gaby move out of her place in the circle in a purposeful and entirely un-Gaby-like stride, heading for the foot of Heath Hill, where the sea roses tossed in the dark.

"Nononono!" she whimpered. "Guardian, make him stop!"

I swallowed and spun back. Ramendysis lifted an urbane eyebrow.

"Let her go," I said, my voice rattling like dice in a cup.

"In due time, Princess," he said calmly, and turned to observe Gaby's progress across the sand.

She had reached the roses, and I watched as she extended a hand. Fingers shook as she fought his will—and I knew, yes, I knew *exactly* what that felt like. The boil of loathing in your stomach; disbelief that your will is not enough to command your body. Despair.

Gaby staggered one more step into the knot of roses, held tall and unyielding by a will not her own. Her hand darted out to seize a vine, fingers crushing it into her palms.

I bit my lip, feeling the thorns as if they pierced my own flesh. Gaby howled, her hand fisted around the vine. There was a slight shiver in the dead air, and the stench of rotted vegetation.

"The guarantee that I will give you," Ramendysis said, his voice waking thunder in the cloudless sky, "is precisely this: If that rock is not opened, and speedily, or if I am in any way impeded in recovering that which is mine, I shall make it very easy for those of your own Land who wish to destroy you to do exactly that. They will drain marshes, cut trees, poison streams, and sow the soil with salt. You motley collection of earth spirits and low fae—all of you!—will fade; the land will gibber and scream, and there will be none to succor it. *This* is your guarantee."

I'd wondered, back when I was newcome to my mother's Land, and hearing Gran tell the story of how the Ozaliflame came to be 'prisoned in Googin Rock, why a bunch of powerful, savvy adults hadn't Just Said No to Ramendysis.

Sure, he'd been able to eat *my* lunch, but I'd just been a kid. It had seemed to me that the *trenvay*—especially Gran and Nerazi—standing secure on their own land, and at the height of their powers—not to mention those Ozali present who had disagreed with the whole procedure—it had seemed to me that they simply hadn't tried very hard to put Ramendysis in his place.

Now I knew why they'd folded. Nothing was going to stop Ramendysis—not good sense, not the threat of retaliation, or even the Wise. He would have his way, he would not be gain-said, nor would he spare a moment to remorse, should he kill an entire town.

Around the circle, the *trenvay* stood silent and horrified. Her will returned to her, Gaby had fallen to her knees by the roses, bent over her mangled hand, keening.

Then, as quickly as it had died, the breeze freshened and the sense of doom lifted. I gratefully filled lungs aching with several minutes of shallow breathing with untainted air. Ramendysis smiled, and bowed, robes rustling.

"Princess Kaederon, shall we proceed?"

It was a phrase out of nightmare—it had been what he had used to say right before, before...

The land thrust itself into my attention. I centered myself, and considered those standing in circle, grim and horrified, most, and none of them a match for Ramendysis, any more than I was...

A forest, Gran observed from memory, *is stronger than any single tree, no matter how old, no matter how wise.*

I took a breath.

"Your assistance will not be necessary," I said, as cool as I could manage it. Ramendysis arched an eyebrow.

"I recall that two were required to open the rock anon," he said. "The Lady of the Wood, as she styled herself, and a certain... sea spirit."

"Seal Woman," Nerazi murmured, from beyond Borgan, "Your Lordship. It will not have escaped your attention that both the Lady and myself were firmly rooted in this Land. While you are, of course, more powerful than any other who stands in circle, your origin lies elsewhere, and the things of this Land may therefore defy you."

"Certainly Princess Kaederon must bid the rock to open, for it is she who may command the land. However, a child can see that the work in question is intricate in the extreme, and requires the hand of a master upon it.

"I am, as you say, the most powerful of those gathered here, and as such I willingly offer my skill in service of this task. All that is needful is for Princess Kaederon to submit her will to mine, and we shall speedily—"

A black pit was opening in the sand about an inch ahead of the toes of my sneakers. *No, no, no. Not again. I won't. Not for anything. Not for life it—*

"Prince Borgan," I gasped, and felt the land leap and go intensely still.

I paused, to give Borgan a chance to back out. He didn't speak, though, and neither did Nerazi.

I took a breath and made it official. "Prince Borgan will assist me."

"Oh," Ramendysis said, and ran a slow and faintly disbelieving gaze over Borgan. In the Land of the Flowers, that kind of look is fightin' words. "Will he." He returned his attention to me, and inclined slightly.

"Forgive me, Princess Kaederon, but what I see here is a—worthy, no doubt!—*low fae*. What is needed for this project is a marriage of *jikinap* and such power as may be resident in this... place. I fail to see any way in which *Prince Borgan* will be able to assist you."

"Well, then," Borgan said, coming up beside me, "I guess it's a good thing that's our problem." He gave me a nod. "Ready when you are, Kate."

I took a deep breath. "No time like the present. Stay a step behind, all right? The Rock's looking ugly tonight."

In point of fact, Googin Rock was looking every bit as crazy as Ramendysis, as if the Fire Ozali imprisoned there knew that his ancient enemy was within reach. And, for all I knew, he did. Gran had never been clear on whether the Ozaliflame was aware or asleep in his binding. If Ramendysis had the choosing of it, he'd have bound him awake and aware. The Ozaliflame's soul, though—such as he might have had—that, he had freely given into Gran's keeping. Surely she would have granted him what mercy she could.

I left my place in the circle and walked down to the Rock, Borgan one step behind.

The wonder of it was that Ramendysis stood where he was and let us go. Maybe he figured we'd fail and he'd get an added tickle from me coming back to beg for his help.

If it came to that, I'd rather Googin Rock blasted me out of time and space.

The shield curtain parted before me, and fell closed behind Borgan. I paused, feeling safer with a little bit of spellcraft between me and Ramendysis, and considered the task before us. Imprisoned fires blew and danced in a silent ballet of malice, by turns illuminating and obscuring the treacherous surface. Above it all, the working shone like moonlight, impenetrable, cool, and hopelessly complex.

"I don't have the faintest idea where to begin," I breathed, and heard Borgan laugh beside me.

"Not as bad as it looks," he said. I turned to look up at him.

"I'm sorry to drag you into this," I said. "I—don't think very well around Ramendysis. Nerazi was the one who helped Gran with the binding. If I'd had my wits with me, I'd've—"

"You did exactly right," he interrupted. "Taste that armor and tell me what you think."

"*Taste* it? The other morning, I slid right off it."

"Must've tried to budge it, then. What you want to do is just open up and let it come to you."

It wasn't like I had a better idea. I took a breath and hauled the old lesson up from the depths of my memory. Right. I remembered this.

Once again, I pictured myself in the schoolroom at my grandfather's house. But this time, instead of looking down at the garden and the maze at its heart, I just leaned forward—and opened the window.

Sensation flowed through me—a hint of green growing things, damp soil, and humus, which I knew for Gran's magical signature; and an effervescent tang, salty, rich. Pleasing. And completely unfamiliar.

"That's not Nerazi," I said.

"Sharp as a needle, our Kate," Borgan said fondly. I resisted the impulse to kick him.

"Who, then?" I asked instead.

"Me."

I thought about that while I overlooked the Rock and the binding. "I'm going to want to hear the story that explains why Ramendysis thinks it was Nerazi who sealed the Rock with Gran."

"I'll be glad to tell it to you," he said, "but first we'd better settle this business before Mr. Wonderful back there has a conniption and does himself a hurt."

"It's not him doing *himself* a hurt that worries me," I muttered, and moved gingerly forward, Borgan at my back.

I took my time crossing the bladed surface, placing my feet carefully, avoiding knife-sharp ridges slicked with seaweed, and numerous tidal pools. A starfish waved at me from a puddle almost too small to hold it; fingerling fish swam in another; a tiny crab sheltered beneath some weeds in a third, everything perfectly clear in the blare of the balefire. I kept my eyes on my route, feeling Borgan behind me, moving light and sure.

In the center of the Rock, there's a hump, but instead of showing edges like the back of a stegosaurus, it's smooth and slick as a bottle. Anyone stupid enough to try to scale it was likely to fall off—right into a field of wicked stone blades.

Up I went, proving once again that as a race the Archers have more hair than brains, and knelt on the glassy knoll, my right palm flat on the surface.

The Rock was hot; it always is. The filthiest deep winter snowstorm lacks the power to freeze it. Which would, of course, be the Ozaliflame bound into the heart of the thing, giving out his heat.

Borgan knelt across from me and put his left hand next to mine, palm against the Rock.

"It'll prolly go easier if I show you the way," he said slowly, and raised his head to look into my eyes. "I'm saying, *show you*, Kate."

Meaning, no submission necessary. I gave him a grin and a nod, relief flooding through me like sea water.

"You're definitely the elder of we-who-are-about-to-be-incinerated," I said. "You were here when this thing was built and you invested your power into the work." I took a breath. "Tell me what to do."

He smiled. "First thing you'll be wanting to do is raise your magic."

I closed my eyes and concentrated. A sense of disorienting power began to grow at the base of my spine, washing up my backbone with the inevitability of the tide. Heat licked along my nerve endings, and my palm warmed of its own, giving the Rock heat for heat.

The *jikinap* rose, ravening and shapeless. I enclosed it, focused it, and looked into the Rock.

Living flame danced across my vision, throwing heat shadows along the jagged interior. I focused more tightly, trying to see past the flames, to identify the source—but they were everywhere, sourceless, disorienting...

"Kate?"

"Got it," I managed. "How long I can keep it is another question."

"Doing fine," he said. "Now. Hold out your left hand. I'm going to link us."

Dazzled by flame, I held my hand out. Calloused fingers closed around mine. Through the flames, or in them, I saw a warrior, tall and supple, confident in his powers, steady in his regard, his leathers white as moonlight. A loon nested on the ground at his feet, ruby red eyes sapient and alert.

"Look close at that binding," the warrior said in Borgan's voice. "What do you see now?"

I drew back until I was focused above the flames, almost, but not quite on the surface of the Rock. I saw the interwoven lines of force, shimmering, turning, becoming something else even as I watched them.

Becoming—a door.

A sea-battered wooden hatch, that was its seeming, secured with a massive iron padlock. I tried to touch it, but it slid away from the power I had raised.

"I see it," I thought or said. "A sea hatch. It's padlocked."

"That's right." The warrior looked down at the loon. "Find the key," he said, "and bring it here."

The bird shifted and was gone in a blur of unexpected motion. Hand in hand, the warrior and I waited, while the sweet agony of power seared the surface of my soul and filled me with dreadful hunger. It would be so easy to widen the channel of power that linked us and drink of that warrior's life force. So easy...

I pressed my hand onto the surface of the Rock, relishing the heat, directing my attention again to the fiery interior, finding as before that my senses were confused and confounded.

At last, the loon returned. It laid something at the warrior's feet, and nestled again into the grass.

The warrior raised the object, allowing me to see...

A key. Just an old-fashioned padlock key, slightly rusty with age. Pardon me—half of a key. As the door was a melding of magics, so the key would also be a melding. All I had to do was complete the pattern.

I considered it carefully, noting the loose ends, comparing fragment against function.

High Magic is a system of protocol and function—a lot like programming, really. Define the need, then design—or in most cases tweak a design already in place—a solution. Since I didn't have the code book, I'd have to work out my own solution—which was fine. I'd always been good at hacking.

It was the work of moments to examine the key and understand its logic. When I had it—its structure and its intent, I reached out, but not for the *jikinap* burning in my blood.

I reached out to the land.

There was a frisson, a spark, and a whole key spun in the space between the warrior and myself, wet and gritty with rust.

"Good," Borgan said approvingly. "Now, let's get this business done."

"One..." he said or I did, as we reached forth with one will and heart "...two..." The key slid into the lock.

"...three..."

There was an instant of resistance, as if the insubstantial lock had rusted shut, then the key turned, the shackle sprung, and the door unraveled.

Jikinap and land magic streamed past us in a spark-ridden gale. There came a fearful rumbling from the depths of the Rock, setting waves dancing in the tidal pools and putting small lives in danger.

I slipped on the glassy knoll, and Borgan grabbed my arm, holding me steady as fire blossomed above us—red, silver, azure, and green. Burning streamers touched the sea, hissing into extinction, explosions boomed, echoing back from the inland hills. Dark wings swept past on the tumultuous air—a bat, perhaps—and then all was dark and still around us. Even the sea seemed to be holding back its next waves, waiting...

Cautiously, I stepped Sideways, searching—but the only *jikinap* I sensed was the bonfire which was Ramendysis, on the shore, and a few scattered threads of what had been the binding spell, dispersing as I watched.

I re-entered my body, opened my eyes, and looked around at a changed landscape.

There was no fell-fire dancing over the surface of Googin Rock; there was no hiss of steam when the retreating waves struck the far ledge, nor any suggestion of intelligent malice. Littered about the dark surface were all manner of objects, glowing with internal luminescence: a casket carved of precious woods; a silver bowl heaped with pearls; glittering lapis bottles of rare perfume; silken pillows; leather-bound books, jeweled chessmen, and other such things as might amuse or comfort a prince...

But of the Ozaliflame, who had been bound in full sight of Ozali and *trenvay* more than a hundred years ago, there was no sign.

THIRTY-THREE

Wednesday, April 26

"Very well, Princess Kaederon," Ramendysis said. "You have had your joke. I advise you now to speedily produce either the Ozaliflame or that which I seek. If you produce the thing itself, I shall overlook the fact that you and your land are forsworn and in forfeit. If you produce the Ozaliflame, the fates of you, your land, and the various earth spirits will hang upon the tale he chooses to tell me."

I staggered as I came off the Rock onto the sand. Borgan caught me under the elbow and more or less walked me six paces up the slope, until I was as close to Ramendysis as I could bear without throwing up.

"No joke," I said, hearing my voice shake. I was having a hard time focusing, Ramendysis kept flipping back and forth between an urbane and elegant Ozali and a seething black vortex through which thick worms of *jikinap* burrowed. I raised a hand, and pointed shakily at the Rock.

"It seemed to me that there was an awful lot of power loosed when we released the bindings. Are you sure that none of those treasures is your lost toy?"

"Treasures!" Ramendysis spat. "Trinkets! As for the *power,* as you care to style it, which was loosed—misdirection and noise, only. The Ozaliflame has long been absent from his prison. If, indeed, he was ever bound there."

"Your Lordship was present," Nerazi said from her place in the circle, "and witnessed the event himself."

"The details of your dishonor are of no interest to me," Ramendysis stated. "I await the return of my property."

"If you don't tell me what it is, how can I return it?" I asked tiredly. "And as far as the Ozaliflame goes—you're right. It looks like he flew the coop and isn't available to answer questions. There's nothing else you can do about it."

"There, Princess Kaederon," Ramendysis purred, "you are in error." I felt his *jikinap* ooze over me, calling up unclean memories, and shivered, reaching for the comfort and the strength of the land. It was hard, my will was sluggish, and the touch, when I finally managed it, was tentative and wavery.

"What I *can* do is take you hostage to your land's honor. While you repose as my guest in the Land of the Flowers, these your minions will search for and recover that which is mine. When it is returned to me, you will be returned to them." He smiled, and I wanted to scream, but I didn't have enough willpower. "If you so choose."

Okay, this was bad. I concentrated, trying to get a firm connection with the land, but his *jikinap* was coating me now, a viscous membrane slowly filling my ears, my eyes, leaching my will. Enclosed, I struggled—which was exactly what he wanted me to do. If I fought and lost, he'd absorb me—*jikinap, voysin,* soul, and whatever might be left of the intelligence that called herself Kate Archer...

"Hostage!" Borgan yelled indignantly, and stepped between us, the better to get in Ramendysis' face. "How's that s'posed to work, exactly? You expect us bunch of *earth spirits* and *low fae* to be able to find your missing ticky-toy? If anybody here can find it, it'll be Kate—but not if you go hauling her off to Flower Land!" He snorted derisively. "Exactly the kind of harebrained idea you'd expect from a man who lets his magic do his heavy lifting for him."

"Why, you insolent—" Ramendysis was breathless—and madder'n hell, which I knew because his *jikinap* receded, like the tide going out, called back to drive whatever horrible thing he was about to do to Borgan.

Leaving me at liberty.

I threw my will into the land, and the land leapt to do my bidding, simultaneously serving warning to the gathered *trenvay*. They vanished between one eyeblink and the next, with the notable exception of Borgan, who stayed right where he was, watching interestedly as a sinkhole opened beneath Ramendysis' feet, and he was abruptly neck deep in sand.

"Behave yourself while you're on my land, damn you!" Brave words—unfortunately marred by the chattering of my teeth. I'd blindsided Ramendysis, hit him from an unexpected direction while his attention was focused elsewhere. I wouldn't be able to surprise him a second time. And if he decided to expend just a tithe of his power right now, the beach would be fused into glass, and I would be dead. If I was lucky.

For one of the longest minutes of my life, it hung in the balance. The air sparked with unexpended *jikinap,* and the land crouched, ready and eager to finish what it had begun. Borgan was poised on the balls of his feet, the sea breeze fingering his braid.

To my enormous astonishment and unbounded relief, Ramendysis blinked first. The air became less . . . electric. The sense of impending doom lessened. He inclined his head with a fair imitation of graciousness, despite his position.

"Very well, Princess Kaederon. You make your point eloquently. I will, indeed, behave myself while I am on your land. Pray, loosen my restraints."

I didn't want to. I wanted the land to swallow him so deep there'd be no getting him out, ever again.

Unfortunately, I couldn't. Burying Ramendysis would be like burying an atomic bomb. All that *jikinap*. It made me sick to my stomach just thinking about the harm . . .

Hating it, I asked the land to release its hold. With visible reluctance, the sand around Ramendysis shifted, grains roiling, and little by little he rose, until he was once again standing on the beach, his fine robes rumpled and gritty.

He looked down at himself, flicked his fingers as if brushing a speck of dust off his sleeve—and his robes were pristine and fresh once more.

"Prince Borgan's point is also well made," he said. "It would indeed be folly to remove from the search the one person best suited to locate that which is mine. You may stay in this benighted land, and search, Princess. I do regret that such influence as I may have had over my associates here on your land is...not as firm as you might wish, as a result of this morning's work." He smiled, and bowed slightly.

"When you locate that which I seek, you will deliver it to me—and receive your token in return."

"Token?" I eyed him. "What token?"

"Merely a ritual assurance of your good faith—it need not be anything of consequence, really..." He looked about him, making a show of it, like he couldn't see behind his head and through stone if he wanted to, just by calling up a little power.

His eye lighted on Borgan, and my chest squeezed so tight I thought my heart would burst.

"Ah," he said. "Prince Borgan's jacket will do nicely, I think."

"No," I said flatly, and in the same breath Borgan said, "All right."

I grabbed his arm. "Borgan—no. Trust me, you do *not* want to do this."

"But he has already given his word," Ramendysis purred. "Surely, Princess, you would not wish him to be forsworn."

As if what I wanted mattered; Borgan was already taking off his jacket.

Far too late, he hesitated, like he'd come to his senses at last. He tipped his head and considered Ramendysis.

"You'll take this here instead of Kate, will you?"

Ramendysis smiled. "It will be my very great pleasure to take that there instead of Kate."

"Borgan..." My voice was shaking. He threw me a look over his shoulder.

"It's all right, Kate. Just a formality, like the man says."

I shook my head, dumb with horror.

Without his skin, Borgan wouldn't be able to shift into seal form. But that wasn't the worst of it.

A selkie's skin is his nature—his soul.

And I knew too well what Ramendysis did with souls.

"Here you go, then," Borgan said, and tossed the jacket, none-too-gently. Ramendysis caught it against his chest.

"You take good care of that skin, hear me? I'm wicked fond of it."

"Be assured that I will lavish upon it all the attention it deserves." Ramendysis inclined his head, courtly and elegant. "Princess

Kaederon. I will await delivery at my primary dwelling. You will remember it as House Aeronymous." He smiled once more, which was about all my nerves could stand. "Search quickly. I know you wouldn't wish me to become... bored."

With that, he was gone, leaving behind an acid spatter of rain and the boom of distant thunder.

My legs gave way and I was kneeling on the sand, retching, arms wrapped around my middle, the land whining and nuzzling me.

"Kate?" The land showed me Borgan settling onto his heels, to the right and facing me. "You all right?"

"All right?" I raised my head and stared at him. He looked like he always did; radiating calm upon the land. "Borgan, Ramendysis has *your skin*. You gave it to him willingly."

"That's right," he said, like it mattered not one bit.

I took a breath, decided I wasn't going to be sick right then, and sat back on my heels. "Dammit—don't you know what he'll *do*? He can call you to him wherever he is—destroy you on whim—make you, make you—"

"Kate, it's all right."

I shook my head, hard enough that my hair whipped my face. "You had to have known!"

"Well, I knew there was a risk, though not as much as letting Mr. Wonderful take you off to Flower Land." He shrugged. "I can get another jacket easier than Archers Beach can get another Guardian."

"Another jacket..." I repeated. "Can you get another *nature*?"

Silence. Borgan glanced away, over toward Googin Rock, sitting dark and quiescent in the rising tide.

"He's going to force you," I said, panic rising again, despite the land's ministrations. "You saw what he did to Gaby. He'll use your skin—"

He looked back to me, shaking his head so that the braid snaked along his shoulder. "No, now see, that's where you're wrong. He won't—or he might, but not the way you're thinking." He sighed. "Kate, I'm not a selkie."

"Not a selkie," I repeated, just to make sure I'd heard it right. "When we went off the Pier," I said, very carefully, "you turned into a seal."

He nodded. "You got me there. I did turn into a seal. But see—you seemed to have your heart set on a selkie, and I don't like to disappoint a pretty lady."

Right. "So, what are you, if you're not a selkie?"

He laughed, deep in his chest. "Here you're a Guardian of the land and it never occurred to you that there're those of us with the same tie to the seas?"

"Did you..." I heard Gran's voice just as plain as if she sat on the sand beside me. "Did you pay your respects to the sea?"

I thought Gran'd told me everything about the pleasures and perils of Guardianship. Maybe she'd figured to let me settle first, and heal the deep hurts. Of *course* I was drawn to Borgan, and him to me.

The land and the sea...that's an old, old alliance.

"The whole Atlantic Ocean?" I asked, and his laugh this time was right out loud.

"Mercy, woman! Gulf of Maine's enough trouble for me."

Cape Cod to Halifax is a considerable swath of living water. And he'd counted himself equal to Nerazi, which was very likely understating himself by a bushel or six.

"Ramendysis is still going to use your jacket to entrap you."

Borgan gave me the grace of a nod. "Well, he's welcome to try," he said, "though I don't say I'd rather he didn't. I'd count it a favor if you'd find Mr. Wonderful's shiny thing for him before he starts in to experimenting."

"You'll notice he never did say what he was looking for," I pointed out.

"He is looking," a voice spoke from the dark, "for that which he must not find."

I came to my feet, and Borgan rose beside me. A shadow moved against the dead black cinder that was Googin Rock. Yellow hair blew like sparks in the star-breeze; dark coattails swelled.

He walked toward us, lithe and luminous, clad all in black leather, and a dark-winged bird on his shoulder. When he was six steps out, he stopped, and lifted a pale hand to stroke the bird's chest feathers. His face was smooth and ageless, his mustaches red as fire. Azure flames danced in his eyes.

My throat closed, and my ears rang; my chest ached. The dark bird cocked its head to a side and considered me out of one bright orange eye.

"Good morning, Katie dear," the Ozaliflame said, and his voice, God help me, was the same that had soothed my childhood fears. "How's my favorite black-hearted pirate?"

"Mr. Ignat," I whispered, and then shook my head. "No, I guess that's not your name, is it?"

"It's near enough," he said softly, and extended a hand. "I'm sorry, Katie."

"Sorry." I stared at the offered hand—so smooth; so pale and shapely. An Ozali's hand, that had never known work or weather. I drew a hard breath.

"You're *sorry* that Ramendysis has my mother and, for all we know, Gran, in his keeping? *Sorry* that Archers Beach is about to be flooded with vandals, the land poisoned, and the trees knocked down? You're *sorry*, are you? Well, that's just dandy."

He sighed, and raised his hand to scratch the bird again, his fingers glowing like pearl against the sooty feathers. I felt the *jikinap* stir at the base of my spine, questing—and forcibly reined it back.

"Sorrier than you know," he said. "Bonny and I took a risk, doing what we did. We knew it was a risk, but I'm afraid we only thought in terms of risk to *us,* and to those who had willingly aided us." He smiled, wry beneath the flaming mustaches. "We thought the innocent would be protected by their innocence."

I stared at him. "Like that ever happens."

"Sometimes," he said. "Sometimes, it does."

"Right." I shook my head. "Do you know now why you gave me that whiskey?"

"It was the least I could do for my granddaughter," he murmured, his fingers nimbly dodging an irritable peck from his avian companion.

Shock, cold and bracing. I might've gasped, because he sent me another wry look.

"How—" I raked my fingers through my hair, trying to order the hundred or so questions that were crowding my brain. "You were never in the Rock."

A real smile this time, blue eyes sparkling. "As it happens, a good bit of me was in the Rock. I'd given my soul into Bonny's keeping. She drew out the *jikinap*, just like we'd done to make the whiskey, only...a great deal...more—and sealed it in a casket made from the wood of her own tree. What was left after that was done was—a man of the Changing Land, no longer young, and not quite right in the head."

I shivered. "Did you know? I mean—"

"I suspected that I would be diminished, but it would only be for a few hundred years, at most. And, truly, Katie, it was a boon. I'd been Ozali for a long, long time."

Meaning that the *jikinap* had begun chewing holes in his brain, and every heartbeat brought a new struggle for domination. I shivered again, and tucked my hands into the pockets of my jacket. My fingers touched something smooth and cool. Foreknowing, I sighed and pulled the gloves out.

They were cunningly crafted of supple red leather, the wide blue cuffs lavish with embroidered golden flames. I held them out to . . . Mr. Ignat'.

"I'm guessing these are yours."

He nodded, making no move to take them. "They were. Keep them. They become you."

I considered him, uneasily aware of the questing hunger held in check by my will. It came to me that I could take him, absorb his *jikinap*, thereby growing in power and—

I gagged, exerted my will and dominated the insidious whisperer. Gasping, I shook my hair out of my eyes, and found Mr. Ignat' watching me with grave sympathy.

"I'm sorry for that, too, Katie," he said. "But you're strong enough to handle it."

"Gee, thanks," I muttered—and gasped, my head suddenly filled with the land's shrieks and horrific images—trees burning like brands in a conflagration too vast to contain.

"Smoke!" Borgan said sharply, and then, "Gas, too."

"They're firing the Wood!" I yelled, and ran, Borgan and the Ozaliflame on my heels.

THIRTY-FOUR

Wednesday, April 26
High Tide 10:33 A.M.
Sunrise 5:42 A.M. EDT

Flames leapt against the dawn-pearled sky; fire swirled amid the tree trunks, feeding on twigs, acorns, pine cones, saplings—

Inside the conflagration, trees screamed, sap boiled, and new leaves went to ash. I ran until the heat stopped me, Borgan and the Ozali who had been Mr. Ignat' somewhere back and behind me, forgotten in the gibbering of the land, the agony of the trees.

Power was churning in my blood; more power than I had a right to—and so very little, against the rapacity of the flames.

My first thought was to smother them, but no Word rose to my tongue, the speaking of which would transform an inferno into a candle flame to be pinched out at my leisure. I would need to create a working, then—and I didn't know how.

A tongue of flame licked upward, and the land brought me the sound of laughter from further up the hill. Joe Nemeier's boys and girls, having themselves a party by the bonfire.

I raised my right hand, noting distantly that, sometime during my headlong bolt up Heath Hill, I'd pulled on the Ozaliflame's gloves. There was only one thing that I knew I could do.

Centering myself, I extended my will, seeking a connection with the fire.

"Katie!"

Black wings beat against my face. I threw my right arm up, concentration shattered, feet tangling in the unruly grass.

"Kate!" Borgan grabbed my left arm, keeping me on my feet by main force.

"Katie." That was Mr. Ignat', coming up on my off side. "Wait."

"*Wait*? Can't you hear the trees? They're dying in there—"

"I hear them," he said mildly. "And you've forgotten something." He lifted his hand, and the big black bird came to his fist, orange eyes sparkling.

"What did I forget?" I demanded, while seedlings died in torment.

Mr. Ignat' smiled. "I'm a fire elemental," he said, and snapped his arm skyward, releasing the bird in an explosion of wings.

It soared, silhouetted against the flames, spiraling against the pale stars until it was well above the blaze. There it hung for a long moment or three, as if assessing the situation.

Then, it folded its wings and plummeted into the heart of the fire.

I screamed and jerked forward, held back at first by the iron grip on my arm—and then by unadulterated wonder.

Between the trees, the flames leapt, the bird a fleet shadow dancing 'round them. Slowly, at first, and then more quickly, the flames began to die back, the panic of the trees began to ease.

The black bird made a tight turn amid the trunks, and was lost to my outer eyes. Inside my head, the land showed me a flash of brilliant orange wings weaving between the trees. Secret tongues of fire guttered as the bird swept past, consuming them like a barn swallow chows down mosquitoes.

I breathed, and looked to Mr. Ignat', standing cool and calm at my side, watching the progress of his pet.

"A phoenix?" I asked.

"Not exactly," he answered, absently.

Right. Well, *that* seemed to be under control. I turned my attention uphill, where quite a number of folks were gathered on the patio, watching the show, occasionally enlivening the proceedings with a catcall or a shouted obscenity.

I stepped Sideways and took a good look at the densely worked protections enveloping the house. They were not only dense, I saw after a moment's study, they were . . . bloated. Power fairly dripped from them, like grease from a roasting pig.

A blink and I was back in my body, taking a deep breath. "Borgan."

"Yep."

"I'm going to rip a hole in the protections over that house. Would you ask our friend the fire elemental if he'd do me the favor of igniting the roof when he has a couple seconds free?"

"Hmm," said Borgan. "Check me. From what you said yesterday morning, seems to me that tearing up his works would only make Mr. Wonderful that much stronger, not to say even more irritable than he was when he left us. Did I get that wrong?"

Ah, hell, I thought, and gave myself a brisk mental kick. *Honestly, Kate. You can't even keep track of your own theory?*

"No," I told Borgan, "you got it right. There's a hell of a lot of power tied up in that working. It's probably to our benefit to leave it right where it is."

"I can see where it might've relieved your feelings," he said sympathetically, and I laughed.

The not-exactly-phoenix had been busy while I'd been considering an assault on the house. The woods were dark, and though the trees were still quivering in horror, they were already taking stock among themselves. The land, too, had quietened; I had a sense of it collapsed in a corner of my head, like a puppy worn out with the excitement of the day.

I was beginning to relax myself, when a flicker of orange threaded rapidly through the woods, shooting up, up, above the tree tops—and turned lazily in the sea breeze.

To say it was beautiful would be as inadequate as saying that the ocean is wet. Every feather was a distinct, tiny flame, gold and scarlet; its crest scintillant. Six times it turned over the wood, then Mr. Ignat' thrust his arm up.

It folded those marvelous wings and fell out of the sky, taking control of its dive at the last possible second and landing light as a mother's kiss on the outstretched fist.

Mr. Ignat' brought it down to shoulder height, and there it sat, preening.

"Pirate Kate?" Mr. Ignat' said quietly. "Do you know who dared to defile your grandmother's Wood?"

"I do," I admitted, perversely pleased by this evidence of shared bloody-mindedness. "They're right up the Hill, there. But. Ramendysis has gone to a lot of trouble and expense to protect the house and the men, and as Borgan points out, it might be best for the moment to let sleeping dogs lie."

"Indeed," Mr. Ignat' murmured. He turned his head and glanced up to Joe Nemeier's house. I had a momentary feeling of absence as he slipped Sideways; then he was back with us, sending a quizzical blue glance into my face. "That working is dangerously over-powered."

"Noticed it myself," I told him. "Still, while it's all twisted around the house, it's power he doesn't have access to."

"True." He turned and caught Borgan's eye. "I am afraid, since we cannot return the gift, that it must go somewhere, before it again becomes an active danger. May I impose?"

Borgan tipped his head slightly, eyes narrowed, as if he were hearing something no one else could hear. Which he probably was.

After a moment, he blinked and gave Mr. Ignat' a nod. "We'll take it."

"Thank you." He brought the bird close, and stroked the brilliant head with a gentle forefinger. The bird cocked an eye—and was gone in a boom of fiery wings, climbing into the dawn.

At the very edge of my vision, when it was only a glittering orange speck against the pale pink sky, it suddenly flared, and fell, a gaudy orange meteor, challenging the dawn; outpacing it for brilliance and beauty—until it was extinguished by the sea.

I sighed, in mingled regret and admiration.

"Useful bird."

"In fact, he is," Mr. Ignat' said. "I wonder, Katie dear, if I might have your attention for a moment?"

I eyed him. "What now?"

"It occurs to me, since we are presently denied the pleasure of dealing with our enemies as we would like, that the Wood requires protection. Attend me and I will teach you what you must do."

"Why me?"

"Because I cannot," he said crisply. "Now, attend." He raised a slim, white forefinger.

"What I would like you to do is lay a line of power in the pattern I will show you. Can you do that?"

Surprisingly enough, I could, since this was the usual way of teaching neo-magicians basic spellcraft.

"We're weaving a protection for the Wood," I said, to make sure we were both on the same page. "Nothing else."

"That is correct."

"All right, then." My blood was still hot with power; it wasn't raising it that was going to be the problem. "I'm ready when you are," I said.

The pale finger moved. Keeping the *jikinap* ruthlessly in check, I laid it down as I'd been bid, taking some small pride in the evenness of the thread.

It was a deceptively simple pattern, and probably it didn't take more than five minutes to lay out. Subjectively, though, we worked for an hour, and I was sweating and shaking by the time Mr. Ignat' said, "That's very good, Katie. Now tie it off."

Tie it off I did, and tripled the knot, too, on the theory that you can never be too careful; then stood panting as I waited for my next instructions.

"Bold lass. The worst is behind you, Pirate Kate. All that remains is to seal it. After, I swear to you, we'll all three of us go down to Bob's for breakfast."

My memory of sealing a work was dim, but I retained the strong feeling that it wasn't nearly as easy as he was making out—which just goes to show how wrong childhood memories can be. All I had to do was step Sideways and raise the working until it hovered over the Wood. A snap of insubstantial fingers and the spell expanded, accommodating itself to the physical parameters of that which it had been crafted to protect.

"Well done!" Mr. Ignat' applauded as I stepped back into my body. I let myself sag against Borgan, who put an accommodating arm around my waist while continuing to stare uphill.

"They went into the house, but I'm thinking they'll try again, sooner rather than later," he said.

"Which is what the protection spell is for," I pointed out. Absurdly, I felt lighter, as if the *jikinap* in the spell were an actual weight that I had put aside.

"Hmm," said Borgan.

"We may only do what we can do," Mr. Ignat' said. "Now, I don't know about the pair of you, but I could use a grilled blueberry muffin."

"Breakfast sounds good," Borgan said. "Bob's oughta be open."

"Excellent."

"What I could use," I said, as we turned and headed down Heath Hill on the easy side, "are some explanations."

"Explanations, Katie dear?" asked Mr. Ignat' as we cut across the vacant lot next to Gentleman Johnnie's. "What explanations would those be?"

I looked over to Borgan, who was politely walking on my left hand, next to the empty street. "Fork over. Why did Ramendysis think it was Nerazi who helped Gran with the binding?"

He looked down at me with a smile. "To be fair to the man, it *was* Nerazi who went through the shield curtain with your Gran and Ozali Belignatious, here—they'd set the curtain in place to protect the common folk from the working, see?"

And also, I was betting, to somewhat obscure what was happening on the other side. Except—"Ramendysis and the other Ozali of the posse—they ought've been able to see through the curtain."

"In the normal way of things, that'd be the case," he agreed. "But there was so much power in the air that night I could hardly see my hand in front of my face, much less be certain of something going on fifty yards away and on the other side of a shield. No reason to think there was anybody else on the Rock than the three who'd started out."

I chewed on that a minute while we continued walking up Grand Avenue. The street lights were going out, one by one, as we approached each, like a special effect in a cheesy horror flick.

"Okay," I said eventually. "I'll buy that. I imagine it was a pretty wild night."

"Right. So, it was your gran and Nerazi and the Ozali who went out to the Rock. But even Nerazi can't be in two places at once, and she was needed at the Boundary Stone to take things in hand there. Once they cleared the curtain, she went into the sea and I came out, with no one on shore the wiser."

I thought about that, turning it this way and that to look for holes and omissions as we cut across Fountain Plaza. "What did Nerazi have to take care of at the Boundary Stone?" I asked.

"She had to catch old Ignat' and keep him from doing himself a hurt," the Ozali Belignatious said quietly. "It was quite a working we'd embarked upon, Katie. We'd planned as well as we could, but we still might have failed that night without Borgan's help."

"Really?" I flicked a look up into Borgan's face. The side of his mouth quirked.

"Wicked rough seas that night," he said, and then, "Here we go."

Mr. Ignat' opened the door for me and the two of them stood

back and let me walk into Bob's first. The heat was blasting down from the overhead, which was a blessing and a mitzvah, and on WBLM, Ric Ocasek was crooning "Magic." Four guys who looked to be regulars were having an earnest conversation over their coffee and pancakes in the first booth; they didn't even look up when I went past, heading for the back.

I slid into the shadowed booth nearest the kitchen. Borgan took the seat next to me, and Ozali Belignatious sat across.

"All right—" I began, then closed my mouth as Bob popped out of the kitchen, a bowl of baked beans in hand.

He paused and shot me a quick glance over his shoulder.

"Everything okay, Kate?" he asked.

"Working on it," I told him.

He considered that briefly; nodded.

"Be right with you," he said, and went on down to the front. I leaned back in the booth, rested my head against the vinyl and closed my eyes. Despite having had what anybody might call a full couple of days, and not a shred of sleep for more than twenty-four hours, I was feeling—good. Frantic, but good. On WBLM, "Magic" segued into "My Best Friend's Girl." Great, a Cars block.

"All right, Kate," Bob said briskly. "What can I get for you?"

I opened my eyes, but didn't bother to lift my head. "Cheese omelet, homefries, grilled blueberry muffin, and a cup of coffee."

He nodded, wrote it down, and looked at Borgan.

"Pancakes, egg over easy, bacon, coffee."

Another nod, a note, and a glance at Ozali Belignatious.

"A grilled blueberry muffin and a cup of coffee, please," he said sweetly.

Bob snorted. "You were gonna start eating something with that, remember?" he said, in that half-worried, half-scolding voice I'd heard from him—had it only been Monday morning?

Mr. Ignat' raised his eyebrows. "A side of bacon?"

"That's better." Bob made the note and stuck the pencil behind his ear. "Coffee'll be right out," he said, and left us.

I turned my head to follow his progress into the kitchen. As soon as the door swung shut after him, I turned back to Mr. Ignat'.

"He didn't see anything different," I said.

He nodded. "Protective coloration. It wouldn't do for old Ignat' to disappear, when there are so many people looking after him."

Not to mention that it might not be altogether smart for an

Ozaliflame to suddenly appear, not when every *trenvay* in Archers Beach knew that Googin Rock had been empty. Still—

"Somebody's going to smell the illusion," I said. "Then what?"

"If it were an illusion, I would have cause for concern," Mr. Ignat' answered placidly. "As it is, I'm merely allowing people to see what they've seen for many, many years."

I opened my mouth—and closed it as the kitchen door swung open and Bob whisked past on his way to the counter.

Next to me, Borgan sighed and rolled his shoulders. "Finn's gonna get tired of fishing for me," he said conversationally. "And he don't do as good a job for Mary as he ought."

I turned my head to look at him. "He stints her on the catch?"

"No, now, none of that. It's just that he doesn't put himself out in the matter of catching them."

"Oh." I frowned. "How long are you going to fish for Mary, now that Hum's gone?"

"Contract's for seven years," he said. "Be done three this summer. I—" He stopped as Bob put steaming mugs and a generous handful of creamers on the end of the table.

"Food's coming," he said, and moved down to check on the first booth.

"Then what?" I asked Borgan.

"After the contract?" He shrugged, and slid a mug over to me, along with four creamers. "Might go back up to Halifax. Might not. Depends on where I'm wanted."

Across from me, Ozali Belignatious claimed a mug, and wrapped his long, white hands around it. Mr. Ignat' had always drunk his coffee black, even Bob's coffee, and it appeared the full Ozali edition shared that preference.

Borgan had better sense. He dumped three creamers into his coffee, and looked pensively into the swirling depths, as if debating the merits of adding a fourth.

I sat up and dealt with my own mug, then slid it to one side so I could lean my elbows on the table.

"Mr. Ignat'," I began, and shook my head in frustration. "I can't keep calling you that."

He looked up, smiling slightly beneath the flame-red mustache. "Why not? It's what you've always called me, and I don't mind."

"I didn't call *you*— Argh." I put my head in my hands, fingers raking through my hair.

"I must say that it was very brave of you to try to absorb that fire, Katie," he said, while I was still wrestling with philosophy—and losing. "Unfortunately, it was also foolish. Even I would hesitate to absorb such a fire."

Fingers still tangled in my hair, I looked up at him. "What made that fire more dangerous than any other fire?"

"It was created in malice, and charged to consume everything in its path. Fire is quite sensitive to nuance. And while you were not strictly in its path, you did place yourself in a vulnerable position with relation to— Ah, breakfast!"

Bob clattered plates down, Borgan passed mine over, and the utensils rolled up in their paper napkin. Mr. Ignat' had already started on his muffin, and I didn't blame him one bit. Granted, we were all going to die, just as soon as Ramendysis got tired of waiting for us, but for the moment, I was *starving*. I broke the paper tape, pulled out my fork and got down to cases.

THIRTY-FIVE

ᴥ

Wednesday, April 26

We made short work of our meals, while the locals filtered in by ones, threes and twos. Raucous, subdued, and half-asleep, they dealt themselves out into their usual places, ordering, when it was their turn, without bothering to look at the menu. On WBLM, the overnight guy signed off and the morning crew signed in, maintaining a steady stream of classic rock in between the weather report, sports scores, and wisecracks.

"All right." I pushed my plate aside and gave Ozali Belignatious a stern look. He raised his eyebrows.

"So *fierce*, Katie . . ."

"Gran is still missing," I said, in case he hadn't noticed. "Ramendysis is not happy with us, and he left in a flurry of threats. Even if he can't get at Borgan through his jacket, which—" I let Borgan have some of the glare. "—it's likely he can, even if only through association." He raised an eyebrow and I sighed.

"Granted, it might take him a while. *Even so*—Ramendysis has Gran and he has my mother—or whatever my mother's become. Also, he didn't waste any time ratcheting up mischief, Joe Nemeier style. This morning's little campfire was by way of a demonstration that he can do whatever the hell he wants to do, however the Law reads or the Wise forbid."

"I don't think that Ramendysis has Bonny," Mr. Ignat' objected. "He would have shown her to you if he did, to be certain you were suffering as you should."

Which was a pretty accurate reading of Ramendysis' character. "All right," I conceded, "maybe he doesn't have Gran. But we know he has my mother."

"It is likely that Nessa is one of the matters in hand he referred to, yes," Mr. Ignat' conceded in his turn.

"But he didn't show her, either," Borgan pointed out.

"He probably thinks Gran told me all about it," I said, gloomily. "He thinks she told me all kinds of things she didn't; what's one more, among enemies? Dammit!" I shook my head, and tried for some humor. "Why didn't Gran ever get a cell phone?"

"She did," Borgan said from beside me. I turned on the bench to stare at him.

"What?"

"Bonny had a cell phone," he repeated. "You didn't find it at the house?"

"I think hell just froze," I said, and pulled my cell out. "You wouldn't happen to have the number, would you?"

"Sure thing." He flipped his phone open, worked the keypad and a heartbeat later I had Gran's cell number in my phone book. "Right," I said, and hit "send."

What should've happened was exactly what did happen. I heard a couple rings, then an automated voice telling me that Bonny Pepperidge was out of range and would I like to leave a message.

Well, why not?

"Gran, it's Kate. I'm back home and I need you to give me a call. It's urgent." I recited my cell number and hit "end" with a sigh.

"Okay, *that* was a dumb idea," I said, flipping my phone closed and slipping it away. I looked between Borgan and Mr. Ignat'.

"If either of you has a better one, sing out."

Not surprisingly, neither did.

Well. I leaned forward, and made earnest eye contact with the Ozali, suppressing a shudder at the blue flames dancing in his pupils.

"What does Ramendysis want?"

He gave me a beatific smile. "I'm sure young Borgan will be

happy to pick up the tab, Katie. After all, you paid for breakfast yesterday."

"That was Monday," I told him; "and you're dodging—"

"C'mon, Kate," Borgan interrupted, sliding out of the booth and heading for the register. "Let's take a walk."

A walk, forsooth. I grumbled my way out of the booth, and paused to watch Borgan walk over to the register. Ozali Belignatious, on the other hand, seemed immune to pleasant scenery. He was already halfway to the door, and I wasn't about to let him vanish without answering my questions.

I followed him, leaving Borgan to find us or not, as the whim took him.

But it appeared that Mr. Ignat' was perfectly willing to wait until our team had re-assembled before continuing on. He was loitering near the curb, gazing up into the pale, cloudless sky and in imminent peril of tumbling into the street. Not that there was any traffic to speak of, but—

"If you fall and break your ankle, I am *not* carrying you home."

"Of course not, Katie," he said absently, "I would never ask it of you." He snapped his fist into the air, and a feathered form burst out of the sky to land on it, light as a soap bubble.

The bird was once again the color of soot; seen in the light of day, it bore a passing resemblance to a common Maine raven, with its long-fingered wings and cruel, heavy beak. The eyes, though, were like chips of topaz, and alert beyond a raven's intelligence.

"What's his-or-her name?" I asked as the bird walked up the Ozali's leathered arm and settled on his shoulder.

"Arbalyr," Mr. Ignat' murmured. "But it's best, Katie, not to speak it aloud, except in times of great need."

Great. Another secret I didn't want. The bird cocked an eye at me, as if it had read that thought and found it amusing.

"All right, then." Borgan came up on my right side, and jerked his head up Dube Street, toward the ocean. "Little walk on the beach to settle the digestion?"

"Excellent," Mr. Ignat' said dreamily, and gave Borgan a nod. "Lead on."

This, Borgan did, leaving me to walk beside Mr. Ignat'.

"What," I said again, and in my best brook-no-nonsense tone, "does Ramendysis want?"

Mr. Ignat' flicked a flame blue glance along the side of my face.

"He wants the Opal of Dawn, Pirate Kate."

"The...Opal of Dawn," I repeated. "And that's what, exactly?"

"Perhaps," he said, "we should wait until we're on the beach."

I sighed, but took the hint, and eventually we were crossing the dunes, single file on the boardwalk, straggling out when we hit the beach.

The tide had turned, but the water was still 'way out. Borgan was standing on damp sand, looking—maybe at the islands, or the lighthouses, or the glitter of sunlight on the waves.

"All right," I said when Mr. Ignat' and I had reached his side. "No more dodging.

"Ramendysis," I said to Borgan's glance, "wants the Opal of Dawn."

"Does he now?" he said politely. "And that would be what?"

"Mr. Ignat' was just about to tell us," I said and turned to give him a glare.

He smiled and raised his hand as if he were warding my power. Which was a joke. I hoped.

"The Opal of Dawn," he said, "is a jewel of great worth, which rightfully lies within the honor of Mergine, High Queen of Daknowyth."

"Hold it." I held my hand up. "Ramendysis says that he's looking for something that belongs to him."

Mr. Ignat' pursed his lips. "To be fair, he does have some reason to believe that the Opal is his. Mergine agreed that he might have it, if he met certain conditions, which he has."

"Changed her mind?" I guessed.

"Given her choice, Mergine would have never pledged the jewel. However, she was in an untenable position, having taken a war into the Land of the Flowers so cleverly that she very nearly established herself before the Great Houses banded together and drove her back."

"I remember my grandfather telling the story of the war with Daknowyth," I said. "Ramendysis was a hero."

"That's very true; he was." Mr. Ignat' turned and strolled up-coast, and Borgan and I, perforce, went with him.

"Since he had shown so well in the war," he continued; "it was Ramendysis whom the Council chose to carry the terms of defeat to Mergine." He paused, reaching up to stroke his bird's feathers, a line between his golden brows.

"The Council's terms were harsh—harsher than many of us had argued for, reasoning that clemency might win us an ally where spite would only confirm a foe. However, there was wounded pride to be salved, and Ramendysis was one of those strongest in support of stern measures. In the end, the vote went his way, and he carried the terms to Mergine, who would have no choice but to accept them."

I took a breath and put my hands in my pockets.

"But," I said.

He smiled. "But, there was the Opal, treasure of Mergine's house, and which Ramendysis, in his ambition, desired. He showed the Queen the Council's terms, and offered to return and plead clemency—on condition that she cede the Opal."

"Tough call. But I'm guessing she agreed to it, to spare her people what she could."

"You were raised to be a princess, Katie. In fact, that was her reasoning. The Opal's virtue is such that Mergine rightly feared what might happen to Daknowyth—and to the very forces that bind the Six Worlds—should Ramendysis come to possess it. So she bargained, and in the end she gave Ramendysis a Word as surety that she would deliver him the Opal when two conditions were met." Mr. Ignat' stopped and turned to face us, raising a slender forefinger.

"One. That Ramendysis win from the Council gentler terms for defeated Daknowyth." The middle finger rose. "Two—that he achieve ascendancy in the Land of the Flowers, for only a master of men and of *jikinap* could hope to command the Opal."

I closed my eyes, and took a step closer to Borgan. He put a hand on my shoulder and warmth radiated through stiff muscles. "This is why Ramendysis started snacking down Ozali, isn't it?"

"It is." Mr. Ignat' paused. "To be just, Mergine believed he would either fall in pursuit of his goal, or that he would attain so much power that it would turn on him. In that light, her gamble wasn't as wild as it may seem to you. No one could have foreseen that Ramendysis could have achieved and contained so much—"

"...without his head exploding," I finished, and opened my eyes. "So Mergine realized that she'd misjudged, and hid the Opal?"

"In essence."

"Great." I rubbed my forehead. "And it's in Archers Beach."

Mr. Ignat' turned away and recommended his stroll. I glared at his back, then moved out from under Borgan's hand, half-running to catch up.

"Gran agreed to hide it here. In fact—" Mr. Ignat' stopped so suddenly I damn' near fell on my nose. "In fact," I repeated, breathlessly, "she talked it over with you—asked your advice. You do know where it is, don't you? That's why Ramendysis wanted to chat with you."

"I knew where it *was*," he corrected me. "Where it is now, and how it has responded to the virtue of this land—that I don't know, Katie."

"Responded—" I stared at him, realized my mouth was hanging open, and closed it. Briefly. "Mergine hid an Object of Power in the Changing Land," I said, the meaning of that finally hitting me like it should, whereupon my stomach tried to escape through the bottoms of my sneakers. "Is she nuts?"

"No more than any of us who have achieved the heights," Mr. Ignat' murmured. "But it may be that she was crazy like a fox, Katie, and wished, rather than hoped, that Change is inevitable."

"That way, she'd still spike Mr. Wonderful's guns, even if he found the thing," Borgan said, and lifted a shoulder when I looked up at him. "Gutsy lady."

"Yeah." I shook my head in equal parts admiration and frustration, and focused on Mr. Ignat'. "All right, where *was* the Opal?"

He tipped his head. "It may no longer be there. Bonny could well have moved it. In fact, it's almost certain that she did."

"I'll take the chance," I said briskly. "Where *was* it?"

"Would you give the Opal to Ramendysis, Katie, knowing that the Six Worlds may cease to exist if you do?"

I blinked. "Define 'cease to exist.'"

Mr. Ignat' inclined his head, but it was Borgan who spoke, in the ritual cadence he had used to tell me the creation story.

"The Wind that Blows between the Worlds will die, and the power of each World will crumble. The Shadows will eat our hearts and the stars will dance in our dust."

"Right." I took a breath. "And that's what will happen, give or take a poetic allusion or two, if Ramendysis gets the Opal? Even if it's been Changed?"

"Katie," Mr. Ignat' said reproachfully. "You know as well as I do that no one can predict what Change might work upon an object. It may have rendered the Opal useless, true. But it's just as likely that the Opal has become...even more powerful."

"Terrific." I closed my eyes. "Just—If I don't give Ramendysis *some*thing, Archers Beach is going to cease to exist, and it's going to hurt like a sonofabitch, too. We *can't* stand against him—"

"Maybe," Mr. Ignat' interrupted softly. "Maybe we can."

I opened my eyes. "If you've got an idea, bring it on out where we can all take a look at it."

But he shook his head. "Give me a day's grace, child. It may be that our case isn't as hopeless as it seems."

"I don't *have*—" I began, and this time it was Borgan who interrupted me.

"Let's look at tactics, Kate," he said, and glanced over my head to the Ozali. "If you give Mr. Wonderful what he wants, he's got no reason to keep his side of the bargain, such as it is. He didn't give you a Word to hang him with if he doesn't behave himself. Not to mention there's your gran still on the wrong side of the Wall..."

"Young Borgan is correct, Katie." Mr. Ignat' took up the argument. "I believe our first order of business must be to fetch Bonny home. The choices before us may be clearer if we leave no hostages in Ramendysis' hands."

Which, I had to admit, only sounded like good common sense. Unfortunately.

"All right," I said slowly, "we get Gran out of the Land of the Flowers first. The question is *how*. Ramendysis will know the second I hit town, even if I don't use the Gate. He'll be expecting me to deliver the Opal, double quick, and he's not going to be a happy camper when he finds out I just dropped by to take in the scenery."

"I'll go," Mr. Ignat' said quietly. I looked at him.

"No."

"It's his mess," Borgan said reasonably. "He's got a right to clean it up."

"The Opal being here is partially his doing," I said, keeping a sharp eye on Mr. Ignat', who only smiled at me wistfully and stroked his bird. "But there were at least three other people in on it, which is why it's the great big, grand old calamity that it is, instead of your garden variety catastrophe. Gran going over the Wall, though—" I laughed shortly. "The letter she left me—she apologized for leaving a mess for me to clean up."

"I'll go," Mr. Ignat' said again. I shook my head.

"What if Ramendysis catches you and drinks your power?"

His smile went from wistful to savage, and the bird started from his shoulder, black wings grabbing air. "Why then, he will be sore amazed, as little as he'd gain from me."

"Which is another argument against your going," I said sternly, and sighed. "All right. Take your day. Let's all three meet at Tupelo House at midnight, and share what we've got. Maybe we can come up with a plan that doesn't involve one or all of us getting eaten alive. And, hey—it'll give Gran a chance to check her messages."

Borgan laughed, and after a moment, Mr. Ignat' joined him. I managed a grin of sorts before I put my hand on Borgan's arm.

"All right," I said when he smiled down at me. "I'm going home. I'm going to take a shower and get some sleep." I looked at the Ozali. "Anything else you want to tell me?"

"Why, yes," he said, and gave me one of Mr. Ignat's charmingly extravagant bows.

"I honor, respect, and stand in awe of you, Katie. And I love you, very much."

He turned while I was still gaping, and walked away up the beach, a slim golden youth all in black leather, bright hair blowing like sparks on the breeze, and the dark bird flying overhead.

THIRTY-SIX

Wednesday, April 26

As I was taking my shower it occurred to me to wonder what crime Ozali Belignatious had committed to get himself sentenced to Googin Rock.

At a conservative guess, I'd heard the story of the Ozali in the Rock about a thousand times while I was growing up. Now that I thought about it, Gran had always been vague on the point; the why of the chase lost inside the how of The Fire.

The subtext of the story, though, had been that the Ozaliflame was framed, going to the Rock innocent and meek. And yet—they'd had time to plan, Ignat' and Gran. I hadn't seen it, but I was betting that the working which separated the Ozali from his power had been several orders of magnitude above non-trivial. Not to mention the time and care that had likely been required to distill a bottle or six of *jikinap*-laced whiskey...

What if, I thought, as I toweled dry—what if it hadn't been the Ozaliflame who had been framed, but the posse that had been hoodwinked?

The Six Worlds don't exactly match up, time-wise, nor does cause in Sempeki necessarily equal effect in Cheobaug. What if, in fact, Gran and Ignat' had engineered the whole farce, up to and including his imprisonment before a cast of dozens in order to demonstrate that he couldn't possibly have been the author of some subsequent action?

"And what if pigs can fly, Kate?" I asked my reflection irritably, as I dragged a comb ruthlessly through the mass of tangles that was my hair. "The problem of the day is getting Gran, and Mother, out of the Land of the Flowers. Focus."

Back in my code jockey days, when my brain got to working overtime on an extraneous, trivial problem it usually meant that the grunt work on the real problem was being done in some sleazy back room tenanted by unsavory thought processes, and that sooner or later, if I just went with the flow and didn't jostle their grubby elbows, they'd fork over with a solution.

I was really, really hoping that was what was going on now.

In the meantime, I got dressed, checked the answering machine, and walked up to Heath Hill.

The sea breeze had cleared away most of the smell of gasoline, smoke, and charred greenwood. Uphill, Joe Nemeier's house slumbered, its protections so dense they were nearly visible to the unaided eye.

I slipped Sideways as easily as if I'd just danced a step across the grass, squinting in protest of the proliferation of workings, laid one over the other with a trowel, apparently; their disparate functions co-existing uneasily, and the whole structure an offense to the senses, not to mention aesthetics. I had expected a mage of Ramendysis' age and abilities to have developed some elegance in these matters.

But the lack of elegance wasn't really the interesting thing. The fact that Joe Nemeier's house had seen a hundredfold increase in protection *since early this morning—that* was interesting. I made a note to mention it to Mr. Ignat'.

Then, I turned my attention to the Wood.

In comparison with the sloppy gobs of power dripping over Nemeier's house, the protection above the Wood was a thing of spare beauty. Enough power to do the job, and no more, the working itself a marvel of silken impenetrability. I couldn't have managed anything nearly so comprehensive and thrifty on my own.

Now that I'd had *jikinap* thrust upon me, it would seem I could do a lot worse than ask Ozali Belignatious to teach me spellcraft.

Assuming I, and Archers Beach, managed to survive our various current difficulties.

I stepped back into my body with a sigh, blinking at the disordered trees. Slowly, so as not to pluck raw nerves, I approached. The working fizzed as I passed through, which was the *jikinap* recognizing me as its all-too-temporary master.

Inside the Wood, the trees were a-twitter. I kept carefully to the path, tallying the damage as I went. The young trees had fared worst, and oldsters with not much sap left in them. For the most part, though, the harm seemed gratifyingly slight. Which was all due to Mr. Ignat' and his feathered friend. I shuddered to think what might have happened if I'd had to handle the fire alone. Assuming that I had managed not to incinerate myself.

At length, I came to the Center. Here, the fire had snacked on last year's leaves and dry twigs, leaving the trees unmolested. I put my hand against the trunk of Gran's ancient tupelo, and gave a sigh of absolute relief to find the wood warm and welcoming. Not so comforting was the blight that teased the edge of my vision. Was it bigger? Darker? Deeper? I hoped it was only my imagination that made it seem so.

"I've come," I said to the trees, "as Guardian of the land and granddaughter of the Lady. Tell me what I can do to help you, and to mend what may be mended."

A breeze rustled through the leaves—a particularly frisky breeze, and flexible as to direction. But if the trees were speaking, they didn't choose to speak to me.

I waited, listening to the sounds of the small lives—squirrels in the high branches, chipmunks scrabbling in the mold. Somewhere among the deep trees, my friend the pileated woodpecker started laughing at his own joke, and I saw the tender curls of fern and wood herbs pushing out from beneath the leaves on the forest floor.

Finally, the breeze came 'round to me and tickled the inside of my ear.

We note the protections in place. The trees are grateful.

"I regret that I didn't foresee the attack against the trees and provide protection beforehand."

We each put down roots where it seems best, seedling. Even the Lady errs sometimes.

What . . . a novel thought. I wondered how Gran would take knowing that the trees forgave her.

And I'd be willing to do damn' near anything to find out.

There are some few places which may benefit from the Guardian's hand, the voice of the wood murmured.

"Show me," I said.

Across from me and to the left of a particularly robust fir, the undergrowth rustled, leaves and branches pulling back. Opening a path for me.

I touched the land, taking comfort from the presence inside my head, and went where the wood desired.

It was four-thirty when I got to the carousel, having gone around by Grand, instead of trying to cut through Fun Country's tourist-clogged avenues. The U.S., Maine, and Canadian flags were snapping smartly in the breeze when I crossed Fountain Circle, and there were people waiting patiently in line next to the fountain itself. I ducked between a plump lady with bright white hair and twinkling brown eyes and a slightly thinner edition—sisters, maybe, I thought as I smiled and nodded my thanks.

Nancy saw me coming and pushed the gate open. I slipped into the control booth and parked my rump on the stool.

"Has it been like this all day?" I asked, scrapping damp hair out of my damp face, discovering bits of leaf and twig in the snarls.

"Pretty much," she said, and tapped the ticket box with the toe of her sneaker. "Already emptied this twice. Chits went down to the office by runner." I nodded.

Nancy touched the switch and the bell rang twice, signaling the end of the ride.

"Today's the day everybody was s'posed to arrive," she said as the carousel glided to a stop. "So now we got the early birds *and* the folks who waited 'til the opening was official." She reached over to unhook the chain.

"Ticket, deah," she said to the first in line. I was quiet while she counted them in, rehooked the chain, rang the warning bell and pushed the stick up.

"Hey, somebody's riding the batwing."

"Been so busy, they've gotta ride her, though some have waited for the next ride," Nancy said. "I think it's the fangs that unnerve 'em."

"Could be." I sighed and stretched, carefully. I wasn't any closer to a brilliant idea for bringing Gran out of the Land of the Flowers, but at least the Wood was squared away. The trees could take it from here. I used my chin to point at the ticket box.

"Why not take those down to Marilyn and go on home? Your shift's almost over."

"About that," Nancy said, and I looked at her, eyebrows up.

"Might as well go over to Tony and Anna's and get your supper. I'll stay on 'til six."

"I appreciate it, but why?"

"Park's open 'til midnight," she said. "Marilyn sent 'round a notice..." She wormed a hand into her front jeans pocket and pulled out a rumpled piece of yellow paper.

I unfolded it and read as much of the good news as was visible. Somebody was determined to wring the last drop of ink out of the Chamber's printer cartridge and no mistake.

Park open noon to midnight for the next three days, was the gist of it. Fireworks every night at ten, weather permitting. Ticket booklets were being sold at group discount, and shares would be adjusted accordingly. At the bottom of the sheet was a breakdown of earnings since Monday.

I blinked. "I want these folks back next year."

"It's been a good start to the Season," Nancy agreed.

"Oh," said the person at the head of the line—a trim matron with violently blue hair—"I love coming to places early! This is my third pre-Season with the Fun Lovers and I always have such a marvelous time!"

"Well, we're having a marvelous time, too," I told her. "Your group's been something special."

She smiled, pleased, and Nancy rang the bell.

Business started slowing down around 11:30, as the tourists sought either their beds or the headier entertainments of the bars. At ten 'til twelve, the carousel was empty for the first time since I'd taken over from Nancy at six. I did a fast tally and bagged the tickets, leaving them on the stool for Marilyn's helper to pick up in the morning.

Across the way, the lights went out over Tony Lee's Kitchen, and a heartbeat later, I heard the night gate rattle down and lock. Summer's Wheel was at rest, platform lights out, though I could hear the rumble of the cars down at Dodge City, and the

distant metallic clatter of the Galaxi roller coaster at the far end
of the park.

It looked like the carousel was done for the night. I crossed
the enclosure and pulled the first two storm gates closed, latch-
ing them together. That done, I stopped at the main switch and
turned off the outside lights. I was about to do the same for the
running lights when there was a movement to my left, and the
sound of a soft consultation.

The land obligingly brought me their words.

"A merry-go-round! Remember our first date?" she asked softly.

"Think I'd forget it?" he responded.

"I wish..." she said, and let it drift off. "But they're closing for
the night, aren't they?"

I turned my head and gave them a smile—white-haired, the
two of them, she comfortably rounded, he stick-thin and slightly
stooped; wearing matching dark blue windbreakers, sensibly zipped
right up to their chins. They were holding hands.

Something clenched inside my chest: So ordinary, the two of
them, with no eyes for magic. Ordinary people, enjoying the late
hour and the sea air, remembering their first date...

"Got time for one more ride," I said, my voice a little hoarse.
"Before midnight."

They smiled, guileless as children, and went over to drop their
tickets through the slot. I walked back to the operator's station
and took hold of the stick while they climbed aboard and chose
their mounts. I looked to make sure they were settled—her on
the unicorn, him right next to her, mounted on the bobcat—and
threw the switch.

The carousel spun, the woman laughed out loud, clutching
the brass pole as the unicorn started moving up and down. He
rode quiet, his eyes on the side of her face, while the orchestrion
played "Daisy, Daisy." I leaned against the ticket box and watched
them, wondering what it was like to be ordinary—*really* ordinary,
blind to magic and oblivious to power. Life would be simpler,
I thought...or maybe not. If Ramendysis fulfilled his threat to
lay waste to Archers Beach, the ordinary people would suffer as
much as the *trenvay*—and never know why.

By the time the carousel had stopped, most of the midway
lights were out; and I heard the rattle-bang of the night gate
being pulled across the park entrance.

"Better step lively," I told my customers, as they came off the platform—him first, then turning to offer his hand and steady her. "They're rolling the gate closed. You don't want to be locked in."

They exchanged a private glance, and laughed together. "No," said the man, "don't want to be locked in." He gave me a jaunty grin, and a wink as they passed; the woman put her hand on the ticket box, and patted it as if it were a favored grandchild.

"Thank you," she said, softly. "Thank you very much."

Then they were gone, slipping into the darkened midway, hand in hand.

I shook myself and went over to close the rest of the gates and put the carousel to bed.

I locked the hatch behind me, and looked around. The midway was silent, all the rides were closed, and the rolling gate was across the entrance way. Shaking my head, I turned right and was soon in the deeper shadows behind Summer's Wheel, feeling for the breach in the fence. I slipped through to the beach, and turned my face north, toward home.

The Pier was lit up like Christmas Eve, music and voices clearly audible. The shops and eateries would be closed by now, but the bar and casino were open, according to today's memo, 'til two. I angled down to the firm sand, moving briskly. From my right came the gentle plash of waves against the sand. Tide going out.

Now that I was alone, worry rushed back in. The unsavory crew in the back room of my mind had let me down. I didn't have one idea, bright or otherwise, how to fetch Gran home. Or to keep Ramendysis from destroying Archers Beach, either. In fact, the only thing remotely useful I could think to do was to call in the Wise.

Risky—always risky to deal with the Wise. On the other hand, dealing with Ramendysis was looking to become lethal.

I entered the noisy light-striped darkness beneath the Pier, hands in my pockets, knuckles resting on the soft leather gloves. Useful things, and comforting, like the knife in its nestle against my spine.

As I stepped out from beneath the Pier, I became aware of a presence on my right hand, and turned my head.

"Good evening to you, Heeterskyte," I said politely to the small creature.

"Evening, deah," it answered. "Wanted to let you know that I put the question about, and there's neither news nor hint of the old lady to be had."

"Thank you," I said. "I've got good reason to believe she's gone across the Wall, to the Land where the Black Dogs live."

"Huh." It paced in silence for a moment or two, then said, "That would make some sense of a tale I had from a tern, who claimed her tree was ailin'."

I swallowed. "It would, at that."

Silence. I began the long angle toward the dunes, the heeterskyte trailing a bit behind.

"Also," it said. I paused, turning to look at it where it straddled the line between the dry sand and the wet. "We see you've put some effort into clearing out the bad rubbish. Them Dogs are no good for nothing, but the snallygasters are purely wicked. We're obliged."

"It was a team effort," I said, somewhat unsteadily. "But you're welcome, Heeterskyte."

"I'm sorry not to have better news," it said, "to balance out the debt."

"Those things don't belong on the land," I said. "No debt, Heeterskyte."

"Well, that's kindly said. Still, we're not the ones to stint a neighbor. Call on us, if you come to have need."

Good God. That was damn' near unprecedented. I managed a nod, and a grave, "Thank you, Heeterskyte."

"Nothin' to it. Goodnight now, deah."

"Goodnight," I said, but it had darted away, chasing the dark waves.

I shook my head and continued across dry sand, looking homeward. The light was on in Tupelo House, shining out from the open French doors. My heart clenched, then stuttered into its normal rhythm. Mr. Ignat' had a key, of course. Always had. I stretched my legs, moving as quickly as I could through the dry sand.

My cell phone whistled, so unexpected and unlikely a sound that I jumped and damn' near fell. I clawed it out of my pocket and flipped it up, glancing at caller ID—

"Hello?" I said cautiously, my pulse pounding in my temples. *Easy Kate,* I told myself. *It could be a trick. Probably is a trick…*

Static filled my ear, the shadow of a voice beneath it.

"I can't hear you," I yelled, putting my free hand over my open ear. "There's too much—"

"I said," my grandmother's voice snapped, as clear as if she was standing next to me, "we're on the way home. Open the Gate."

The connection went dead.

Not possible, I thought. On the other hand, it was hard to see how it could've been a joke.

I turned and ran back the way I'd come, slipping and sliding until I was all at once on firm sand and running hell for leather back toward Fun Country.

According to the tales that were being told long before the first Archer set foot on the land and so found his destiny and his doom, anybody with a pinch of magic can sing themselves down a hole, or up a tree, or into the sky, in order to visit neighboring worlds. You can do it that way, even now, though it's risky—and unregulated. Which is why the Wise created the Gates.

In Archers Beach, the Gate is the carousel, and if Gran was *on her way,* whatever that meant in terms of the mismatch of time and geography between the Land of the Flowers and the Changing Land, I'd better open it ASAP.

Under the Pier I went, running across light-striped sand, between the shrouded pilings. I was almost through when a shadow lunged out of the greater darkness, grabbing my arm in a grip that threatened to break bone.

I kicked, making solid contact with something yielding; the bruising fingers relaxed just a little and I twisted, my free hand snaking under the jacket to yank the knife free.

Before me, in a haze of dèjá vu, stood Joe Nemeier's errand boy. This time he was holding a gun.

I sighed. "I so do not have time for you," I said.

He smiled. "That's good, because you don't have any time left."

I saw his finger tighten, and reached out to the land. The beach trembled under my feet and I threw myself sideways, rolling until I was on dry sand, coming up onto my knees—and looking back.

Joe Nemeier's boy screamed as he struggled in knee deep sand, his voice lost in the greater uproar from the Pier above. As I watched, he sank to his waist, and then to his shoulders. His head went under and I was on my feet, running full speed for the carousel.

THIRTY-SEVEN

Thursday, April 27
Low Tide 5:06 A.M. EDT
New Moon

For the second time in slightly less than a day, I raised power in order to manipulate a Major Working. The seal on Googin Rock had been complex and tricksy. Damned impressive, too—for the naive work of unlettered savages.

The Gates, though, had been built by the Wise. Not only did that mean it required a mage of a certain level of talent and control to even *see* them; it meant their construction was elegant, balanced, and—if mishandled only a little—deadly.

They were also, truth be told, noisy. There wasn't any question of stealth when opening a Gate. Presumably the Wise had wanted it that way, to ensure that the comings and goings between the Worlds were public and aboveboard. Not that everybody cared to use them—witness Ramendysis.

Whatever the reasoning of my betters, as soon as I opened our Gate, every mage, and a good many of the more sophisticated *trenvay*, were going to know it.

And if I screwed up—well, they'd know that, too, along with the entire mundane population of Archers Beach, just as soon as the Rescue was called out to hose down the smoking crater where the carousel used to be.

High Magic: not for the fainthearted. Or the sane.

I stood at the center of the carousel—the center of the circle—the *jikinap* flickering along my nerve endings, hungry, like it's always hungry. My hands glowed faintly blue in the illumination of the safety lights, and sparks dripped from my fingertips, snapping when they met the sea air. No doubt I had the power. The talent and, more importantly, the control? Well, we'd see now, wouldn't we?

I closed my eyes, took a breath, held it, and breathed out. In Beautiful Theory, along with that breath went all my worries and everyday cares: The imminent destruction of the universe as we know it; the Wood smoldering on the Hill; vandals and condominium developers poised to rape and ravin the land. Gran on the road and the Gate sealed against her...

Breath two—in and out. I felt slightly dislocated, but calmer. Good.

Breath three. I opened my eyes and stepped Sideways.

The Gate hung before me, a thing of grace and beauty, the forces absolutely aligned, subdued and elegant; a mosaic of High Magery, perfect— Well, no. Not quite perfect.

A single tile was missing from the mosaic. A tile bearing exactly the correct load of magic, bound and elucidated in precisely the correct manner.

Cautiously, not daring to hurry, I did the math, brought the power between my palms and painstakingly formed a tile. I weighed it, tasted it, and fired it in the crucible of my will.

Then I gingerly slid it into the place that had been left to receive it.

The world blew apart into brilliant ribbons of lacy nonsense, rippling in a hot, driving wind. I threw a hand up to shield my eyes, squinting into the confusion. Beyond the gusting ribbons of reality, I could see the pennant-crowned spires of a Great House soaring bold against a cloudless green sky; the breeze brought me the nerve-wracking tinkle of merrybells; and the ululating howl of a hunting hound.

I flinched, and the Gate shivered in response, teetering on the edge of implosion—then stabilizing as I flexed a little magical muscle, holding it open between two mutually incompatible worlds. Around it all, the carousel spun, disorienting as it passed through the spires and the pennants; the strains of the "Too Fat Polka" mixing weirdly with the high nattering of the bells.

Excepting that single howl, there was no sign of life beyond
the Gate. The spires, the pennants, the sky—where the hell was
Gran? Had I missed her? The time, the damnable mismatch of
times, what if— There.

Something moved in the gauzy distance; moved with purpose
and against the whim of the wind. Slow . . . agonizingly slow. I
strained to see better through the blowing tatters of reality—and
my heart sank. For it was only a dust devil moving along the
road, glittering with the crystalline particles that passed for soil
in the Land of the Flowers.

The Gate shuddered, sensing weakness in my disappointment,
shrinking dangerously.

Be stern, Keeper, the batwing murmured snidely between my
ears. *Be strong and bold of heart! Waver and you destroy not only
your unworthy self, but the great experiment of the Wise!*

I ground my teeth.

"Shut up," I gasped and thrust the voice out of my head, nar-
rowing my focus to encompass the Gate, the road beyond, and
nothing else. I pushed, forcing the opening wide by brute force—
and held, though I tasted blood at the back of my mouth, and
felt the sear that came of channeling too much power.

I wasn't going to be able to dominate the forces much longer,
and the question became—how long *should* I hold the Gate? The
Wise had never meant for us to just prop the damn' thing open
like a screen door and leave it. Soon or late, it would close—and
if I tried to oppose it—well, let's just say that's one of those things
it's better not to think about.

Carefully, I took a breath, tasting not the wholesome tang of
ocean air, but the cloying sweetness of ambrosia. I sneezed, the
Gate shook—and the dust devil was suddenly nearer, spinning
against the current of the wind, and it seemed to me that I saw
a glint of green among the glittering swirls.

Behind it, moving much more rapidly, came a brace of the
great hunting hounds of the Ozali, their tongues running scarlet;
their eyes molten gold.

"Gran!" I shouted. "Hurry!"

A hand fell on my shoulder, *jikinap* flickered along my nerves,
and a quiet voice said, "Hold the Gate, Katie. I'll bring them in."

He stepped past me, walking tall into the wind, hair streaming
and coat snapping. Down he went to meet the dust devil. I lost

him momentarily among the glittering motes, then found him again, a shadow against the walls of the twister. Then he, and it, were gone.

The hounds howled and leapt forward, teeth bared now. Far back, but fast gaining, I saw horsemen—the hunters, following the hounds. I couldn't see their weapons, but I didn't have to; I remembered too well the great black bows, and the burn of Elfshot...

I shook the memory of agony away, bit my lip, and held the Gate, my lungs burning with effort.

The whirlwind touched down on the threshold of the Gate. Crystalline dust blasted everywhere, opening a thousand tiny cuts in my face—then it was gone, and they were through, past me. Safe.

I stepped back, withdrawing my will with a vengeance as the first hound leapt for the Gate.

Air displacement knocked me off my feet; I fell messily, whacking my head a good one on the edge of the orchestrion, stars chewing the edges of my vision. A howl escaped the closing of the Gate and I whimpered, untangled myself, and pushed upright with arms that shook, blinking to clear my sight—

"Gran—" I started, and stopped.

She turned. Her face showed every one of her years; the front of her dark hair had gone silver to the width of my hand; her skin was bloodied and streaked with grime; her clothes scarcely more than rags. Her eyes, though—her eyes blazed with triumph.

I got my feet under me and walked across the carousel to her side, taking her hand between both of mine. She was cold; I could feel the fragile bones beneath her skin as she tugged me forward to where Mr. Ignat' knelt on the floor, cradling a twisted, brittle stick in his arms like a child.

"Your mother's alive," Gran whispered. "My Nessa." She bent abruptly, her free hand fisted in her mouth, tears cutting the silver dust masking her face.

There wasn't anything to say, and only one thing I could think to do. I gathered her in my arms and held her while she cried.

"Six months?" she asked some while later, in a tone of dizzy disbelief. "It didn't seem any longer than two weeks." She took a breath. "Two weeks from Hell, mind..."

"Yeah, well..." I sighed and shook my head. I'd dragged the stool out from the control booth and gotten her to sit on it, then lowered myself to the cold concrete floor, so that the three of us formed an awkward triangle. My nerves were a-twitter; I expected that the Gate would at any moment open from the other side, admitting an outraged Sempeki Gatekeeper, flanked by two of the Wise, all of them after blood.

"We'll need to go to the Wood," Gran said. "My Nessa needs healing."

Right. I frowned at the dry stick still cradled in Mr. Ignat's arms. It didn't look to be in good shape. At all.

"You should know," he said softly, "that there was an attempt to burn the Wood earlier today."

Gran paled beneath the grime; I saw her shoulders rise as she took a breath.

"The trees still stand." Not a question.

"They do," he agreed.

"And those responsible? Their names are known?"

"I know who they are," I said. "Unfortunately, they're under the protection of Ramendysis—" I looked over to Mr. Ignat'. "—who's seen fit to increase the wardings over the house by an order of magnitude since this morning."

He smiled.

"I...see." Gran bent her head, hands knotted on her lap; thinking or recruiting her strength, or both...

I sighed, quietly, and turned my attention again to the stick. Unlike Gran, my mother'd been only half a dryad. I'd thought—and Gran had never seen fit to correct me—that she'd been born of a liaison with an ordinary citizen of the Changing Land.

My own private guess had been that my paternal grandfather was an Emerson—say, Henry's great-great-grandfather. The possibility that my mother's father was Ozali—and a Fire Ozali, at that—had never crossed my mind.

Regardless of who or how, Nessa's state of half-dryadness meant that her fate and her life weren't tied to a tree like Gran's was. She had been, however, remarkably attuned to growing things. Her smile could bring a rosebush into full bloom, the touch of her hand brought forth lilacs, no matter the season. All growing things loved her, and wanted only to please her.

That said, the idea that my mother had somehow transformed

herself into this spare, drying twiglet, with scarcely a leaf to bless itself with—made my head hurt.

I queried the land, but the land was as baffled as I was. Carefully, I extended a tendril of *jikinap*, questing toward the twig—

"Stop that," Gran snapped, without lifting her head. "You'll have the round tale in good time."

I took a breath, and slid a glance over to Mr. Ignat'. He was watching Gran with an expression of intent interest that I'd never before seen on his face.

Gran sat up straighter on the stool, lifted her head and looked at us, one after the other.

"Bel, you're scarcely a candle to Kate's bonfire."

"True. But I have age and guile on my side, while Katie is an innocent, black-hearted and ruthless though she be."

"Innocent," I repeated, too tired to get mad.

"Indeed. And I am remiss, Katie—my apologies. Young Borgan asks that you call him, when you have a moment free."

"Right." Borgan would've heard the Gate open, just like Mr. Ignat' had. However, being the bright laddie that he was, he'd chosen *not* to come rushing down to watch the fun. I didn't blame him in the least; in my book, it's always best to view explosions and mayhem from a safe distance.

Joints creaking, I stood, fishing my cell out of my pocket. Mr. Ignat' rose as I wandered a few paces away, and bent to place the rickety little bush into Gran's arms.

I stopped by the utility pole, pulled Borgan's number up on the phone, and hit "send."

"Kate, where are you?" He sounded worried, which was gratifying.

"The carousel," I said. "Gran's back, with . . . my mother. It looks like we'll be going up to the Wood to do some planting. Where are *you*?"

"I'm to home. Thought I'd best be on the sea, in case there was—"

Arm yourself! the batwing shouted, while the land shrieked bloody murder, and the storm gate directly across from me went to mist. The blast of hot wind knocked me backward. I snatched at the pole for balance and the cell flew out of my hand. The wind caught it and spun it away beneath the carousel.

Mr. Ignat' whirled between Gran and the breach as a blue-black storm-beast cleared it, Ramendysis on its back.

Flames burst on the busy air: blue, orange, and yellow. The storm-beast swirled them away, and Ramendysis launched a handful of lightning and sleet. Mr. Ignat' parried the bad weather as coolly as if he were playing a casual game of badminton. Behind him, Gran and my mother vanished inside the leaf-green swirl of a protection spell.

I blinked Sideways, noting the thinness of the protective walls of power. If one of those bolts got past Mr. Ignat', Gran's shield would crumple like so much wet tissue.

I touched the land, formed my request, and felt it rush to do my bidding. Around Gran's position a grove of ancient trees snapped into being, trunk to trunk and impenetrable, drawing their strength from the soul of the land itself.

That taken care of, I turned back to the main battle.

In Sideways sight, the Ozaliflame burned like a hearth fire; competent, clever—and small. His opponent, on the other hand, was rogue-crazy, 'way too hot, and looking to destroy everything in his path. Ozali Belignatious was as crazy as Mr. Ignat' had been, if he thought he had a snowball's chance of surviving so unequal a contest.

Ramendysis launched another attack—a net woven of pure *jikinap*, cast from his hand as if he were trawling for herring.

The spell was heavy, the strands over-coated with *jikinap*. It was ugly, unsubtle, out of balance—and good enough to do the job.

But Ramendysis—and I—had reckoned without the Ozaliflame's superior knowledge of spellcraft. The working began to settle, wobbling a little, and abruptly stiffened, frozen in place, locked by a sliver of *jikinap* no longer than my least finger.

It seemed to me that Ramendysis laughed. He dismounted and the storm-beast dispersed, flowing back through the misty wall. A hand wave and it was solid again, ordinary and everyday.

"So, you were in the Rock," he said, conversationally, and cast another net, every bit as heavy and unsubtle as the first.

Once again, Mr. Ignat' caught and locked it.

But the orientation of the two frozen nets formed a right angle; and I could see where Ramendysis was going with this.

If a net wouldn't do the job, then a cage would serve just as well.

"Come, Belignatious!" Ramendysis said. "We aren't savages; we are Ozali. There is no need for me to destroy you. Only tell me where the Opal has been hidden, and you may go your way unmolested—and your low-fae doxy, too."

"What Opal is that?" Mr. Ignat' asked. "Old friend."

Ramendysis threw another net, and four more in such rapid succession I could barely track them.

Four froze as they unfurled, laying inert atop the others, dripping malice. The fifth, though, very nearly did the job, and I couldn't help but notice that the spike that immobilized it was less substantial than the others.

Mr. Ignat's power was visibly depleted, the hearth fire guttering and pale. Ramendysis, by contrast, burned as bright or brighter than before; undiminished by his reckless expenditure of power.

Ramendysis smiled.

"Forgive me, but it seems you have a limited reserve. Would it not be best to husband your resources? You know you cannot stand against me. What is an old oath to the loss of your life and the death of your child?"

He flicked his fingers, tossing another working negligently into the growing pile, where it was skewered in its turn.

"When your last sliver of power is gone into my net, what then, Belignatious?"

"An excellent question," Mr. Ignat' answered. "Shall we find out?"

Might one break silence to point out that you are unprotected and unchampioned, Keeper? The batwing's thought was strained; I could almost hear it stamping its dainty hooves in distress.

And what it said was certainly true. I was wide open. I should, I thought, do something about that.

Across from me, Ramendysis shook his head, lightning threading his thundercloud curls.

"This grows tiresome," he said, and lifted his hands.

Power swirled and flowed between his palms, more power and even more, forming a great, sticky mass, gray touched with pink, like the sky before a thunderstorm, and laced with smoking black threads. Elfshot. I could see its intent as clearly as if I'd built it myself. Released, the sticky mass would pass through the gaps and omissions in the larger workings as separate globules, each containing its tithe of poison. It would stick to whatever it touched, and it would burn, and burn—and, eventually, kill.

Magical napalm.

Trapped between the bars of *jikinap,* Mr. Ignat' took a breath, foreknowing his doom.

Ramendysis paused, the ball spinning between his palms, and tipped his head.

"One more chance. Old friend. Where is the Opal?"

Mr. Ignat' shook his head, golden hair crackling.

Ramendysis released the working.

The Word flamed out of my throat, burning my tongue; the bomb fried in mid-flight, charred bits drifting in the unsteady air.

Ramendysis didn't bother to turn. I saw him raise a finger— then I stumbled as a blade of pure energy swept out of the ether, thick with *jikinap* and ablaze with malice.

I parried clumsily. The next strike came as a hammer blow, and again I barely turned it. My blood was hot now. I yearned to contest against Ramendysis fully, I wanted to crack him open, suck the power out of him, and become, become—

To me! the batwing screamed between my ears. *To me, as you love your life and your land!*

I jumped for the carousel, smelled ozone, and leapt astride the batwing's back.

"Go!" I yelled, and cut the ties that bound it.

THIRTY-EIGHT

Thursday, April 27

The batwing threw itself into the air, heading straight for a distressingly solid metal wall. I shouted a Word; the metal went to mist; leather wings swept down—and we were outside, airborne, and climbing, in starlight almost as bright as day.

He will pursue us.

"Good. We want him to pursue us."

Do we? If this is your unruly blood speaking, Little Ozali—

Far below us, the roof of the carousel enclosure vanished in a blast of sleet, and Ramendysis was rising, a dust devil his steed, and lightnings in his hands.

Your wish is answered. Now what?

Good question. Memory replayed Borgan's voice: *Thought I'd best be on the sea, in case . . .*

Keeper? The batwing's thought was sharp enough to cut.

"Go out—over the ocean," I said.

The batwing turned neatly, furled its wings, and angled downward, right under the noses of the dust devil and its master. Lightning knifed around us; I smelled scorched hair in the racing air, then only the complex scents of the sea.

I flattened myself along the slender neck, my fingers twisted in the silken mane.

"Skim the surface," I panted into a back-swept ear; "as close as you dare. Go north."

The sea rose with dreadful speed, and behind us came Ramendysis upon his beast. Power flared all around, and a *jikinap* net formed on the surface of the waves.

"Watch out!" I yelled, but my mount had already taken evasive action: A strong beat of the wide wings, and we were up, in the middle air again, and blasting north at approximately the speed of sound. Behind us, Ramendysis was gaining.

"You see that notch in the shore up ahead at eleven o'clock?"

Yes . . .

"That's a creek. Follow it inland."

'Ware!

The batwing twisted in mid-flight, and the net fell past, its strands woven with elfshot. Ramendysis was so close I saw him smile.

Too close.

I snatched power into my hands and hurled it like a softball, directly at that hateful smile. Ramendysis raised a negligent hand and absorbed the blast, laughing—and then not, as a black shape whisked out of the star-mantled sky, directly into his face, talons raking and cruel beak slashing.

Mr. Ignat's bird. Arbalyr.

"Go!" I yelled, but the batwing needed no encouragement from me. Leather wings thundered as they cut the air, thrusting north with a vengeance.

I dared a quick glance over my shoulder as we skated messily into the mouth of Carson Creek. Ramendysis was some distance back, his mount at a stand, patterns of power stitching the night sky in what I hoped was a vain attempt to ensnare the bird.

Carson Creek is a twisty snake of a waterway, and the batwing flew the course with all the panache of a veteran stunt car driver, arriving at Heron Marsh with no pursuit yet in sight.

"Hover over that clump of salt hay, there," I directed. "And don't make any sudden moves. I've got to visit a friend."

I thrust my will into the marsh, not caring about the noise or the rude disturbance, and as I expected, the mad *trenvay* rose to meet me.

The water freshens, Guardian.

"Good," I said. "One comes behind me. He would see you strangled, the marsh filled and the small lives slain."

What would you have me do?

"Everything that is in your power."

There was a small silence, while the *trenvay* weighed his indebtedness, then—

Guardian, I will do all that I might.

"Do that, and your debt is canceled," I said, and would have added something more about the nature of our pursuer, but a familiar voice interrupted me.

He comes! He rides on the back of the wind!

I hurled myself into my body, retching with the suddenness of it, snatching the silky mane, which had to have hurt, but the batwing made no complaint. Wind gusted, throwing dust and debris into our faces. Beneath us, the weeds and reeds flattened, and the sluggish water showed white-capped waves. My mount danced back a few nervous, mid-air steps.

"Steady..." I murmured, and threw a hand up to shield my eyes as Ramendysis blasted into the marsh.

Kaederon... the batwing implored.

"Steady..." I answered, like my stomach wasn't tied into fifteen knots, and the kid who had been his plaything wasn't gibbering at the back of my mind, screaming at me to run, run, *hide!*

A gout of black slime erupted from the depths of the marsh, coating Ramendysis in an instant, tightening into a tentacle. The wind steed bucked, roaring like a locomotive. Encased in slime, Ramendysis twisted, one white hand breaking free, power sparking along his fingertips, an edge of violet light, growing.

Another tentacle burst from the depths, wrapped 'round that slender hand. Ramendysis shouted something I couldn't hear above the roar of the wind. If it was a Word, though, it missed its mark—and in a blink he was gone, sucked under, vanished within the embrace of tentacles, the flare and flash of incomplete workings shredded on the violent air.

I took a breath, tasting dust and ozone, and said, quite calmly, "Begone."

The wind died; the murky waters stilled.

Batwings beat, one...two...three.

I counted, slowly, to one hundred.

Beneath us, the marsh was calm, the reeds in their small group-ings, upright, and the peepers took up their interrupted chorus.

Is the deed so easily done, then?

"I'm not sure," I admitted. "I don't *think* we can bury him so deep he'll never get out. He's just too powerful. And I wouldn't sleep real sound, knowing he was underfoot." I took a breath, tasting the musk of weeds and mud. "What I'm hoping is that he had to go back across the Wall to disengage. Give us some time to regroup."

Regroup? I have knowledge of your allies, Little Ozali. What do you imagine they might do to thwart so cruel and determined a mage?

"Damned if I know." I sighed, contemplating the quiet waters of the marsh. The smart money said that Eltenfleur wasn't going to be able to hold Ramendysis long. The *trenvay* altogether hadn't been able to thwart him. "We'll have to call the Wise, is what?"

And the Wise, the batwing said delicately, *will do—what?*

Well, that was always the question, wasn't it, with the Wise. I sighed again.

"Let's get out of here."

A sweep of wings and we were rising, the swamp and its secrets shrinking below us.

What direction?

"Back to the carousel," I said, and tensed for an argument.

But all I got from the batwing was a courteous, *Of course.*

The light inside the storm gates was an unsettling shade of violet, rippling off the *jikinap* bars in pulsating sheets. Ozali Belignatious looked up from inside the cage—and visibly relaxed.

"Well met, Pirate Kate."

I slid off the batwing's back, and threw a glance around.

Beside the nasty illumination, everything seemed all right. The protective ring of trees still stood at the back of the enclosure, Arbalyr the not-quite-phoenix roosting in the topmost branch of the tallest. I sighed in relief, and bowed when he cocked a bright eye at me.

"Thank you," I said.

He closed his eye, and I turned back to the trap and its contents.

"Thought you'd be out of there by now," I said to Mr. Ignat'.

"Alas, there is far too much power in the working," he murmured, and I saw then that he was sweating. "It yearns to consume me—which it will do, and speedily, if I dare try to absorb it."

I blinked. "You're Ozali—"

"I *was* Ozali," he corrected me. "I am an empty vessel, Pirate Kate—or near enough. If I wish to re-establish myself, I must take small bites, over time. Such a feast as this will surely end me."

He speaks sooth, the batwing murmured between my ears. *Lesser power yields to greater.*

"What about the flask?" I asked.

"I have it," he said, and I could hear the strain in his voice. "Do you counsel me to throw a match into a gas tank?"

Right.

His will wavers.

It certainly seemed so. As I watched, the bars contracted. The Ozaliflame closed his eyes.

"Tell me what to do," I said, and watched in horror as the bars contracted again; the nearest barely a cat's whisker away from a leather sleeve. "Mr. Ignat'!"

He didn't answer me.

Lesser power yields to greater, the batwing said again. *You have the means, Little Ozali. Do you have the heart?*

"What do you mean?"

A feast lies before you, in all ways suitable to your station.

Despite its recent assistance, the batwing horse had good cause to want me incinerated. It had every reason to lie. I did know that.

On the other hand, I couldn't think of anything else to do.

Except stand there and watch him die.

I swallowed, and took three steps forward.

The air crackled as the *jikinap* took note of me, and my power rose to meet it.

I held my gloved hands before me, opening my fingers wide. *Think you can take me?* I thought, watching the bars of the cage twist and reorient, seeking, as power always does, to merge with more of itself.

"Come on..." I heard myself croon, and at the same moment felt a weight settle on my left shoulder, and the prick of claws against my skin. Arbalyr, throwing in with the challenger.

I just hoped I wasn't about to get us all fried.

Black lightning leapt from the power caging Mr. Ignat'. From my fingers, an electric blue bolt leapt to meet it. The air ignited even as I drew a breath to scream. My blood flared and the world vanished, lost in a crazy electric dazzle. I was caught, unanchored, bodiless, one spinning spark in a vortex of power—

Knives pierced my shoulder. I gasped; clung to the pain, embraced it—and so found my body, and my mind.

The knives in my shoulder became claws. The air I drew into parched lungs carried the tang of the sea. I was on my knees on the concrete floor. Directly before me a bright haired man with red mustaches stood unrestrained and free. I gasped at a sudden shove, and gasped again as a fiery bird flamed into the air, beating upward until it passed through the roof and was lost to sight.

I took deep, deliberate breath. Hungry...I was so *hungry*.

"Katie!"

Power flickered feebly against my skin. A tithe of my own flowed outward, to capture and consume—

"Command yourself, Pirate Kate. You'll not be unmanned by such a scurvy strike as that."

Damn' straight I wouldn't, I thought laboriously, closing my eyes as I struggled to impose my will, to control my hunger, to remain in control. The *jikinap*; I'd taken too much, I—

I wasn't hungry.

Cautiously, I raised my head, tasting blueberries, or maybe fiddleheads. In the back of my head, the land purred like a contented Maine coon cat.

"Excellent," Mr. Ignat' said approvingly. "Now, look at me."

I opened my eyes and focused on his face.

He was smiling, the blue flames dancing in his eyes.

"Thank you, Katie," he said.

"I'm not sure you're welcome," I said, slowly coming to my feet. It was nothing short of amazing, how well I felt. "We left Ramendysis in the marsh, but that's not going to hold him long. Gran needs to call the Wise."

He shook his head. "That might not be to the best good, Katie."

"We've got no choice," I snapped. "Ramendysis is the one who's tearing up the place, against Law, custom, and the Word of the Wise. They're gonna throw the book at him."

"We daren't risk Nessa," he said, simply, and I felt suddenly not *quite* so well.

Ramendysis would claim Nessa had been stolen from him—as, indeed, she had been. There was nothing that the Wise could do, *except* find that she be returned to his care. She had, after all, given him her soul.

"Mr. Ignat'—"

'Ware! A storm rises from the north!

Hailstones hammered against my greatly enhanced senses, and I lurched to my feet.

"Get Gran and Mother to the Wood!" I yelled at Mr. Ignat' and threw myself across the batwing's back. "We'll pull him off!"

The batwing danced under me.

"Katie!"

Leather wings boomed, and we were airborne. I looked down in time to see Mr. Ignat' throw something that flashed silver upward. The wall was 'way too close; I shouted a Word, caught the flask, and shoved it into my pocket as we rocketed into the night.

Power bloomed around us like fireworks, boxing us inside bars of living fire. The wind blew down the stars, and here came Ramendysis, a working of compulsion and servitude hanging like a lariat from his fingertips.

"Shit."

I brought my attention closer, grasped the structure of our prison and threw power against it, meaning to destroy.

Only the bars didn't shrivel under my assault; they drank what I used against them, growing stronger with every strike.

"Princess Kaederon," Ramendysis crooned, and raised his hand to me, as if inviting my company in a dance. "You may yield."

I do NOT yield!

The batwing threw itself forward. I wrapped my arms around its neck—and a good thing, too. Sharp hooves battered the fiery bars of *jikinap* as if they had physical being. Ramendysis shouted, and I felt the night swell with the speaking of a Word, but the batwing was having none of it.

One last kick and we were out, free; flying for our lives and more. The wind roared and capered, hurling trash, stones, and broken glass at us. I was as flat as I could be, bleeding from a dozen cuts, and there was blood mixing with sweat on the batwing's silver neck. Gasping, I brought power into my hands, and hurled a fireball into the teeth of the wind.

Enough! Would you feed him still more?

The metal maze that was the Galaxi's framework loomed before us, and we were zooming straight for it.

I took a deep breath. Held it.

The batwing horse furled its wings and shot into the maze, weaving expertly between the metal struts. It seemed that the wind died somewhat, and I dared a glance over my shoulder.

The good news: Ramendysis had fallen behind.

The bad news: He was rising above the maze.

"The ocean!" I yelled into the batwing's ear. "Now!"

Obediently, it banked, rising as I fought to keep my seat.

Up we went, and out, the wind screaming like a freight train behind us. I snatched the flask from my pocket, pulled the cork with my teeth and spat it out.

Lightning flared to the right. The batwing never slowed.

I brought the flask to my lips, and drank.

Thunder roared. Ahead and down, the reflected stars sparkled and swelled.

My steed folded its wings—and fell.

Beneath us, the ocean...shrugged.

Leather wings snapped out, clawing us to a stop, the batwing dancing backward on panicked hooves, while the water shrugged once more, surged...

And rose.

A hundred feet and more, it rose, a skyscraper lifting out of the ocean, water sheeting from it in truckloads. Snout, flukes and tail, it rose, toothy maw gaping.

Ramendysis threw his working at the rising leviathan, blasting the creature with unformed bursts of power. He might as well have been throwing water balloons, for all the attention it paid to him.

He was still hurling great gobbets of power down the beast's throat when the mighty jaws closed around him, and the whale crashed back into the sea.

Water geysered, swamping us. The batwing reared, wings working. I slipped, grabbed, lost the flask, but somehow kept my seat.

We dare not hope that this will keep him any longer than the other, the batwing panted. *What now?*

The night crackled with possibility; distracting and delectable tidbits of power drew my eye, and I felt—bloated, too big for my skin. I blinked and looked down at my hands, gloved fingers gripping the dusky mane, blue flames dancing merrily along the leather, illuminating the intricate embroidery.

Even as I watched, the flames faded, and I was comfortable

inside my skin once more—if terror and exhaustion could be said to equal "comfort."

The plan bloomed then, like a dark and wondrous flower, and I knew what had to be done.

"House," I said, my voice rasping and raw.

Wings snapped against the pregnant air, and we rose toward the stars.

Attend me. The batwing's thought was strained. *The sea will not hold the Storm Lord long. We cannot outrun him. A plan would be—*

"House," I repeated, and hauled on its mane, yanking it toward Heath Hill and the snake's nest of power enclosing Joe Nemeier's abomination of a house. "No time to lose."

THIRTY-NINE

—— ✺ ——

Thursday, April 27

Googin Rock lay black and baleful in the restless sea; its bladed surface slick and sullen.

I slid off the batwing's back and dropped to my knees on the glassy knob, the outgoing waves lapping, ice cold, over wrists and legs.

I closed my eyes, the better to see the wall I had built. A wall of sheer willpower, with me on one side and all the power I had drunk on the other. It was not an optimum arrangement, and it wasn't going to last long.

I just hoped it would last long enough.

This is not, the batwing said, its thought coruscating against the breeze, *a very good plan.*

I leaned hard on my hands, feeling the rock through leather-covered palms.

"You have a better," I managed, wincing away from the resonance of my words, "plan?"

There was a pause, during which I touched time and drew my will along its delicate strings, watching the notes as they thrummed across the waters.

No. The batwing's voice recalled me from my game.

"Right, then," I said, struggling to keep the words flat; uninformed by power. "You'd better go."

No, the batwing repeated. I saw it lift in the darkness, and settle carefully amid the blades directly behind me. It folded its wings, and shook its mane into order. I saw all this without turning my head. The power showed it to me. Just as the power showed me the turmoil on the ocean's floor and the belch of brimstone storming toward the surface.

If the Ozali can absorb your gift? the batwing asked. *What plan, then, Kaederon?*

There was no other plan. This was my best shot: Overload Ramendysis with *jikinap* and watch as his head finally and oh-so-deservedly exploded. If the plan failed—

Power shattered the star-shot night. Lightning ran my blood, rising to meet and join with itself, bearing me along like storm wrack, all I could see was blare and blaze.

Flowers filled my vision, and a running carpet of springtime green. A gull laughed, peepers sang; waves stroked the shore.

I gasped, reached out and wrapped myself around the land like a kid clutching a teddy bear.

Out by Blunt Island, a waterspout rose.

I might have screamed. Certainly, I wanted to. The wind whipped, lightning stitched the sky, thunder crashed.

I held my breath, the land a comfort at the back of my power-dazzled mind.

A wave broke hard over the Rock, sudden as a gunshot. Mist swirled, but not so much that I couldn't see the figure kneeling on the broken surface below me—and now was my chance.

Power smoked my blood, rising fast, hungry and hateful. I raised my hands, and threw it—all of it—at that quiet, kneeling figure.

The blare of power burned away the mist, igniting the air like a meteor—

No! screamed the batwing, but I had already seen—it wasn't Ramendysis kneeling there—

It was Borgan.

I flung my will after the bolt of *jikinap*, desperate, not caring that it burned as I snatched it back—snatched too little back.

My power struck him mid-chest, burning, toothy, and full of malice. I saw his eyes widen, that was all, then he was down, a dark huddle among the stony knives.

The sea went still.

"No," I said. Shivering, I got my feet under me on the glassy rock. "No."

The land whined like an abandoned hound; behind me I heard hooves clatter against stone. Down among the stone blades, a dust devil swirled into being beside the still huddle that had been Borgan, and just as suddenly died, leaving Ramendysis behind.

He held a leather jacket negligently in one hand, and he was smiling.

"Well done, Princess Kaederon," he said, and bowed.

He made a marvelous target, standing there, so near I couldn't possibly miss. If I had any power left me—but I'd given everything that I had to Borgan.

Ramendysis dropped the jacket—one more rag onto the heap—and stepped forward until he was at the base of the center hump on which I uncertainly stood.

"Yield," he said, just an ordinary word, drawing its power from old horror, and present despair.

"No," I said, and reached beneath my jacket, snatching Mam'selle free of her nestle against my backbone and throwing her in one motion.

She tumbled once, and buried herself in the center of Ramendysis' chest; a true strike, even in the Land of the Flowers.

Ramendysis laughed.

"Stupid child. I can no more be broken by the toys of this sorry land than Prince Borgan could resist the call of his skin."

He extended one long, white hand, not even bothering to pull Mam'selle from her resting place. There was no blood.

"Yield."

My stomach cramped, bile rising. I averted my eyes, but that was no better, because there on the broken surface was Borgan, dead by my hand. A warrior in white leathers crouched beside him, loon tucked into the crook of an arm.

He met my eyes, and in the eerie silence made by the absence of waves, I knew what I had to do.

I turned back to Ramendysis, and held my hand out to him.

"I yield," I said, "and freely give everything that I am."

Kaederon! the batwing screamed, but it was too late.

Ramendysis had already taken my hand.

I smiled, and relaxed my will, allowing the peculiar virtue of this, my Land, to fill me utterly, and flow to our enemy.

The land buoyed me, submerged me, fragmented me. I was the beach, and the leading edge of the shore, yearning for the caress of the absent waves. I was Googin Rock, sullen and dangerous. I was pebble, thorn, and sand. I was every living thing that set roots in the land, and every living thing that moved upon it. I was the tourists in their beds, the *trenvay* at their service, the plover on their nests. I was a calico cat slinking toward home; I was the warrior in his white leathers, kneeling among the broken knives of his vanquished foes.

Briefly, I was Kate Archer, shivering in the chill air, fingers crushed in a blazing hot grip. I had eyes, and I opened them, saw *jikinap* rising up to the stars like sea mist, and the blood, rich and red, staining the front of Ramendysis' robe.

It was something of a shock to open my eyes and take in pale sky laced with dawn fog. Waves plashed near at hand, and hissed along the sand. Somewhere, a gull shouted good morning.

"There, she's coming around now," said a deep comfortable voice.

Breath-caught, I turned my head. Borgan was lounging within arm's reach, his head propped on his fist and his face drawn with exhaustion.

"'Mornin', Kate. You were right about that jacket."

"I would have rather been wrong," I told him truthfully. "Where's Ramendysis?"

"He has," came an accented, murmuring voice that seemed eerily familiar, even though I was pretty sure I'd never heard it before. "I believe that he has become Changed."

"That had been the plan," I allowed. "But—don't you know?"

"Little Ozali, I do not."

Ice ran my backbone. I rolled to my knees in the sand, and stared at the lady seated on a drift log. She smiled, displaying dainty fangs. Seated as she was, still she was tall, her dark skin iridescent in the borning light.

They probably heard the penny drop in Bangor.

"I wouldn't," I said delicately, "be addressing the Opal of Dawn, by any chance?"

The smile widened, and she shook her silver hair back, revealing a narrow face tapering to a pointed chin; her eyes a milky, sight-less blue.

"You are, indeed." She inclined her head. "I will not forget, Princess Kaederon. Come to me, when your duties allow. And bring your rogue of a grandfather."

"Not sticking around?" I asked.

"I think not," she answered. "Now that the threat to Daknowyth has been retired, I ought return and take up duty."

She rose as if she were leaving immediately and shook out her dappled robes.

"What an extraordinary Land this is," she said, and bowed. "Princess Kaederon. Prince Borgan. Long may your powers delight you."

The mist thickened slightly, then blew apart.

I was alone on the beach with Borgan.

"Nice lady," he said. I laughed—or at least I tried to; it came out kind of choked and mangled.

"I thought I'd killed you," I said.

"Near thing," he answered with a tired smile. "Pulled your punch at the last, though."

"Ramendysis," I began—and stopped when he shook his head.

"He's Changed, all right. Changed from being so full of power he was barely alive, back to the man he might've been. Your lady knife made a difference to him, then."

I felt a rush of relief—of liberation—so vast that I think I could've flown at that moment, if I'd've had the wits to spread my wings. As it was, I blinked a couple of times, clearing the tears out of my eyes, and brought my attention back to Borgan.

"You look like hell," I said, after I'd studied him a long moment.

He laughed, kind of breathy and thin.

"I just guess that I do," he agreed, and sighed. "I'd best be getting in, if you'll lend a hand and a shoulder?"

"Sure." I came to my feet, surprised at how light and limber I felt, held my hand down and braced myself.

He levered himself to his feet, moving slower and more care-fully than usual, his grip not as firm as I'd like. When he was upright, I moved closer, and he put his hand on my shoulder, leaning like he meant it.

"Where's *Gray Lady*?" I asked, as we moved down toward the waves.

"She's to dock," he said. "I'll just go into the water here, Kate. You might not see me for a day or six."

"I'll see you after, though?"

He smiled. "Oh, aye. You'll see me after. The land and the sea, you know—there's no keeping 'em apart."

I nodded, and walked with him into the surf.

"See you," I said.

"Soon," he answered, and waded out into the breakers. When he was waist deep, a wave broke over his head, and he was gone.

FORTY

Thursday, April 27

The trees let me in with a welcoming murmur, and opened a path to the Center.

Gran and Mr. Ignat' were sitting on the ground, their backs against the ancient tupelo tree, Arbalyr roosting, head under wing, on the branch over their heads.

Mr. Ignat' saw me first; he touched Gran on the shoulder, and helped her to her feet.

"Everything all right here?" I asked, embracing her. She'd lost weight, but when I touched her tree with my thought, I found no sign of blight.

"We'll be a little while mending," Gran said. "You can handle the carousel?"

"Been doing it this long," I said, like it had been nothing. There would be time for stories over the long winter.

"Good," she said, and cupped my face in her hands. "I'm glad you came home, Katie."

"Me, too," I said, truthfully.

A rustle brought my head around, as Mr. Ignat' stepped 'round the tree, a careful arm around the waist of a frail woman wearing the tattered dress of House Aeronymous.

Vivid green eyes touched my face and she held out a painfully thin hand.

"Katie," she said, and her voice was as sure as her smile. "How you've grown."

ABOUT THE AUTHOR

Sharon Lee has been married to her first husband for more than half her lifetime; she is a friend to cats, a member of the National Carousel Association, and oversees the dubious investment schemes of an improbable number of stuffed animals.

Despite having been born in a year of the dragon, Sharon is an introvert. She lives in Maine because she likes it there. In fact, she likes it so much that she has written three novels set in Maine; mysteries *Barnburner* and *Gunshy*, and *Carousel Tides*.

With the aforementioned first husband, Steve Miller, Sharon has written seventeen novels of science fiction and fantasy—many of them set in the Liaden Universe®—and numerous short stories. She has occasionally been an advertising copywriter, a reporter, photographer, book reviewer, and secretary. She was for three years Executive Director of the Science Fiction and Fantasy Writers of America, Inc., and was subsequently elected vice president and then president of that organization.